MERCY WILL
FOLLOW ME

PRAISE FOR SARAH HANKS
MERCY WILL FOLLOW ME

Get ready to have your perceptions challenged. *Mercy Will Follow Me* will provoke you to see the world from multifaceted perspectives. Things are not always what you think they are. There are at least two sides to every story.

~ Dr. Rene Burress, PhD

Sarah takes three ordinary people, shaped by their upbringing, surroundings, and the events of their lives and weaves them together. You can never be sure what's coming next. You do however sense that there is something going on in the background. Enjoy the read.

~ Cheryl Brockwell, author

Mercy Will Follow Me weaves tragic events from the past and present into a compelling tale of forgiveness and freedom.

~ Georgia Schmeichel, author

I have been very deeply touched by this book. It's entertaining and well-written, but it also just shows so much skill. Sarah Hanks explores so many complicated and touchy subjects in this story, but she does it with such grace and compassion that everything comes together beautifully and with such complexity. I'm in love with these characters and the mercy of God in their lives.

~ Paige Duke, editor

Sarah Hanks is an expert storyteller. After reading *Mercy will Follow Me,* I feel like I know the characters. I found myself rooting for their success, and feeling sadness over their failures and disappointments. Sarah has tackled some very sensitive topics in this story, but she has woven it all together so delicately. It's easy to be drawn into the storyline, and hard to put the book down. This is a real page-turner! I not only enjoyed the story aspect but also found myself asking the deep questions about how I would handle some of the situations the characters found themselves in. I love it when a book is not only entertaining but causes me to think deeply and ask the hard questions. *Mercy Will Follow Me* is just such a book. This is a story that needs to be told, and one that you will be glad you read.

~ Melissa Jacobs, Author of *Livin' the Dream*

Mercy Will Follow Me is captivating, drawing readers in from the outset. A riveting read.

~ Kim Rees, author

Mercy Will Follow Me grips hold from the start, challenging rough, hidden corners of belief, and following the reader well beyond the turning of the final page. The characters are tangible, their journeys compelling and beautifully navigated. The author opens the eyes of your heart to look past ingrained assumptions and prejudice to see with eyes of mercy, insight, grace, compassion. You cannot walk away from the reading of this novel without an enrichment of your view of fellow man and a burning desire to do better than has been done, to throw off the old bitter ways and walk forward renewed as mercy follows.

~ Shannon Lugger

Mercy Will Follow Me is filled with unforgettable, multi-faceted characters and shows us that a look into the past can teach us about ourselves in the present and change our futures forever.

~ Jill Tilley

Sarah Hanks has woven a beautiful story that stretches past the boundaries of time, race, age, and class. She tells a difficult but long-needed story that proves truth and courage are eternal things that can turn. Being a rape survivor myself I really appreciate the tender way she handled a devastating subject. *Mercy Will Follow Me* will leave you believing hope cuts through the darkest heart and faith can build a bridge to impossible places.

~ Angie Stumbo, author

Sarah Hanks has produced an incredible account that takes you from past, to present, and back again through the eyes of her characters in an indelible way. I found myself deeply immersed in each character, and couldn't wait for the next chapters to be reviewed! Her careful research into the history of the characters—into their lives, their perspectives, and into their loves—shows clearly in the story, and it's impossible to read the books without finding yourself in their pages. Although these books tackle generations' worth of difficult situations and struggles, Mercy (as it will) wins overall. These books were a wonderful read, and I eagerly anticipate their conclusions.

~ Cassidy Cooley

MERCY WILL FOLLOW ME

SARAH HANKS

SonFlower Books

DEDICATION

I poured over very many narratives of enslaved African Americans when researching for the historical fiction portion of Mercy Will Follow Me. This book is dedicated to these resilient people — brave, beautiful, human — and to their descendants. May mercy follow your family line, and may the Lord grant you peace.

NOTE TO READER

The characters in this fictional storyline chose not to continue pursuing prosecution against a serious crime, and the author created a poignant tale of redemption and forgiveness through the traumatic rape that the main character experienced. The need for redemption and forgiveness is real and applies to every human for we have all sinned (Rom. 3:23). However, forgiveness is not diametrically opposed to justice under the laws that govern us. The author is not attempting to make that case or to discourage anyone from seeking prosecution of a crime. Rape and any form of sexual assault are serious, criminal offenses.

1

———

Friday
April 9, 2010

nticipation brewed in Natassa's gut. Yes, Brandon was reluctant, but he hadn't said no. Not officially. Just: "We'll talk more about it later."

Well, tonight they were going to do more than talk.

Things couldn't be working out more perfectly. Natassa had been charting for months. She had always thought her cycles were irregular. It turned out she just hadn't been paying enough attention. They were consistent, and this time around, everything lined up perfectly with her ten-year anniversary.

Natassa was going to seduce her husband.

Once she was pregnant, if she got pregnant, he would warm up to the idea. They were blessed with the means to support a fifth child. He couldn't use money as an excuse. Brandon was well established in his career as a computer programmer at a national bank, always speaking technical jargon Natassa couldn't begin to comprehend. They could easily turn their extra guest bedroom into a nursery. No, finances couldn't be the reason for his hesitation.

He was also an excellent father, doting on his two daughters, wrestling with his two sons. His face lit up when he helped build a snow fort with them in the backyard or when their three-year-old princess fell asleep in his lap on page three of a *Curious George* book. Brandon went after his role as a father like he did everything in life: with passion and purpose. He dove in, fully involved in the lives of his children. When they were younger, he helped change diapers. Now that the boys were older, he sat with them, hashing out math problems for hours if necessary. He couldn't claim he wasn't doing a wonderful job with the kids he already had. Another one to love? Yes, he'd be thrilled ... eventually.

She tried to push the rest of their heated conversation out of her mind. He had been unreasonable. He'd said she was never satisfied. Why couldn't she be content with the four children they had? *Insatiable.* It wasn't true, at least not in the way he meant it. What was wrong with wanting another child? If she hungered for it, it was only because God put that desire in her. He would come around. He had to. He couldn't make good on his threat to not sleep with her until they worked through this disagreement. He was a man, after all. And she planned to work all her womanly charms on him tonight.

Natassa tore through her walk-in closet looking for the red dress. They'd seen it while shopping one day. "That would look good on you," Brandon had whispered in her ear. She'd thought so, too, and had gone back the next day and bought it, hiding it in the back of her closet.

She couldn't wear it to church. The neckline was too low, and the hemline not low enough. Wear it out in public? She'd feel too exposed. But she'd wear it for Brandon tonight.

She ransacked the master bathroom, looking for her old

makeup bag. Where was it? She didn't often wear makeup. In fact, the last time she used it was probably at her cousin's wedding over a year ago. Finding the bag, she rummaged through it, searching for something daring. Something surprising. Something beyond typical Natassa. She found what she was looking for and glided on the bloodred lipstick, searching her creamy reflection in the mirror. Well, she wasn't twenty anymore, but she didn't look bad. Even after ten years of marriage and four children, she looked like the kind of woman who could turn heads. She shuddered, imagining the unwanted attention. It was only her husband's recognition she coveted, only his approval she was looking for.

She busied herself arranging her wavy brown hair. Half up, half down was how he liked it best. She secured it with a silky red ribbon. With her makeup in place, she found her black heels and grabbed her small black purse.

There. How could he deny her tonight?

She heard her phone belt out the Celine Dion melody reserved for Brandon's ringtone. A giggle bubbled forth as she snatched the phone from her bed and answered.

"Hey, babe." Could he hear the smile in her voice? The expectation?

"Hi, sweetheart. I just wanted to let you know I'm about to head into my last meeting. I'll be an hour, an hour and a half, tops. Gosh, I wish I could get out of it."

She felt his sincerity reaching out to her and loved him for it.

"It's okay."

"I'll make it as quick as I can. I can't wait to spend time with you."

"Right back at ya." She felt her cheeks warm.

"Are the children already at the sitter's?"

"Yep. Dropped them off over an hour ago."

"What are you going to do for the next hour?"

"I don't know. Maybe a crossword puzzle."

Brandon's laugh triggered her own. She enjoyed how their laughter danced together. She always had. "All right, have a blast with that. I'll see you at the hotel in no more than two hours—hopefully less. Love you."

"Love you too," she said before hanging up the phone, smiling and wiggling her toes. What *was* she going to do for the next hour?

Her bag was already packed, her purse already in hand. Maybe she had time to go by the shop in their old neighborhood and grab a bottle of his favorite wine. She rarely visited the city anymore, but the hotel was downtown.

She and Brandon had met downtown just a block away from the hotel they would be staying at that night. One moment she was bent over her laptop hammering out a term paper on cognitive theory, the next moment she heard his voice asking if the seat across from her was taken. Then she saw his face—kind eyes and a sincere smile—and the rest of him, strong and muscular. Her term paper was forgotten, completely overshadowed by Brandon Bloomington. They talked for two hours straight. She couldn't take her eyes off him. His sandy-blonde hair was neatly trimmed, and as she sat there listening to him, she fantasized about running a hand through it. Touching his tanned face. Kissing his mesmerizing lips. They talked so long she was late for her child psychology class. Eight months later, they were married. Three months after that, she was pregnant with David. She never did finish her degree. She didn't mind; her family was everything to her.

Daniel followed David two years later. Nearly two years after that, Faith was born. And then Hope entered their family. Brandon said they were now complete: two boys, two girls. But Natassa just wasn't ready to give the baby clothes away. Their daughter Hope was three already and growing so fast. Natassa missed the sweet baby sounds and the feel of newborn hair and skin. She yearned for more. At least one more. Then maybe the ache would cease, or at least dull to something bearable.

She navigated the city streets, surprised by how much the neighborhood had changed in eight years. Their favorite restaurant had once been on her right, the Italian flag boldly painted on the window. Now the only things on the windows were boards, and several beer bottles lay on the sidewalk in front of the entrance.

Was she ... had she accidently crossed over Park Avenue? Natassa checked the street signs again, mentally racing through her memory of the city layout. No. She'd just crossed King Street and hadn't even hit Winston yet. She was still north of Park, still in safe territory. Perhaps time simply clouded her memory of what the neighborhood used to look like.

A flash of color on the corner of Winston and Fourth stole her attention. A graffiti painting of a cardinal taking flight made her smile. It looked lifelike, as if its wings were flapping wildly. Then she looked underneath the bird and spotted the figure the bird had been nesting in. A skull. Ew. She turned her thoughts back to her mission.

"This is dumb. It's probably not even open," she mumbled to herself. But as she turned the corner, there it was: Edison's Wines. Natassa parked in front and got out, making sure to lock the car door. A few minutes later, she emerged onto the street, wine bottle in hand. She started for her car and then wondered if Merrie's Berries was still in operation. Brandon relished the chocolate-covered strawberries served there. If she remembered correctly, it sat just around the next corner.

Glancing at her watch, she thought she had enough time for a quick stop. She imagined how he'd appreciate her thoughtfulness, how he'd show her that appreciation tonight. And maybe she'd come away from this weekend with a new life inside her, slowly blossoming into a new blessing, the next addition to the Bloomington family.

2

———

Red lights flashed in DeAndre's rearview mirror as he turned left onto Dover Street.

"What'd I do?" he mumbled to himself as he pulled to the curb. He hadn't been speeding; he knew that much. His '96 Corsica had seen better days, but he was sure it was up to code. Had a taillight burned out since last night? He had checked everything before venturing into suburbia. At least he was dressed in a shirt and tie. Pale blue. Non-threatening. Respectable.

The officer came around to his window, eyeing him suspiciously. "License and registration," he demanded.

Apparently, they were skipping pleasantries and getting right to the point.

"Excuse me, sir, but what is this about?" DeAndre asked in as polite a voice as he could muster. He handed his license and insurance cards to the cop, noticing the sweat beads near the man's bald brow.

"Why are you in the area?" the officer probed.

Why are you ignoring my question? DeAndre wondered,

biting his tongue to keep from voicing that bit of internal dialogue.

"I'm looking for a job. I heard there were a few fast-food joints out here hiring."

"You aren't from around here, are you?"

"No, sir." *Of course not. My skin's too dark to be from this hood.*

"Why aren't you, uh ... looking for employment closer to your home?"

What could it hurt to tell this cracker the truth?

"I'm trying to make a better life for myself, officer. Nothing good happens in the neighborhood where I live."

The wariness in the cop's eyes remained. He wasn't convinced. "You hold tight, you understand? I'm going to run this."

"Yes, sir," DeAndre managed. He watched the cop swagger back to his car, watched car after car of white folk drive by. Reg had told him this was a bad idea, a fool's errand. Reg told him a lot of things. Like nothing was ever going to change and the world wasn't going to do nothing but push you down.

"Why you tryin' to escape it, D? Ain't no way you gonna just waltz up there and get handed a job. No one hands us anything, D. It's a white man's world. The best you can do is work for Boss and get a little something to make it all a bit more bearable." Yeah, Reg said a lot of things. A lot of things DeAndre didn't want to believe.

Things could be different, right? If he dressed nice, sounded articulate, smiled, and said "Yes, ma'am," and "Yes, sir," he could get out of the hood. Sure, flipping burgers wasn't much of a career, but maybe he could work his way up. Those places were always hiring for management positions, right? *Manager.* Sure would be better than getting shot dead on the street like his pa. DeAndre would take the smell of grease any day.

The officer returned, looking slightly annoyed. He handed DeAndre's license and insurance back. "You fit the description of someone we're looking for," he explained. DeAndre knew what description that was: black male.

"Pop the trunk," the cop demanded. DeAndre complied without comment. What did he think he'd find? Drugs? A gun? Maybe a ski mask? Indignation began to boil in his belly. Reg was right. Life just wasn't fair.

The cop came back to the driver's window. "You're free to go," he admitted.

"Yes, officer," DeAndre eked out. Slowly and carefully, he pulled back into the lane, going five miles under the speed limit lest he have to go through the ordeal again.

* * *

DeAndre sauntered down the street, walking in the opposite direction of his car. He should leave, go back to his hood. He wasn't welcome here. The stares were enough to prove it. A few mothers even grabbed their children, holding them close when they saw him coming. He had filled out four applications. Now he just had to wait for a call to set up an interview. One of the managers was even cordial, giving him a sliver of hope. The others ... well, he wasn't welcome here. But he wasn't eager to drive back to his crib either.

Walking these streets lined with shops of all kinds, he could almost imagine living a different kind of life. There weren't boards or bars over the windows. He could hear birds chirping and the sound of pleasant conversation wafting through the air. A young child laughed in the distance. He paused, listening more intently. Yep, no gunfire. He took a deep breath, inhaling the aroma of barbecue coming from a nearby restaurant. This felt right, this life. He wanted to grab hold of it.

Spotting a convenience store in the distance, he started for it. He could go for a snack. In reality, he could go for anything that would prolong his visit to suburbia. He entered the store, and a bell jingled overhead. "Hello," a voice called from the checkout counter. A middle-aged woman sat behind the counter, engrossed in a book. She didn't look up.

DeAndre wandered over to look at the chips, surveying his choices. At the other end of the aisle, a teenage girl with an unzipped hoodie ran her fingers across the candy. Hmm, maybe he'd have a Snickers bar instead of chips. As he walked further down the aisle, the girl turned toward him, giving him a generous view of her slinky red shirt that did little to hide her ample cleavage.

That girl needs to make use of that zipper on her hoodie. Why doesn't her mama make her put some clothes on? Still, she smiled slyly as she caught him glancing at her chest. He hated how his body responded to the invitation in her eyes. *How am I supposed to not look when you got it all hanging out there like that?*

She winked at him and then stuffed a bag of M&M's in the pocket of her hoodie. Did she—? Was she—? She then grabbed a Twix bar and stuffed it in her other pocket. She looked around then, and their eyes met again. She put a finger to her pouty red lips.

If she thinks I'm going along with her game, she's got another thing coming.

"I'd put that back if I were you," DeAndre whispered to her. Her mouth opened in surprise. She glared at him. She made a beeline out of the aisle, pockets still bulging with her five-finger discount. DeAndre shrugged. He wouldn't get into it. He'd stay right there and mind his own business. Now, what candy was he in the mood for?

He heard a voice from the next aisle. "Mom, let's go. That guy over there came on to me. When I tried to move away he threatened me."

Guy over there? Was she talking about him? That little lying

...

"He threatened you? What guy?"

"The guy in the next aisle. Please, Mom. Let's just go."

Their voices were getting louder. "If he said something to you, we need to tell someone, Christina." Footsteps. DeAndre debated ditching the candy and getting out of there. But he hadn't done anything wrong. This was ridiculous. Better just play dumb and go about his business. He grabbed a Snickers bar and made his way over to the soda. As he rounded the corner, the lady from the counter stopped him in his tracks.

"I think you should leave." She stood tall, but her voice wavered. Was she afraid of him?

"Leave? Look, lady, I didn't do anything wrong. I'm just grabbing a snack and I'll be on my way."

"No, you need to go right now. Leave right now, or I'm calling the police."

"You serious? I'm a paying customer."

The woman rushed back to the counter. *She's calling the cops! I didn't do nothing wrong, and she's calling the cops.* Indignation rose up within DeAndre. His ears warmed until he felt like they were on fire.

"I didn't do anything wrong!" he shouted. No one was listening. It was just like Reg always said. No one ever listened to them unless they did something to get their attention. He dropped the Snickers, picked up the Coke in front of him, and threw it against the glass beverage case. As he watched the bottle plummet to the floor, brown liquid fizzing and oozing from the sides of the cap, he saw his own rage. He was close to exploding from the injustice of it all. Storming to the counter, he threw a five-dollar bill down in front of the cashier. "I'm leaving. $1.75 is for the Coke on the floor over there. The rest is a tip for your excellent customer service."

The jingling bell over the door that had sounded so welcoming on the way in grated now. *A fool's errand.* Reg was right.

* * *

Clouds crept in, obscuring the sun as DeAndre drove back to the city. He tried to remember what the bird chirps sounded like less than an hour ago, but the rumbling inside of him drowned out any recollection. He felt like a caged animal, trapped in his skin, trapped in a life he didn't choose. Trapped. All the anger inside him had nowhere to go. And it was building. It was as if darkness swirled around him, beckoning him to give into it—darkness so deep it threatened to suck the marrow from his bones, feed on his very soul.

If only he could cry, leak the steam out of him through tears. But he couldn't. The hood had stolen that from him long ago. You had to be hard when gunfire was your lullaby. The only hope he had of softening was stolen from him, pickpocketed like that candy.

DeAndre had never stolen anything in his life, though he'd watched Reg do it. Loyalty ran deeper than laws where he came from. He'd come to Reg's defense many times when he was clearly in the wrong. Not that DeAndre was entirely innocent. He managed to stay out of trouble for the most part, though, packing down his latent temper, whitewashing it with a type of watered-down optimism he didn't fully believe. Yet it only took a night of disillusionment and vodka plus some punk kid talking smack about his pa for DeAndre to let his fists do the talking, Reg egging him on the whole time. Sometimes in his dreams he still saw the blood oozing out of that fool's mouth. Four years later, DeAndre still hadn't taken another sip of vodka.

Reg? Now Reg was a different story. He might be full of vice, but Reg and DeAndre were like brothers, closer even. Reg never knew his daddy, so he'd gravitated toward DeAndre's like a moth to a flame. DeAndre's family absorbed him when he was only a little boy with a mom turning tricks on the street.

The boys grew up together, got to where they knew each other's minds even though they thought so differently. Reg, cynical and jaded. DeAndre, optimistic if not hopeful. Not because life had taught him there was anything worth hoping for but because if he didn't he'd drown.

Reg had been with him when Pa died. They were playing a video game, and for a moment DeAndre hadn't distinguished the gunfire on the screen from the gunfire in front of their high-rise apartment. Then his gut plummeted and he scrambled to the window, trying to see in the dim lighting. From the fifth floor, it was hard to tell it was his daddy. If not for the orange sweatshirt, he might not have known. Then he heard Mama screaming from the kitchen, and he scrambled toward the front door. Reg held him back, saying whoever shot a good man like him wouldn't blink an eye at shooting his boy too. They held onto each other, guttural noises of their rage echoing in each other's ears.

"Don't you cry, D. Don't do it. Don't give them the satisfaction." DeAndre knew Reg would say the same thing right about now.

DeAndre pulled up in front of the house Reg and he rented together. It wasn't much, but it was the only sanctuary he had. Several pieces of once-white siding hung loose in front, and there was a hole the size of a cannon in the wooden porch, right to the left of the door. The bottom step was broken, too, the board splintered in half. At least the house had most of its windows. There was only one missing, and it was upstairs, so no one bothered to spray-paint graffiti on the board covering it. And, yeah, the grass was overgrown, but his mower was busted, so it was going to stay that way for the time being.

Though Reg's gray Escort was outside, DeAndre found the house empty. He grabbed one of the last five beers from the fridge, plopped down on the sofa, and picked up the remote. He turned on the news, but when another story of a shooting a few blocks away from his house came on, he turned it off. He looked around. Sagging furniture, a kitchen table that didn't match the chairs, stained linoleum, carpet with cigarette burns —this was his lot in life. He had to accept it, had to let the dreams of sun-bathed streets, fresh air, and new beginnings wither away and die. There was no room in that world for the likes of him. Finishing off the beer, he crushed the can and grabbed another one. Then another.

"Hey, D, how'd it go?" Reg blew in the door, his jeans low and his smile broad. Until, that is, DeAndre clued him in on the events of the afternoon. Then he saw a storm brewing in Reg's eyes, the same kind of storm that brewed in his own gut. Reg stormed to the fridge.

"We out of beer?"

"Yep." DeAndre tossed a crushed can in his direction.

"We need more. Or something stronger. You wanna walk or drive?"

"Drive. I done enough walking today."

Ten minutes later they were pulling up outside the liquor store, in front of where the old video game store used to be. When they were young teens, this place had been their favorite hangout. The white folk might have been able to keep them from renting north of Park Ave., but they couldn't keep Reg from crossing their imaginary boundary line. While most people DeAndre knew accepted the way things were, keeping to themselves on the south side of Park, Reg never paid much attention to norms and rules. Eventually, the lines blurred and budged, not that it was some great victory.

The video game store shut down several years ago. Everything on the street had. Now it was completely deserted, nothing but boarded-up windows and memories. Reg and DeAndre still found themselves gravitating toward the familiar, even if it was empty, loitering on St. Anthony Street. Forty minutes later, they were still there, now loaded with whiskey and brooding. DeAndre wasn't ready to go home yet. Cigarette butts on the ground didn't bother him as much as cigarette holes in his carpet.

Reg returned from DeAndre's car, where he'd disappeared a minute earlier.

"Here, drink this," Reg said, handing DeAndre another shot of whiskey.

DeAndre tipped it back, feeling it burn all the way down. Minutes later, his heart began to race. He felt strange, like he could catapult into the sky. He gaped at his feet. Were they still on the ground?

"It ain't fair. Nothin' is fair, D. Not for us. You waltz down there. You do everything right and what happens? You get kicked in the teeth. I'm telling you, it's a white man's world. Ain't no one gonna do nothing for us to help us get ahead. You gotta take what you want, D. No one's gonna hand it to ya." Reg paced the sidewalk, fury radiating from him.

"I'm so mad. I'm so mad I can't see straight, can't think straight."

"Bro, you can't see straight 'cause you drunk. Or something." Reg laughed. DeAndre knew he had never been able to hold his liquor as well as Reg. He rarely had anything stronger than a beer. But Reg was right. He felt stronger, more empowered with the whiskey coursing through him. Maybe what he needed was to be bolder like Reg.

"I'm not just drunk. I'm ticked. I don't think I've ever been this mad in my life. It's like everything's been building up inside me for the past ten years. I'm tired of holding my peace."

"Yeah? Well, what ya gonna do about it, D? Let it eat you alive?" Reg stopped midstride and whistled low. "Well, lookie here. Somebody's in the wrong neighborhood, and it ain't you this time."

DeAndre followed Reg's gaze and saw a white woman sauntering down the sidewalk in some fancy getup, phone in one hand and a bottle of wine in the other. He laughed. "She lost for sure."

"What do ya say we teach her a lesson about wandering into our hood?"

"What are ya saying, Reg?"

"I'm sayin' ... Look at her. So high and mighty. She's the kinda girl that gets whatever she wants. Look at that red dress. Those shoes. Who does she think she is prancing her fancy self down here? I say we teach her a lesson."

DeAndre hesitated. Reg wasn't serious, was he?

"Get behind the car. If she ever took her pretty eyes off her phone long enough, she'd see us."

DeAndre complied, still feeling woozy.

He looked at the woman, sauntering down the street in her slinky dress. She wasn't hiding her goods much better than the little tramp in the convenience store. So this is what white women were like. They wanted to use their bodies like weapons against men and then accuse the men of the worst intentions. If he was going to get accused of it anyway, why not just do it? If someone was going to be the victim in this equation, why did it always have to be him?

"But what if—"

"Shhh ... Why you always worrying? She ain't gonna know who we is." He pulled his shirt off and ripped it down the middle. The woman came closer and closer, never taking her eyes off her phone, her pretty little nails texting in a flurry. "I'm gonna cover her eyes. You grab her hands behind her back."

DeAndre downed the last of the whiskey. Adrenaline coursed through him as Reg's plan unfolded. Reg snuck up behind the woman and tied his shirt around her face, blinding and gagging her. The bottle of wine crashed to the pavement, shattering. DeAndre clenched her arms behind her back and shoved her into the back seat of his car. Reg went around the other side and held her arms down.

"Go on. Have at her, D."

DeAndre did. He never would have conceived of raping a woman. That was something Reg would do. Not him. But in the back seat of his Corsica, he channeled all the rage that had been building inside him into this woman. He made his soul stone, and with gritted teeth he unleashed his fury.

When DeAndre was done, Reg yanked the ribbon out of the woman's hair and used it to tie her hands behind her back. Then he shoved her out of the car. The sound of her head smacking the pavement sent a shiver of regret through DeAndre, but he pushed it down.

Reg kicked her until she lay unmoving in the middle of the street.

"Quick, D, get in. We gotta get out of here."

And they did, but DeAndre made the mistake of glancing in his rearview mirror to see the carnage they left behind.

3

———————

Natassa lay still, silent, as if playing dead. The rumble of the motor faded in the distance, but still she didn't move. Not yet. She started trembling and couldn't stop. Her teeth chattered, amplifying the dull ache in her head. Now were they gone? Could she be sure they were not coming back? She waited a few minutes more and then wrung her wrists until she freed her hands from the ribbon. She uncovered her eyes, blinking to adjust her vision in the surrounding dusk. She was in the middle of the street. Where was ...? Her eyes scanned the scene until they found shards of glass on the sidewalk a few yards away. The bottle of wine. And beside it, her phone. And beside that, her small black purse. Still trembling, she crawled toward it.

Her hands shook wildly as she picked up her phone, the teal case glinting from the streetlight. A surge of relief coursed through her as she pushed the button and was greeted with a soft glow of light. *It survived the fall.*

She hit the text icon and held back a sob when she saw the text she had sent right before being attacked. I HAVE A SURPRISE FOR YOU. The surprise had been the wine, now no more than a stain pooled on the pavement. There had been no Merrie's Berries. Now there was no wine and no anniversary celebration, just a raw ache and pervading fear. Slowly, methodically she typed I NEED YOU TO PICK ME UP. Then, straining to see if there was anyone in the distance, she forced herself to stand.

"One foot in front of the other. One foot in front of the other," she whispered to herself. Her head pounded and her stomach churned. She just had to make it to her car. Then she could lock herself inside and wait for Brandon. It was just around the corner. She could make it. She would make it. She heard the chirp of her phone but ignored it, intent on her mission. "One foot in front of the other."

Finally, she rounded the corner and saw her maroon Audi SUV. Reaching into her purse, she grabbed her keys and hit the unlock button. She dove into the front seat and slouched low, locking the door behind her. Finding her phone, she read Brandon's reply. PICK YOU UP WHERE? WHY?

How could she answer that? How in the world could she even begin to answer that? *IN THE CITY. WAS RAPED?* Or *IN FRONT OF THAT OLD LIQUOR STORE WE USED TO FREQUENT. BECAUSE I'M SHAKING TOO BAD TO DRIVE?* She should just call him, but she didn't want to talk. She didn't want to do anything but curl up in a ball and sleep. She found a bottle of Excedrin in her purse and swallowed three pills, washing them down with the remnants of melted ice from an old cup of iced tea. Her phone chirped again. NATASSA? R U OK?

No. She wasn't.

I'M IN MY CAR IN FRONT OF EDISON WINES. WILL EXPLAIN WHEN YOU GET HERE. HURRY.

A minute later, her phone began to ring. She ignored it. She turned it on silent, made herself as small as she could, and surrendered to her drowsiness.

* * *

Natassa awoke to pounding on her window. Her heart hammered, and her scream pierced the air.

"It's me! It's me! Unlock the door," Brandon pleaded with her through the glass. She put her hand on her heart, attempting to force her breathing to slow. She hit the unlock button, and all at once he was there—her rock, her safe place. "Natassa, baby, what's wrong? What happened?"

That's when she began to sob.

He shushed her gently in a way that felt comforting, not demeaning, and she clung to his crisp white shirt, pressing her face against his chest. Then all at once she realized where she was and where she wanted to be.

"The hotel. Take me to the hotel. Now, Brandon. Let's go to the hotel."

"Okay, okay. We can go. You'll tell me what's going on?"

"I will, but let's just go."

"You want me to drive? Your car ... We shouldn't leave it here. This isn't the best neighborhood." He paused, surveying the surroundings. "You know what? I'll call Brett and see if he and Laura can come by and get it. They have an extra key."

She nodded, not at all caring what happened to her Audi. She just wanted to get as far away from there as she could, as quickly as possible. Brett was Brandon's older brother and a police officer. Let him handle the shadows of that neighborhood. Or not. So what if thugs desecrated her car? They had already taken something far more important.

She started shaking again and grasped Brandon's hand.

"Honey? What happened to you?"

She opened her mouth, but nothing came out.

"Okay, let's get out of here. I'll call Brett on the way."

He gently picked her up and carried her, just as he had ten years before when he carried her over the threshold on their wedding night. She bit her lip to keep from wailing. She couldn't help thinking about how his gentleness contrasted with the harshness of her attackers, the love of their union contrasted with the violation of the assault. It was too much to bear. He placed her tenderly in the passenger seat, buckling her in as if she were a child. She almost wished she had hit her head harder—lost consciousness, lost the memories. That might have been a kinder reality than the one she was faced with.

Brandon started the car and spent the next few minutes talking to Brett and explaining the location of Natassa's car. She relished not having to say anything for the moment. How would Brandon react to this? Would he see her differently? Treat her differently? She was thankful when they pulled onto the interstate. Even though their hotel was only two exits away, it felt like another world.

He hung up the phone. "Brett said it's no problem. They'll drop by, pick it up, and park it at our place. No worries."

She hadn't been worried. Not about the stupid car.

"Now will you tell me what's up?"

She took a deep breath. It was better just to say it, right? Just get it out. It's not like she couldn't tell him. She *had* to tell him …

"I … I wanted to surprise you. So I stopped by Edison's and grabbed a bottle of that Harvest wine you used to like so much."

He eyed her warily, no doubt wondering where the wine was now.

"Then … Well, do you remember Merrie's Berries?"

He nodded.

"I wanted to go there and get their chocolate-covered straw-berries. I thought I remembered it was just around the corner, so I thought I'd walk. Only I couldn't find it. So I was walking back to my car when …"

"When what?" Brandon asked, glancing at her with worry etched in the lines around his eyes.

"I was … I had just texted you … I was trying to text with one hand because I was holding the wine in my other hand. I wasn't paying attention to what was going on around me. Then—" Natassa covered her face. She couldn't say it. It was too horrible.

"Then what?" Brandon's voice held an edge of urgency, overriding the gentleness.

They were pulling up in front of the hotel. Timing saved her. "I'll tell you inside."

"What? No, Natassa! Tell me. What? Were you mugged? That's it, isn't it? You were robbed."

Yes. Someone stole something from her, but not from her wallet. She almost nodded, but just as the valet attendant came around to Brandon's side of the car, she shook her head no instead.

They checked into the hotel without any of the anticipated excitement. She felt drained. He seemed withdrawn. They didn't touch.

Once inside their room, Brandon barely waited until plopping the bags on the floor before turning to her and saying, "Continue."

She sat on the edge of the bed, looking at the picture of a lily on the wall. She had to just get it over with, say it as fast as possible with as little feeling as possible. As if she were reading off a grocery list. "Someone grabbed me from behind, put something over my face, and grabbed my arms. Then they shoved me into a car and raped me. Then they pushed me out of the car and drove away." She felt a traitorous tear slide down her check. Not quite emotionless.

"What?" Brandon came around in front of her, blocking her view of the innocent flower.

"Do you really need me to tell you again?"

"You were raped?" His voice sounded softer now, familiar.

She nodded.

"Oh, honey." He sat down beside her and held her again, rocking her and patting her hair. She let the tears loose once again, leaning into his strength. She didn't know what to say, and she was thankful he didn't try to say anything to make it better. What a futile, awkward effort that would be.

Finally, he pulled back and searched her eyes. "Why didn't you tell me?"

"I did." She looked back at the painting, mesmerized by the gentle white petals blurred by her tears.

"I mean right away, when we were there. Or when you texted. When it happened. Why didn't you tell me? The police —we could have called them right away. They could have caught the lowlife ..."

She took a deep breath, unsure of how to explain that justice hadn't been at the forefront of her mind, only safety. "I don't know."

"It's not too late." Brandon stood and began to pace. "We can call them right now. You should go to the hospital. Right now. They can collect evidence. You can give a police report."

"Brandon, no." She shook her head, her eyes wide and pleading.

"No? What do you mean, no?"

"Haven't I been through enough tonight? I don't want to go to the hospital. I don't want strangers examining me, prodding me ... asking questions. I don't want to have to tell the story again and again. Not tonight. I just want to take a hot bath and go to bed." With that, she made a beeline for the bathroom, locking the door behind her.

"I'll call Brett. He'll know what to do."

Natassa cringed but knew she couldn't stop him. There was no way she'd be able to keep this from her brother-in-law. She just hoped that was as far as it had to go. She didn't want anyone else to know, didn't want them to look at her differently or to pity her. She couldn't stand pity.

She caught a glimpse of her face as she passed by the mirror. She stopped. Stared. A red scrape stretched across her right cheek. A faint blue bruise was forming near her hairline on her forehead. *That* would look just lovely tomorrow. But what captured her attention the most was the bloodred lipstick staring back at her, mocking her. It was barely even smeared. Her lips still looked as if they were ready for a sweet anniversary getaway with the love of her life, a night on the town.

She retched into the toilet.

After rinsing her mouth out in the sink, she took a tissue and rubbed the lipstick off. She knew she should be gentle with herself, yet she scoured her face, finding a twisted measure of comfort in pain that she could control.

There. With the lipstick off, she looked nearly as awful as she felt.

Her bubble bath sat with the rest of her toiletries in her suitcase next to the bed. She debated getting it but didn't want to risk further interrogation by Brandon. Hot water and a bar of hotel soap would have to do. It would have to be enough to erase the remnants of the horrible ordeal from her body. She turned the water on full blast and heard Brandon talking to her through the door. She couldn't make out what he was saying and didn't put any effort toward deciphering it. Ignoring his voice, she sank into the tub and let the scalding water bury her. She looked at her body, disgusted. Did she actually have the thought earlier that she might be an attractive woman? She felt ugly now. Ugly and small.

When the water got too high, she turned the faucet off. Brandon's voice was instantly pressing through the door. "Natassa! Why didn't you listen to me? Brett said do not take a bath. You're not in the bathtub already, are you?"

"Yes, I am."

He let out an expletive that she rarely heard him use. "Seriously, Natassa? That's just great. You just ruined the chance of collecting evidence on this loser."

For the first time she could remember in their ten-year marriage, she was thankful for the lock on the door keeping her husband at a distance. She pulled the lever to drain some water from the bath, thinking she could drown out the sound of his voice for a few moments more. It wasn't loud enough.

"Okay, wait. Natassa? Brett says if we bring your clothes and underwear they might still be able to get a sample." Her cheeks grew hot at the thought of her husband discussing her underwear with her brother-in-law. It was completely mortifying. And her dress? If she presented her slinky red dress for inspection, what would they think? That anyone who dressed like that deserved what they got? And then she'd hand them her underwear, carefully chosen with their anniversary night in mind? Wait ... She leaned over the tub, surveying the floor.

"I don't have my underwear!" she shouted in a panic.

"What, Nat?"

"I don't have my underwear. It must be in that car. They ripped it off." Hot tears pooled. For some reason, the fact that her underwear was in the back of some rapist's car made her feel all the more violated and exposed. Trashy. As if there was still a part of her out there she couldn't get back.

"Okay, Brett says that isn't the worst thing. It gives the police something to look for."

"Look for?"

"Yeah. They're going to find the guy. Brett's going to make it his mission to find the son of a—"

Natassa turned the hot water back on and sank down low. She should be thankful she had a husband and brother-in-law committed to justice. She should consider other women. The rapists needed to be caught before they could attack someone else. All she wanted, though, was for the horrible nightmare to go away. She didn't want a righteous vendetta hanging over their family. She didn't want any ties to that horrible night. It was bad enough it had to happen on their anniversary. Now every time they celebrated their marriage, she'd have to push dark shadows away from her consciousness. That seemed enough of a battle to wage.

4

———

DeAndre catapulted out of bed in a cold sweat as the pounding at the front door jarred him from a restless sleep. They found him. The cops had finally found him. He looked around wildly. *For what? What exactly do you think you're going to do? Fight them off? Escape into the night?* The pounding continued, and adrenaline shot sharp pains into his chest. Just that morning he had been innocent, falsely accused. He was filled with righteous anger at the injustice. Now? He deserved whatever he got. He was as guilty as they came. Might as well face it like a man. He pulled a sweatshirt over his bare chest and forced himself to walk deliberately to the door. Bracing himself, he unlocked the deadbolt and flung the door open.

Reg stood on the doorstep.

"What took you so long, D? You gonna make me stand out here forever, bro?" Reg shoved his way inside, closing and locking the door behind him.

DeAndre pressed his hand over his heart, taking a deep breath, telling himself to snap out of fight-or-flight mode. He slid his fingers between the blinds, prying them open. Everything was quiet out front.

"I got it taken care of," Reg said.

"Got what taken care of?"

"Everything. I got your back, D. They ain't gonna find out."

"Who?"

"No one's gonna know. You get it? It's just between us."

"How can you be so sure, Reg?"

"I drove by there. She's gone. The only thing there was the broken bottle of wine and the hair thing. I grabbed it. Burned it. Burned the panties. Even burned your clothes just in case. Cleaned the car. You're good, bro. You're good."

"What if someone saw you? Or saw us?"

"No one saw nothing, D. I was watching. I'm smarter than you give me credit for. You think I'm just gonna do that with a bunch of witnesses around? C'mon. And she didn't even have the wits to scream before I gagged her. Didn't fight much neither. You know there's no one on St. Anthony Street 'cept on Sundays."

DeAndre looked down at his hands, which weren't being swayed by Reg's logic; they were shaking.

"I don't know. I wish I could relax."

"Dude, I know. I feel ya. The first time I did something like that, I had trouble sleeping for a few nights. It gets better, believe me."

"The first time? Do I want to know?"

"You remember Shante? We dated for a while, and you remember how she was. She was always acting like she wanted some, dressing like she wanted some, sending me all kinds of signals. Then what does she do when I try and make a move? Let's just say I got tired of being told no. I been told no all my life, D. All my life. Done sick of it. I slipped her something one night. She didn't remember in the morning, but man I was paranoid for a while, wondering if it worked or if I was about to get busted. 'Course that was different, but I'm telling you, it gets easier."

DeAndre didn't know if he wanted it to get easier. He didn't want to be like Reg, conscience seared beyond recognition. He wanted to go back in time, to tell Reg to get his own godforsaken beer. He thought he felt trapped earlier, but he had never felt as closed in as he did right this moment—closed in by his own stupid, shortsighted choice. He needed a drink.

* * *

Natassa tousled David's hair and adjusted the collar of Daniel's shirt. "Be good," she admonished.

"We know," David groaned. "We always are, Mom." She pressed her lips tightly together and nodded, then forced a smile. He was right. They were such good boys, popular and well behaved with good grades. She hoped they would never know the darkness she had experienced on St. Anthony Street downtown.

They hadn't known what to tell the children, so by default they told them nothing. This necessitated acting as if nothing had happened. Everything was fine. C'est la vie. Brandon said this would help her move on with her life—that and bringing the criminal to justice.

"Go on now, you two. Mrs. Laurel is waiting." She halfheartedly shooed them out the door, wishing she could shelter them in their safe haven of a home instead of sending them to school. At least it was a Christian private school, and at least they didn't have to take a bus. Amanda Laurel did drop-off for carpool, and Natassa did pick-up. Or at least she had until *the event* happened and she became afraid to leave the house. Brandon was doing it for the time being. She needed to think of a convincing excuse to explain this development to the boys. On Monday, Hope was sniffling, so when the boys asked why she wasn't there to pick them up, she said their sister was under the weather. But now it had been nearly a week, and Hope was clearly on the mend. She needed to think fast.

Her phone buzzed in her pocket. *Breanna.* She knew without looking at the picture of her friend's straight jet-black hair streaked boldly with red. But Natassa pulled her phone out just to see Breanna's face again. It had been too long. The nose stud glinted back at her as did the sparkle in her eyes. Natassa sighed. She wished she could answer it. But to answer the phone after six days of silence would mean answering all kinds of questions she wasn't ready for. It ate away at her insides to keep such a big event from her best friend. But how could she tell her? She wanted everything to go away, and that was only possible if no one knew. More people knowing meant more people who could bring it up in conversation. Or worse, not bring it up and leave it hanging awkwardly in midair, both of them trying to avoid something as unavoidable as the air around them.

No, it was best she didn't know. But it would take Natassa more time or inner gumption to be able to hide the truth from the girl who befriended her at their high school lunch table, the one who stood up for her when the popular girls snubbed her. Breanna had been the maid of honor at her wedding and was the godmother of her children. She was the only one Natassa truly confided in, the only one who would think to ask, "How was your anniversary getaway?" knowing what Natassa had really been after. So how could she talk to Breanna right now? And how could she *not* talk to her?

Natassa shoved the phone back into her pocket and went to survey the damage left from breakfast.

"Mommy, Mommy, Mommy." Hope tugged on the pocket of her hoodie, beautiful blue eyes wide and expectant. "Read this book to me."

"Read this book to me ..."

"Pleeeease!" Hope corrected with a grin.

Kitchen forgotten, Natassa curled up on the couch and pulled Hope onto her lap, wrapping them both in a blanket.

"What do we have here?" Natassa asked, pulling the library book from Hope's chubby fingers. "*My People* by Langston Hughes."

Natassa started at the face of the black child on the cover. The slight smile, the hopeful eyes. She was mesmerized. The little girl was beautiful. Her skin, her eyes ... The man who raped her and his accomplice had been black. She could never recall an image, no matter how many times Brandon tried to get her to remember the details of the attack. She hadn't seen them, but she'd heard their voices. Well, she only remembered one voice. "Have at her, D." That voice belonged to a black man, she was sure of it. Was this where prejudice came from? But the face in front of her was so innocent.

"Mommy, are you going to read?"

Suddenly, she wasn't ready for this. She wasn't ready to open the cover and look at more faces. "You know what, Honey Bunches of Hope? I'm just in the mood for *The Very Hungry Caterpillar*. Can we read that instead?"

As soon as the words were out of Natassa's mouth, Hope was off her lap, thumbing through the bookshelf for her "most favoritest book." It hit Natassa that the house was far too quiet and she hadn't seen Faith in a while. "Faith? Hope, honey, where's Faith? Where's your sister?" Hope ignored her, searching intently for the caterpillar, deaf to the world.

Natassa got up and began her search. Faith was always wandering off, fluttering like a fairy in her own make-believe world. She had the wild imagination of an artist, and perhaps ADD. "Faith? Faith!" Natassa called as she looked upstairs in the girl's bedrooms and downstairs in the playroom. She wasn't in the boys' rooms either; the bathrooms, kitchen, office, and den were empty. A wave of panic rose within Natassa, churning her stomach. Their home was safe, right? A haven. A shelter.

She looked out the back window again. She didn't see her daughter, but she decided to go in the backyard and look. Thrusting on her flip-flops, she admonished Hope to stay right there and jogged out back.

"Faith?" Natassa's heart thumped in her chest, and the feelings of helplessness that had assaulted her days ago came flooding back. Then she'd been paralyzed by fear, unable to scream or fight, move or think. Now, she forced herself to do all of the above. She ran around the giant birch tree, the shed, and the bushes in their back garden. No sign of her little girl. Just when she was about to head inside again, she saw a pink plastic slip-on shoe peeking around the corner of the side yard. She sprinted to the spot. Her sweet daughter lay in the grass, clothed in a princess costume and holding a wand in her right hand.

"Faith!" Natassa screamed, shaking her daughter.

"No, Mommy. You're not supposed to shake me. You're supposed to kiss me. I'm Sleeping Beauty." Natassa's breath caught as tears pooled in her eyes. She grabbed her baby girl, smothering her with kisses. She held her tight and rocked her.

"Mommy, what's wrong?" Faith asked innocently.

What was wrong? All her life she had believed in God, had prayed for God to protect her. Every night she prayed for the safety of her children. She had trusted God to keep her safe ... and He hadn't. Not at all. How could she ever trust Him again? How could she trust Him with her children? Yet, if she couldn't trust God, then it was all up to her. How could she keep all the evil of the world away from the four little people who meant everything to her? She couldn't. She knew that. She would go crazy trying.

That's what was wrong. She couldn't trust God. But she couldn't trust herself to be God either.

5

———

The doorbell rang, interrupting Natassa's afternoon routine of slicing apples to pair with her homemade peanut butter dip for the children's snack. Brandon had taken Faith and Hope with him to pick up the boys from school, and she'd been relishing the rare silence. She hesitated. Who could be at the door? A salesman, maybe. She wasn't expecting any deliveries. What if it was—no, it couldn't be *him*. She was safe in her home. She had to stop being ridiculous. She wasn't putting herself in danger by answering the door. Still, she was home alone ...

The doorbell chimed again. Natassa bit her lower lip and wrung her hands on the kitchen towel. She walked slowly toward the front door, being careful to avoid the creaky board in the center of the walkway. She would just peek through the peephole and see.

"For the love of all that is right and good, Nat, open the door!" Breanna's voice called through the crack. Natassa released a breath she hadn't realized she was holding. Bre. It was Bre. She flung open the door, momentarily forgetting this was the person she had been avoiding for an entire week. In seconds, Breanna's tattooed arms were around her, squeezing her so tight her ribs ached.

"What are you doing here?"

"I'm on a rescue mission. Or a spy mission. Something. You disappear off the face of the earth for a week, don't return my calls or my texts, and don't so much as post one picture of the girls on Facebook, so I got desperate. I called Brandon. He wouldn't tell me what's up with you but said we should talk, so here I am."

"Yeah, I guess we should. Talk, I mean. But they'll be home any minute, and—"

"Ahh, but that's where you're wrong, friend. Brandon and I planned this great conspiracy. Your hubby and kids are staying the night with my hubby and kids."

Natassa snorted. "That should be interesting." Though in truth, Breanna's husband, Jack, and Brandon got along well enough, considering their personalities were polar opposites. Jack was an artist, and Brandon was ... not.

"And," Breanna continued, "we are having a girls' night, complete with a sleepover. I brought ice cream and a wide variety of chick flicks." She held up a plastic shopping bag and duffel bag as proof. "And before you start with your excuses, I made sure Brandon packed toothbrushes and vitamins. You know, so the world doesn't fall apart and your children don't wither away overnight from malnutrition."

Natassa found herself smiling, even though she was trying not to. "It's nice to be with someone who knows me so well."

"That's what I'm here for."

"We haven't had a sleepover since, when? The night before your wedding?"

"Hey, you've dozed off at plenty of our New Year's Eve parties. I think that counts."

"Not hardly! There are a million people at your New Year's Eve parties."

"Ah yes, but I only have eyes for you." Breanna's exaggerated wink highlighted her aqua eye shadow and dark mascara.

Natassa shook her head. "I could never pull that off."

"What?" Breanna asked.

Natassa gestured to her eyes.

"Oh! The makeup. Do you like it? It's from our new line."

"It looks great on you."

"It would look fabulous on you too, dear. Or even the azure color. You'd love that one. I'll doll you up tomorrow. Show you some simple techniques to make your eyes pop."

Natassa didn't want her eyes to pop; she didn't want any part of her to stand out, but she said nothing. Hopefully, Breanna would forget about it by the morning. Breanna ran a successful small business selling makeup and skin care products. She wasn't one of those slick and sleazy salespeople oiling their way into people's pockets with empty promises and a cheap stick of eyeliner. She was the real deal: professional and successful to the tune of six figures, aided by her exemplary people skills. But Natassa was one woman Breanna couldn't win over as a customer, no matter how hard she tried.

Breanna breezed past her, plopping the ice cream in the freezer, tossing her bags on the floor by the kitchen island, and grabbing herself a glass of water. If Natassa were a good friend, she'd have a Snapple in the fridge for Breanna, but she didn't want the girls getting into it. So, she didn't.

Breanna plopped down on a barstool. She took an apple slice sitting in front of her, dunked it in the peanut butter dip, and took a bite.

"Ugh! Oh my gosh, Natassa! This is disgusting! How can your children eat this stuff?"

"It's healthy," Natassa said with a shrug.

"Ewww. What, do you buy that peanut butter that you have to stir first? The kind that you keep in the refrigerator that doesn't spread, right?"

"It's organic, and it doesn't have all those added sugars in it."

"Which is why it tastes disgusting."

"My children like it."

"That's just because you shelter them and they don't know any better. Are you going to eat this?" Breanna asked, gesturing to the platter of apples and dip in front of them. "Because I'm certainly not going to."

Natassa shook her head and covered the dish, sliding it in the fridge.

Natassa sat down on a barstool across from her friend, admiring Breanna's tight topknot with a stylish stray red hair dangling down the side. With her hair up, her silver crescent moon earrings loomed large. "How are you even a mom? You look like you should be on the cover of a magazine. You can't even tell you have two kids, what with your skinny jeans and shimmery blue top. I look frumpy compared to you."

"First off, I've had five years, almost six, to lose the baby weight. Jesse will be six years old this summer."

"I can't believe it."

"I know, right? I'll have a nine-year-old and a six-year-old. I think that officially qualifies me as a grown-up. Anyway, you have a great figure yourself. You just choose to hide it. So don't you go talking about my skinny jeans. And stop stalling. Spill it. What happened to you?"

Natassa stared at Breanna's moon earrings a moment longer, gathering up her courage. How much should she tell? This was her Bre. How could she keep anything back? So, of course, she told everything. Unlike when she reported the story to Brandon, and later to the police, she was not emotionally distant. By the time she finished, she was clutching a wad of tissues she hadn't even seen Breanna grab for her. She tasted salt on her tongue. If she was worried about how she looked before ... Then again, Breanna's mascara didn't look so hot anymore either.

"But you did give a police report?" Breanna asked, her face twisted in sympathy.

"Yes. The next morning we left the hotel early and ... Oh, Bre. I don't even want to talk about it. It's like I had to relive everything all over again. I know they were just doing their job, but ..." Natassa shuddered.

Breanna squeezed her hand. "I am so, so sorry, Nat. I don't even know what to say. Except that you are strong and brave, and you're going to get through this. And you don't have to do it alone."

She asked some questions about Brandon's reaction and the police report and then gasped. "Nat!"

"What?"

"What ... what if you're pregnant?"

"No." Natassa shook her head, sliding off the barstool and walking toward the living room. "No. No. No. No. No."

Breanna came around in front of her, putting her hand on her shoulders, prodding her with her eyes. "Natassa, you can't make the pain of this go away by not telling anyone about it, and you can't make yourself not be pregnant by denying that it's even a possibility. I mean, it is a possibility, isn't it? You said yourself that you were hoping to get pregnant that night."

"Not like that!"

"Of course, not. But ... I mean, you've thought about it, right? Did they try to give you something at the hospital?"

Natassa sidestepped her friend, slumping onto the couch. "I wouldn't take it."

Breanna sat down beside her. "Then you did at least think about the possibility?"

"I don't want to talk about this right now."

Breanna threw her hands up in the air. "You're impossible. Really, Natassa, you've got to talk to Brandon."

"I can't. You have no idea how much he would freak out. And for what? Probably for nothing, right? So why bring it up?

Not until I know for sure, which won't be for another week or so."

"Why? Because Brandon doesn't like surprises, does he?"

"No."

"That would be a pretty big one."

"But at least that way I can act surprised too."

"Oh, Natassa, you've got to work this whole thing out with Brandon one way or another. I've told you over and over again—it's going to drive a wedge between you. You two need to have an honest conversation. You need to tell him the truth."

"I know. I just don't know how. He's been … different since the … incident. Angry, I guess. I don't know. He can still be really sweet to me at times, but then sometimes it's like he doesn't even see me. Just a crime scene."

"People work through things differently. It's only been a week. Give him some time."

"Okay, okay, sage. Can we watch some mindless movie now and forget about all of this for a while?"

"All right, one movie. Then we're going to come up with a game plan for how to get you out of this house without fearing for your life. Deal?"

"It better be a really good movie for that deal."

"Your pick. *Bride Wars*, *50 First Dates*, *Return to Me* …"

"You got *Little Women*?"

"You know it. Just for you."

"Deal."

* * *

"And they kiss in the rain. The end. Next pick is mine. I want to laugh. Enough sentimental tearjerker stuff."

Natassa picked at the fringes of the knitted blanket wrapped around her. Her mind had been miles from the movie, rehearsing what she might tell Brandon and how. Then she'd been planning what to say to Breanna when the credits rolled.

"I lost Faith," she said.

"Oh, Natassa. You didn't lose faith. You still believe. Anyone who has been through what you've been through is going to have some questions for God, some doubts. That's okay. He's not upset by that—"

"No, I mean, my daughter. I lost Faith," she said, gesturing to Faith's picture on the wall. Her hair was in twin French braids, her two front teeth were missing on the bottom, and her small dimple gleamed on her left cheek. Was there anything more beautiful to her than her children?

"Oh. What do you mean? Where?"

"I was reading to Hope, and then I realized Faith was gone. I looked all over for her. I eventually found her in the yard ..."

"Wait, so you didn't actually lose Faith. She was here all along. You just lost sight of her for a little while."

"I guess. But it just felt like she was gone. I don't know how to describe it, Bre—" Natassa shuddered, "—anna."

"Wait, why did you just do that?"

"What?"

"That! Bre—anna?"

"I don't know. It just ... saying your name just ... made me remember ..."

"Remember what?" Breanna prodded, her eyes a storm of gentleness and fierce protectiveness.

"'Have at her, D.' The guy who ... did that to me. His name was D. I just can't say ... out loud."

"Ohhh no. No, ma'am. No, sir. No way! That lowlife stole so much from you, Natassa. I am not going to let him take this. Not from us. That was my nickname first—has been since high school—and I am not letting that jerk hijack it. I'm Bre. You know me. I'm safe. That loser can shove it."

Natassa's eyes pooled, and she looked at the murky blanket, noticing the pattern of purple and green on the fringe.

"Look at me, chicka."

Natassa complied, the blue and black around Breanna's eyes puddling together through her tears.

"Who am I, Nat?"

"You're my best friend."

Breanna reached her hand out to Natassa. "And what's my name?"

Natassa took a deep breath and took Breanna's outstretched hand. "Bre."

"That's right, baby. Nat and Bre are a team. We're a team. No one is breaking us apart. Got it?"

"Yeah."

"Now, we've got to get you out of this house. You can't live like this forever. If you do, it's like he won. It's like the enemy won, and that is just not okay with me. It shouldn't be okay with you. So, here's what I think we should do. We should dive into that tub of rocky road, pop in something light and laugh our pajama pants off, and then conk out. Tomorrow morning, I'm doing your makeup, and then we'll get in my car and just drive by the scene of the crime. We won't get out. We won't unlock the doors. We'll just drive through the neighborhood as fast or as slow as you want."

"I don't know ..."

"The best way to get over your fears is to face them, right? I think you even told me that when you were taking some class. Face fear head on so that it loses its power over you. I'll be right with you. Nothing is going to happen."

"Brandon wouldn't like it."

"Why not? Does he want you living like your home is a bomb shelter? Does he enjoy leaving work every day to run carpool?"

"No. He thinks I should just get over it."

"Well, dearie, that's completely unrealistic. But we're going to take the first step in that general direction."

"Okay."

"Okay?"

"Yes."

"Score! All right, I'm grabbing spoons, and we're eating straight out of the carton. I'm feeling wild and crazy tonight."

"You're always wild and crazy. You fascinate me," Natassa shouted after her.

Breanna's laugh echoed off the walls. Natassa felt her body relaxing.

* * *

Natassa fiddled with her seatbelt. She felt cramped in Breanna's yellow Charger. She was claustrophobic and conspicuous. Was this truly a good idea? Two pasty white girls cruising by in the Sunmobile. Just passing through. Nothing to see here.

"Maybe we should take my car." The second the thought was out of Natassa's mouth, she vetoed it. She didn't want any unnecessary familiar associations. She hadn't driven her car since that night.

"Chill, will you?"

"I hope no one recognizes me. Do I look ... different enough?"

"If by different you mean that you looked hot then so you need to look frumpy now, then yes. I wish you would have let me do your makeup. I always feel better with some color on my face."

"It's not my thing."

"Don't knock what you won't try."

Natassa worried the sleeve of her oversized sweatshirt. Okay, so the sweatshirt paired with her yoga pants and tennis shoes did have her looking a bit frumpy. Her messy bun completed the ensemble. She just didn't want to take the chance of anyone recognizing the woman who'd walked that street the other night. Getting dolled up, looking attractive—see what that got her? She was retreating to the safe and familiar, but it didn't feel right. Nothing felt right anymore.

"Take a left on Winston," Natassa directed.

Breanna did so without comment. As chatty as Breanna normally was, she seemed to understand when silence was needed. The only words spoken were Natassa's directions, more frequent as they got closer.

"There it is. Edison's Wines. I parked in that spot and went in and bought the wine. When I came out, I walked around there," she said, pointing.

Breanna slowly drove around the corner and up St. Anthony Street, past the scene of the crime.

Natassa pressed her forehead against the window.

"Are you okay?" Breanna asked.

"I need some air." Natassa gasped and motioned for her friend to roll down the window.

With the window down, it was all too close, the feeling of being pushed from the car onto the hard pavement. Falling. The openness of the air around her when she couldn't see, the contrast of the back seat and the empty street. All of a sudden, she felt like death was strangling her. *I'm going to pass out. I'm having a heart attack. I can't deal with this.* Her vision tunneled, and her hands and feet tingled. She could taste metal in her mouth. She was dying. She had to be dying.

"Nat? Nat!" Breanna's eyes widened in panic for a split second before narrowing in resolve. She gunned it down the road and pulled into a parking lot at the end of the street.

"Natassa, take my hands. Look at me." She grabbed Natassa's hands in hers, moving into her line of sight. "You're okay. You're safe now. Take a deep breath. That's good. Another one.

Good girl. Keep going. You're okay. It's over. It's all over. Keep breathing deep. In and out."

Natassa continued breathing slow and deep, and her heart rate began to slow. As her vision cleared, she peered around. They were in the parking lot of a beautiful old church with stained glass windows depicting dark-skinned angels in sun-kissed skies. Natassa admired the intricate designs and colors, amazed that something so beautiful could be just down the street from the place where something so ugly had been done to her.

Breanna broke the silence. "I'm not a proponent of lying. You know that. So, if Brandon asks, 'Natassa, did you and Bre drive downtown to the neighborhood where the incident happened?' I absolutely want you to tell him the truth. But if he doesn't happen to ask, I don't think it's completely necessary to volunteer the information, right?"

Natassa never answered. She was still thinking about the window and how it was made of hundreds of pieces of broken glass, yet somehow arranged in such a stunning way. She caught a glimpse of the side window as Breanna drove away. It had the shape of a cross in it and was yellow like the sun.

6

———————

"I'm worried about her. She's afraid of her own shadow."

"It's Natassa. She's always been timid. And seriously, Brandon, can you blame her? You've just got to give her some time," Breanna whispered in reply.

"Time to what? Completely turn her back on everything she's always believed? She won't go to church. She hasn't even picked up her Bible since then."

"Her faith isn't lost. She thinks she lost faith, but it's just in the backyard. It's out of sight at the moment, but it's still on the premises. Give her time, Brandon. And space. To grieve, you know? She's got to work through this in her own way."

"You're a good friend to her, Breanna."

"Nat's the best. Hey, I've gotta run, but let me know if you guys need anything. A babysitter, maybe. A date night might do you good. Seriously, I'm on speed dial."

Natassa slowly pried her ear from the bedroom door and tiptoed back toward the bed, stepping over the princess Barbie lying in the middle of the floor. She was supposed to be napping, not straining to catch pieces of the hushed discussion going on down the hall. As soon as Breanna and she had arrived home, she made the excuse of a headache and plodded to bed with a wet rag pressed against her forehead.

She did have a headache, but she wasn't tired, just weary of conversation. She didn't want to talk to Breanna about what happened on St. Anthony Street, and she didn't want to talk to Brandon about her girls' night with Breanna. She didn't want to talk to anyone, but she couldn't resist eavesdropping when her husband and her best friend were talking about her.

She hoped Breanna was right. Didn't they say time healed all wounds? Maybe time was all she needed. She laughed humorlessly into her pillow. Some wounds cut too deep.

Natassa lay in bed and listened to the sounds of her family, her happy family. Faith and Hope's light footsteps scampered back and forth on the hardwoods. David and Daniel's tennis shoes trampled through the gravel out back, where they took turns pitching to each other. Occasionally, Brandon would laugh at the girls, and one of them would erupt in a fit of giggles. Once she heard him call out the back door for Daniel to watch his follow-through. Natassa could picture the look of concentration on her boy's face as he squinted into the sun, bony elbows sticking out, ready to swing at whatever ball his little brother could manage to throw to him.

She'd had a great life, one many would envy. Until she put on that blasted red dress.

* * *

Natassa rummaged through the pantry in frustration.

"Why are you growling, babe?" Brandon came up behind her and kissed her cheek.

She screamed and jumped, startled by his display of affection. He had barely touched her since *the incident*.

"Nat, it's okay! It's just me."

"Sorry." She put her hand on her chest, willing her heartbeat to slow. It took her a minute to get her bearings. She angled herself back toward the pantry, attempting to rein in her mind and focus on what she had been doing before Brandon threw her off.

"Uh ... I ... I didn't growl. Okay, I did. We don't have much for dinner. I'm trying to figure out what I can scrape together."

"You know, that's the crazy thing. When you don't go to the grocery store, the food magically runs out."

She spun around, intending to retaliate when she saw him wink. *He's messing with me. Like he used to.* She found a smile.

"Guess what?" Brandon walked up to her, grabbing her hands in his. "It doesn't matter because we are not eating dinner here. We are going out to eat. Just you and me. A date."

A date. She swallowed hard. What was wrong with her? Shouldn't she be happy to be going on a date with her husband?

"Let me guess, Breanna's babysitting." She managed to keep her voice even. Neutral.

"Yep." Brandon's grin only served to make her feel more ashamed.

It was on the tip of her tongue to say, "But she only offered yesterday," but she didn't want to give away the fact she had been eavesdropping.

"So where are we going?" Natassa asked instead.

"I don't know. Breanna said you had something you needed to tell me, so I guess somewhere with some privacy."

Natassa could feel dread welling up inside her. *I could strangle her. I'm going to strangle her. Somewhere private? Yeah. What about a desert island?* How could she have this conversation in public?

"How about you choose the place, just this once?" Brandon asked.

"No. Please don't, Brandon. You know I hate to make those decisions. I'll be fine with whatever you pick."

"Baluchani's?"

"Fine. Good." She nodded, thankful the conversation appeared to be over.

"Great. Now, make a list of what we need from the store, and this knight in shining armor will valiantly brave the public to retrieve those items to feed his starving family for the week. Maybe next week you'll be up to going yourself."

Natassa shrugged. She wasn't about to make any promises.

* * *

Brandon took Natassa's hand from across the table and found her eyes. "Baby, I know this has been the week from hell, and I'm sorry for that. I'm so very sorry, Nat. But we're going to get through this together. Me and you."

His voice was soft, so soft she felt she could melt into it, make reality disappear for a moment. Maybe he was right; all they needed was each other. He stroked her hand softly with his thumb, and her eyes were drawn to the small act of gentleness. The candlelight flickered and illuminated the diamond in her engagement ring.

"What are you thinking about, babe?" he asked, his thumb still caressing hers.

"I'm just remembering how you used that same wording when you proposed. 'No matter what obstacles come our way, we'll make it through together. Me and you.'"

They shared a small smile of reminiscence. That night under the glow of the sunset, she'd accepted his proposal, kissed him, and agreed that nothing would ever break them apart. She was giddy and drunk with new love that night.

She'd never envisioned this obstacle.

Her stomach churned. How could she do this? How could she ruin such a tender moment by initiating a conversation that had proven to be so explosive in the past?

She managed a weak moment of eye contact and a nervous smile before grabbing a roll and ripping it into small pieces, eating each one slowly. She caught Brandon's eye again. He was staring at her.

She needed to attempt conversation.

"So how was work?"

"Nat, don't do this. Breanna said you needed to talk to me. Something's obviously bothering you. Didn't you hear what I just said? Whatever it is, we'll get through it together."

"I just ... I just don't have a grid for this, Brandon. I know you want me to move on like nothing ever happened—"

"I didn't say that."

"You kind of did."

"No. That's not what I said. I didn't say act like it never happened. I said don't let it change you. There's a difference. You can't let external circumstances control you. You have to take the reins of your own life."

Natassa closed her eyes and sighed. "You know what? Forget it. I can't talk to you."

"What do you mean? Of course you can talk to me."

"Really? Because I'm trying to talk to you now, and I don't feel like you're listening. And the last time I tried to talk to you about how I wanted another child, you nearly bit my head off."

"Oh, come on! I did not. Good grief, Natassa. You said you wanted a baby. I said I didn't. It was a disagreement."

"A heated one," she whispered, hoping Brandon would take the hint that his voice was a tad too loud for *this* conversation in *this* setting.

"It wouldn't have been if you had respected my decision and stopped pressing the issue," his voice was quieter but held the same edge.

Natassa reached for another roll. Brandon intercepted her, grabbing her hand again. It didn't feel quite as tender this time around.

"Look, I'm sorry. Tonight wasn't supposed to be like this. We get along great most of the time, don't we? There's just this one issue we can't seem to see eye to eye on. We're just going to need to work through it. I told you I would pray about it, and I am. I told you that I wasn't going to sleep with you until I got some peace, some direction for all of this, and I'm still holding to that—"

"That's not even biblical. You know that, right? You're trying to sound all holy or something, but doesn't the Bible say 'Do not deprive one another?'"

"Don't start throwing Bible verses at me, Natassa. Not unless you want the ones about submitting to your husband thrown back at you. You're the one who doesn't want to take any kind of birth control."

The waiter stopped by, refilling their water glasses and asking if everything was okay. She wanted to tell him that, no, everything was most definitely not okay. She only smiled and nodded.

Brandon took a sip of his wine. "How come you haven't touched your wine?"

Deep breath. Here it goes. "Because I think I might be pregnant."

She felt Brandon release his grip on her hand. She held her breath and waited. He leaned forward, teeth clenched. "What?"

"I could be. Maybe not. But possibly. The dates line up with my cycle ..."

"You were ... on our anniversary." He closed his eyes, and Natassa cringed as she imagined him working it out in his mind. He shook his head. "You had a plan. You wanted to trap me into another child."

"I wanted a baby, Brandon. I wanted *your* baby." She leaned forward, pleading for understanding with her eyes. "Because I love you. Because ... because we're good together. Because—I don't know—something feels like it's still missing. I know you think that's crazy, but it's real to me. I know you said you didn't want to ... until we worked things out between us, but I thought if I dressed up for you and got your favorite wine, I thought maybe there was a chance."

"Why would you do that to me, Natassa? To us? Even before we had that conversation you were supposed to tell me when it was safe each month. Do you really think it would be good to start a child's life in such a deceitful way?"

"What were my options, Brandon? I tried talking to you about it. I tried telling you how I felt, and all I got was a fight. What was I supposed to do? Just give up? Oh, it's just Natassa. Her opinion doesn't really matter anyway. Her feelings don't count. She always ends up caving to what other people want. She can't even pick the restaurant, for goodness' sake! Well, maybe for once I didn't want to be steamrolled over." Natassa caught her own voice rising and hushed her volume.

She saw the waiter approaching in the distance and watched as Brandon closed his eyes for a moment and took a deep breath. When he opened his eyes again, it was as if they were clear of the previous conversation. Cool and collected Brandon returned, Etch-A-Sketch clear of negativity.

The waiter placed their meal on the table, giving Natassa room to escape the suffocating conversation. She smiled politely and told him her salad looked delicious, all the while thinking of how everything was falling apart around her. She was thankful he turned to leave before her eyes began to well with tears.

They ate in silence for several minutes before she spoke again.

"What if I am pregnant, Brandon? You don't seem to be worried in the slightest."

"I'm not." He took a bite of his steak.

"How come? How can you be so laissez-faire about this?"

"Natassa, you're not pregnant. You don't feel sick, do you?

You're eating that salad just fine. You haven't been falling asleep at six o'clock in the evening. You're not showing any signs. We've been through that four times. I remember what it's like."

"It's too early for signs."

"Besides," he continued, as if she hadn't spoken, "God is good. He's not going to let that happen to you, to us. He's not going to let you get pregnant by some rapist. You're a good, godly woman."

Natassa dropped her fork and sat back. "Do you realize how ridiculous that sounds? How callous? Oh no, God would never let you get pregnant, Natassa. He's good. Far too good to let that happen. Just not quite good enough to prevent you from getting raped!"

"Honey, I didn't mean—"

"What did you mean, Brandon? Hmm? Are you going to give me the line about everything working out for my good?"

"Natassa, you know—"

"What do I know? Because this good God who is supposed to protect His people? I don't think I know Him anymore."

Natassa grabbed her purse and slid out of the booth, knocking over her glass of wine in the process. She barged out the front doors and stood stiffly in front of the restaurant, wondering what to do next. She heard footsteps behind her, and a shiver went up her spine. Spinning around, she saw a middle-aged couple walking back to the parking lot. Her eyes told her she wasn't in danger, but her pulse still galloped and her senses were on high alert. She couldn't wait out here.

But she had made a scene. After worrying about the volume of Brandon's voice, she was the one who drew attention to their conversation. She was more embarrassed to go back in, fearing all eyes would be upon her, than she was afraid to apologize to her husband for her outburst.

She ducked back inside and into the bathroom.

She texted Brandon: LET ME KNOW WHEN YOU'RE READY TO LEAVE.

She spent twenty minutes mindlessly staring at her phone before she saw his return text pop up.

NOW.

7

———————

DeAndre woke with a start.

"So you gonna do it? You gonna do a run for Boss?" Reg came bursting through the door at four in the morning, flipping on the light and talking up a storm like DeAndre had nothing better to do than sit on the edge of the couch and wait for him to come home.

DeAndre flung his arm over his eyes. "Turn the light off, man. My head's killing me."

"I never thought I'd be the one saying this to you, but you need to lay off the booze, D."

"I know." He just didn't know what else to do to drown that caged feeling he'd been living with ever since that night on St. Anthony Street.

"So, is it true? Blane said he heard you was in, but you know how he is. That boy can talk, and half the time he don't know what he talking about. I can't believe Blane Thomas would know you running for Boss before me."

"I said I'd think about it. I didn't say I'd do it."

"Well, that's something coming from Mr. High and Mighty."

"I'm not so high and mighty anymore, am I?"

"Come on, D. You've got to get over this. Move on. It wasn't even your fault. Blame it on me if it makes you feel better. I liked you better with your head in the clouds."

"The air was pretty thin up there."

* * *

DeAndre's head was still throbbing when his phone rang at 9:30 the next morning.

"Hello?" DeAndre rubbed his eyes, wondering who would be calling him from that area code.

"Hello, am I speaking with DeAndre Scott?"

"Yes. Who is this?"

"My name is James Witherton. I'm the manager of Java Joe's Coffee Shop in Crawford County. How are you?"

"Uh … fine, sir. What's this about?" Had some other white chick accused him of stealing her coffee or something?

"We had a barista put in her two-week notice yesterday. She loved working here but got accepted to a college on the East Coast with a great academic scholarship, and it was an offer she couldn't refuse. You know how it is."

No. He didn't.

"She's got family out that way, so she's leaving us already and getting settled out there. Anyway, I came across your application and was wondering if you were still interested."

DeAndre pulled the phone from his ear to check the number again. This wasn't one of the boys playing a joke on him, was it? Paying some white boy to call?

"You're kidding, right?"

"No."

"You know I'm black, right?" Might as well lay all his cards on the table. Or at least the only card that seemed to matter in Crawford County.

"Yes, I do. I also know you drove twenty miles and dressed

up in a tie just to fill out an application. That says something about you."

Something more than that he was a fool on an errand?

"The starting pay is nine dollars an hour. I'm looking to fill twenty to twenty-five hours a week to start. I'm not sure if you were hoping for full-time hours, but there's a possibility you could do that in a couple of months. Are you interested?"

"Interested? Yes! Yes. When do I start?"

"Janell—she's the one who is moving to the East Coast— she can train you. Can you come in tomorrow morning? Around 8 a.m.? We can work out your schedule for the next couple weeks from there."

"Tomorrow? Sure. I can come in tomorrow."

"Great. I'll see you then."

"Thank you, sir. For the opportunity."

DeAndre hung up the phone and did a little dance. A barista. He was going to serve a bunch of uppity white people their vanilla frappuccinos. He had a job. A real, bona fide job. He was moving up in the world—up, up, and out of the neighborhood that was pulling him down. Look at him soar. DeAndre's head was back in the clouds, right where it belonged. He had to tell Reg.

He burst into Reg's room and flipped on his light. Reg let out an expletive as he rolled onto his side. "What you doin', D? Leave me alone."

"I'm not going to work for Boss. You know why? 'Cause I got my own boss, and his name is James. Oh yeah! This brother's gonna be working his black tail off at Java Joe's in Crawford County."

Reg propped himself up on one elbow. "You serious?"

"Yep. Just got offered the job."

"You mean to tell me you are going to get in your car every day and drive yourself up to the same neighborhood you nearly got kicked out of the other day? You crazy? You gonna get pulled over every day, D? What you gonna say to the cop the next time those lights flash in your rearview mirror? What are you gonna do the first time some sassy white chick gives you a condescending look? Or purposely goes to the line with the white guy waiting on her even though it's twice as long just so she won't have to deal with your black hands touching her drink? And what if you want to grab a Coke after work? Are you going to stop by the friendly neighborhood convenience store?"

"Shut up, Reg. You're not going to ruin this for me." DeAndre flipped off the light and slammed the door on his way out.

* * *

DeAndre had left his home forty-five minutes earlier than he probably needed to, but he wasn't sure what the traffic would be like that time of day in Crawford County. He didn't want to risk showing up late on his first day. His shirt was pressed, his shoes shined. He might not have much in the way of possessions, but he was going to make sure that what he did own was well taken care of. He was out to make a good first—or second—impression. And he drove five miles under the speed limit just to be safe.

He practiced his introductions in the car. It was especially important that he got along well with his coworkers. A cantankerous customer could make his life difficult for a few minutes, but a bad relationship with a coworker could ruin the whole deal and send him back to the Boss with a capital B.

DeAndre checked his smile in his review mirror. "Hi, I'm DeAndre. It's a pleasure to make your acquaintance," he practiced. No. Too formal. He was trying too hard. He caught a glimpse of flashing lights behind him. His smile dropped. His heart began to pound.

No! Reg can't be right again! His sweaty palms stuck to the steering wheel. This time everything was different. *"You match the description of someone we're looking for."* It could very well be true. He had to stay calm. That was the only way out of this. He could not lose his cool. He slowed down and began to pull over when the police car sped past him.

DeAndre checked his rearview mirror to be sure. The cop was gone. He hadn't been pulled over. Not today. He placed a hand over his racing heart. Reg had a point. Was he going to go through this every day? It would give him a nervous breakdown, the paranoia of being pulled over, of being found out. They would get used to him eventually, wouldn't they? Crawford County would get to know him, and when they did, they would accept him for who he was and not reject him for the color of his skin. He wanted to believe that. He used to believe that, but now he wasn't sure he was worthy of their acceptance. Maybe he was exactly who they thought he was.

* * *

"So, isn't it, like, a super long drive for you?" Janell asked while wiping down the counter.

"It's about twenty-five miles. It takes about forty minutes if there's no traffic, probably a bit longer to get home tonight."

"Gosh, that's so far. Rob and Patrick are looking for a roommate. You should move in with them. They only live a block away from here. You could walk on nice days and be here in five minutes."

DeAndre laughed.

"I'm serious! Hey, Rob!" The dude with bleach-blonde spiky hair turned from the table he was bussing. "You're still looking for a roommate, right?"

He eyed DeAndre curiously before answering. "Yeah. We are. Why?"

"DeAndre will be driving forty minutes or more every day

just to get to work. Why don't you give him the scoop?" Janell tilted her head toward DeAndre, lifting her eyebrows in a plea.

"Oh, I don't know." DeAndre didn't like putting Rob in an uncomfortable position on his first day there. "I live with my best friend, Reg. We go way back."

"Why don't you just come by and see the place after work?" Rob asked, to DeAndre's surprise. "It's just down the street. Rent is $300 a month. There's actually four of us living there, or there will be when we find another roommate. Patrick works here, too, but only on weekends, and then Eddie doesn't work anywhere. He's in school full-time."

"His parents foot the bill. They pay for everything. He's so lucky," Janell said.

"What do you say? Want to have a look?" Rob shifted the rag he was holding from one hand to the other.

DeAndre hesitated. "I wasn't planning on moving."

"You'll spend $300 a month on gas if you keep driving that far."

Janell had a point. An exaggerated one, but a point just the same.

"Do you offer everyone a room on their first day on the job?" DeAndre asked, skeptical at their trusting nature.

Rob chuckled. "Hey, James vouched for you. The boss is a great judge of character. He doesn't hire just anyone. So ..."

"I guess it wouldn't hurt just to look at it," DeAndre said.

Rob came up to him, shook his hand, and gave him a friendly pat on the back. That show of solidarity felt good, so good he wanted to rush out and look at the house right then. He was just looking, right? It wouldn't hurt to look.

Unless he liked it. Unless he went through with it. Unless his dream of walking those streets and living in that neighborhood actually came to pass. Because if that happened, he could only imagine how Reg would react. He'd never before considered that every dream had a price.

* * *

Oh, yes. He could see himself in this crib. His room would be in the basement, the finished basement. DeAndre admired the hardwood floors with those fancy throw rugs. The couches were leather, and not the kind with cracks in them. He spied granite countertops in the kitchen, a flat-screen television in the living room, and plush towels in the bathroom. There was not a leaky sink to be seen. The refrigerator was even the kind that spit out ice and water for you. If Reg were here, he'd ask where the button was to change the setting to beer.

Reg.

What am I doing? I can't turn my back on Reg now. I'm the only good thing he's got going in his life. Yeah, he's got faults, but he's loyal. He's been through stuff these white boys probably can't even imagine. He's stuck by me through everything. They might not have much, but they had each other.

"What do you think?" Rob asked, voice full of expectation.

"It's a great place. It looks like a palace compared to where I come from. I just don't think I'm ready to move right now."

Rob's shoulders drooped and his smile faded. "I understand. We've been looking for a roommate for a few months now, but no bites yet. If you change your mind, there's a good chance the spot will still be open."

"Thanks, man." DeAndre held his hand out to Rob for another handshake but was met with a less-enthusiastic response than before. *I've disappointed him. Trying not to disappoint Reg, I let Rob down.* DeAndre wasn't sure he was going to do so well navigating between two worlds.

* * *

"How was your first day in Whitey World?" Reg was reclining on the couch when DeAndre walked in the door from work.

"I had a great first day of work, Reg. Thanks for asking. What are you doing home so early?"

"Waiting for you. I missed you, D. You didn't get tossed to the curb?"

"Nope." In fact, not one person had been rude. Most people looked at him with only slightly veiled curiosity. He felt like an animal at the zoo, the new attraction to Crawford County. However, no one refused to have him wait on them or called him a thug or a hoodlum.

Or a rapist.

Had he almost forgotten that's what he was? Yes. One day out in suburbia and he was under the illusion that he was just another nice guy serving up fancy coffee. How he wished it were true. That sinking feeling returned to his gut. He felt like he had gained twenty pounds in an instant.

"The gas station on Washington and Ninth is hiring," Reg said.

"You mean the one that was robbed last week?"

"Yeah. Max don't work there no more."

"I wonder why. Might have something to do with having a gun pointed at his head."

"Hey, I'm just trying to give you options."

"I got options." Options. Earlier that day, he believed he had choices laid out in front of him. In Crawford County, he had believed he was the master of his own destiny, that he could make things different simply by choosing a different address. He had forgotten the streets he was from were made of quicksand. His hood had already sucked him under, made him another statistic. A criminal. And criminals didn't deserve clean air.

"D, you don't belong there. You belong here, with your people. Those white folk, they don't know what it's like to be you. They don't know the first thing about living in your skin. They don't know what you been through. Not like we do here."

DeAndre eyed his friend, sitting forward, looking at him expectantly. Reg was scared, wasn't he? Scared of losing him. That had to be it. In this crazy hard world, all they had was each other. How had DeAndre even thought of hightailing it out of there, of planting his black behind in suburbia for good? He was tied to these streets, whether he liked it or not, and to one street in particular. How could he ever have wings to fly after what he did on St. Anthony?

* * *

DeAndre's hands were shaking as he opened the door of Java Joe's the next morning. He told himself to calm down. *Everything's fine.* He hadn't been pulled over, but a cop had trailed him for a good six miles. He wanted this job—oh how he wanted it—but he wasn't sure how long he could go through the stress of the commute without having a nervous breakdown.

"Good morning, DeAndre!" James called out from behind the counter.

"Good morning."

DeAndre's attempt to play it cool must have failed miserably because James stopped restocking the napkins at the end of the counter and walked up to him, brows knit with concern. "Are you okay?"

"Yeah, boss. I'm fine."

"You look shaken up a bit. It's okay, DeAndre. You can talk to me."

Could he? Really? DeAndre contemplated replaying this morning's commute day after day and weighed the stress of that situation with the risk of looking bad in the eyes of his new employer. James looked as if he sincerely wanted to know what was going on.

"The thing is," DeAndre began, weighing his words, "when

I drive in this neighborhood, I'm likely to get pulled over by the police."

"Pulled over? Why?"

"Well, because of the color of my skin, sir. It's an unusual sight in Crawford County."

"What? I had no idea. I never thought ..."

"It's okay. Why would you? Think about it, I mean?"

"That's not right."

DeAndre gripped the back of his own neck, kneading his tense muscles. "It's the way it is. But it makes for a stressful drive up here."

"How can I help?" James asked.

DeAndre shrugged. What could James do for him? Paint his skin?

James's eyes lit up. "Why don't we go down to the station. I'll introduce you to the officers, let them know that you're working for me, vouch for you. I'm good friends with Brett, one of the officers there. If they know who you are and what you're doing here, they should leave you alone, right?"

"Yeah." Hopefully. DeAndre smiled in relief.

"You're working until noon, right? We'll go when you get off."

James gave DeAndre a friendly slap on the back then instructed Janell to show him how to work the cash register during his shift. It wasn't until an hour later that DeAndre realized he would be going directly to the place he wanted most desperately to avoid: the police station.

* * *

DeAndre ran his hand over the leather seat of James's jeep before hopping inside. The interior was meticulously maintained, not a crumb nor crack to be seen. It even smelled new, as if James were just taking it out for a test-drive.

As James got in the driver's side, DeAndre whistled. "Sweet ride. Did you just buy this baby?"

"I've had her about a year now."

DeAndre raised his eyebrows. "Doesn't smell like it."

James pointed to the air freshener hanging from the rearview mirror. "New car scent."

"You're kidding. I should get one of them for my beater. Then I could close my eyes and pretend I'm driving your jeep."

"Not a good idea to drive with your eyes closed."

He wouldn't have to drive. He could just park in Rob's driveway and imagine a different life. A life he gave up the right to reach for when he made the biggest mistake of his life. He should just turn himself in at the station. Save himself the torment of fearing being found out.

His hands began to tremble again.

"Hey, don't worry about this," James assured him. "It's no big deal. Brett is a great guy. I don't know the others that well, but I'm sure they'll be cool about it."

"Okay. Thanks," DeAndre said, but his insides were in turmoil.

"So, you live in South City?"

"Yes, sir."

"I know a couple that used to live down there. Right around Myrtle Tree Park. Is that near where you live?"

"No, sir, not really. That is South City, technically, I guess. But I live on the other side of Park Ave."

"The other side?"

"Park's kind of a dividing line in the city. They don't rent to people like me on the north side of Park."

"I had no idea."

"You don't have to worry about those kinds of things in Crawford County. That's why I came here."

"I understand."

DeAndre didn't think James understood, but he was trying

at some level, and that meant something. Some things you couldn't truly understand unless you lived them. James with his sweet jeep, that new car smell in his nostrils, and the possibilities of the world at his fingertips ... envy threatened to gnaw away at DeAndre's gut. He didn't have time to grow embittered, though. The police station appeared in the distance.

"You don't even have to say anything if you don't want to. Just let me introduce you to the guys," James instructed.

DeAndre nodded, unsure he could trust his voice to come out smooth and clear anyway.

James led the way into the station and asked to speak with Brett and the other officers there. When a group of five officers gathered, James introduced DeAndre and explained that he was the new employee at Java Joe's. DeAndre forced himself to smile, nod, and shake each officer's hand. He didn't see the cop that had pulled him over his first day in Crawford County.

"I just wanted you guys to meet him. DeAndre is an excellent employee. He's well mannered, responsible, and dependable. He'll be putting in a good twenty-five to thirty hours for me, maybe more, so you'll be seeing a lot of him around here. He drives a blue Corsica. Please don't give him any trouble. I'd hate for him to be late for his shift. I depend on him. And, as you can see, he's no criminal." James smiled and laughed, and the officers chuckled nervously. DeAndre held his pasted grin, all the while feeling his stomach sink.

If James only knew.

One of the officers thanked James for the information and promised to pass it along to the other officers.

"That was easy, huh?" James said as they left.

DeAndre nodded, still not trusting his voice to even eke out a "Yes, sir."

8

The moment Natassa had been dreading for weeks crept upon her. She had to do it; she knew she did. Breanna would be waiting for a text from her. If she didn't text, Bre would badger her. She couldn't avoid it.

Hope was napping. Faith was watching *The Princess and the Frog*. Natassa set the security alarm so she would be alerted if her little wanderer got distracted and decided to take a field trip, but she doubted that would happen. Disney princesses captured Faith's attention quite well. Natassa probably wouldn't be interrupted for a good half hour or more.

Her hands shook as she took the pregnancy test out of the box.

Maybe she should wait. Weren't these things more accurate if you took them in the morning anyway? She could get up before Brandon tomorrow and do it then.

Her phone chirped. She checked the text. From Breanna, of course.

DON'T CHICKEN OUT.

Can she read my mind?

Natassa wished Breanna were there with her to hold her

hand. She looked at the pregnancy test and tried to summon the courage she knew her best friend would give her if she were there. "It's just you and me, locked in the bathroom together. Let's do this."

As the wand sat on the counter, far away from her, she felt the minutes tick by. She was afraid to look. There she was, sitting on the bathroom floor, running her hand over the plush teal rug in front of the sink. It had been ten minutes, well over the required waiting period, but she couldn't bring herself to look at the results. She needed to get this over with. She didn't know how long Faith would remain occupied, but she didn't have all day.

She'd made it this far. She could do this. She had to do this. Taking a deep breath, Natassa forced her eyes to look at the test.

Two blue lines.

The tears began to pool. *I'm pregnant.* How she had longed to say those words. Just not like this. Natassa lay down and pressed her face into the rug, allowing her grief to express itself in moaning and tears. After the rape, all she wanted was for no one to know what had happened to her. Now everyone would know.

Her cries came louder, faster, harder.

She heard music in the living room and felt the freedom to not keep quiet. Faith wouldn't hear her above the song.

"God! How could You? How could You let this happen to me? I trusted You. I followed You. O God! I'm Your child? Aren't I Your child? And this is how You treat Your children? I want to erase this horrible, brutal attack that You stood by and watched, never lifting one finger to stop. And now this! This will follow me for the rest of my life!"

Mercy will follow you.

It wasn't an audible voice, but clear and straight to her heart. She knew that voice, even if she hadn't heard it in some time.

Wasn't that a verse? She grabbed her phone from the vanity and searched the Internet, looking at the words on the screen through her tears.

Surely goodness and mercy shall follow me
All the days of my life;
And I will dwell in the house of the Lord
Forever.

—Psalm 23:6, NKJV

Goodness. Mercy. Those were two words she didn't know how to reconcile with her present situation. Her belly would grow, and people would ask questions. They would talk. Strangers would make innocent remarks.

Mercy will follow you.

Every time she looked at her belly, every time she looked at her baby, she would remember—with excruciating clarity—the details of the attack. How would she ever be able to heal with such a vivid reminder facing her day after day?

Mercy will follow you.

She would give birth to a baby with skin a different color than her other children, a different color than her own. Her baby would have a different texture of hair, different facial features, different DNA. How could she explain that to her children?

Mercy will follow you.

But Brandon? What about Brandon? How would he feel putting his hand on her belly and feeling a baby he had not helped create kick inside her? How could he welcome a child who had nothing of himself inside its being? How could she even ask such a thing of him?

Mercy will follow you.

Mercy.

Natassa closed her eyes. A picture filled her mind. A little girl with black curly pigtails held her hand, trailing just a few steps behind her. Mercy. Following her. Her breath caught. She was shocked at the swelling of love in her heart at the simple beauty. She put her hand on her stomach and smiled through her tears.

She didn't have any of the answers to her other questions or objections, but she suddenly knew the child inside her was a girl. And she knew what she would name her.

Natassa went to rest in her bed. She laid her head back and closed her eyes. A moment later, her phone chirped, but she ignored it. She was certain it was Breanna. She couldn't tell Breanna before she told Brandon, and she couldn't tell Brandon ... well, until she figured out how to tell Brandon.

They hadn't talked about the possibility since their dinner discussion at Baluchani's. He didn't know Breanna bought the pregnancy test for her or that she planned on taking it that day. He hadn't said one word about it. They had spent the past week tiptoeing around the minefield of the issues brought up that night. As long as they steered their conversations toward the safe and familiar—their four children, his job, her cooking—a tentative peace remained between them. Natassa's focus had been not rocking that boat and keeping all dialogue regarding the subjects of another child, the attack, or what could come from it to short conversations with Bre or in the echoes of the own mind.

"Mommy! Mommy!" Faith came bursting into her room, leaping onto her lap, and wrapping her arms around Natassa's neck. "My movie is over. Will you read to me? Read to me, Mommy!"

Natassa smiled. Her stomach remained in knots, but she'd had time to settle herself down and dry her tears. After seeing that picture of what her little girl might look like, she felt some kind of peace. It wasn't pervasive. She wouldn't put her whole weight behind it, but it was more than she had experienced since the night of the attack. As she had slowly made her way from her bathroom to her bed, she'd come to have the inkling of hope that life would move on.

"Sure, FaithCakes. Grab Mommy a book, and we can snuggle here in bed and read together." Natassa relaxed against the pillows.

A minute later, Faith came flying into her room again and tossed *My People* by Langston Hughes onto Natassa's lap. As Faith lay down beside her, head on Natassa's shoulder, Natassa surveyed the cover again. A daughter with this pigment in her skin was growing in her womb right now. How dark would her skin be? How different would their arms look when held next to each other? It didn't matter. She would be beautiful. She would be hers.

"Yes, Faith. Let's read this one," Natassa said, turning to the first page.

* * *

"What are you waiting for? The water is already boiling."

Natassa startled at the touch of Brandon's hand on her shoulder. She hadn't even heard him come in.

"Whoa. You're edgy today. You must have jumped five feet in the air. What are you daydreaming about?"

"Daydreaming?"

"I'm assuming you're not so bored that you make it a habit to watch water boil."

"Oh." Natassa's nervous laughter nearly made her choke.

"Nat, what's up with you today?"

"Nothing. Just tired, I guess," Natassa cracked the spaghetti noodles in half and dumped them into the pot. Having something to do with her hands kept them from shaking so noticeably.

Brandon just stared at her. She could tell he wasn't buying it. Conversation. She needed to make conversation. Something. Anything.

"When is David's game?"

"Saturday. Two o'clock. Why? Do you think you'll come?"

"I'm thinking about it." She hadn't given it a single thought until that moment, but it seemed as good a distraction as any.

"It would mean a lot to him. I'm sure he misses you rooting him on at his games."

"I've only missed two."

"So far."

She didn't need the guilt trip but bit her tongue to keep from saying so. They'd had enough arguing lately. She stirred the pasta silently. If he wanted conversation, he'd have to make the effort. She stirred mindlessly, watching the timer flip from four minutes to three.

"Natassa," Brandon called out warily from the direction of their bedroom. She took a deep breath and made her way to the sound of his voice, spoon still in hand. She rounded the corner of their bedroom to see him standing in the doorway of the master bathroom holding something.

"Were you planning on mentioning this to me?" He held out the pregnancy test. Her stomach dropped. *Oh no! I remembered to hide the box but not the test itself.*

"Eventually. You just walked in the door." She shifted her wait from one foot to the other.

"You could have called."

"Yeah. That would have made a great telephone conversation."

"Well?" Brandon crossed his arms, as if in a challenge.

"Well ... I'm still processing. It's a lot to take in."

"I can't believe this!" Brandon kicked the doorframe, sending a shiver through Natassa. "That no good son of a—"

"Brandon, please. The girls are just in the other room. Can't we talk about this later? I need to check on dinner." Natassa waved the spoon in emphasis and turned to walk out of the room.

"I'm going to Brett's. I can't believe he hasn't caught this creep yet. There's got to be something he can do to ramp up the investigation."

Natassa nodded wordlessly, but she doubted Brandon even noticed. He didn't seem to need her permission for anything, even something that so personally concerned her. Were they even speaking the same language? She said *baby*, and he heard *criminal*.

Natassa returned to the kitchen and busied herself with the task of feeding her family, minus the man who was supposed to lead and protect them all.

* * *

It was after ten o'clock by the time Brandon returned. Natassa was lying in bed but not sleeping. Sleep was far from her; all her thoughts, fears, and hopes collided like crashing waves. She sat up when Brandon opened their bedroom door, unsure of what to expect, afraid to make the first move.

"Why didn't you take the pill they gave you? To make sure this wouldn't happen." He rubbed the back of his neck, the stress of the day etched in the lines on his face.

"Hello to you, too."

"In the hospital. Why didn't you take it? Brett asked me, and I didn't know what to say."

"Because it's wrong, Brandon. Come on, you know that. It's wrong to end a child's life."

"In most instances, yes. If it's because of convenience, of course. There are bad reasons to have an abortion, but you were raped, Natassa. Raped. No sane person would blame you for taking that pill in these circumstances."

"Who are you?" Natassa couldn't believe that those words had just come out of her husband's mouth. Brandon Bloomington. He gave generously to pro-life causes, taught a Bible study at their church. She was shocked by the idea that her husband believed it was perfectly moral to take the morning-after pill in some instances.

"I could ask you the same thing."

"It's still a baby, and it's not the baby's fault."

"Well, it's not your fault either. Is it?" His eyes sliced through the distance between them. She pulled the covers over her further, feeling exposed.

"Is it, Natassa? You did fight back, didn't you?"

She opened her mouth, but nothing came out.

"Please tell me you kicked or clawed, something!"

"I ..."

"You know, maybe it is your fault. You in your sexy red dress. You don't seem to mind. You got what you wanted, didn't you? Your fifth baby. And you don't care who you hurt in the process."

"Brandon—"

He stilled and raked his hands in his hair. "I shouldn't have said that, but I can't do this Natassa. Not now. I'm sleeping in the den tonight."

Natassa listened to Brandon stomp out of their room and down the stairs. After the attack, she had turned to her husband to be her safe place. Where was her safe place now?

9

____

"Are you sure you don't want to go to church with us?" Brandon asked, straightening his tie.

"I'm sure." Natassa sat cross-legged on her bed, braiding Hope's hair. Brandon had come up that morning as if nothing happened between them the night before, as if they hadn't spent the night apart for the first time in their marriage. And he wanted the family to go to church together as if things weren't unraveling? No thank you. She'd stay in her pajamas.

"Why aren't you coming with us, Mommy?" Hope asked, turning to face her.

"Hold still, please."

"Mommy's not feeling great this Sunday, but I'm sure she'll be back to her old self next week. Right, honey?"

"All done, Honey Bunches. You can go get your shoes on." Natassa smiled at Hope, ignoring Brandon's comment. Hope scampered from the room, leaving the two of them alone.

"You haven't been to church in a month. People will start to talk."

"I know." She'd better get used to people talking. "Call me

when you're on your way home, and I'll get lunch ready for you."

"Oh, I almost forgot. I talked to your mom. She wants you to go over to her house for lunch today. You and your sisters. One thirty."

"You talked to my mom?"

Brandon shrugged.

"She called you? And invited me to lunch?"

"One thirty," he repeated before walking out the bedroom door.

"Strange," Natassa whispered to herself.

Brandon peeked his head through the doorway. "It'll be good for you. You haven't left the house without me since that night."

That wasn't true, but he didn't know about her trip downtown with Breanna.

Trip downtown.

Natassa closed her eyes and remembered the stained glass windows of that church. She wondered if it was abandoned or if they still had services. She wondered what it looked like when the lights were on inside, what it sounded like during worship. What songs did they sing there?

She began to form a plan.

* * *

Thirty minutes later, Brandon and the children were out the door and on their way to the contemporary church they had been attending faithfully for the past six years. With a congregation of around four hundred—made up mostly of upper-middle-class white families—Natassa knew Brandon was right. People would begin to talk. After the third worship song, there would be time for worshipers to turn around and greet one another. She could almost feel sorry for Brandon, fielding the questions from people—some well meaning, others downright nosy—about where she had been. Thankfully, the meet-and-greet time only lasted four minutes. Brandon wouldn't have to shift his weight and make awkward excuses for too long before the band began to play their short interlude, signaling the sermon was about to start.

Natassa waited a full ten minutes after Brandon pulled out of the driveway to make sure he didn't forget anything. When she was certain he wasn't coming back, she scoured her closet for something to wear—something dressy but not attractive. Could she do that? Could she pull that off? She settled on black dress pants, a modest black blouse, and a blazer to match. There, she looked like she was going to a funeral. Perfect.

She went into the bathroom and surveyed her hair in the mirror. Running a brush through it, she sighed. She really should shower, but she didn't know if she had time. Probably not. Instead, she rushed back to her closet and found the old black straw hat her mother had given her. Appropriate since she would be seeing her mother today. Back to the mirror, and ... Great, now she looked like an old lady going to a funeral.

She didn't have time to change her mind. She brushed her teeth, slid on her black flats, and grabbed her keys. She had already turned the ignition before she began to question what in the world she was doing. *I'm crazy. I'm willingly driving this car onto that street? What's gotten into me?*

What had gotten into her was a baby, planted in her in that neighborhood, on that street. She felt drawn to that place now, as if it were a magnet attracting the growing life inside her womb. She *needed* to drive down St. Anthony Street, but her hands shook on the steering wheel.

I can't believe I am doing this. She contemplated turning her Audi around, maybe spending the morning with a caramel macchiato and a scone instead. But no. Hadn't Breanna told her the way to get over her fears was to face them? And Brandon was wrong about some things, but it was true that she couldn't avoid her life forever. Carpool. Grocery shopping. Baseball games. Church. Life had to move on, and though this seemed to be a completely illogical first step, something inside her told her it was the right one. Even if she was terrified.

"My doors are locked. I'm safe," she reassured herself as she entered the neighborhood. "Plus, I have mace." Brandon gave her the pepper spray the day after the attack. She remembered how she had stared at that little bottle, feeling cynical. Brandon acted as if this would solve all her problems, but if she couldn't even scream and kick when threatened, how could she trust herself to use mace? It brought little comfort.

Instead, she remembered how Breanna had coached her on taking deep breaths, and she did so then, imagining her friend beside her. What would Bre say when she heard this story? She wanted to have another slumber party and a long heart-to-heart with her friend. She needed Breanna's strength to lean on. She wanted her advice. What should she do about Brandon? How could she make him see beyond the crime and get to her heart? Breanna always knew what to say, what to do.

Of course, Natassa still hadn't told Breanna she was pregnant. So, there was that.

Natassa instinctively drove more slowly as she got closer. The streets were quiet, hardly a person to be seen. She noticed the graffiti spray-painted on the side of some brick buildings, some names or words she couldn't quite make out next to a cartoonish picture of a big brown eye looking to the sky. She did a double take at the eye before driving on, mesmerized by the details of the lashes and how the artist captured such a feeling of desperation in a simple cartoon picture.

As she turned the corner onto St. Anthony Street, the sun shone directly into her field of vision. She grabbed her sunglasses from the dashboard, sliding them on. Strange how the street didn't seem so menacing in the path of the blazing sun. Her heart was still pounding, though, and she felt her pulse in her throat. But she could breathe. And she did—slow, deep breaths. She didn't look to the right, where she had been grabbed from the sidewalk. She didn't look to her left, where she had been carelessly discarded in the street. She looked straight ahead, toward the church at the end of the street, its tower rising above the ugliness she had experienced, its bell clanging a beautiful melody.

Its bell? Interesting. She hadn't noticed a bell before. Yet there it was, looking ancient and heavy. It sounded so inviting; it was so mesmerizing that Natassa pulled into the church parking lot before thinking twice about driving past the crime scene. She made it.

"I did it!" she whispered to herself. Her fingers trembled slightly in response. She put her car in park but didn't kill the engine. "Now what?" She hadn't completely thought this through. The entrance to the church was directly to her right. There were a few people milling around the front of the church. She noticed they were all black people. She averted her gaze, staring straight ahead. What did she, Ms. Don't-draw-attention-to-yourself-Natassa, think she was doing showing up at a black church? Did she think she could just waltz in there in her granny funeral outfit and slip in the back unnoticed? Her thumb caressed the gearshift. She could just shift into drive and forget the whole endeavor. She bit her lip, debating.

Then she heard ... yelling? Out of the corner of her eye, she saw a woman waving. Was that woman waving at her? Natassa looked down, grabbing her phone from the passenger's seat and mindlessly fiddling with it, attempting to ignore whatever was going on in the parking lot. Why would anyone be waving at her? The woman had to be trying to get someone else's attention.

A knock on her passenger's side window made her jump and gasp.

"Sorry to startle you, sugar," a woman said through the glass. Her silver hair fell in gentle curls around her shoulders, matching her stud earrings. Her long green dress billowed in the breeze. She had skin the color of pistachio shells, and her teeth gleamed when she smiled, which she was doing while signaling for Natassa to roll down her window. Natassa hit the button.

"I said I's sorry to startle you. Are you lost?"

"Lost? Uhh, no. Not really. I'm not lost."

"Really? 'Cause you look like you don't have a clue where you is. Are you joining us this morning?"

"Me? Oh, I wasn't really planning on ... I have somewhere I need to be in a little while. I just ... I was just admiring the stained glass windows of your church. They are beautiful ..."

"We won't bite, sugar. You can come out of that fortress of yours."

"Oh, it's not that. I don't have a lot of time."

"It's Sunday morning, honey. Ain't nowhere better to be on the Lord's day than in His house. Ain't that right?"

Natassa cautiously returned the woman's broad smile.

"Now, come on out of there so I can shake your hand all proper like."

Even as Natassa said "I don't know," she was unlocking her door. The magnet inside her was being pulled in the direction of this enchanting woman, or of the church in general. She didn't know which. Natassa got out of her car and, wrapping her arms tightly around herself, walked to the passenger's side where the woman was standing.

"Welcome to St. Anthony's Baptist Church. My name's Bethany, like Mary of Bethany. You know your Bible, don't you, sugar?"

"Mostly," Natassa replied, though she had an inkling she didn't know her Bible as well as the woman standing before her. "I'm Natassa."

The church bell sounded, startling Natassa yet again.

"You'se a little jumpy there, darlin'. You're not from around here, are ya?"

"No."

"But you'se not lost?"

"No."

"Maybe you is and you just don't know it yet. Never mind that, sugar. You'll be finding your way. Come here. Let me introduce you to some folk."

Natassa walked with Bethany toward the stone steps. There was a beggar sitting on the ground by the bottom step, hat upside-down on the ground to his left. His scraggly gray hair stuck out in all directions, and a gnarled cane lay to his right. His gray dress pants were too short, exposing half his calf. He wore a white dress shirt with a dingy maroon sweater-vest on top. Natassa imagined that if she pulled at one of the loose threads hanging from it, the entire vest would unravel with little effort. He wore dark sunglasses and stared straight ahead.

"Who do we have here? What's your name, child?" the man asked as she approached.

"Who? Me?" Natassa looked nervously at Bethany. Had the man just called her a child? Or was he talking to someone else?

"Oh Lawdie, Old Ezra! Have we got one for you today! This here is Natassa with a T. I bet this one's gonna stump you good!" Bethany's laugh rang out even louder than the church bell, it seemed. Natassa had no idea what they were talking about, but she wanted Bethany to keep laughing.

"Natassa, you say?" The old man fingered the whiskers on his chin. "That is a tough one, but not too tough. Variant of Anastasia. Greek. Means 'Resurrection.'"

"You serious?" Bethany looked back and forth from the old beggar to Natassa. "You got another one! There's no stumping you, is there?"

"Stumping him? What do you mean?"

"This man knows the meaning of every single name known to mankind. You tell him a name, and he can tell you what it means. You got yourself an unusual one, and he still knew. Your name means 'Resurrection.' Did you know that, sugar?"

"No, I didn't."

"Well, fancy that. You didn't, but he did."

Natassa choked back a wave of tears that threatened to surface. Resurrection. Rebirth. New beginnings. How she needed that. Ever since that night, she felt that some part of her lay dead or at the very least in critical condition. Maybe Bethany was right. Maybe she was lost and she just hadn't realized it.

The church bell rang again, bringing her back to the old beggar and the eccentric woman in front of her.

"That's my cue for a quick smoke." Bethany pulled out a pack of Camel cigarettes and lit one in a flash. The very sight of it jarred Natassa. She did not expect *that* from this woman.

"I know, I know. With all the Good Lord delivered me from, you'd think I would have given up these cancer sticks a long time ago. Seems like it's just that one pesky thing that's still got a hold on me. Don't you worry none, though. We gots five minutes still, and I'll be done with this old thing 'fore the music starts playing."

Natassa chuckled nervously, embarrassed that her surprise had been so apparent to Bethany. She needed to attempt conversation.

"So, how did you come to know the meanings of names?" she asked the old beggar.

"That's an interesting story. I was born in '34—"

"Oh no, Old Ezra. I done told her we only got five minutes. This story takes far longer than five minutes!"

"I grew up during the Depression, you see. I wanted to go to school, but my pa needed me to help him in the fields."

"What he's gonna get around to sayin' eventually," Bethany

interrupted, "is that he never did learn how to read until he was all grown up. He couldn't get his hands on hardly any books, but one day some missionary society ladies came, and they gave out some books other people didn't want anymore. Old Ezra here got stuck with some name meaning book."

"I read that book cover to cover, over and over again 'cause it was all I had. I got real good at reading with that book, and while I read it, I remembered what I read is all. Then when I lost my sight, I kept all those names in my head. That way I can give out their meanings like gifts to the people I meet."

"Oh!" He was blind. How had she missed that? She reached inside her purse and grabbed a ten-dollar bill. Moving toward him as silently as she could, she placed the bill in his hat. He had given her a gift. It was only right that she reciprocate.

"Hey, Mazy!" Bethany shouted across the parking lot as a thin woman wearing enormous heals made her way to the church's entrance. Her hair was styled in a sleek bob, and her skin reminded Natassa of the midnight sky, so dark and enchanting. Everything about the woman spoke poise and sophistication as she sauntered ever closer in her buttoned blouse and navy skirt.

Bethany pointed her cigarette in Natassa's direction, ash sprinkling to the concrete steps. "This here's Natassa with a T. Natassa, this is Mazy—fashionably late again, I see," Bethany said with a smile.

"Oh, I'm not late. The music hasn't even started. I bet I have a good minute and a half." Mazy smiled back at Bethany and then held her hand out to Natassa, who shook it, noting how smooth Mazy's hand felt. "Nice of you to join us, Natassa."

The earnest look in Mazy's eye as she said this made Natassa feel that maybe it was true. Perhaps she wasn't out of her mind to be there, though she hadn't actually had any intention of going inside the church. How could she get out of this situation now? Standing outside on the steps was one thing;

going inside to the church service was quite another. She watched as Mazy gave Bethany a pat on the back and then slipped inside the heavy wooden front doors.

She heard a bar of music from inside. *That's my cue.* Natassa looked for a way to escape to her car. Bethany quickly put out her cigarette, smooshing it with her shiny black low-healed shoe. She looked down to see Old Ezra picking up his cane and standing to his feet. To her horror, she saw him grab his hat and put it on his head. Her ten-dollar bill floated gracefully to the pavement. She felt her cheeks go hot. He wasn't a beggar at all! He was just a man waiting outside for church to start, and she had put money in his hat! It was definitely time for her to leave —and not come back.

"Time to go in, sugar!" Bethany's voice rang, sweet with expectation. There was her new friend, holding the door open for her, inviting Natassa into her world. But she couldn't; she didn't belong. Did she? She was too ... white.

"Oh, sugar, looks like you done dropped your offering on the sidewalk. You'd better grab it before it blows away." Bethany nodded to where the bill lay, shamefully fluttering in the breeze.

Did she see me put it in Old Ezra's hat? What must she think of me?

"Your money for the offering," Bethany said again. "You better grab it quick. You can put it in the basket when they pass it around." Bethany met her eyes and smiled. So, she did see. She was giving Natassa a graceful out. But to take it would mean that she would have to go inside.

10

He was seeing things. Crackin', pure and simple. DeAndre rubbed his eyes and looked out at the street again. Yep, the car was gone. *She* was gone. Must have been a figment of his overactive imagination, brought on by stress. And guilt. Oh, the guilt gnawed his insides raw until he wasn't sure there was much of anything left.

He took another swig of his beer, knowing he shouldn't, aware that there wasn't enough booze in the world to drown the ache inside of him. It was futile, yet he didn't know what else to do. He wasn't drunk, not really. Buzzed a little like he was on most of his days off. If he wanted to get drunk, he'd reach for the harder stuff. He'd venture across the street and around the corner to the liquor store Reg and he had used to fuel their fires that night. But no. He'd vowed never to set foot in that store again.

He stared out the broken glass to where the old video game store used to be, remembering better times. More innocent times. St. Anthony Street. What was he doing here? He couldn't stay away. It was as if something was drawing him back to the very place he knew he should be avoiding. Reg said the cops were prowling for clues. Even if they weren't, did he enjoy torturing himself? Yet there he was, sitting in a beat-up chair in an abandoned building right across the street from where he helped grab that woman and shove her in his car.

When he had walked by earlier, the board had been half hanging off the window. It hardly took any effort to pry it loose and climb inside the place that used to be a little mom-and-pop ice cream parlor. It afforded him a secluded viewpoint of St. Antony Street and the perfect little haven to brood.

And hallucinate, apparently, because not more than ten minutes after he sat down, he thought he saw the same woman he raped driving her fancy SUV down the street. Right. As if she just happened to take a Sunday morning drive in her favorite friendly neighborhood.

DeAndre groaned. Maybe he needed to see a shrink. He was losing it, clearly. No sooner did the idea cross his mind than he dismissed it. Even if he had the money for a shrink, even if there was one besides someone at the income-based mental health clinic with a waiting list years long, what would he tell the guy? The truth? The shrink would have to report the crime to the police, and where would that put DeAndre? In prison. And once he served jail time, he could kiss his dreams of getting out of this hood goodbye. Getting a job with a criminal record? Forget it. There was no way he could move up in the world with a record trailing him.

He would have to live with his hallucinations. They were his punishment for what he'd done, and he needed to take it like a man. If he could take it back, he would. If he could apologize, he would. But what could he do? He took another drink.

The church bell chimed down the street. That old Baptist church was still going strong after all these years. The whole neighborhood had crumbled around it, and yet that bell still rang out every Sunday morning. That was something, wasn't it?

He wasn't much for church anymore, but even he could admire that in all the mess around him there was something stable, something a person could hold on to.

DeAndre looked down at the bottles of spray paint lying at his feet. Maybe it wasn't the smartest idea—he was supposed to be keeping out of sight—but it felt right somehow, at least better than sitting here thinking about how his life got off track. Perhaps he could make some sort of atonement for himself. He wasn't worthy to set foot in that church, but he could bring a piece of the church right where he was.

He grabbed the paint, climbed out the window, and went to a good, solid section of brick wall. He turned his back on the street where he'd made the most horrendous mistake of his life and began to paint.

He painted the church with its stone steps and black railings. He painted the stained glass windows in front. He painted the bell on top. And right there on the side, unfit to even set foot inside the painted building, he painted himself on his knees begging for mercy.

* * *

DeAndre tossed the cans of spray paint inside the old ice cream shop and walked toward home. He felt life in his veins, art flowing through him. His fingertips buzzed from it even then. He couldn't wait to tell Reg he'd painted another one. He'd been in a slump lately. It had been— what? Three months since he painted that eye looking up to heaven.

Reg hadn't been too impressed with that one, come to think of it. "He look like he got his head up in the clouds, same as you, D."

Reg much preferred the Black Power fist DeAndre had done on Ninth or the caricature of Malcolm X on Park Ave. He'd done those at Reg's request, and they turned out all right. But he hadn't felt this energy charging from him after he painted those.

No, this was different—special somehow. And as DeAndre turned the corner and saw the dilapidated house in the distance, he decided not to tell Reg at all. Reg wouldn't appreciate it, wouldn't see the beauty. His best friend saw no need for redemption nor mercy. DeAndre had never kept much of anything from Reg before, but maybe it was time to start.

DeAndre stopped halfway up the steps to his house, realizing it must be well after noon. Reg wouldn't be home, and he didn't want to sit alone in an empty house. As much as it goaded him to visit Pa's shop on a Sunday, he found himself walking in the direction of Seventh and Elm, making a game of kicking every stray beer bottle and coke can he passed on the way, just like he used to do as a boy visiting Pa at work. But never on a Sunday.

He called Elm Street Automotive "Pa's Shop," though of course his father had never owned the place. His dad worked there as a mechanic for as long as DeAndre could remember, maybe even before he was born. He didn't have all the facts straight. All DeAndre knew was that Pa always talked about them working together at his shop someday, and DeAndre always assumed that's what would happen. It was as good a trade as any, a far better outcome than what many other black men from his neighborhood found. It would have been a good life, working beside Pa, coming home covered in car grease, full of stories.

The thing was, Pa had this natural love for his job. Fixing a car was like putting together a puzzle for him. DeAndre would watch his face and see that spark in his eye when he figured out what was wrong and how to fix it. DeAndre kept waiting for that magic spark, something to light him up, make him excited about wrenches and carburetors. He never found it. He thought he had more time, that if he let it come to him, Pa's enthusiasm would catch on eventually.

When Pa died, DeAndre realized he hadn't paid a bit of attention to the vocation Pa was so passionate about. He knew little more than how to pop the hood. But Reg—Reg was different. He was the son Pa never had. While DeAndre had been in his room doodling in his notebooks and "messin' around," as his mama always said, Reg would be by Pa's side, watching and soaking it all up. And now? DeAndre was aimless, not sure what he wanted to do with his life, save get away from the neighborhood that haunted him. And Reg? Reg was following in DeAndre's father's footsteps. He worked in Pa's shop and footed most of DeAndre's bills.

The thought of it stung with humiliation, served with a heaping side of regret, but DeAndre couldn't hold it against Reg. His best friend had loved Pa deeply, like he was his own father. No, the only one DeAndre could blame for this one was himself. No wonder he couldn't stop dreaming of hightailing it out of there and leaving it all behind.

DeAndre turned the next corner, and there it was: Pa's shop. Reg would be the only one there today. The others who worked there were older men, friends of Pa. They held hard and fast to the Sunday Sabbath rule. Just like Pa would have been, they'd be with their families today.

DeAndre saw Reg bent over an engine, his overalls and white muscle shirt smudged with black splotches. His ball cap was turned backward and his brow pinched in concentration. It was strange how Reg could wear the same attire as Pa had. Could there be two different men? DeAndre could remember his father cursing twice in his life. Reg cursed twice in a sentence a lot of times. His dad was a man of hard work and integrity, a man who believed that if you did the right thing, good would come of it in the end. Of course, he got shot dead in the street, so DeAndre couldn't blame Reg for not holding fast to that conviction.

Even so, Reg cut corners in a way that would make Pa shake his head and sigh if he were alive today. DeAndre could almost see the old man grabbing the back of his neck, hear him saying, "What we gonna do with that boy, Dre?"

DeAndre didn't know what to do about Reg's ethics, but he did know that without this job, without Pa's legacy to carry on, Reg would be running for Boss for sure. There wasn't anything keeping him from it, save the memory of Pa leaning over an engine, wiping his forehead with an old rag, and saying to Reg, "I want you to make something of yourself. Hear me, boy? I don't mean you got to be famous or nothing like that. I just mean you got to work with your hands and stay out of jail. Be better than what everyone thought you'd end up like, you hear?"

Reg now had someone he didn't want to disappoint, even if that someone was just a memory.

And yet, DeAndre knew Reg was tight with several drug dealers. He'd look the other way, even cover for them just the same as he'd do for D. It wouldn't take much to get sucked in, and that wasn't all DeAndre had to be afraid of. It was dangerous just having those connections. How long could Reg go on that way without getting caught in the crossfire?

Then again, their pa hadn't had any connections to the drug culture, and yet, a stray bullet found the back of his head. No one was safe around here. You could play by all the rules and still end up burying the people you loved the most.

"Whatcha doin' here, D?" Reg spotted him just as DeAndre set foot in the garage.

"I was bored. Thought I'd see what you were up to."

"Alternator's out on this one. I'll fix 'er up real quick then we can grab a bite to eat if you want."

"Sounds good."

"Wanna help?"

"Aww shush, boy. You know I don't know the first thing about any alternator."

"It's easy. C'mon, give it a try. First we got to use this serpentine belt tool to loosen the belt here, see. Then we move it off the pulley of the alternator."

DeAndre leaned over, watching Reg carefully. At least now he knew what an alternator looked like.

"Now, we gonna put these bolts back. Why don't you do that, D?"

"Me?"

"Yeah, you. Who else 'round here is named D? I think I can trust you to tighten a couple of bolts. That's hard to mess up."

DeAndre wasn't too sure, but he did as Reg asked. It was easier than it looked, and as Reg continued to walk him through replacing the alternator step by step, DeAndre started gaining a small amount of confidence. He wasn't about to attempt anything without Reg right next to him giving him a tutorial, and he certainly still didn't feel called to this line of work, but pride rose up within him when the new alternator was in and he turned the key to the car. Being greeted by the purring sound of the engine was akin to hearing Pa's old jazz music pouring through the speakers. He felt connected to his father in a way he never had before. Too bad Pa wasn't alive to see it.

11

———

Natassa's phone buzzed, still on vibrate from the church service. She reached to grab it but then changed her mind. She knew she was late. She didn't need to be reminded. Or badgered. Still on a high from the "Bapticostal" service, as Bethany called it, she wasn't ready to be deflated just yet.

Her plans to sneak in the back and slip out after twenty minutes or so had been demolished when Bethany hooked Natassa's arm in her own and led her straight to the front pew. Even though they were some of the last to arrive, Natassa found that Bethany had a special place in that church and a designated spot front and center. So much for being inconspicuous.

Natassa didn't have time to look around self-consciously. As soon as she set her purse down, Bethany shoved a faded lime-green hymnal in her hand and told her to turn to page twenty-two. Natassa couldn't remember the last time she had sung a hymn, much less sung out of a hymnal, but as her fingers caressed the threadbare spine, she tentatively added her soft soprano to Bethany's alto. The sounds coming from the organ up front threw her for a moment, so foreign from the keys and electric bass she was used to hearing at her church, but as she closed her eyes, she had to admit it was endearing in a way. Authentic.

Natassa sat in her car, still grinning from the wave of contagious joy that washed over her during the service. Natassa had felt too awkward to lift her voice in agreement during the sermon like many of those around her were doing. She wasn't used to the congregation being so vocal. However, in the car by herself, she allowed it to bubble out of her. "Mmm hmm. That's right. Amen!" She laughed at the sound of her own voice. It felt good to let loose a little.

Her phone buzzed again. Natassa checked the time. The clock read 1:50, and it would be 2:10 by the time she got to her mother's house. She needed to answer it.

"Hi, Mom."

"You're late."

Natassa wanted to say, *And you're annoyed, as usual.* Instead, she said, "I know. I'll be there in twenty minutes."

"Twenty minutes? Natassa! The food will be cold in twenty minutes."

"Go ahead and eat without me. I'll just heat mine up when I get there."

"Don't be ridiculous. We'll eat as a family. We'll wait. I just can't imagine what on earth would cause you to be so late. Your church must have ended over an hour ago."

"Yeah." *Must have.* "I was out doing something, and it took longer than I thought. I'll see you in a bit."

"Maureen and Olivia got here before one o'clock."

"I'm sure they did, Mom. Hey, I'm driving, and I know you don't like me to talk on the phone when I'm driving, so I'm going to let you go now. See you soon."

Natassa hung up before her mother could remind Natassa how she was raised to be punctual or probe into where Natassa had been or what she'd been doing. She wasn't about to share this morning's adventure with her mother. Or her sisters.

Maureen was three years older than Natassa and married to a handsome hunk of a man. Charles was a successful real estate investor; Maureen, a successful CPA. They didn't have any children and didn't want any. Their tunnel vision on the corporate world fit with what Maureen had always been like: president of National Honor Society, class president, and valedictorian. And Natassa? Natassa was "Maureen's sister."

That is, until Maureen graduated and Olivia came into high school two years behind Natassa. Olivia made the cheerleading squad and the volleyball team her freshman year and then started dating the lead quarterback of the football team. So, of course, Natassa was then known as "Olivia's sister."

Olivia married Chase, a chef in an upscale Italian restaurant. She was a hostess there part time but mostly doted on their three-year-old son, Marcus, who modeled for various catalogs. Olivia didn't currently use her bachelor's degree in marketing, but at least she had a degree. That was more than Natassa could say for herself. And, of course, Olivia managed to keep a thriving social life, something Natassa hadn't been able to master either.

Natassa never did manage to make her own mark in high school, but her sisters were quite impressed when she announced her engagement to Brandon. She could still remember Maureen's response verbatim: "How did *you* ever manage to snag *him*?"

Yep. It still stung.

But one way or another, she made it, didn't she? Her house was just as nice as Olivia's. And though she didn't live in a gated community like Maureen, she wasn't embarrassed to have her older sister over.

Ugh! She was thirty-five years old. When would she stop riding the comparison train? Wasn't the last stop in the teenage years? As Natassa pulled into her mother's driveway and parked behind Maureen's silver Corvette and Olivia's Lexus, she let out a sigh. It was completely pointless, anyway. Comparing herself to her sisters would always—always—leave her in third place.

Natassa sat there, not eager to leave the solitude of her car and face the three women inside. She studied the modest split level in front of her. Three bedrooms, pale-blue siding, two-car garage. Three rosebushes lined the walkway in front, expertly trimmed. Though the house seemed cramped compared to Natassa's—it was less than half the square footage of the home she and Brandon shared—her mother maintained it immaculately. She always had been the model housekeeper, an administrative dream machine.

Natassa's gaze drifted to the window above the garage, to the room she used to share with Maureen and Olivia. She used to be so mad their father commandeered the third bedroom as an office instead of letting the girls spread out, but their mom insisted there was no fair way to do it otherwise. Someone would be whining that someone else got her own room, so to solve that problem they all had to put up with each other while their father stretched his legs in the extra room. If their mother thought it would bring them closer, she was wrong. Still, Natassa could understand her mother's reasoning; she could see herself making a similar decision under such circumstances. She'd been fortunate enough to know from the beginning that each of her children would have a separate bedroom.

A flash of movement from the living room caught Natassa's attention. She spotted her mother peeking through the curtains. Natassa looked at her and forced a smile. "Here we go," she said through clenched teeth.

Natassa was halfway to the front door when her mom flung it open, releasing the tantalizing aroma from the kitchen. She wore her classic red checkered apron over her knee-length forest-green swing dress, simultaneously bringing Natassa's mind to both the fifties era and to the Christmas season.

"Wow, Mom! Where'd you get the dress?" Natassa asked, leaning in for a pat on the back and a peck on the cheek.

"Oh! EBay. I get most everything on EBay nowadays."

"Really? Wow."

"Come in, come in. Lunch is—"

"Getting cold. I know." Natassa hung up her purse in the entryway and then followed her nose into the kitchen. Her sisters were at the kitchen table, deeply engrossed in conversation, which they briefly interrupted to say hello, then quickly resumed.

Her mother came up behind her, grabbing a dish from the oven. "It's ready, of course. We can eat. Today we have Lemon Chicken Piccata with angel hair pasta and roasted asparagus. I hope you enjoy it. It's a new recipe."

"Well, it smells amazing," Natassa said. Her sisters agreed. Their mother said grace, and as they passed around the food and exchanged small talk, Natassa's apprehension waned. No one even ventured into the forbidden territory of the attack. As long as they kept the conversation light, she didn't mind the company. Maybe the three of them had never been the best of friends, never had the close relationship the books she read and movies she watched made her envious for, but they were sisters. They were on the same team, shared the same memories and history. They would be there for each other, wouldn't they?

As soon as Natassa finished her last bite of pasta and put her fork down, her mother swooped down, grabbing the plate and silverware and depositing them in the sink. Natassa finished last, as always. As Olivia continued to update them on Marcus's upcoming modeling shoot, Natassa watched her mother rinse her dish off and place it in the dishwasher. Quick and efficient. They had literally finished eating less than five minutes prior, and the kitchen was spotless. No one would be able to tell a meal had been cooked in it. Her mother set the bar high.

"Now," her mother said, sliding gracefully back into her seat across from Natassa, "it's time to discuss the reason we're all here today."

Natassa sat back in her chair, eyeing her sisters. She hadn't been told there was a specific reason for the gathering, but judging from the way Maureen and Olivia shifted nervously in their chairs, she deduced they knew. Her stomach sank.

Her mother reached across the table and put her hand over Natassa's. "Natassa, dear. We are all so very sorry about what happened to you."

"I'm so sorry, Nat. I can't even imagine how horrible that must have been for you." Olivia's eyes held concern.

"We all feel terrible for you." Maureen looked as uncomfortable as Natassa felt.

Natassa felt overly warm under their pity. She didn't know what to say or how to get out of the situation. She opened her mouth, knowing she *should* say something, but nothing came out.

"I guess I don't understand what you were doing in that neighborhood to begin with." Maureen didn't seem to have trouble finding something to say.

"Maureen!" Olivia looked at her eldest sister in horror.

"What? I don't mean anything rude by it. It's just ... Why *were* you there, Natassa? It's a valid question."

"I ... uh ... I was getting Brandon his favorite bottle of wine from Edison's. We used to live down there, remember?"

"Oh, yeah. But that was before the neighborhood went downhill. Back then it had kind of an eclectic feel, didn't it? A lot of small, family-owned shops and whatnot? You had to realize it wasn't like that anymore. Didn't you notice that while you were driving around down there?"

"Um, well ..."

"Maureen," their mother interjected, "we all know Natassa isn't the best at paying attention to her surroundings. She can't go back now and do anything differently, so there's no point in this line of questioning. What we can focus on is the decisions that lie in the future."

"Decisions?" Natassa asked.

"Yes, honey. Decisions. Brandon informed me not only of the ... attack ... but also of the fact that you were ... impregnated through it. He also said that you have some moral reservations about terminating the pregnancy."

Natassa put her head on the table, fighting a wave of nausea. This was a setup. Brandon had set her up. She tried to take a deep breath but ended up holding her breath instead. She was starting to feel lightheaded.

"Natassa? Are you okay?" Olivia asked.

"Natassa? Are you even listening to me?" Her mother's far more impatient voice collided with Olivia's compassionate one.

Natassa forced herself to breathe and lift her head, but she could not look her mother or her sisters in the eye.

"As I was saying, I know that you are pro-life."

"We all are," Maureen said.

"Yes, we all are. But this is not a mother taking the life of her baby because of selfish reasons related to convenience. This was a brutal act of rape. No one would expect you to go through with this pregnancy, Natassa. God would not expect you to go through with this pregnancy."

Natassa gripped the edge of the table, trying to stop the sensation of the room spinning around her. It didn't work.

"Plus, think of Brandon," Maureen said. "Think of how he feels. You can't expect him to raise another man's child, a rapist's child. You can't expect him to be okay with this. You've got a good husband, Natassa. A real good one. He's successful and smart and handsome. He could have chosen any number of women to marry, and he chose you. Don't give him a reason to question that decision. If he were to leave you over this, what would you do?"

"Leave me? Did he say that to you?" Natassa looked back and forth between the women sitting before her, eyes wide.

"No, honey. Of course not. No one said anything about leaving. That's quite unnecessary. Now, there are two clinics in the area that will take care of the termination for you. Either one would be fine. They both do great work. I've taken the liberty of writing down the information for both of them so you can choose which one you want to go with. Now, if you'd like me to make the appointment for you, I can do that—"

Natassa took a deep breath, gripping the edge of the table again as she stood up. She cast a glance at her mother but couldn't bring herself to hold her mom's gaze. "No, Mom. That's quite unnecessary."

"Natassa, you don't know what you're saying. Think of Brandon and the children. Think of our family." Her mother's voice sounded much the same as it had when she'd scolded Natassa as a child. "And if you need a driver, any of us would be happy to help you in that way."

"Thanks for lunch, but I've had enough of your 'support.' I'm going to go now."

"Natassa, wait. You can't run away from this." Maureen started to stand up, but their mom put her hand on Maureen's shoulder, settling her back in her seat.

"Don't worry. She'll come around."

Shaking and holding back tears, Natassa walked to the front door, grabbing her purse and letting herself out with as much composure as she could manage. Her mother and sisters didn't even say goodbye, or maybe she finally tuned them out. She figured she should have learned to do that a long time ago.

* * *

Natassa grabbed her phone as soon as she got in the car, thankful Breanna was number three on her speed dial. Her hands were still shaking too much to dial more than one number. The phone was ringing before she pulled off her mother's street, before she even put words to the emotions brewing inside of her. Breanna would help her process through the storm. She had to.

"What's up, buttercup?"

What's up? Oh, yeah. You don't even know! Where do I start?

"I need to vent."

"My place? Yours? The park?"

"Timberlake Park sounds good. Twenty minutes?"

"Wow! Look at you! All decisive and everything. I'm impressed! Okay, I'll be there in twenty with chocolate."

"Love you, Bre."

"Right back at ya, chicka."

Natassa made it to Timberlake in fifteen minutes and surveyed her surroundings from the safety of her car. Their bench sat next to the massive weeping willow tree, unoccupied. All she had to do was force herself to make it over there. After all she'd been through today, she could walk over to a bench, couldn't she?

The park teemed with activity. People walked dogs, children played on the playground, kites danced in the air. This was far from a deserted street in the city. She pressed her lips together in resolve and hit the button to unlock the car door. She estimated it couldn't be more than twenty steps to the bench, but as she counted each one, she found herself whispering the number thirty-two before sitting down. Never mind. That only made the victory sweeter.

Now, to wait for Breanna. Natassa picked up a white dandelion, twirling it between her fingers, then blowing and scattering the seeds in the wind, just like she used to do as a little girl, when dreams just seemed like they'd take flight.

"Made it!" Breanna plopped a one-pound bag of M&M's on the bench before flopping down on it herself, out of breath, Snapple in hand. Wisps of hair cascaded out of her bun, and the light breeze played with them, tossing them about. "You don't give a girl much time."

"Sorry."

Breanna half sat, half lay on the bench eyeing Natassa. "What are you wearing?"

Natassa's hands flew up to her head. The hat. Then she looked down at her outfit. She had completely forgotten what she was wearing and why. She burst out laughing and couldn't stop—the kind of side-burning, belly-cramping, tear-inducing laugher that was contagious. Breanna started laughing too.

"Okay, seriously," Breanna said when she caught her breath. "What's with the outfit? Did you rob a senior citizen at a country club?"

Breanna's question only made Natassa laugh harder. She was surprised she could laugh at all after lunch at her mother's. This friendship proved medicinal.

After they both calmed down, Natassa found that she didn't feel so heavy inside. Saying what she needed to say wasn't much harder than blowing on the dandelion.

"Breanna, first off, I'm pregnant. I don't know why I didn't text you back."

"I figured you were. I knew it would be an easy text if that test were negative. Not so much if it were positive."

"Well, Brandon freaked out. He went all CSI on me, going back into 'we've got to find the criminal' mode. He wants me to have an abortion, Bre. I can't even believe that he's suggesting it. I thought he didn't believe in abortion. He says he doesn't, except in these kinds of circumstances. I said I wanted to keep the baby. He said maybe this was all my fault. Then he sets up this meeting with me and my mother and sisters and has them try to pressure me into getting an abortion. That's where I just came from. They're telling me he's going to leave me if I don't go through with this ..."

"Wow." Breanna opened the bag of M&Ms and held it out to her. Natassa picked out a handful of blue ones, waiting for her friend to say something that would make everything make sense.

"You don't really want to raise the baby, do you? I mean, that was just something you said in the moment, right?"

"No. I want to."

"I don't think that's such a good idea."

"What? You sound like you're on their side."

"No, I'm not on their side. I'm on your side. Bre and Nat. Always. It's just that you've got to look at things from their perspective too. Can you blame your mom for not exactly embracing a black grandchild? Or Brandon for not wanting a child that's not his?"

"Okay, first of all, a *black* grandchild? Is this about race?"

"That's not what I meant—"

"I hope so. I mean, I know you're not an overtly racist person. But she'll be biracial, you know. That means, yes, half black but also half white because, what everyone seems to completely disregard is that this child is a part of *me* too. And, yes, Brandon is not the father, but he loves *me*, right? And this baby has my DNA in her. So, can't he learn to love her? For me?"

"That's a lot to ask, Nat."

"Too much, you mean. You think it's too much to ask."

"Maybe. Don't take this the wrong way, but you're being kind of self-centered here. This is a decision that doesn't just affect you. It affects your entire family, everyone around you."

"Selfish. It's selfish to want my husband to love me enough to fight for me in this instead of against me?"

"Okay, maybe selfish isn't the right word. But, Nat, are you even thinking this through? This baby would remind Brandon of what happened. Every day. It would remind you of what happened. Constantly. Are you absolutely sure this is what you want?"

"Yes," she whispered, fighting back tears. She had never been so sure of anything. Despite everything. Only ...

"Do you think he'll leave me over it?"

"Oh, come on, Natassa. You guys have been happily married for ten years. There's got to be another way around this thing. You'll find your way."

"You mean I'll cave."

"I didn't say that."

"You didn't have to."

Natassa wrapped her arms tightly around herself as she powerwalked back to her car, leaving Breanna and the bag of M&M's on their bench.

12

Natassa drove aimlessly through subdivisions, her emotions in turmoil, her heart not yet leading her home. So much for processing through everything with Breanna. Bre's lack of empathy for her side of the story had hurt, but the tears on her cheeks hadn't taken long to dry.

Breanna wasn't the one who made her hot with anger.

She should have expected as much from her mother and sisters. She learned long ago that her family would not be a safe place for her soul, even if they were all churchgoing people who professed to follow the same God Natassa served. She couldn't even be too mad at them for being who they had always been. Olivia seemed a bit softer than Natassa remembered, but she still sat there with the other two, her silence speaking judgment in volumes.

But Brandon. Brandon had orchestrated the whole plan. He had trapped her unaware. Her knuckles turned white on the steering wheel. Oh, how she wished she could say what she wanted to say to his face. What would that sound like?

"How could you? How could you set me up like that? That

was low, Brandon. Real low. You just can't stand not having your way, can you? You can't stand me not bowing to your every whim. You have to be in charge of everything, always. That's why you married me, isn't it? Because I take the back seat and let you do what you want, don't put up a fuss. You wanted someone easygoing, good natured, someone who wouldn't challenge you. A trophy wife to smile at your side."

"'Natassa, we should move out of the city.' I say okay."

"'Hey, honey, I don't think you should pursue a career right now.' I say okay."

"'Natassa, what do you want for dinner?'"

"Whatever you want, Brandon. Whatever you say, Brandon."

"Well, maybe I'm sick of it! Maybe I don't want to be pushed around anymore! Maybe, for once, I have something I feel is worth standing up for. For once, can't you listen to me? Can't you take my feelings into consideration? Do I always have to be an extension of you?"

A honk sounded behind Natassa, startling her out of her monologue. She had gotten so wrapped up in shouting at the not-present Brandon that she had forgotten to keep driving. *I must look like a nutcase, talking to myself, waving my arms all over the place. I hope that anyone who saw me assumed I was on the phone.*

She felt better after releasing the steam that had been building up inside her. Could she actually do that in real life? March up to Brandon and say those things? She thought again about that niggling comment Maureen had made. *Don't give him a reason to leave you.* Would he? Would he just up and leave them like her dad left their family? Find some skinny blonde bimbo ten years younger than himself and never look back? Of course, her father had waited until she and her sisters were grown before abandoning them.

Brandon wasn't like her father, was he? As mad as Natassa

was at her husband, she had no grid for her life without him. They had built something beautiful together. She loved him. He loved her. Didn't he?

She put her hand instinctively over her abdomen. Would she have to lose this new part of her life to make sure the rest of her life stayed intact? But what about the voice?

Mercy will follow you.

She hadn't told anyone about that voice. It seemed too sacred to go tossing it around here and there. She wasn't sure anyone else would get it or appreciate it like she did. But maybe they would feel differently if she shared.

Natassa drove toward home with renewed purpose. She wasn't sure if she was ready to see Brandon. She didn't figure she would ever be ready for that confrontation, but she had collected herself to the point where she could greet the children without bursting into tears.

As she pulled into the garage, she noticed she had missed a text from Breanna.

I FELT SO BAD I ATE THE WHOLE BAG OF M&M'S. ALMOST THE WHOLE BAG. SAVED YOU THE BLUE ONES. SORRY I WAS A SUCKY FRIEND TODAY.

Bre's text was complete with a sad face and a picture of the bag of now only blue M&M's.

Natassa smiled and texted back SORRY I MADE YOU EAT ALL THOSE CALORIES. GOOD THING YOU CAN EAT WHATEVER YOU WANT AND NEVER GAIN WEIGHT.

Bre texted back immediately. DID YOU TALK TO BRANDON?

Natassa gathered her things and answered while walking to the door. NO, BUT I YELLED AT HIM WHEN HE WASN'T THERE. EFFECTIVE, HUH?

A laughing emoji greeted her in reply, followed by THERA-PUTIC. KEEP ME POSTED.

* * *

The clock read nearly 5:00 when Natassa walked through the front door, and she hadn't even given a thought to what to make for dinner. Faith and Hope careened into her, thrusting their arms around her and bombarding her with questions about where she had been and why. She artfully changed the subject by asking to see the papers they colored at Sunday school, which they scampered off to retrieve. David and Daniel were lounging on the couch watching a game. They greeted her with a quick "Hey, Mom," their eyes never drifting from the screen.

When the girls returned, Natassa made much of their rudimentary pictures and then asked where Daddy was.

"He's in the kitchen," Hope said.

"Making dinner," Faith added.

Natassa took a slow, deep breath and went to find him.

"Hey, babe!" His face lit up when he saw her. It took her off guard, and she could feel herself softening toward him despite herself.

"Hi. What are you making?"

"I found some frozen pizzas in the deep freeze. Is that okay?"

"Well, it's not Lemon Chicken Piccata with angel hair pasta and roasted asparagus, but it will do." She felt the edge of her mouth turn slightly upward in a traitorous smile.

He came over to her and kissed the top of her head. She felt the warmth of his lips long after he pulled away. She watched him for a couple minutes as he grabbed plates and checked on the pizzas. He looked funny wearing her apron, and all for sticking a couple of frozen pizzas in the oven. Cute. Endearing.

If only they could stay in this space and not move into treacherous waters.

"How did lunch at your mom's go?"

So much for that thought.

"Honestly, Brandon, it wasn't what I was expecting." Natassa paused, giving Brandon a chance to jump in and apologize for the way he set her up. If he would just say he was wrong and that he was sorry, maybe they could go back to the warmth that had existed between them just minutes ago. But he said nothing, just busied himself with taking the pizzas out and slicing them. So, she continued.

"But it was exactly what you were expecting, wasn't it?"

Brandon sighed and briefly made eye contact before once again finding his job as master chef all-consuming.

"So, are you going to make an appointment?"

That was it? No discussion about how he had gone behind her back to convince her family to pressure her into getting an abortion. No conversation about it at all? His only concern was if there was an appointment on the books?

"I'll take care of it." Natassa's voice sounded small. She felt small.

He sighed again and looked up at her, relief clear in his expression. "I knew you'd come around."

"Join the club," Natassa murmured while turning to walk to her bedroom.

It was time to take off her ridiculous outfit. Though, when she thought about it, she had dressed as if for a funeral, and she felt like she was laying something to rest: a piece of herself.

* * *

Natassa's alarm went off, and she snoozed it, annoyed to be shaken from such a sweet dream. Brandon's arms were wound around her, tight and secure, his breath tickling the back of her neck. In that odd space between sleeping and waking, she drifted, her heart soaring at the peace and love between them. As she roused into fuller consciousness, she turned on her back and felt his side of the bed. It was still warm from his presence.

She realized then it had not been a dream, not entirely. Brandon had held her close last night, pulling her body tightly against his own.

It was a simple gesture, one that had been repeated on hundreds if not thousands of nights in their marriage, but it was the first time he had held her since the rape. There had been a few tender moments between them since the incident, but nothing that intimate, nothing that truly gave her the assurance that they would be okay—even come together again as husband and wife, eventually. She wasn't quite ready for that, especially with the tension between them lately, but feeling close to her husband again made her realize how much she had missed him.

But had he only drawn near to her because she had agreed to make an appointment? Was he "rewarding" her for acquiescing? Would he still have held her if she didn't? She doubted it.

As Brandon showered and got ready for work, Natassa attempted to read her Bible. She was distracted and found herself reading the same verse over and over again, trying to ascertain the meaning in her cluttered mind. Eventually, she gave up and tried to pray, but that didn't go over too well either. She asked God to show her what to do, to make the path clear before her. How was she supposed to honor her husband if she felt like he was telling her to do something that was wrong? She couldn't seem to find peace in prayer and eventually gave up and went to the kitchen to get breakfast ready for the children.

Brandon came in looking handsome as ever in his dress shirt and silk red tie. He walked straight up to her and kissed her full on the mouth, taking her breath away.

"Brandon!" She was embarrassed she hadn't showered in two days and hadn't brushed her teeth that morning.

"I love you. You know that, right?"

A wobbly smile was her only reply. She used to know that.

She thought she still did, but confusion lay on the outer rim of that thought.

* * *

Natassa knew she had to make the call. She had put it off for over a week and was getting tired of fielding Brandon's questions and her mother's texts. She had to at least tell them she had an appointment.

Naptime afforded the perfect opportunity to get it over with. Natassa picked up the phone and called the first number listed.

"Hello, All Women's Health Center. This is Dee. How may I help you?"

Natassa's heart hammered in her chest.

Have at her, D.

Her throat went dry. Her palms, clammy.

"Hello?" Dee's voice sounded pleasant and concerned, but that did little to comfort Natassa.

"S—Sorry. Wr—Wrong number," Natassa stammered. She hung up the phone, willing her heartbeat to return to normal.

Definitely the wrong number.

* * *

Brandon greeted her that evening with a peck on the cheek as she scooped quinoa onto the dinner plates.

"Did you make an appointment?" he asked in her ear, as he had every evening since she told him she would.

"Not yet." She focused her attention on adding the perfect portion of steamed vegetables, making sure Hope's veggies didn't touch her quinoa.

"I thought you were going to."

"I made a call. It wasn't the right place." She reached into the drawer to grab silverware but dropped the handful of forks on the floor. The clatter sounded overloud to her ears. Brandon didn't seem to notice.

"Do you want your mom to do it for you? Or Maureen? Or Olivia?"

"I'll take care of it," she said, picking the forks off the floor.

"Breanna might even help you out."

Natassa snapped her head up, finally looking Brandon in the eyes. "Please don't bring Breanna into this. I said I'll take care of it."

"The longer you wait, the harder it will be, babe." He loosened his tie as if they were having just another casual conversation.

"I understand."

He tilted his head, eyeing her.

"What?"

"You're not sick or anything, huh?"

"No, just tired." On so many levels.

"Still too early for signs?"

"No, not really. I was nauseous with the others by now."

"But you aren't bleeding or anything? No signs of ... you know."

She shook her head. "There's been no bleeding. Why do you ask?"

"It would just be great if God would just take care of this naturally, you know? Maybe there's something wrong. You could just miscarry it, and we could both go on with our lives."

Natassa just stared at him. Was that what he wanted? For God to "take care" of it?

"What?" he asked when she didn't comment.

"Have you prayed for that or something?"

He shrugged. "Maybe. I don't know if it was really a prayer or maybe just kind of a hope. It would sure be merciful of God, though, wouldn't it? It would save you the trouble. Maybe you could pray for that."

What would that prayer sound like? *God please kill this baby so I don't have to?* Natassa cringed at the thought. There was no way she could ask God for that because that's not what she wanted. She didn't want to miscarry this baby, and she didn't want to abort this baby. She wanted to figure out how to do her wavy black hair and walk into St. Anthony's Baptist Church with her little girl on her hip. But what she wanted seemed to be irrelevant to everyone but her.

* * *

Natassa finished singing to Faith, tucked her in, and meandered to Daniel's room, gazing at the family pictures hanging in the hallway. Dimples. All her children had the most adorable dimples. *So far.* She sighed. She really did have a beautiful family. *I hope I'm not tearing it apart.*

After praying with Daniel and singing to him, she stepped next door into David's room. He briefly glanced up from the book in his hand and mumbled, "Night, Mom."

"Oh, you know you don't get off that easy." She held back a smile when he rolled his eyes.

"I'm nine years old. You don't have to sing that baby song to me anymore."

"You know my rule. I'm going to keep singing to you until you're taller than me. Then, and only then, can you tell me to stop." He huffed, but Natassa saw the edge of his mouth tip upward in a slight smile. He could pretend to be exasperated all he wanted. She knew he enjoyed their nightly routine.

She sat down next to him on his bed, ruffled his hair, and sang to him their own special, personalized version of "You Are My Sunshine." She sang it three times through, then prayed with her eldest, the little boy who had made her a mother for the first time. She kissed his forehead then left the room, strolling down the hallway past the pictures again, whispering the song to the one child she hadn't sung to yet while rubbing her belly.

She stared at Brandon's face in their family picture then added, "Please don't take her away."

13

———

"DeAndre, I need you on drive-through."

"No problem, boss."

James patted DeAndre on the back as he passed by. "I appreciate your hard work and great attitude. Keep it up."

DeAndre smiled to himself. It felt good to be praised for a job well done. He walked to the drive-through window and donned the headset. He had only worked the drive-through once before, but he enjoyed it. He stood ready and waiting, though they were in a lull at that time of day.

"Hey, DeAndre, what do people call you for short?" Rob asked, leaning against the counter, keeping an eye on the door in case a customer came in.

"My buddy Reg calls me D. Always has. My Pa, though," DeAndre said through a smile, "He called me Dre."

"Dre." Rob nodded, a grin spreading across his face. "I like it. Mind if I call you Dre?"

"Aww, I don't know, man. No one's called me that for a long time. Most people just stick to DeAndre."

"But Dre is cool. It fits you." Rob lifted his right shoulder and tossed out an idea, "You could just try it out today and see if you like it. You know, like trying on a pair of jeans at the store. If you don't like it, don't buy it. Just go back to DeAndre."

"You mean use the name Dre here at work today?"

"Yeah, man. See how you like it. See if you think it fits."

DeAndre grabbed hold of the thought and examined it. Perhaps a "new" name would pave the wave for his new life. "All right. Yeah."

Just then the bell jingled over the front door, and Rob stood up attentively. A few minutes later, there was a string of customers in the drive-through lane. At first DeAndre felt strange saying, "Hello, my name is Dre. How may I help you?" A couple of times he forgot and used his full name. However, after an hour or two, it started to feel more natural.

Using Pa's nickname for him made him feel more connected to his old man somehow. It was as if in some small way, he was doing his part to keep his Daddy's memory alive, same as Reg was doing by working in his shop. Yeah, it fit. Like his favorite Chicago Bulls sweatshirt that used to be his pa's. All the soft stuff had worn out of that old sweatshirt, and yet the familiarity of it made it the most comfortable thing DeAndre owned.

"Hey, Dre," Rob called when there were once again no customers. "You like it?"

"Yeah, man. I like it."

Rob grabbed a roll of masking tape out of the drawer, tore off a piece, and stuck it over the front of DeAndre's name tag.

"Now it's official. You're Dre." Rob's cheesy grin made DeAndre bust out laughing. That boy was so different from Reg, but he was fun to be around.

A beep alerted DeAndre to another customer in line. "Hello, this is Dre. How may I help you?" he asked, traces of a laugh remaining at the edges of his voice.

A pause and then, "I'd like a caramel macchiato, please. Grande. Shoot. Scratch that. Make it a short."

"Absolutely. Would you like anything else?"

"No, thank you."

DeAndre gave the customer her total and made the drink, still smiling from Rob's earlier antics—until he saw a maroon Audi SUV pull around. He froze.

It can't be her. What are the chances?

DeAndre willed himself to smile, to act natural, to do his job. But as she came into his direct view and lowered her sunglasses, he saw that it was indeed the same woman he had attacked on St. Anthony Street. His stomach dropped like lead. He stared, blinked, felt his pulse in his throat.

What was he supposed to do now? Oh, yeah. Remind her of her total. DeAndre cleared his throat and did so. As she handed him her card, he noticed the wedding ring on her left hand. She wasn't a tramp; she was someone's wife. And from the looks of the car seats in her SUV, someone's mother as well. He normally slid the cards without paying any attention, but this time he snuck a glance at the name. Natassa Bloomington.

Aww shoot. Why'd he do that? Now she had a face and a name. His nightmares were about to get twice as vivid.

He handed her card and receipt to her and grabbed her drink. His hands shook, and a little coffee sloshed out.

"I'm so s—sorry, ma'am," he said as he wiped the edge of the cup with a napkin and handed her the coffee.

"No problem." She smiled up at him, seemingly oblivious to his inner turmoil.

She doesn't know it's me. She didn't see me that night. She doesn't know.

She thanked him again and drove away. He watched her car until it disappeared in the distance.

"Dude, did you see Patrick's new tattoo?" Rob asked, nudging DeAndre on the shoulder.

He only coughed in reply.

"You okay, man?"

"Bathroom." DeAndre took off his headset and handed it to Rob, making a beeline for the restroom at the back of the restaurant.

Thankful it was a one-person restroom, he locked the door behind him and splashed cool water on his face. *She thanked me. "No problem," she said. "Thank you," she said. After what I did to her, she had the audacity to thank me.* DeAndre paced in the tiny quarters like a caged animal.

I came all this way to escape what happened down in my hood, and here it comes staring me in the face. Natassa Bloomington. My God! The woman drives an SUV. She has a family! A life. And I ... I ...

DeAndre sucked in his breath. He could not lose it. He could not cry. Not here and now. He was at work, and he had a job to do. He tried to picture Reg standing in front of him telling him not to give into tears but found that Reg wasn't who he wanted to be thinking of just then. Switching from grief to anger might be effective in keeping tears at bay, but it always left DeAndre feeling empty inside.

Instead, he looked at his name tag. Dre. His pa's boy. He knew his dad would still love him, even after the horrible stunt he pulled. He knew it because his daddy loved Reg like he was his own, and Reg was forever doing foolhardy things. Pa would be disappointed, no doubt about that. But DeAndre knew if Pa were here right now, he'd tell DeAndre to hold his chin up. "It ain't where you been. It's where you're going."

And right now, DeAndre was going back to work.

* * *

DeAndre managed to make it through the rest of his shift, but the boys didn't engage in any more lighthearted banter during off-peak times. Rob asked him several times if he was okay, and DeAndre assured him he was. They both knew he wasn't, but

Rob didn't call him out. For the first time since he had started working there, DeAndre felt relieved to clock out.

On the drive home, paranoia set in, and he took note of every maroon vehicle he saw. What if he was wrong? What if she *did* know who he was? What if she was tracking him? Her innocent face remained embedded in his mind. More like haunting him. He couldn't get away from her, couldn't run from what he'd done. She must hate him. And her husband must loathe him as well. DeAndre could only imagine the rage that the Bloomington family held toward him. Completely justified, scathing rage. And what did he have? Enough regret to bury him.

Reg's car was out front when DeAndre pulled up, and he steeled himself for a few minutes before going inside. He and Reg had been off lately; they weren't jiving like they used to. He couldn't seem to make Reg see what he saw ... or maybe it was the other way around. Either way, DeAndre wasn't eager to spend an extra couple hours of quality time with his best friend that evening.

Reg was in the kitchen nuking a hot dog when DeAndre walked in.

"Hey, D! Want a dog, man?"

"Nah. I'm all right."

"You sure? I was just about to watch last night's game. I didn't know when you'd be home." Reg had already changed out of his work clothes and into sweats.

"Yeah, I'm fine."

"Look at you, all fancy in that getup. How was your day in Whitey World?"

"Work went well. Thanks for asking."

"What's wrong with your name tag? You got something on it."

DeAndre's hand instinctively went to his name tag. He felt

the masking tape before he saw it. "Rob did that. He wanted me to try out a nickname ..."

"Rob?"

"Yeah, Rob."

"You on a first-name basis with those white boys now?"

"Well, yeah. What do you want me to call him? Whitey?"

"I would."

"I bet you would."

Reg walked up to DeAndre and inspected his name tag. "So, this Rob calls you Dre now?"

"Yeah. It fits."

"And you're letting that WASP there call you by the special name Pa used to call you? That don't bother you none?"

"I like it, Reg."

"It's lowercase. On your name tag."

"So?"

"You know why I call you D?"

"Why?"

"'Cause you Da Man with a capital D!" Reg smiled and took the piece of masking tape, moving it from the front of DeAndre's name tag to the back, covering up everything but the first letter of his name. "Come on now, D. Watch the game with me."

Reg grabbed his hot dog and plopped down on the couch, grabbing the remote and flipping on the game. DeAndre just stood there, trying to figure out what had just happened inside him and how the placement of a little piece of tape could make him feel so different. Here he was. D, Reg's best friend. His name tag even said so. Yet, he felt out of place. Right there, in his own living room.

Reg scarfed down his hot dog in three bites and said, "I need a beer."

DeAndre feigned interest in the bouncing orange ball on the screen, still standing in the same spot Reg had left him as Reg scoured the fridge.

"Oh no! We're out of beer again. Pause the game, will you, D? We got to go get us some booze."

DeAndre's mouth went dry. He bit the inside of his cheek to assure himself that this was not another one of his nightmares, not some strange version of déjà vu. Reg was grabbing his keys and walking to the door.

"You go ahead. I'll stay here," DeAndre managed.

"What you talking about? Come on, D." DeAndre hadn't moved to pause the game. Reg grabbed the remote and did so himself.

"I don't want any booze tonight, Reg. I'm working the early shift tomorrow."

"Okay, Mr. Straight and Narrow. Come keep me company then."

"I don't think so. I'm just going to relax here. It's been a long day."

"What's this about? Really? You too good for me now? Is that it? You don't want any schnapps 'cause now you making fraps?"

"I'm tired, Reg. I just got home. I don't want to go out."

"You know what I think? I think you've changed, D. Or should I say Dre? You've gotten all uppity, looking down your nose at where you come from. Your new friend—Rob, is it? I'm sure he's a great guy. But he don't know you like I know you, D. What would he think if he knew everything? Would he still be all buddy-buddy with you then? Before you go looking down your nose at the brothers in your hood, you might want to remember that you didn't have a job for over a year. I was the one fronting your bills. And who do you think bought you that nice shirt and tie so you could even go on that interview? You might want to remember where you came from, bro. That's all I'm saying."

"I hear you, Reg. But I don't want to get booze with you. It didn't turn out well last time."

"It didn't turn out too bad either. You didn't get caught, did you? Thanks to me."

DeAndre laughed without humor. "Thanks to you."

"Fine. I'll get my own beer." Reg slammed the door on his way out.

DeAndre took the tape off his name tag, wadded it up into a miniature ball, and threw it in the general direction of the trash can.

14

Natassa took a sip of her caramel macchiato as she careened into a parking spot at Timberlake Park. When Breanna had offered to watch the girls so Natassa could get some alone time, Natassa jumped at the chance. She felt like she hadn't had a minute to herself to think or process things since her Sunday escapade weeks ago. And that day had been too chaotic to do much reflecting.

As Natassa exited her Audi and locked the door, she surveyed her surroundings, relieved to see more than a dozen people milling about. She inhaled deeply through her nose, let the breath out through her mouth, and gave herself another internal pep talk.

It's okay, Natassa. This isn't some deserted street in the city. This is a crowded park in a good neighborhood in broad daylight. It's the same park you've been to a hundred times over the years.

Taking courage, she walked toward the lake, armed with a journal, pen, and her steaming cup from Java Joe's. The smell alone relaxed her, which was ironic, considering how nauseated the smell or even the thought of coffee had made her when she was pregnant with the others. Natassa wondered again if the child inside her was okay. It was strange for her to be seven weeks pregnant and not bent over the toilet bowl several times a day. Not that she was complaining. She just wondered ... Was Brandon onto something? Was God going to "take care of it"? Brandon thought it would be a sign of God's mercy, but Natassa couldn't imagine how heart-wrenching it would be to miscarry this child. Would Brandon be wanting to give her a high five while she was doubled over in physical and emotional pain?

Breanna insisted Natassa look at things from Brandon's perspective, and she was trying to, but her emotions were so swollen at the moment they were hard to see around. Her heart was tender to the touch. At least *that* was one pregnancy sign she confidently displayed. Those pregnancy hormones must be in full swing.

Natassa was pleased to find the bench Breanna and she claimed as theirs empty. Setting her journal down, she decided to just take a few minutes to sip on her coffee and people watch. *The caffeine won't hurt the baby, will it? I think my OB said a cup a day was fine.* All the thoughts surrounding miscarriage were making her paranoid. And did it even matter? Brandon would probably have her drink a couple gallons of coffee and hope for the "best."

Oh no. She was getting cynical. And bitter. *Lord, help me. I don't want to be this way.*

Natassa turned her thoughts to the people around her. There was a man jogging with his Golden Retriever, a couple of young children tossing a Frisbee back and forth, two older women in jogging suits walking side by side. All white. Nearly every single person she encountered in her neighborhood on a daily basis was white.

It had thrown her for a minute, being waited on by a black man at Java Joe's. She suspected his voice sounded African American, but in Crawford County? She thought she must be mistaken. Then at the first sight of his dark skin, her pulse skyrocketed, her body flashing back to the night of the attack, completely bypassing her conscious mind.

But then ... then she talked herself down from the precipice. That young man in the sky-blue Java Joe's shirt didn't look frightening. He seemed nervous. She assumed it was because he was new to the job and was still learning the ropes. He had a kind face and sympathetic eyes. She couldn't afford to have prejudices against people of a different race, not when a child with different racial make-up was growing in her belly. So, despite the butterflies in her stomach, she had thought of Bethany and the others at St. Anthony's Baptist Church and smiled at the barista.

She thought that if she had a chance to raise the child growing in her belly, she would have to take her outside of their county to see anyone with a darker skin tone. And she would want to do that, for her daughter. She wouldn't want her growing up feeling like the only one with pigment in a white world.

But maybe things were changing in Crawford County. Maybe things were becoming more diverse. She'd never given it a second thought until someone of another race invaded her isolated world. But now she wanted more color in her life, more diversity. For her daughter, yes, but as she thought about her experience at St. Anthony's Baptist Church, she had to admit she wanted it for herself as well. She smiled to herself as she pictured Bethany swaying and clapping to the music.

How she wished she could introduce her other children to Bethany. She wanted them to be enveloped in the peace she'd found under that woman's wing. She just didn't see any way of making that happen. Brandon obstructed the way. *Brandon.* What should she do about Brandon? And about the baby?

Natassa thought of how her mother had taught her that all of life's problems could be solved by making lists. That was only a slight exaggeration. Her mother made lists for everything; that was how she made nearly every decision, and she'd taught her girls to do the same. Were you trying to decide which shoes to purchase? Make a list of pros and cons. What college should you attend? List the positive and negative aspects of each choice. When Olivia had to choose between two men who wanted to pursue a serious relationship with her, she sat down with their mother and made a list. It was how they'd always done things in their family.

Natassa picked up her journal and went to work mapping out two columns. She labeled one "Keeping the baby" and the other "Not" because she couldn't bear to put the other option being forced down her throat into print. Under "Keeping the baby," she listed things such as "seeing her smile," "feeling her hand in mine," "hearing her laugh," as well as "a clear conscience," and "doing the right thing." She also thought about the positive impact that adding a biracial child could have on their family and added "broadening my other children's world" and "teaching them to love people who look different from themselves."

She then moved to the "Not" column. At the top, she put "Saving my marriage." Was she being melodramatic? She didn't know. She wished she could see into the future and could tell how things would play out if she moved forward in that direction. Would she break their family apart? She also put "not having to explain what happened," a scenario she could not avoid if she brought home a child with darker skin. Her girls were so innocent, and she hated the thought of exposing them to the reality of rape. If she continued with the pregnancy, not only would she have to explain the situation to her children, she would have to explain it to everyone: acquaintances, friends, doctors, and even some strangers. What else could she put in this column? "Making my mother happy." That was lame and she knew it, but she put it down anyway, knowing that she still had issues to work through in that regard.

Natassa sat back and looked at her lists. The problem with lists was that they weren't weighted. Shouldn't her marriage carry more weight than anything else? And could she still have a clear conscience if she deliberately went against her husband? What if he divorced her because of it? What if he broke their family apart and scarred their other children over it?

"Have mercy!"

Natassa snapped her head around to see who had said that. A man stood on the jogging trail to her right, bent over, hands on his knees. The sweatband on his head couldn't contain all of his perspiration, and some dripped onto the track below. Another man stood upright next to him.

"You've got another half mile. You can do it. Keep pushing. Don't give up on me now."

"I can't do it, man."

"Yes, you can. Keep moving. One foot in front of the other. Here," he said, handing the winded man a water bottle. "Drink."

The winded man stood up straight and guzzled half of the water and then started jogging again. Natassa watched the two of them, the man's words echoing inside of her. *Have mercy. Have mercy. Have Mercy.*

* * *

Natassa had dinner waiting for Brandon when he got home from work. She wore her hair half up, half down with just a touch of color on her cheeks. She managed to cook dinner without getting even a smudge of ketchup on the silver blouse Brandon liked so much on her. Her long black skirt swished around her ankles with every turn. The girls had remarked that she looked pretty. She hoped Brandon would think so too.

Her stomach fluttered as she heard him at the door.

"Wow! Something smells good in here!"

"Dinner's ready, honey. Meatloaf," Natassa called out. She took notice of his footsteps nearing the kitchen, the fluttering intensifying. Brandon rounded the corner, and his eyes took her in, a smile spreading across his face.

"Meatloaf? My favorite. What's the special occasion?" He leaned against the counter, not taking his eyes off her.

She shrugged. "No occasion."

"No occasion?"

"No." She smiled, and her cheeks warmed under his perusal.

"Okay, then." He walked up to her, wrapping his arms around her, tilting her chin up, and kissing her soundly. She allowed her body to melt against his, hungry for him in a way she hadn't realized until that moment.

"I miss that," he said.

"Me too."

He threaded his fingers in hers, caressing her thumb with his.

"So," he said, pulling back, breaking the spell, "did you make an appointment?"

"Yes. I did." She forced herself to make eye contact, even though everything in her wanted to look away, to hide.

"You did?"

"Yes."

"Why today? What made you do it?"

Natassa turned and busied herself with putting the meatloaf onto plates, talking over her shoulder. "I made a list and decided what was important to me."

"When is it? The appointment."

"Next week. Thursday."

"Not until then? Why?"

Natassa shrugged again. "That's when they wanted to see me."

"Huh. Okay. Well, at least that's taken care of."

"Yeah." Natassa added a scoop of mashed potatoes to each plate then reached for the corn.

"Who's taking you? Your mom?"

Natassa nodded, unable to speak past the lump in her throat.

Brandon put his hands on her shoulders and turned her around, looking into her eyes. "I know this is hard for you, babe, and I'm sorry. But it's for the best. You'll see."

"Okay." It was all she could say, but not all she wanted to say.

"Okay. Now, let's enjoy this dinner. It looks amazing. Thank you, honey." He kissed her forehead and went to tell the children it was time for dinner. As soon as he was out of sight, Natassa touched her forehead and then put her hand to her belly, as if trying to transfer his love from her to her child. A single tear trekked down her cheek. She wiped it away and grabbed the silverware.

15

———————

"Hey, sugar! So good to see you!" Bethany shouted from the top step of St. Anthony's Baptist Church, cigarette in hand. "Old Ezra! Natassa-with-a-T is back!"

Old Ezra mumbled something Natassa couldn't make out as she walked up to greet them, but his smile held warmth and welcome.

"You look better today, sugar. You ditched the hat, I see. Now I can see your pretty face better."

"Thank you, Bethany. You look lovely as well." Bethany's emerald wrap dress crested at her ankles, its purple sash matching her head scarf.

"You hear that, Old Ezra? I look lovely today, she said." Bethany smiled broadly, encouraging Natassa's smile to widen as well.

"Of course, I hear that. I'm blind, not deaf." Ezra chuckled at his own remark.

Bethany waved him off, along with a puff of cigarette smoke just as the bell began to sound.

"You got babies, Natassa?" Bethany asked. Natassa resisted

the instinctual urge to place her hand on her belly. Though the changes in her body weren't yet visible to the casual onlooker, she noticed them. She had been opting for elastic over the past week due to the thickness around her middle.

"Babies? Well, I have children at home, but they're not babies anymore. They're nine, seven, five, and three."

"Oh, honey, they'll always be your babies. What you got? Boys or girls?"

"The two oldest are boys, the two youngest are girls."

"What are their names?" Old Ezra chimed in.

Natassa sat down on the step next to him. "Well, the girls are easy. Faith and Hope. My nine-year-old is named David."

"Beloved."

Natassa smiled. "You don't miss a beat, do you?"

"I told you he don't!" Bethany called out from above them.

"My seven-year-old is named Daniel."

"God is my judge."

"Wow. Really? I didn't know that." Natassa shuddered, feeling exposed.

"Yes, ma'am. Those are some good names. Biblical names." Old Ezra nodded his approval then grabbed his cane. "We best be heading in now. Service is about to start."

"Why don't you bring your babies with you sometime, sugar? Your hubby too? We'd sure like to meet them."

"I'd like to," Natassa said, and she meant it. She felt horrible for ducking out of time with her family. She just couldn't resist the pull of the peace she found in the old Baptist church. She wanted her children with her, by her side as she walked through those heavy doors. She just didn't see that happening. Ever.

She'd had to lie to even make it out there that morning. Remembering how she faked a sick stomach so that Brandon would take the children to church and leave her behind made her face flush with guilt.

"I thought you weren't feeling any signs," Brandon had said.

"I wasn't." But then she had run into their bathroom and made retching noises, running the sink and flushing the toilet repeatedly to convince Brandon that she wasn't fit to accompany the family to church. All so she could go to a different church behind his back. What was wrong with her? Why couldn't she just tell him the truth?

Because she knew he wouldn't understand. And there was no way he would accompany her here.

Would God forgive her for lying if it was for the purpose of going to church? Did the ends justify the means in this case? If God was her judge, what was His verdict?

"Come on with you, sugar. The music's starting. We best get ourselves in there." Bethany crushed the butt of her cigarette with the heel of her navy platform shoe.

"Here I come." Natassa stood and dusted herself off from the grit on the steps. Her forced smile morphed into a genuine one as Bethany threaded her arm through Natassa's and the two women walked to the front pew together.

When the service was over, Bethany took the liberty of introducing Natassa to each and every parishioner in attendance as they milled about, chatting with each other and waving bulletins in front of their faces to provide respite from the stuffy air.

"Hi, Bart! This here's Natassa-with-a-T. This is her second time here, but last time she had to dart out real quick so I didn't have time to show her off."

Bart's bald head glistened under the overhead lighting as he smiled warmly at Natasha. He took her petite hand in his muscular one, shaking it gently. "Nice to meet you, Natassa. I'm glad you could join us this morning."

"My pleasure."

"Bart is in construction and fixes things up around here when they break down. He's a real gem. If you ever need a handyman, Bart's your man. Give her your card." Bethany nodded to Bart, and he pulled a business card out of his wallet, looking a bit sheepish.

"If you ever need anything at all," he said, handing it to her.

"Thank you." Natassa smiled and put the card in her purse as Bethany moved on to the people in the next pew.

When they were halfway to the door, Natassa snuck a look at her watch. One-thirty! Her phone was on silent, but she was sure Brandon had already left her a handful of texts and voice mail messages questioning where she was. She hadn't meant to stay the whole service, much less afterward. She'd intended to be home before they were; she'd just lost track of time.

The crowd thinned out, and only a few people stood between her and the door. She could make it home by quarter after two. She had the entire drive home to think of a good excuse as to where she had been. She shifted her weight from foot to foot, smiling politely and shaking hands while mentally preparing for the interrogation she knew was coming.

The pastor stood at the door, the last handshake between her secret life and her real one.

"I'm so glad you came back."

"I'm glad too. I enjoyed your sermon today, Pastor. Thank you."

"Different than what you're used to?"

"Much different. In a good way."

Pastor Jaden loosed a full and hearty laugh, tossing his head back and slapping his leg. "Good! You come back now, you hear?"

"I plan to!" Natassa laughed as well, joy bubbling up from within her, pushing back her anxiety.

"Hey, sugar, you like chicken salad?"

"Um, sure." Natassa squinted into the sun, looking in Bethany's direction.

"Why don't you come over for lunch? I sure would like to

get to know you better. I made some chicken salad yesterday and got some of those good Hawaiian buns. Your family can spare you for a little bit longer, can't they?"

Natassa hesitated, glancing at her watch. What did it matter if she was an hour or two later? She would still have to explain to Brandon where she had been. There was no getting out of it. She might as well enjoy her afternoon before going in front of the firing squad.

"That sounds nice."

"Follow me then. I only live a couple blocks away. That's me," Bethany said, pointing to a red Volkswagen Bug in the parking lot.

"Sure thing. I'll follow you." Natassa slid into her Audi and followed Bethany's red Bug with the Christian fish on the back past boarded up buildings and windows with bars on them. She heard her phone buzzing in her purse but ignored it. When her eyes began to drift to her surroundings and her heart began to beat a bit faster, she forced herself to look straight ahead. She could see Bethany's purple head scarf, and she focused on that. She felt safe with this woman, even if the neighborhood put her on edge.

What Bethany said was only a couple blocks away seemed longer, whether from Bethany's exaggeration or from Natassa's nervousness, she couldn't tell. She was relieved to finally pull into the parking lot of an apartment building. She parked right next to Bethany and waited until the older woman gathered her things and got out before opening the car door herself.

"I'm on the fourth floor, sugar. Hope you don't mind climbing steps 'cause the elevator is out again. They not in any hurry to fix it neither. Never are."

"Oh, I don't mind."

"Do you ever put up a fuss about anything?"

Natassa winced. "Not often."

"Did I hit a sore spot?"

"Kind of."

"Good."

"Good?"

"Sore spots—they show us just where we need healing, my dear. If it weren't for them, we'd walk around broken inside forever. God has a way of bringing those broken things to the surface. So He can heal them."

Natassa filed this away for further inspection as she hiked up the four flights of stairs, Bethany huffing and puffing at her side. She reached out to grab onto the railing, but Bethany stopped her.

"I wouldn't grab onto that if I were you. It's wobbly. Liable to go crashing down any day now. I put in a request for them to fix that months ago, but like I said, they ain't in no hurry to fix things around here."

When they finally reached Bethany's apartment and Bethany unlocked two separate locks, they plopped down at her kitchen table.

"Give me a minute, sugar. I'll be getting you lunch after I catch my breath."

"It's fine. Take your time."

"So, tell me what your church is like. You said it was different, huh?"

"Yes. Very. Pastor Keith, our pastor, he's a very good teacher. He gives these organized sermons. You know, with Roman numeral outlines. We have bulletins with blanks to fill in. It's all very orderly and methodical. And biblical, that's what I like about it. He's solid in his theology. It's very ... very Brandon. Brandon is my husband. He's a computer geek and likes things in a three-point outline like that. And I don't mind it. I just ... there's something about the way Pastor Jaden gets all worked up ... how he takes off his jacket and dabs his head with a rag because he's so passionate about what he's saying. It's refreshing. He's a preacher as opposed to a teacher, and I enjoy it."

"That's the most I heard you talk since I met you, sugar!"

"Oh, sorry. Am I talking too much?"

"Shoot, girl! No! I want to hear what's on your mind. Don't you go apologizing."

Bethany got up and started on lunch, asking Natassa questions about her children as she did so. Natassa was happy to answer; she could talk about her "babies" all day. Natassa managed to get a couple questions of her own in as they ate. She found out Bethany had two grown children and three grandchildren. Her oldest son lived in Detroit with his wife and two daughters. She only saw them around the holidays. Her younger son had moved to Boston a few years ago. He had a son with an old girlfriend but didn't have custody. The mother still lived in town, and Bethany got to see her grandson whenever Mom needed a babysitter or got herself into trouble.

"Do you have other family around here?" Natassa asked.

"Oh, sure. I've got cousins and a couple aunties and uncles. But my church family, that's who I lean on the most."

Bethany took their plates to the sink and then returned to the table. She sat down, folded her hands in front of her, then looked at Natassa intently. "Now, are you going to tell me how you ended up at my church and why?"

What was it about Bethany that made Natassa comfortable enough to let down her defenses and unfold the layers of her heart like the petals of a rose in bloom? Natassa had no intension of ever telling Bethany what had happened that night on St. Anthony Street, and yet there she was, sobbing into a fuchsia handkerchief and spilling one horrid intimate detail after another. Well, not the pregnancy. That detail could be her secret.

"That's right, sugar. Let it all out. You done needed a good cry." Bethany had moved her chair around next to Natassa's and sat rubbing Nat's back, her voice low and soothing.

"This doesn't make much sense, does it? You asked why I

came to your church, and here I am telling you why any sane person would avoid that street forever."

"First of all, it don't got to make sense. We're talking about pain and matters of the heart. When hurting gets involved, sense ain't got much of a say. But also, baby girl, you've got to believe there's something bigger going on than what you can see. All that's before your eyes is the ache of it all, but God's got His hand on you, and He ain't letting go. He's moving things around in ways that might only make sense to Him right now, but one day you're gonna look back and see how He took the ugliest, most awful thing you could ever imagine and made something beautiful."

Natassa nodded and wiped her eyes. "Baby girl?"

"Oh, I know you a grown woman, but you look like you can use a mama about now. You don't mind if I adopt you, do ya?"

"Not at all." Natassa found a semblance of a smile.

"Now, what's the baby's name going to be?"

"Baby?" Natassa's gaze snapped down to her belly. "What? I didn't tell you I was pregnant." Natassa sat upright, eyes wide in panic.

"I read between the lines."

"Oh, my gosh! Am I showing? Do you think everyone can tell?"

"Relax, sugar. You as skinny as a rail. I just get a sense about these things. Your secret's safe, for a little while longer at least."

"I can't believe you could tell," Natassa said, relaxing back in her chair a bit.

"So, does this baby have a name yet?"

"Well, yes. Kind of. I mean ... It's complicated, but if I get my way, I want to name her Mercy."

"Mercy?"

"Yes. I know it's not a conventional name, but—"

"Whoo-ee, Sweet Jesus! Mercy!" Bethany sat back in her

chair, tilted her head back, and smiled up at the ceiling. "Yes, Lord! I know what to do. You sent her to me for sure!"

"What? What's going on?"

"Mercy, huh?"

"Yes. From the verse 'Surely goodness and mercy will follow me all the days of my life.'"

"I gots to give you something, sugar. I think you'll like this." Bethany got up and went into the other room, leaving Natassa to percolate in her curiosity.

Bethany came back a few minutes later holding a portfolio. She set it on the table in front of Natassa.

"This is Mercy's journal. Well, not the original, of course. Great Aunt Thea has the original, though I guess it should be in a museum somewhere. We never wanted it to leave the family. My son Grant done typed it all up in that fancy font and put it on that stick thing he plugs into the computer."

"A flash drive?"

"That sounds right. Anyway, he printed out copies for the family, and now we each have our own. You can take this one, and I'll just have him make me another one."

"But you said you wanted to keep it in your family."

"Baby girl! Didn't I tell you I done adopted you? You are family now, sugar. And this belongs to you. It was written by a relative of mine, a mulatto slave girl named Mercy. She been through some stuff, and she learned some stuff too, just like you is learning. You take it home and read it. Let me know what you think."

"Sure." Natassa picked up the portfolio. It had a clear cover so that she could read the title of *Mercy's Journal* in elegant script on the first page. "Do you mind if I look at it now?"

"Girl, I don't mean to kick you out or nothing, but your phone's been buzzing like there's a bee trapped in your purse ever since you got here. I'm thinking your husband is wondering where you is."

"I guess he is."

"And I'm guessing there's a reason why you ain't answering it."

Natassa sighed. "You're right. I should go home now. Thank you so much for lunch. And for listening. And for this," she said, grabbing the portfolio.

"You're welcome here anytime, you hear? Anytime." Bethany wrapped Natassa in a bear hug and kissed the side of her head.

Natassa glanced out the window to where her car was, remembering what neighborhood she was in.

"Why don't I walk down with you?"

"Oh, I don't want you to—" Natassa started to say, but then just said, "That'd be nice. Thank you."

"I've got to have a smoke anyway. I don't smoke in the house, seeing as how my grandbaby visits, and that second-hand smoke ain't good for him."

Natassa smiled.

"Oh, I know. The firsthand smoke ain't good for me either. I'll be quittin' one of these days. One of these days."

As the two women parted, Natassa thanked God for placing Bethany in her life, no matter the path it took to get her there.

16

____

Natassa waited until she was on the highway and out of Bethany's neighborhood to check her voice mail. She noted that she had eleven missed texts as well, but she didn't check texts while driving. She listened to Brandon's four voice mail messages, each one sounding more panicked than the last. Breanna had left a message, too, stating that Brandon had called her to ask if she knew where Natassa was and that Nat better call him stat.

Natassa sighed. How could she possibly get out of this one? She pulled off at her exit with no more of an idea of what to tell them than when she had started driving. Her phone buzzed again, and she groaned. She needed to answer it before Brandon had the police go looking for her.

Seeing a McDonald's in the distance, Natassa instantly craved a cookie. _What is wrong with me? Even my pregnancy cravings scream avoidance._ But she went through the drive-through and texted Brandon and Breanna a quick I'M ON MY WAY HOME. SORRY. WILL EXPLAIN LATER. How she would explain, she had no idea, but she figured her text would buy her a few extra minutes. She was only five minutes away from her house, and she was insanely curious as to the contents of *Mercy's Journal*.

Natassa pulled into a parking space with her chocolate chip cookie and opened to the first page.

Mama always said, "Everybody talk 'bout joy and pain like they's opposites, but they ain't really. Not to me. Not less you talkin' 'bout opposite sides of the same coin." She'd talk 'bout how if she'd have a big eraser and could 'rase every bit a sorrow in her life and in her past, people might think she'd have a right pretty picture. But she ain't. Alls she'd got would be a big white space. Empty, that's what'd be. Joy and pain—those threads are woven so tightly together ain't no one can get 'em apart. If I close my eyes, I can still hear Mama sayin' those things. I didn't know what in tarnation she was talkin' 'bout when she rambled on, but now I'm thinkin' she was talkin' 'bout me the whole time.

I miss Mama something fierce. Don't think I'll ever be able to wrap my heart 'round the day when she sent me off, eyes shimmerin' like the moon, shoulders shakin' like she trying to hold the force of the whole world back up in her body. Her kerchief around her head— blue with white little daisies, or at least what once was white daisies 'fore the dust settled on them and her apron. Who knows what color that used to be, if it ever were white or if it came cream like my skin to begin with. I looked back over my shoulder as the wagon pulled away, and everything I knew faded like a dream.

Mama said it was for my good. Reckon I was too young to under-stand it then, but now I see she was right. The Missus might have killed me if she had half a chance and another year or two. I ain't never seen hate spew from someone's eyes like it did from hers. Poison. Mama knew it was deadly and aimed right at me, so she begged Old Master to sell me to a couple from Nashville who'd come callin'. I begged Mama to keep me with her, holding onto her dusty ankles, my tears making mud as they spattered on the ground. She stood as still as stone. Just said, "I love you, Mercy. That's why I'm doing this."

Out of all Old Master's slaves, my mama was the only one who had the gumption to ask anything of him. Everybody knew she was his favorite to bed with. The Missus knew, too, and knew that Old Maser's blood ran in my veins. That's why she was hell-bent on making me suffer. I think she would have skinned every bit of cream off me if she could. Oh, she wanted me black. She used to make me roll 'round in the mud with nary a bit of clothes on, telling me I was no better than a filthy pig. Then she made me sleep outside, the caked mud the only thing keeping me warm as I shivered from the cool breeze and fear of the sounds in the dark. Each cracking twig, no matter how far off, made me squeeze my eyes shut so tight I saw white spots floating by. Funny how after all the beatings the Missus gave me, the memories of her that burn hottest in my chest are the ones where she humiliated me by treating me like an animal, as if I had nothing inside me to give me even a scrap of dignity.

Natassa's phone buzzed again, and she snapped the portfolio shut, startled and undone. Mercy, this Mercy, had been a child of rape as well. Natassa trembled, picturing this little slave girl begging her mother not to send her away. What had that been like for Mercy's mother? Natassa felt her emotions churning—grief, fear, loss, and uncertainty crashing in her gut like waves. She pushed them down. She had already done her crying for the day. Right now she needed to take a deep breath and drive home. She stashed the journal under the driver's seat.

* * *

"Where were you?" Brandon paced the living room, his dress shirt untucked and his tie loosened around his neck. "You scared me to death! I checked with everyone I could think of."

"Did you check with my mom?"

"Your mom? No. Why? You were at your mom's?"

"I had lunch at my mom's." Natassa reasoned to herself that

it wasn't completely a lie. Bethany said herself that she was Natassa's adopted mother.

"I thought you were sick!"

"It's called morning sickness for a reason. I felt perfectly fine at lunchtime." Again, it wasn't *exactly* a lie. Some women did only get sick in the morning. With Natassa's other pregnancies, the sickness hit at all times of the day, but that wasn't true for everyone. And Natassa did feel perfectly fine at lunchtime.

"Why didn't you call? Text? Leave a note? Something!"

Natassa walked up to him and buried her face in his chest, wrapping her arms around him. He hugged her back tightly, possessively, as if he were afraid she would slip out of his grasp.

"Honey, I'm so sorry. I really am. I don't know what I was thinking. I guess I wasn't thinking. My brain isn't working right lately. I don't know if it's the hormones or the stress or what. My phone was on silent …"

Brandon put his fingers on the bridge of his nose. "At least you're okay."

"Brandon, are you crying?"

"I'm okay," he said, but she heard a small sniffle in his voice. "You're safe."

Safe.

"Where are the girls?" Natassa asked, looking around. She knew the boys were at their friend's house, but it was odd not to be greeted by her girls upon returning home.

"They're in the playroom. They're playing house."

"Are you sure?"

"Yes. I just checked on them a few minutes ago."

"Faith wanders. She's there one minute, and then the next—"

"Shhh. Honey, listen."

Natassa quieted and strained to hear downstairs. She was greeted by the faint sound of giggling.

"No, Hope. Babies can't do that. You're supposed to be a

little baby! Stop being so silly." Faith sounded like she was trying to be exasperated but was too amused by Hope's antics. Natassa felt herself relax. Brandon was right. They were fine.

"See? We're all okay. And, hey, at least you're home in time to make dinner. We're out of pizza."

"No problem. Let me put on my superhero apron and save the day."

"It actually might take super powers of some sort. We're about out of food again. It's time for a grocery run. Do you think maybe you could do it this time?" Brandon asked tentatively, his arm still around her like he was afraid she would bolt if he pressed the issue too hard.

"I don't know ..."

"You're apparently not afraid to leave the house anymore." He stroked her arm with his thumb, his tone laced with gentleness.

"I'm getting there."

"What if Breanna went with you?"

She nodded. "Yeah. That could work. I think I can do that. Now, let me see what I can scrape together for tonight."

She moved toward the kitchen, but Brandon grabbed her hand and pulled her back toward him.

"I love you, Natassa Bloomington." He stroked the side of her face and kissed her gently.

"I love you, too."

* * *

"Thanks for coming with me," Natassa told Breanna as she pushed the cart down the cereal aisle.

"Are you kidding? One-on-one time with my BFF? It's not like you had to twist my arm. What are we buying anyway? You probably have a list, right?"

"Of course." Natassa pulled the neatly folded paper from her purse and handed it to Breanna.

"Wow. Numbered and—what is this? Organized by aisle? How come it's not alphabetized? Did you run out of time?"

"Oh, shush."

"Okay, so three boxes of cereal." Breanna grabbed two boxes of Fruit Loops and a box of Apple Jacks and threw them in the cart. "Next!"

"Breanna! Those must have over twelve grams of sugar per serving."

"Oh, sorry. The list just said 'cereal.' It didn't say 'cereal that tastes like cardboard.'"

"My children like regular Cheerios just fine. Or Rice Krispies. Those are fun."

"Oh yeah. Snap, Crackle, Pop! They're a blast."

"How about I do the shopping and you just keep me company?" Natassa said as she put Breanna's selections back on the shelf and added her more-sensible ones to the cart.

"Whatever makes you happy, chicka. I'm at your service today."

They made their way slowly and methodically down the aisle, Natassa checking off each item as she placed it in the cart. She had just crossed off Brandon's granola bars when Breanna dove into the subject Natassa had been avoiding.

"So, what did you decide to do about ... you know? Did you talk to Brandon?"

"I made an appointment. That's all I'm going to say." Natassa kept pushing the cart, her eyes straight ahead.

"What do you mean that's all you're going to say? Come on, Nat, it's me! You've got to talk to me. How do you feel about all of this?"

"I love you, Bre, but I don't want to talk about it, and if you press me on it, I'll just shut down and not say another word to you the rest of the day."

"Okay. Okay, fine. You made an appointment. That's all you're going to say. Which means you're not going to ask me to go with you. Which means, what? Your mom is taking you? But you're not going to answer that, are you?" Breanna sighed. "You're probably right. It's probably for the best. For everyone."

Natassa didn't comment, but Breanna's words cut deep. She leaned over the cart, putting her head on the handle, squinting her eyes shut tight to keep back the tears.

"Sorry, Nat. I keep botching things up. Are you okay? Breathe, baby. Breathe." Breanna rubbed her back, her hand moving in slow, rhythmic circles. "I'll shut up now. We'll keep it light and get through this list. This is your first real public outing since everything happened, except for that disaster of a lunch at your mom's. And the park. Those don't really count. Oh, and you went out to dinner with Brandon. But anyway, we just need to get 'er done. Get through it. Can you do that?"

Natassa took a deep breath, pushing everything out of her mind except for the items on her list. She nodded. She could do this. She needed to do this.

Breanna stayed true to her word and kept things light. Every time Natassa turned her head, Bre threw a sugary treat into the cart for comedic effect. Natassa took the donuts, suckers, cookies, Toaster Strudels, and cinnamon rolls out but kept the gallon of rocky road for herself.

After they put the groceries in the car, Natassa started the engine but didn't shift out of park. Though she didn't feel at liberty to divulge everything to her friend, she had to get one thing off her chest.

"This wasn't my first public outing."

"Like I said, your mom's house doesn't count. Maybe the park kind of counts, but not really—"

"I went to that church. The one on St. Anthony Street. Brandon doesn't know."

"Wait. You snuck out and went to that church we were in the parking lot of?"

"Twice, actually."

"Why?"

Natassa shrugged. "I felt drawn to it."

"I can't believe it. You hyperventilated when we drove down there. Why would you go back? How did you go back? By yourself? Did you panic?"

"It was scary driving down that street, especially the first time, but I took deep breaths like you told me to. I made it. Once I got to the church, I met this lady who made me feel welcome. Safe."

"I don't know how to ask this after I so badly worded that other question in the park, but is the church ... is it ..."

"I was the only white person there, if that's what you're trying to ask."

Breanna shook her head, her mouth hanging open. "I'm shocked, honestly. I cannot for the life of me imagine you driving by yourself down that street and marching into an unfamiliar church where you are the only white person. I can't wrap my brain around this. Who are you?"

"I didn't exactly march." Natassa closed her eyes and smiled, remembering the feeling of panic she'd had when entering that church for the first time and contrasting it with her second visit.

"Did you prance?"

"Hardly."

"Are you going to go back?"

"As much as I can."

"What about Brandon?"

"I don't know. I'm still figuring that out." Natassa shifted the car into reverse and pulled out of the parking spot. Both friends were quiet during the ride home, Natassa's mind buzzing with questions and uncertainties.

* * *

I never did figure out what the man who bought me was doing so far south. What business did he have with Old Master that caused him to go roaming all about? Never could tell. Regardless, the journey to Nashville took a couple of weeks, I reckon, and that gave me plenty of time to think. I didn't waste too much of it wondering what my new life would look like, 'cause I didn't have a scrap of an idea what to expect. My mind couldn't even imagine a world without Mama in it, so instead I spent the time thinking of all I was leaving behind. It wasn't no paradise. We was slaves there just like I'd be a slave in Nashville, but at least we was together.

I thought mostly 'bout Mama an' how she's so fiercely brave. She done taught herself to read, even though she could get whipped for it. She could have gotten whipped for teachin' me too, but that didn't faze her none. Ain't no one with more courage than my mama. No one I know at least. I reckon that's why it confused me so why she didn't fight to keep me with her. I didn't understand then that sending me away was the bravest thing she could do.

As I watched the wagon kick up dust mile after mile on the road to Nashville, I thought about Pa too. He might not be my pa by blood, but he done raised me, so I reckon he was my pa in all the ways that mattered. I wasn't quite sure if Pa was brave like my Mama. He would take a beatin' without a shadow of emotion passing over his face. He made himself hard as stone. But when Old Master called for Mama, I'd see tracks of tears down his cheeks and hear sounds coming out of him like he some wounded animal. I didn't understand what was going on then, but now I think he'd have wrung Old Master's neck with his thick hands if he could have. But he knew if he so much as said a word 'bout it, Old Master wasn't above havin' a noose hug his neck to show the other slaves who's boss. Mama, too, knew she was helpless to fight it, but she wasn't above negotiatin' for her willingness to not put up a fight.

Reckon that's how she got the book in the first place.

Hidden in my change of clothes, wrapped real tight, was my primer. It's the only book I've ever owned, the only book I've ever touched. Old Master didn't know I had it, and neither did the man who bought me. Mama reminded me never to let on that I could read and to never let anyone see me write anything. Not anything. I done promised her I'd be careful as could be.

The very fact that I had an extra change of clothes said something. None of the other slave children had extra. Was it a sign that my father cared about me? That he thought it proper to provide for me? Or was it just another something my mama bargained for in the night? Did I care where it came from? I guess maybe I do care, since I'm asking that question.

In my best guess, I'm fifteen as I write this. It's been nine years since I've seen my mama's face. Her flesh-and-blood face, that is. I see it in my dreams plenty. I guess the way this thing is supposed to work is I's supposed to write a diary and keep track of everything that happens from day to day. I done seen the Missus doing that very thing, writing the date up top. The thing is, nothing's gone and happened today that's any different from any other day for me. It's my past that eats at me. It's days gone by where all those feelings twist and turn 'round inside me, begging to be let out somehow. So I think I'd rather stuff this book full of memories and let their echoes do the talkin'. If adventure finds me in the days to come, well, then maybe I'll write that too.

Before I left for Nashville, I ain't never seen anything outside of our own plantation. On that first day after pulling away from Old Master's plantation, away from Mama, we passed a line of slaves on that dusty road to Tennessee. We heard them first, singin' a sad song.

Then we saw them, all chained together by their right ankles and their necks. The women had ropes instead of chains, but they still walked like they was weighed down. They only had underclothes on, even the women. With their backs exposed, I saw stripes on more than half of them, cuts so deep and jagged their flesh there was a different color than the rest of them. It struck me then that maybe I hadn't belonged to the cruelest Master in existence. Perhaps there was worse. I'd gotten whipped, for sure, but each time my back healed within weeks, and the faded marks that were left were flat, not puffy like what I was seeing then. And I ain't never been shackled. All of the sudden, I was filled with dread and started breathin' all heavy like.

"Don't you worry." The man who bought me hadn't said more than a word to me until that time, but now he caught my eye and tossed out a small smile of pity. He nodded to the slaves passing by. "If you're a good little girl and you please my wife, you'll never know what that's like. Only bad slaves get sold to a slave trader. Ones who don't obey their Masters. You do as you're told and you'll be just fine. You won't even need a whipping if you're obedient like the Bible says you ought to be."

I nodded, keeping my head down like I's been taught. "I be good. I promise I be good."

"Splendid. I bought you as a surprise for my wife. She's been wanting a young slave girl that she can train to be an attendant. You'll be a great gift for her."

"Yes, sir."

We's didn't talk much the rest of the way, 'cept when we'd stop for the night and he'd bid me to fetch the water and such. But the next time I saw a slave caravan, I didn't feel like all the air got sucked out of me—more like a heavy cloud perched over me, weighing me down with a melancholy wrapped up in a thousand questions. I done looked at each slave and wondered who was they? What was their name? Their real name that they's mama gave them, not no name from any Master. Where did they come from? Where were they going? Did they have a mama who was missing them? Or was they a mama missing their baby? Why was they sold to the slave trader? What did they do that was so bad anyway?

Whatever it was, I wasn't gonna do nothing like it. I was gonna do good. I wasn't gonna end up with no slave trader.

When we finally pulled up to the Big House, part of me was relieved to be done with the riding on the bumpy road, and part of me wished we could go on riding forever. Maybe then eventually we'd end up right where we came from. My new Master told me to hurry along, dust off my dress, and come with him. I done followed him up the steps onto the porch.

"Now, you wait right here by the front door. Don't go anywhere until I call you in."

I done answered with "Yes, sir," like I was supposed to. When he went in, I lifted my head and looked around. The house wasn't near as big as Master and Missus's house back home, but the height of the columns still managed to give it an imposing feeling, like it was standing over me with a switch, watching for me to do something wrong.

I heard my new Master's voice and pressed my ear against the door to make out exactly what was being said as I didn't want to miss him callin' for me.

"Victoria, darling! I have a surprise for you. I know how you've been wanting a young slave girl to train—"

"Oh, Charles, you didn't!" And a giggle.

"Yes, sweetheart. I hope she pleases you well. She seems quite moldable. Just what you wanted."

"Where is she? Let me look at her!"

"Mercy, come here."

I don't rightly know how to justify the feelings that were coursing through me while I's listening to them talk. They's sounded so excited 'bout me, and for a moment I forgot I was a slave and felt like I's joinin' their family, like they were thrilled to have a daughter come into their home. I wanted to meet this lady who sounded over-

joyed with me comin'. I wanted to run in and say, "I's here! It's me. The one you wanted!" I done forgot how sad I was right then and thought that maybe we'd be happy there, the three of us together. I don't know why I thought that. Guess I was just too little to know better.

At any rate, I contained my excitement and walked in all proper-like with my head bowed. I lifted my eyes slightly in acknowledgment and curtsied to the Missus. But she done looked like she bit into a lemon.

"Charles! Oh, no! She's ... she's ... She nearly looks white!"

"Well, yes, dear. She's a mulatto, but I've heard the lighter the better, especially for a house slave. She will be perfect for you, dear."

The Missus shook her head. "No, this will never do. If I take her out in public, someone might mistake her as my daughter. That would be mortifying. Take her back. Or sell her to a trader. I don't care—just get her out of here."

And with a wave of the woman's hand, I was dismissed. I left the house in Nashville as quickly as I came. As I followed Master out to the wagon, I glanced back up at the Big House. It gleamed white in the sun, making my skin look so ... unwhite in comparison. I didn't feel white, but for the second time, the white blood in my veins caused me to be sent away. Maybe that's when the seed of hating white, and hating the white inside, fell into me. Or maybe that's just when it grew thorns.

Being wanted is a powerful thing. It's alls I wanted all my life. When the Nashville Missus sent me away, I wasn't even wanted as a slave. Not even good enough for that. And since that Master said if I did good I would never be sold to no slave trader, well, I didn't have no chance to do good or not do good. It wasn't about my doing. It was about my being. I didn't do bad. I was bad. And that's why I ended up in the slave pen. At least that's how my mind worked things out

back then. If I could have just laid my head on Mama's shoulder, she could have righted my thinkin' for me and told me she loved me and I was worth somethin'. She could have told me again that I's the cream in her coffee. She would have made everything all right. But Mama was gone, and I had no one.

* * *

Natassa stuffed *Mercy's Journal* back under the driver's seat and wiped her wet cheeks with the back of her hand. *Being wanted is a powerful thing.* Natassa stroked her belly, wishing she could rub that feeling of being wanted into the baby growing inside of her. "Oh, Mercy," she whispered, "you aren't unwanted because of the color of your skin or even because of how you came to me." But like the scenario she just read, one spouse wanted Mercy and the other did not. Who would have the final say in their case?

She flipped off the overhead light in her car and snuck back into her home by the light of the moon. Being careful not to wake Brandon, she slipped into bed, traces of dampness still on her cheeks.

17

———————

DeAndre's phone went off in his pocket as he walked toward St. Anthony Street on Sunday morning. He pulled it out, surprised to see his mother's face on the screen.

"Hi, Mama. What's up?"

"Hi, DeAndre. I didn't catch you at a bad time, did I? You're not at church yet, are you?"

"No, Mama. I'm walking in that direction right now. The first bell hasn't even rung yet." He hadn't been to a service since his Mama left, but he wasn't about to break her heart and tell her that.

"Oh, good." The relief in her voice only solidified his conviction that it was better she didn't know he was no longer a faithful attender.

"How's Chicago treating you?"

"All right. But I miss you, DeAndre." He would have said that he missed her too, but he didn't trust his voice not to crack. It just didn't seem right, them being so many miles away from each other. "I got a new job." The pride in her voice helped

DeAndre to focus on the reality of their situation instead of walking down the road of coulda, shoulda, woulda.

"That's great, Mama. Where at?"

"Bobbie's Jazz House. I'm waiting tables there five nights a week."

"But you hate jazz."

"It grew on me. It's amazing the things you can learn to enjoy when you love someone. Working there ... well, it's the closest I've felt to your father since he passed. It's like I can feel him with me, in the soul of the music."

"I thought you moved to get away from Daddy."

"I wanted to get away from how he died, not how he lived, DeAndre. I couldn't stand walking those streets, reliving the shooting in my mind day after day. I needed to get away from that."

"Yeah, well." DeAndre's gait slowed with the downward turn of his mood. "I guess I didn't want to leave him, huh? You've moved on, and I'm still here."

"He ain't there anymore, DeAndre."

"His shop's still here."

"It's not his shop if he ain't in it."

DeAndre sighed, frustrated that he couldn't make his mother understand why he felt tied to his hood and why he felt betrayed when she left. He lost both his parents. He lost Pa to violence and Mama to grief. No wonder he clung to Reg so tightly.

"Reg is doing well with Pa's shop. He does good work."

"Aww, Reg," she said with a smile in her voice. "How is that boy? Is he keeping out of trouble?"

"Mostly."

"You tell him I said hi, you hear? I don't want him to think I done forgot about him."

"I'll tell him."

"Do you think you boys could catch a bus over here and visit me this Christmas?"

"Maybe. We'll see."

"Think about it. I better let you go. I don't want you to be late for church."

"Good talking to you, Mama."

"The phone works both ways, you know."

"I got it. I'll call you soon."

As DeAndre hung up with his mother, he turned onto St. Anthony Street, dragging his feet a bit more than before. He tried not to think about his mama for this very reason. Thoughts of her—and conversations with her—left him melancholy for days afterward. But his mother, working in a jazz club, feeling his daddy through the "soul of the music"? That surprised him.

As he neared the abandoned ice cream shop, a car turned onto the otherwise deserted street. He froze as it passed him. He was staring at the taillights of the maroon Audi SUV.

Are you serious? DeAndre stepped into the alleyway between two buildings just in case she happened to look out her rearview mirror and wonder what the boy from Java Joe's was doing there. Dre. She knew him as Dre. It had been D who raped her, but Dre served her coffee. He watched her car proceed down the street and saw her pull into the parking lot of the church.

That lady goes to my church? Okay, he couldn't exactly consider it his church, but he had gone to the church as a boy, had grown up going to that church. It stood in his neighborhood, not hers. What was she doing down here anyway? Maybe it wasn't even her. He hadn't caught a glimpse of Natassa Bloomington herself. There was more than one maroon Audi in the state, right?

Keeping his head to the side, he walked down the street hoping to get a better look. When he came to the last building on the street, he ducked into the doorway, putting a hand above his eyes to shield him from the sun's glare. There she was. Natassa Bloomington was there, sitting on the step and talking with Old Ezra. DeAndre shook his head, shocked. That first night he thought she was some slut, and here she was sitting on the church steps in respectable clothes.

DeAndre was beginning to think he didn't know anything about anything. The first bell resounded from the church. A wave of nausea rolled over him, and he hurled in the alley, head spinning. What had he done? Attacked a churchgoing woman? Violated some child's mama? Some man's wife? How could God ever forgive him for what he'd done to Mrs. Natassa Bloomington? He squeezed his eyes shut and pressed his forehead against the hard brick wall, wishing he could push himself into another reality.

But when he opened his eyes, the brick wall still stared back at him.

The second bell clanged its melody. DeAndre felt hollowed out, and the sound seemed to echo inside him. He put his hands over his ears, but it did little to muffle the sound.

He had to get his mind off of this, off of *her,* before he went mad. Paint. He needed to paint.

Remembering why he set foot on St. Anthony Street that morning to begin with, he resolved to continue his mission. After hearing strains of organ music drifting from the church, DeAndre cast a furtive glance toward the stone steps to make sure Natassa had gone inside. Relieved to find the steps empty, he walked back to the ice cream shop. He ducked inside and grabbed his cans of paint then got to work. He had been up half the night envisioning this scene. He wanted to go back in time or forward to a better place. Something. Someplace where the streets he was so familiar with didn't make headlines in the news each night. He was tired of hearing about violence and drugs, innocent people fearing for their lives. He felt stuck. He couldn't make things different, but he could at least paint things different.

He used the church scene that he had painted weeks ago as the central focus of a larger scene, working out from there on both sides. He painted children playing in the streets, all smiles, no fear. He painted a woman gardening out front of her home, a house without boards, bars, or holes in the porch or roof. He painted teens wearing hoodies, playing around and laughing to combat the negative stereotypes of black males with hooded sweatshirts. He painted shops open for business. And just because he missed her, he painted his mama sitting on the steps of the ice cream shop, eating a chocolate-dipped cone.

His paintings sprung forth from wishes locked deep inside him. They came forth almost like prayers. He didn't talk to God directly; that felt too presumptuous. Still, it almost felt like speaking to the Almighty, in a roundabout way. He asked for things he wanted for his city, all the while knowing he wasn't worthy to say the words.

It was getting late when DeAndre stepped back to take in his creation. His mind had been moving so fast, he hadn't taken the time he should have to fill out all the detail. He would have to come back and fine-tune it. Still, he was pleased with how it turned out. Yet, it was missing something. He scanned the entire scene from top to bottom, side to side, trying to figure out what the missing piece was.

As the sun began to melt into the horizon, it came to him. He knew exactly what was missing. He would add it on his next day off, only he didn't have the color he needed. He'd have to pick it up first. He set the cans of paint back into the abandoned ice cream shop and walked home, feeling like he had been to church after all.

Reg wasn't home when he walked through the door. The way things had been going between them, DeAndre figured he should be grateful for the reprieve. However, the phone call from Mama left him with an ache only family could satisfy. And Reg was family.

A quick phone call revealed that Reg was still at Pa's shop, so DeAndre grabbed his keys and drove down there, flipping the radio to the jazz station, trying to see if he could feel the soul of the music like Mama did. It was too short of a drive, though, and his thoughts distracted him.

The shop was locked, and DeAndre had to pound on the door before Reg let him in. When Reg opened the door, DeAndre heard music streaming from Reg's headphones. Hip-hop, not jazz. This might be Pa's shop, but this wasn't his pa.

"Sorry, D." Reg fiddled with his phone until the beat stopped busting out.

"Why are you here so late?"

"There's a lot of work to do. Besides," Reg shrugged, walking back to a Corolla, "I wasn't ready to leave. You know?"

"Yeah. I know." Boy, did he know. "Do you need any alternators replaced? I'm pretty good at that." DeAndre smiled at his friend, offering a truce.

"Naw, man. Not today. This baby needs new spark plugs."

"Sounds simple. Let me at it," DeAndre joked.

"And let you melt the catalytic converter? I don't think so."

"Fine. Have it your way." He tried to keep his tone light, but in reality, Reg's brush-off stung.

"How about I work on this and you just keep me company?" Reg popped the Toyota's hood and went to work. DeAndre pulled up a folding chair from the office.

"So, Mama called today." DeAndre couldn't see Reg's expression from where he was sitting, but he noticed Reg's movement slowed a bit.

"What'd she say?"

"She got a job. She's working in a jazz club now."

"Beats that fast food joint she was working at."

"It's weird, though, isn't it? Mama never could stand jazz."

"People change."

"I guess."

"Can you hand me that spark plug socket?"

"The what?" DeAndre asked, looking around him.

"The ... oh never mind." Reg walked over to the table next to DeAndre and grabbed a tool, then headed back under the hood.

"Anyway," DeAndre continued, "she did say she wanted us to take a bus to Chicago this Christmas. She wants to see us."

"Us? She mentioned me?" Reg peeked his head out from under the hood, eyebrows raised at DeAndre.

"Yep. She said to tell you hi. And she wants to see you for the holidays."

"Huh. Interesting. I got a call from my mama the other day, too."

"Uh oh. What did she want now?"

"She's in the slammer again. Wanted me to bail her out."

"Are you gonna do it?"

"She can rot in there for all I care. I'm not giving her a dime."

DeAndre didn't know what to say, so the only sound heard in the garage was the clunking of metal under the hood. He wished he could make himself useful, but whatever camaraderie he and Reg had found the last time they were in Pa's shop together fell flat at the moment. Maybe if DeAndre had just gone with Reg to get that beer, they would be working together under that hood right now.

Reg broke the silence, "Yeah, I'll go with you to Chicago. Heck, I'll go to the moon if that's what your mama wants. I'll do anything for her. She was more of a mama to me than my own mama ever was."

"Yeah, until she left," DeAndre muttered.

"Stop it, D." Reg came out from under the hood, swinging some kind of wrench in front of him for emphasis. "Stop acting like you some orphan, like your mama left poor baby D all alone. She didn't abandon you, bro. You had a mama and a daddy tucking you in at night until you was a teenager. Do you know how lucky you is? Then, yeah, you lost your daddy, and that's tough, but at least you had a daddy to lose. And your mama stuck around here till you was a grown man before she just couldn't take it anymore. She toughed it out for years for you. She made sure you was gonna be okay before trying to find a piece of happiness for herself. Don't you go moping around here like she don't deserve that."

DeAndre bristled under the rebuke. "You're just jealous."

Reg cursed. "Of course, I'm jealous. You wanna switch places with me, D? 'Cause if I were in your shoes, I sure wouldn't be complaining about a mama who loved me, even if she was in Chicago."

"Are you almost done?" DeAndre asked, nodding toward the Toyota.

"I'll only be a few more minutes."

"I'll be outside. I need some air." DeAndre let himself out the front door and walked around the building. Reg just didn't understand. He couldn't. DeAndre didn't want to get into it with Reg, but he didn't want to just sit there while his buddy ran his mouth either.

He eyed the cracked sign out front. The bottom of the E was faded away so it looked like Flm Street Automotive. It could use a new coat of paint.

Paint.

DeAndre walked around to the side of the building that faced Seventh. That side was pure brick, a blank canvas for DeAndre's imagination to run wild. What if? He was still staring at the wall when Reg came outside.

"What you doing, D? You finally crackin' up?"

"I want to paint again, Reg. I want to paint right here. Elm Street Automotive, with the logo right here and, if they'd let me,

Pa's face right here. Do you think the guys would go for it? Will you talk to them?"

"Yeah." Reg nodded his approval. "All right. I'll ask them."

"Thanks."

"Now, how about a beer?" Reg asked, slapping DeAndre on the back.

"Nah. What about a latte?" DeAndre kept a straight face even as Reg widened his eyes and pursed his lips.

"Sure, I'll take a latte. A latte beer."

DeAndre couldn't help but laugh at Reg's cheesy joke as they climbed into DeAndre's car and headed home. There was beer in the fridge.

18

———

Natassa sat in the waiting room, filling out a thick stack of paperwork. *Name. Birthdate. Address. Phone number. Number of previous pregnancies.* She paused, remembering each pregnancy so distinctly. The excitement. The anticipation. It had been different with each child, but it was every bit as present with her fourth baby as it had been with her first. This time was different, of course, and yet ...

"Natassa, you can come on back." The nurse smiled politely. It was just another routine visit for her.

"I've barely started the paperwork."

"It's okay. You can bring it with you and work on it in the room."

Natassa followed the nurse to the back, stepped on the scale, had her blood pressure and temperature taken, and then was left to wait for the doctor. Her heart hammered in her chest, and she turned her attention to the stack of forms waiting to be filled out. When she was halfway through answering the medical history questions, there was a knock on the door and the doctor came in.

"Hello, I'm Dr. Amber. How are you?" The woman's face was

dotted with freckles, and her curly red hair was tamed with a headband.

"Okay. I'm Natassa."

Dr. Amber shook Natassa's hand before sitting on the rolling stool in front of Natassa.

"Good to meet you. I see you're still working on the paperwork, which is fine, but it means I don't have much to go from here. Is this your first pregnancy?"

"No. It's my fifth. I have four children at home."

"Oh! How wonderful. That's lovely. So, are you new to the area?"

"No."

"You just wanted to find a new OB then?"

"Yes. I just ..." Natassa couldn't bear going to Dr. Hill for this pregnancy. Dr. Hill had delivered all her other babies and was an excellent obstetrician, but Natassa needed the shield of anonymity right now. Having Dr. Hill look at her with pity after all of the moments they had shared together? She couldn't do it.

"It's okay. You don't have to explain. How did you find our office? Did someone refer you?"

"No, Google." Truth be told, after going through the search engine list alphabetically didn't work out as planned, Natassa started looking for some sort of sign. Dr. Amber's office was located on Anastasia Boulevard, which was just the nudge Natassa needed. This place had her name on it, or at least a variant of her name—which she never would have known if not for Old Ezra.

"Okay then, this isn't your first rodeo, so I'm sure there's a lot you are already a pro on, but do you have any questions for me?"

"Yes, actually." Natassa took a deep breath, but her voice still wavered. "I haven't felt sick. With my others, I was throwing up all the time, but this time I haven't felt nauseated at all. Is there something wrong? Something's the matter, isn't it?" Her lip trembled, but she didn't cry.

"Not necessarily, but we do an ultrasound this visit anyway, so we'll check and see what's going on in there. Have you had any bleeding or cramping?"

"No. Not at all."

"That's a good sign." Dr. Amber smiled, and Natassa felt herself begin to relax.

After going over Natassa's medical history, current nutritional information, and general plans for the birth, Dr. Amber told her that the ultrasound technician would be there in a minute and asked her to undress and put on a gown for the ultrasound.

"Why do I need to wear a gown for the ultrasound?"

"We do an internal ultrasound for this first time. They are the most accurate at this stage."

Natassa felt panic welling up inside her. The thought of something as invasive as an internal ultrasound brought her thoughts, her emotions, her senses right back to St. Anthony Street that night. She could almost feel herself being shoved in the car, the horror of her underwear being ripped off ... The tears she had held back earlier came cascading out of her.

"Please, no," she gasped. "An external one. Please! Please just do a regular external ultrasound, not an internal one."

Dr. Amber stared back at her, eyes wide. *I'm making a fool of myself and scaring the doctor. Calm down, Natassa!* But the adrenaline coursing through her didn't listen to reason. She knew she was going to have to tell her new OB the nature of this pregnancy eventually. She hadn't planned on doing so this visit, but ...

"I'm sorry. I must sound like a nutcase. I was ... I was raped. This baby is from that rape. It's still so recent, so fresh in my mind, and an internal ultrasound just seems ... violating somehow."

"Oh, Natassa. I'm so sorry." Dr. Amber reached out and grabbed her hand. Natassa looked down at it then up at the woman's face. There was that look: pity. Or was it compassion? Natassa wasn't sure she could tell the difference.

"I didn't want to tell you until I was further along. I didn't want you to try and talk me out of going through with the pregnancy." Natassa sniffled, and Dr. Amber handed her a tissue.

"I'm not in the habit of talking people out of having babies. Delivering babies is my job, and my joy—no matter what circumstances brought them into existence."

"I wish everyone felt like you do."

"Wow. You've been through it, haven't you?"

Natassa nodded. Her tears had slowed, and she willed them not to pick up again.

"I'll tell you what—we'll go ahead and do an external ultrasound. Sometimes we can't pick up a heartbeat this early with those, so I don't want you to worry if that's the case. We'll just have you come back again in a couple weeks and try again. Sound good?"

Natassa nodded, grateful to be spared and thankful to still be able to get an ultrasound. She wanted the assurance that the baby was fine, wanted to lay those worries to rest, bury Brandon's "wishful thinking."

"Since we're doing it this way, you can follow me down the hall to the ultrasound room. Our technician, Sandy, will do the ultrasound. I'll pop in afterward." The women rose to leave, but before opening the door, Dr. Amber patted Natassa on the back. "You're a strong woman, Natassa. You're going to get through this and shine even brighter than before. I know you will."

Natassa bit her lip, holding in another wave of emotion that threatened to take over. The kind words spoken by a stranger pushed at her tender spaces, hungering for affirmation. She tried to formulate words of gratitude, but by the time she compiled a coherent sentence in her head and was ready to speak it, Dr. Amber was heading down the hall. Natassa hurried after her, trusting that the doctor already knew when healing had been given.

Moments later, Natassa held her breath as Sandy the technician squirted cold blue gel onto her stomach and began to move the probe around. She squinted at the screen, straining to make sense of the gray lines and shadows. A little lower, slightly to the left, and there! Natassa recognized the little bean shape that was her baby. She took a breath, but her shoulders were still taught with worry.

"Let's see about that heartbeat," Sandy said.

Was that a flashing heartbeat in the center there? Natassa hoped so, but she couldn't tell. Within seconds, though, she was greeted with the sound of it, like a horse galloping, and her eyes began to mist again.

"One sixty-seven. Perfect." Sandy smiled at her and then went on to complete the other measurements.

"She's healthy? Nothing is wrong?"

"Your baby looks perfect. Why? Were there concerns?"

"It's just that I haven't been having typical pregnancy symptoms. I mean, I've been tired, but not sick."

"Oh. Well, don't worry a bit. Just consider it God's mercy."

Mercy. From God.

The tears began to surface again.

Sandy smiled at her. "It's okay. These ultrasounds make a lot of women cry. You've got a baby growing inside of you, plus all the hormones that go with it." Natassa gave her a wobbly smile in return.

A few minutes later, the gel was rubbed off, and Dr. Amber stopped in to say everything looked great and she'd see Natassa again in four weeks. Natassa left the office on Anastasia Boulevard with a second appointment on the books and three pictures of her baby in her hand.

* * *

The babysitter was scheduled to stay until Brandon got home from work, which meant Natassa had three more hours before she had to be home. She loved her children more than anything in the world, but being a full-time mom day in and day out left her longing for a bit of solitude. She didn't plan on rushing home. She had three more hours to brace herself for whatever Brandon's reaction would be. But first, she had to tell him. Meaning, she had to text him. She wasn't brave enough to tell him to his face.

She took out her phone and snapped a picture of the clearest ultrasound photo. It was still fuzzy, but they'd been through this before; Brandon would know what it meant. Under the picture, she typed the text: IT'S FOR THE BEST. YOU'LL SEE. Adrenaline rushing, she pressed send.

He had set her up, and now she had done the same to him. He might be furious with her, and maybe he had the right to be. She hadn't outright lied. All she'd said was that she made an appointment, which was true. It just wasn't the appointment Brandon thought it was. Okay, so she did nod her agreement when he asked if her mom was taking her. A sick feeling of regret surfaced. She was getting tired of these games. *I made an appointment. I was at my mom's house.* She just didn't know what else to do. He could be so unreasonable, so unyielding. She had spent ten years getting used to just yielding. But like she told Breanna, some things were worth fighting for.

Breanna. She needed to tell Breanna.

She took her phone back out and attached the same picture to a text to Breanna with the text: MY FIRST OB APPOINT-MENT IS OVER. BABY LOOKS GREAT. HOPEFULLY BRANDON WON'T KILL ME. She didn't feel the same amount of trepidation pushing send as she did with Brandon's text, but she still felt nervous. Breanna had said that making an appointment for an abortion was "probably for the best." Was that what she really believed? Or was that just her way of trying to be supportive? Natassa wasn't sure and didn't know how Breanna would react.

But she didn't want to think about that now. Natassa had told the babysitter that if she had any problems, she was to call Brandon. So Natassa turned her phone off, pulled *Mercy's Journal* out from under the seat, and started driving in the direction of the coffee shop.

* * *

That's how I ended up followin' behind the slave coffle, hearing the heavy clink of the chain as the men plodded forward. The women was in front of me, tied together at one hand. I's followed behind them. I ain't had no chain or rope on me. Guess they trusted that I's too small to run away. In truth, I wanted to be where they was headin'.

Lexington.

I didn't do much talkin', but I sure done a heap full of listenin', and I's heard what the trader said to the sellers there in Nashville who cared to ask where the slaves were bound. To Lexington, the slave trading center of Kentucky. And if we's not sold there, he'd be takin' us south eventually.

Now I ain't know much about directions and the like even now, but 'specially then, but I done knew that I came from South Carolina. And I done thought if I could manage to not get myself sold in Lexington then I might be headed straight back there. Straight back to Mama. So, as I walked on at the end of the line, I tried to keep my eyes off their bare backs, puffy scars glaring at me, daring me to freeze in fear. Instead, I kept my head down at my own two feet and tried to think how every step I was takin' was getting' me closer to Mama. If only I didn't get sold 'fore I got there, but I wasn't too worried 'bout that. It went core deep, that knowing that no one wanted me. I was too white. Too unlike my mama. Too much like Old Master. But 'course I wasn't white 'nough neither or I wouldn't be marchin' in a slave caravan.

Every now and then, the driver would command us to sing. I couldn't find my voice, even with fear of a whippin'. I opened my mouth to make him think words was comin' out and tasted the salt of the tears that had been rollin' down my cheeks. He didn't figure out I's not singin'. Or maybe I'd become invisible. I felt that way anyhow.

When we's got to Lexington, all the sudden they started treatin' us like we's important. They fed us real good and gave us new clothes 'fore they closed us in a damp, smelly slave pen. I got a light-blue linsey-woolsey dress, though no one bothered to give us shoes. We all's barefoot since our old shoes gave out along the way. The slave trader told us we'd be on the auction block in the mornin' and to get a good rest. I don't think I slept a bit, though it sure be dark enough. There was signs up and about saying they'd be sellin' wenches and bucks and fancy girls. The signs didn't say nothin' about chillum, so I's wondering if maybe I was safe. But when the sun came up the next morning, another slave was oilin' my face so it'd be shiny and I'd look healthy and that.

"If they ask you if you'd done been whipped, tell them no," the slave said as he rubbed the oil in good.

"But I has been whipped, sir."

"You best not let on. I's just tellin' you what he done told me to tell you."

"My mama done told me not to lie."

He sighed, his eyes all droopy like he'd done seen too much to hold all the hurt in those eyelids. He touched my hair gentle like a whisper. "I had a little girl. She'd be 'bout your size by now, I reckon."

Then he walked away, slumped as if he was melting. Now I's had tears to cry for him as well as my own, but I done tried to hold them in so I wouldn't get in trouble.

It got harder as I watched others go up for auction. A mama stood up on the block with her baby and little one grabbin' round her *leg. No one was buyin', so the trader said he'd go and sell her separate from her chillun. When that babe was ripped from her arms, I felt that woman's screechin' in my very bones. Again and again I heard mamas cry as their babies were taken from them. The pressure kept buildin' in my chest until I couldn't take it no more. I started sobbin', and even the threats of whippings couldn't get me to stop.*

That slave had to come and oil my face again.

"Don't you cry no more, ya hear? If you don't get sold here, rumor is you'll go south."

"I want to go south. My mama's south."

"Girl, listen to me. Down south is harder. It be harder for you. Up here you'se got a better chance. They ain't gonna bring you to your mama. I's sorry. I's so sorry, but it ain't gonna happen that way. You best buck up and get yourself a kind Master here."

I shook my head, but something inside me knew he be telling the truth. Even if they marched me straight up to Mama, she'd likely just send me away again.

By the time it was my turn on the block, I'd stopped my tears from flowing, though my eyes were still wet 'round the edges. I stood there and looked out at a sea of white people, scanning their faces to see if I could find one that looked good and kind.

One man to my right looked at me in a way that made me feel greasy inside.

"Bring her back in a few years," he called. "She'd make a great fancy girl." A few men chuckled in the crowd, and I lowered my eyes.

I didn't know what a fancy girl was, but I done seen that look before when Old Master laid eyes on my mama. I stepped to my left.

One man called out that he'd give a hundred dollars for me. Another called out a hundred and twenty. The auctioneer told them all that the bidding started at one hundred and fifty, and that I was healthy and had never been whipped. Then they called out one fifty, one seventy-five, then two hundred. Just like that, I was sold to another stranger, put on the back of another wagon, and sent on the way to another house unfamiliar to me.

* * *

The man who bought me bought a young man as well. When we's stopped for a meal on the way, he explained that the man was to be a field hand and I was gonna tend to their baby.

"Most Masters here in Kentucky have a handful of slaves. Maybe three. Perhaps as much as six. But I have a large farm. With you two, I will have ten slaves altogether."

I don't know if we was supposed to think he's someone important or we was lucky to be among so many of our own, but I didn't have an ounce of emotion for it. Old Master had over seventy slaves, and it didn't mean a lick to me. I's still lookin' at him, trying to figure out if he was good and kind or whether he'd beat my back till it was all puffy-like.

He told the other slave what he could expect in the field raising corn and sweet potatoes, clearing land, shelling corn, working dawn to dusk with an hour rest during the heat of the day. He told me I'd be in charge of the baby in the evenings, sleeping in the house and tending to her at night. When I wasn't needed for the baby, I was to help cook. I nodded. Said, "Yes, sir." Tried not to cry. Actually, that 'bout sums up much of my days for a good long while. Saying, "Yes, sir." "Yes, ma'am." Trying not to cry.

19

---

aying, "Yes, sir." "Yes, ma'am." Trying not to cry. Natassa released a shuddering breath. She would never presume to compare the hardships in her life to the ones she'd just read about, but she tired of always saying, "Yes, sir," to her husband. But what would be the repercussions of going against his wishes? A mother and her child were meant to be together. Hopefully, Brandon would see that. He had to see that, had to see that ripping her baby from her arms—or her belly—could never be the right thing to do.

Natassa shut the journal, drained the last of her macchiato, and fished in her purse for her phone. What time was it? How long had she been reading, glued to the page? She'd been reading slowly, carefully, soaking up each word. She found her phone and turned it on. Five o'clock. Brandon would be getting off work right about now.

Two missed texts. She opened the one from Brandon.

MEET ME AT MALONE'S AT 5:30.

What? Malone's Bar and Grill? What about the children? She texted back a question mark in response. A minute later, her phone chirped.

BABYSITTER STAYING LATE. C U SOON.

She'd sent him a text about how she had deceived him, and he was taking her out to dinner? She hadn't expected that.

He didn't ask where I wanted to go. He always tries to get me to pick. Not that I ever do. Did he get tired of trying? Or is he afraid I might finally have an opinion? Maybe one that contradicts his own?

She didn't have time to contemplate the possibilities or even rehearse what she might say when she got there. She only had thirty minutes to make it to Malone's, and it was the middle of rush hour. She grabbed the journal, tossed her cup, and was about to hurry out the door when she remembered that she had spent a significant portion of the day in tears. *I must look like death.* She needed to freshen up, and she had to make it quick.

Natassa rushed toward the back where the restroom was, and as she turned the corner, she nearly collided with the young man who had waited on her in the drive-through last time.

"Oh! I'm sorry!" she said, startled and short of breath. Her pulse hammered in her ear.

"No, ma'am. Don't apologize." He stood there, staring at her as if he wanted to say something else. She willed herself to breathe more normally. She wasn't in any danger. She was in a coffee shop. *The poor kid must be bashful.* She smiled at him but didn't have the time to engage him in conversation. She needed to wash her face and get out of there. She turned and entered the bathroom, locking the door behind her.

* * *

Natassa spotted Brandon across the crowded restaurant. He was scanning the room, but he didn't see her. She began to walk toward him, and as she got closer, she saw his legs fidgeting under the table. *He's nervous.* The realization calmed her somewhat. Maybe they were on a level playing field.

She nearly made it to the table when their eyes locked.

"You came."

"You didn't think I would come?"

"I wasn't sure. I just ... I don't know anymore."

"I'm sorry." And she meant it. She felt sorry for how things had gotten so muddled between them, but as she sat down and set her purse on the floor beside her chair, she put her hand in the front pocket where the ultrasound pictures were, fingering their glossy surface, summoning strength from them in case she needed it for battle. She wasn't sorry for not extinguishing the life within her.

"Thank you for coming."

She didn't know what to say to that. Everything felt so unnatural. She picked up what she thought was the menu in front of her, but it turned out to be only the drink menu.

"I already ordered for you."

"You ordered for me?" She pushed the drink menu away.

"Sure. You were running late—"

"Rush hour."

He put up his hand, indicating it was not an accusation. "You always get the club and Caesar salad here. So, yeah, I ordered for you."

"What if I wanted something else?"

"Then change your order when she comes by, Natassa. It's not the end of the world."

She sat back and sighed. "The club is fine."

Brandon stared at her. She couldn't decipher his gaze. She wanted something to do with her hands. Malone's didn't have bread. Or chips. There weren't even crackers on the table. She took her time unwrapping her napkin and spreading it on her lap. *There. That bought me ten seconds.*

Brandon sat forward and laid his hand on the table, palm

open as if in a peace offering. She knew she should put her hand in his, but she hesitated, not sure she could trust him. "Natassa, I am so sorry." His voice faltered, and she leaned forward. "I saw that picture, and I started to … I couldn't believe I … It was so wrong of me, Nat. I should never have asked you to do that."

In their ten years of marriage, Natassa had seen Brandon cry less than a handful of times, yet his eyes were misting. She grabbed his hand and squeezed tight.

"I'm sorry for lying to you. I mean, I tried not to lie. Technically. But I'm sorry for not being truthful."

Brandon shook his head emphatically. "I should never have put you in that position. That," he said, nodding toward his phone on the table, "is a person. A baby. And you're right. That baby didn't do anything wrong."

Natassa smiled, flooded with thankfulness. He understood! He saw her heart. He got where she was coming from. They would make it through this together. She squeezed his hand again then brought it up to her mouth and kissed it.

"But, Natassa, it may be a baby, but it's not *my* baby." Brandon's voice was gentle, but that did little to soften the blow. The hope she had just found plummeted, leaving a sick, sinking feeling in her stomach.

"What are you saying?"

"Honey, try to understand. If we kept this baby, if we tried to raise it—"

"Her."

"Her? How do you know?"

"It's just a feeling I have, but it's a strong one. I really believe this baby's a girl."

"Okay, if we try to raise her as our own, every time I see her, I will think of the men who hurt you, Natassa. I will think about how I wasn't able to save you, to protect you. My job as your husband is to protect you, and I failed. Every time I see that little girl, I will be reminded of that horrible night and my failure. It will kill me, Natassa."

"But Brandon ..." He was afraid that night would follow him for the rest of his life, just as she had been, but wouldn't God's mercy follow her husband as well? She struggled to find the words to convince him that the future with this little girl wouldn't be as bleak as he was painting it.

"Hear me out, Nat. You are a compassionate woman, a good woman. I know you want what is best for this baby. That's why I believe you have to consider placing the baby up for adoption."

Natassa's train of thought screeched to a halt. *Wait. What?* Adoption. It had never even entered her mind. She took her hand out of Brandon's and placed it protectively on her stomach.

"I ... I don't know ..." she stammered.

"Come on, honey. This baby deserves to have two parents who love her unconditionally, without reservation. I don't know if I can do that. I don't know if I could give this baby what she needs."

"But ..."

"Surely you don't have any moral reservations about adoption."

"Moral reservations? No. It's not that." Natassa had always viewed adoption as a beautiful thing. She had just always pictured herself on the other side of it, as herself being the one to take in a child who needed a family. She couldn't seem to wrap her mind around being the one to hand her child to another.

"Then what is it? Because I thought this was a pretty decent compromise."

"Brandon, you took me off guard here. You've obviously been thinking about this, but it's a new thought to me. All I can think about right now is how hard that would be. In ten weeks or so, I'm going to feel her move inside of me. Then she'll move more and more, and I'll get to know her personality a little by her motions. She'll get to know my voice. I've sung to all my babies, remember that? Would I sing to her, too, or ... or not because I wouldn't want to get too attached? How could I not get attached? We are attached! She's inside of me."

"Babe," Brandon said, reaching for her hand again, "I know this is hard. It's crazy hard. But sometimes we need to make hard choices because they are the best thing for the people we love."

Natassa pictured it then, the slave girl Mercy holding onto her mother's feet, weeping and carrying on, begging to stay. And her mother, resolute in her decision to send her away. Natassa was sure that mother's heart was breaking with every single tear her daughter shed. It was a sacrifice for her daughter's best interest. Was God calling Natassa to make a similar sacrifice?

"I don't know ..." She was unsure. But she wasn't sure she had much of a choice.

"At least promise me you'll pray about it."

"Yes. Of course." She would pray. If she couldn't change Brandon's mind, maybe God would.

* * *

Natassa followed Brandon home after dinner, her mind and emotions in a jumble. The rest of their time together had gone smoothly enough. They ate and confined their conversation to the small selection of safe topics. He stopped fidgeting and seemed more relaxed. She, however, couldn't seem to ease the tension gripping every inch of her body. There was a time when she would have asked Brandon for a back rub, but now his touch didn't have the same effect. At least not consistently.

After Natassa parked in the garage, she pulled out her

phone. She had seen Breanna's text earlier but hadn't had time to respond.

WOW. LET ME KNOW WHAT BRANDON SAYS.

That was it. *Wow.* What did that mean? "Wow, that's awesome"? "Wow, you've got some guts"? "Wow, I think this is a bad idea"?

BRANDON TOOK ME OUT TO DINNER. WANTS TO GIVE THE BABY UP FOR ADOPTION.

It only took a minute for Breanna to reply.

THAT'S GREAT! HOW WONDERFUL!

Great? Wonderful? Natassa put a line of crying face emojis but then erased them. Once again, she pictured Mercy's mother standing there straight-faced, holding back the emotion she was surely feeling.

Natassa grabbed her purse and went inside. She never responded at all.

* * *

Walkin' into that house be something entirely new to me. I just stepped right in from the walk to the front door. They don't have no steps or porch or nothin'. I ain't never seen a Master's house that didn't perch itself up on top of the world like it be needing to remind everybody who's in charge. I couldn't figure it out.

Then I walked in and there be no staircase in front. Just a small little front room with an oilcloth to keep the floor clean before you walk straight into the dining room and the parlor. I knew the house went up higher, but I couldn't reckon how without no staircase up front. Turns out they hide the staircase behind a door on the side because they say it keeps things cooler. It's a right pretty staircase too, all twisty-like, and I think it's a shame to be hiding it in a corner behind a door. Right from the start, I noticed these things that seemed strange about this house to me, things I couldn't quite put together in my mind. That should have given me a clue as to what my time there would be like.

* * *

Baby Elizabeth was the prettiest thing I'd ever seen in white skin. I couldn't rightly justify the affection I felt bubble up inside me the instant I saw her perfect little features. She was like the porcelain doll Old Missus used to keep on the mantel, only she wiggled and gurgled and came to life. For all the reasons I had to hate whiteness, I loved her. I didn't even know why 'cept maybe she was too little to know nothing 'bout slavery at all. She didn't look at me no different than she did anyone else.

Cook and me was the only servants in the house, as the rest was needed in the field. Cook said there used to be a lady's maid before the baby was born, but she didn't please the Missus, so she got sent to the field.

Cook shuddered. "Field hands. The lowest of the low. Pray to God that never happens to you."

I didn't say nothing back to her. My mama was a field hand.

* * *

The first day I got there, the Missus took me up the twisty steps to the nursery and taught me how to hold Baby Elizabeth. I gazed into her eyes and touched the little brown curl on the top of her head. She grabbed hold of my finger. I smiled, just straight up grinned up at the Missus, who looked back at me with some strange look on her face.

"That's enough of that for now. Go help Cook." She waved her hand toward the staircase. I nodded, said, "Yes, ma'am," and passed Baby Elizabeth into her stiff arms. As Cook taught me how to wash the clothes with lye soap in the boiling water, I kept thinking about that look on the Missus's face and wondering what it meant. Old Missus in South Carolina hated me, and I could see that in her eyes

plain enough. But this new Missus? I couldn't figure out how she felt 'bout me. She said very little. She didn't ever smile, but she ain't ever screamed at me neither. Not yet. Not yet.

After we's done, Cook took me out back, and we looked out over the field. There were two slaves limping, not much more than boys, I thought. Too young to be walking like they old.

I pointed toward them. "Why they walking like that?"

Cook shook her head, looking far off in the distance as if in another world. "They's got their toes cut off."

"Cut off? Why?" My stomach turned all sour-like.

"They done run off to the woods too many times. Master did the job hisself. Cut them clean off. Not all of them. Just the big ones and the middle ones, I think. Don't rightly matter. They's not running anywhere no more."

I shuddered. Eyed Cook. Thought maybe she was telling me some tall tale. The Master who bought me, who brought me here and told me what to expect, didn't seem capable of such cruelty. His eyes weren't soft and kind, but neither were they hard stones.

I looked at Cook then looked at the men limping. Thought about the way Master looked at me and the way Missus looked at me. I couldn't figure it out. I just knew I missed my mama. I knew how she felt about me and where I stood with her. I started to cry then, thinking about her.

"Now, don't you go carrying on like that," Cook said.

"I miss my mama."

"I bet you do. But the Missus don't want no crying around here. You best buck it up. Put it out of you mind, child."

I tried my best to stop crying, and I did mostly. I managed to keep the tears in when other people were around and let them loose when I was by my lonesome. But put Mama out of my mind? I wasn't never going to do that.

* * *

When I was with Mama, I never did work in the rice field yet. If I had stayed, I wouldn't be far off from being sent down there with the rest of them. As it was, my jobs were to weed the garden, gather eggs from the chickens, tote water, feed the pigs, and milk the cows. So when Cook told me I'd be milking the cow every morning, I didn't bat an eye. I's good at that job. 'Course I didn't realize I'd be so tired from being up in the night with the baby.

Every night I slept on the floor by Baby Elizabeth's cradle. They gave me one blanket, so I had to choose whether I wanted to sleep on top of it or cover up with it or try to scrunch up real little and do a little bit of both. They ain't give me a pillow. My job was to rock Baby Girl to sleep. Then when she wake in the night, I's have to give her some milk and rock her back to sleep real quiet-like so she didn't wake Master and Missus in the room right next door.

Some nights went real smooth-like, and Baby Elizabeth would drink her milk somewhere between wakin' and dreamin', then she would drift off to sleep real peaceful-like. Then some nights, 'specially in the beginning, after she was done with her milk, she'd start opening her eyes wider and wider, looking at me and realizing that I's not her mama. Then she'd start wailin'.

"Mercy! You'd better shush that baby right quick before I come in there and give you a whipping!" Missus's threats made me tremble.

I'd nearly start to panic, but then I'd look at Baby Girl, eyes so wide with wanting. She just wanted her mama. That's all she wanted, and I knowed the feeling. I understood yearning for someone who was outside your grasp.

"I's sorry, Baby Girl. You done stuck with me. I ain't your mama. I's your Mercy."

I tried talking sweet and soothing to her, which calmed her down a little but not enough to keep the Missus from yelling my name again.

That's when I started singing.

"Mercy. Sweet mercy.

Good Lord, we need Your mercy.

Every morning. Every morning.

Your mercies are new."

Mama used to sing that song to me while I drifted off to sleep. My throat got all lumpy, but I's kept singing. Singing and rocking Baby Girl and feeling tracks of tears mark my cheeks as I wondered if Mama sang that song anymore now that she didn't have no baby girl of her own to sing it to.

* * *

No matter how many times I got up with Baby Elizabeth the night before I had to be up before sunrise to milk the cow and help Cook prepare breakfast. I had to go down the twisty stairs then outside and down the stone steps to the basement where the kitchen was and see what she be needing that morning. She might want me to gather eggs from the henhouse or an onion from the garden. I had to fetch water from the creek too, and 'cause I was so small, it took me several trips to get enough. I could only fill them buckets half full or they'd be too heavy for me to carry. I's so tired. So, so tired.

One morning I done fell asleep in the barn while milkin' the cow. That was the first time I got a whipping there. Master gave me that whipping, not Missus. One minute I was dead asleep, the next minute there was a hot flush of pain across my back.

"I will not tolerate laziness in my house. Is. That. Clear?" he asked, a lash ripping between his words.

I's so startled, I jumped up and tried to run, but he caught me around the wrist and grabbed on real tight.

"You will know your place!"

"Yes, sir! Yes, sir! I's sorry, sir!" I was a big crying mess then, all snot and tears as I fell on my knees at his feet, begging for my name-sake. "Please forgive me, Master."

I don't know if he ever did.

"Did you get the milking done?" he asked.

"Some of it."

"Finish up. The Missus and I are waiting on our breakfast."

He turned and stormed toward the Big House before I could even say "Yes, sir."

* * *

I sang to Baby Elizabeth near every night. As exhausted as I was during the day, I looked forward to our time together at night. Sweet Baby Girl loved me. And I loved her. We made space for each other, and in her nursery in the dark of night, our hearts became knit together. She smiled at me, looked up at me as if I's her world and she needed nothing else 'cept my arms. The ache of missing Mama loosened its grip on me when Elizabeth held onto my finger with her chubby fist. And yet it squeezed tight to me all the more when I wondered if Mama had felt the same way when she held me in her arms. I guess love ain't something that's easy to figure out.

Master and Missus were mostly indifferent to me. They didn't say much to me either way, and I's just tried to stay out of their way best I could. I didn't want no more whippings, so I tried to stay awake and do as I's told. Maybe a storm was brewing, and I just didn't see it coming. I was still young. I's trying not to blame myself for not knowing better. I don't know how knowing would have changed anything anyway.

The first time Elizabeth said my name was at night when it was just the two of us. I's got real excited and gushed real proud-like. It sounded more like "Mermy," but I's knew what she was saying. I kept saying, "That's my girl!" and kissin' her cheeks. It was a real special time that night.

The next time Elizabeth said my name was when she was in her Mama's arms and saw me pass by on the way to the kitchen. Now, Baby Girl didn't say much of anything but babble words, so Missus asked her what she said.

"Did you say 'Mama'? Elizabeth, did you say 'Mama'?"

I pretended not to notice what was going on, but then Elizabeth said "Mermy" and reached out for me. She done leaned out of her Mama's arms and toward me. Before I could stop myself, I grinned up at her. Then I saw the Missus scowl, and I wiped the smile off my face and walked straight back to the kitchen. But the damage was done.

* * *

From then on, I could do no right in the Missus's eyes. I didn't bring in enough milk. There were still weeds in the garden. The clothes were not clean enough. They weren't ironed neat enough, though that was Cook's job anyway. I didn't dare tell her that. She'd have just found fault with something else. She whipped me herself for each and every indiscretion, whether it really happened or she just done made it up in her head. Every time the baby fussed at night, she'd call me in for a whipping. Sometimes the baby would be fast asleep, and she'd call me in anyhow saying the baby's crying had woken her up. I didn't dare cry 'bout the injustice of it all or she'd just whip me for crying too. This was the cost of love for me. Me loving Baby Elizabeth. Baby Elizabeth loving me.

It was this way until Baby Elizabeth started walking. Then she done walked straight to me, and the Missus sent me away to be auctioned off again.

* * *

Natassa stared at the crescent moon, her hands stroking the cover of *Mercy's Journal*. Giving up her baby for another to raise. What an inconceivable thought. Natassa imagined Mercy and Baby Elizabeth bonding together all of those nights. Each night, an opportunity Elizabeth's mother gave up, handed over. Could Natassa do the same? Or ... what was the cost of love for her?

20

When Breanna invited Natassa over Saturday night for another girl's overnight, Natassa accepted without hesitation. Her main motivation for going was for easier access to escape to St. Anthony's Baptist Church the next morning. If Natassa had to sit through Breanna talking about the great and wonderful upcoming adoption, well that was the price she had to pay.

Breanna greeted Natassa with a giant bear hug that caught Natassa off guard.

"I am so glad you and Brandon worked things out," Breanna said in her ear. Natassa didn't have time to respond. "Come in! Come in. I banished the boys to the den for the night. They've got popcorn and Dr. Pepper, so that should keep them alive, don't you think? Oh, and they're doing a Star Wars marathon, so we shouldn't hear anything from them at all. I also threatened to take their PlayStation away if they bother us. I'm pretty sure it will be just us girls up here tonight."

"You didn't have to do that."

"Oh, believe me, my pleasure. I need some Mommy time off just as much as you do, chicka."

"So, what's the plan? What are we watching?"

"Watching? Oh, Nat, we've got work to do!"

"Work? What are you talking about?"

"Sit down. Let me grab my laptop."

Natassa sat down slowly on the couch. Though she felt wary, she couldn't help being curious about what Breanna was up to.

Breanna returned, laptop in hand, and plopped down on the couch next to Natassa. "Okay, so, from the research I've done, these two agencies seem to be your best bet. This first one here is local, which is a bonus. The second one isn't, but they work with women across the country. You can reach them twenty-four seven through email, phone, or text. They're a larger agency, which means a greater selection of families to choose from."

"Breanna, what are you talking about?"

"Agencies. Adoption agencies. They are both Christian agencies. I made sure of that. Most of—"

"Breanna, wait."

"What?"

"I'm not ... I'm not ready for this."

"Not ready for what? I thought you said Brandon wants to give the baby up for adoption."

"Yes. Yes, he does."

"Then ... in order to do that, you have to choose an agency. Then you get to pick the adoptive family. Couples who want to adopt put together profiles. You look through their profiles, and you get to choose who you think would be the best fit. I think it could be quite a healing process for you."

"But I'm not ready. I'm not ready because *I* don't want to do this!"

"Nat, I know you had this fantasy in your head of having this baby and it just becoming part of your family like it was always meant to be there—"

"She. The baby is a she." Natassa's voice sounded quiet, deflated.

Breanna threw up her hands. "Whatever! Are you even listening to me? *She* is not going to just be another one of your children, Natassa. I'm sorry, but it's not going to work like that. You're going to have to move on to a more realistic plan for the future. Adoption is a great plan. Think of all the women out there who desperately want children but can't have any. You have four beautiful children. That's such a blessing! Not everyone has that. But you could give someone the chance to be a mother. That's beautiful!

"Or, Nat, if you can't think about the joy you could give to another couple, think about the baby. Maybe there's a transracial couple out there that wants to adopt. Wouldn't this child be better off being raised by a couple who understood and could help sow into her identity as a biracial child? And wouldn't she be better off with a father who wanted her just as much as her mother does? Think about it, Natassa."

"I am thinking about it. It just doesn't feel right."

"Well, you can't always go by your feelings, can you? Sometimes you just have to do what you know is right. Brandon said ... Never mind. Just look at these two agencies, will you? If you don't like either of them, there are others. I just thought I'd save you some of the legwork."

"Wait. What where you going to say? What did Brandon say?"

"Forget about it." Breanna waved her off, angling the computer toward her.

"No, I don't want to forget about it. Wait. Breanna, did Brandon put you up to this? Did he ask you to talk me into going along with an adoption plan?"

"No! No. It wasn't like that. Not really. I mean, he asked if I could help you choose who to go with and everything—"

"I can't believe this! He set me up again? Just like with my mom?"

"Nat! No! This is nothing like with your mom. He didn't tell me to pressure you or anything."

"Really? Because I feel pressured."

"I'm just trying to help you choose an agency."

Natassa wanted to say, "You're being pushy," but she couldn't bring herself to do it.

"I was trying to be helpful."

Natassa stared at her friend. Breanna was just being Breanna, wasn't she? Taking charge. Jumping in the driver's seat and declaring the destination. Throughout the course of their friendship, Natassa had always been content to relax in the passenger's seat and enjoy the ride. Why was it bothering her so much now?

"Okay, fine." Breanna shut her laptop. "You're not ready. I get that. We'll wait. You've got time to make these decisions."

Natassa breathed a sigh of relief.

"So," Breanna said after a few minutes of silence. "Are you going to that church tomorrow?"

"As long as you promise not to tell Brandon."

"I wouldn't do that."

"Then, yes. I'm going."

"I'm still floored by this whole thing, by the way. I can't believe you have the courage to drive down there. Of course, it's not like you're parking in Edison's parking lot and walking down the street like you did that night or anything. You wouldn't be able to do that. But even the fact that you can drive down that same street is really something."

"What do you mean? I wouldn't be able to do that?"

"Oh, come on. You nearly needed me to hold your hand in tenth grade because you were afraid to walk past Rick Goldbee's lunch table when you had a crush on him. I'm just saying bravery has never been your forte, my dear.

They sat in silence for a few minutes, and Natassa contemplated what Breanna had just said. *Bravery has never been your forte.* Did it sting because it was true?

Natassa's thoughts were interrupted by Breanna's playful voice. "Can I do your makeup?"

Natassa groaned.

* * *

On a whim, Natassa pulled into the parking lot of Edison's Wines instead of driving half a block further down and turning right on St. Anthony Street. The parking lot was understandably empty on a Sunday morning, and Natassa pulled into the same parking spot her car had inhabited the night of her anniversary weekend.

She fidgeted with the watch on her wrist, key still in the ignition. *Bravery has never been your forte.* Was it true? Okay, so she would never be the heroine in the story, in anybody's story. More like a bit player with no lines. But maybe she was changing. She wasn't sure if her recent actions were brave or stupid. Perhaps both. Maybe ... maybe she could do this.

The best way to get over your fears is to face them. It was a bright, beautiful sunny day. Natassa knew there would be dozens of people milling around at the other end of St. Anthony Street. No one would give her any trouble with so many witnesses around. If she kept her eyes straight ahead, on the church, just like she did when she was driving, she could make it. She took the keys out of the ignition.

She could be brave. She wasn't in high school anymore.

"God, help me. Be with me. Help me do this." It wasn't her most eloquent prayer, but at least it was sincere. She took a deep breath, grabbed her purse, and got out of her car.

"One foot in front of the other. One foot in front of the other," she mumbled under her breath. Her gaze naturally drifted down to her feet, where her jeweled flip-flops made methodical progression, but she intentionally forced her chin up. A slight breeze played with her hair and ruffled her plain blue silk top. No red dress today, but as she begrudgingly allowed Breanna to put some color on her eyes, she had felt every bit as beautiful.

"One foot in front of the other." There. She was already to St. Anthony Street. She turned the corner, and the church was in sight. She could feel her pulse rise as she laid eyes on the very spot the attack happened, but she took another slow, deep breath and continued walking one step at a time.

She saw the church in the distance, but a flash of color from the corner of her eye caught her attention. She glanced across the street and stopped in her tracks, mouth agape. Painted on the building directly across from her was a gigantic mural that most definitely hadn't been there before.

The mural included a bustling street full of people laughing and having fun. There was the church! The bell, the railings— the detail was exquisite. Natassa gasped. Was that? It couldn't be! But it sure looked a lot like … her!

The mural beckoned her to cross the street, calling out to her like a siren of Greek mythology. Mesmerized, she went over to it, admiring the sum total and all of its parts, trying to make sense of the one white face in the midst of all of the dark ones. It couldn't be her, but it was as if someone made this just for her. Her hand hovered over the artwork. She longed to touch it, to connect with it, but one didn't put their fingers on a master-piece. So she let her fingertips get as close as they dared, the thin layer of air nearly more of a barrier than her heart could stand. It was breathtaking. Someone had put a dream on a wall.

The church bell chimed in the distance, breaking the spell. Natassa blinked and stepped back. She turned and crossed the street, rushing toward the church building. She looked over her shoulder one last time to survey the artistry of painted dreams.

21

———

DeAndre heard the quick smack of her flip-flops as they whacked the pavement in her retreat. He released the breath he had been holding and doubled over, dizzy and nauseated. What the heck was she doing *walking* down that street? Was she crazy? Stupid? Was she onto him? Maybe the only reason she was in the neighborhood at all was to search for evidence so she could lock him away. If that was true, the lady sure had guts.

Her face didn't seem suspicious, though. More like awestruck. She was so close; she could have seen him if she hadn't been so transfixed on the mural. And if she had seen him, what then? Would she have put two and two together? Would he be in the back of a cop car right now?

How he wished he could apologize. Not that an apology was enough to cover over the evil of what he had done, but at least it would be something. When they'd run into each other at Java Joe's, it had been on the tip of his tongue to say more. *Don't apologize* came out in the moment, but what he really wanted to say was, "I'm sorry for everything." He tried to communicate his regret with his eyes, knowing all the while that every intention of atonement would fall flat. She didn't know, couldn't make the connection, couldn't offer him what he thirsted for.

The only way she might put an apology with the crime was if it were offered in the same context of the attack. And how could he manage that? He couldn't paint it on the side of a building for the whole world to see. What if … what if he wrote it in sidewalk chalk? She would have to walk back to her car after church. Would she make the connection? Or …

It came to him then, and he knew what he had to do. It was foolish, for sure. Risky. It might not even work. But it was a shot at absolving his conscience, and he had to take it.

His phone rang. Reg.

"We're out of aspirin, D. Can you pick me up some? My head is killing me."

"Yeah, man. I'll grab you some and run it by."

"Where you at anyway?"

"Just out doing some things. I'll be home in a few."

DeAndre needed to run by the store anyway, and he had some time. He finished off the rest of the beer he had started before he spotted Natassa walking down the street and climbed out of the storefront, intent on his mission.

* * *

DeAndre tossed the bottle of aspirin at the foot of Reg's bed and turned to scrounge around for some scrap paper. He thought he remembered seeing some in a kitchen drawer.

"Thanks, man. I owe you one."

"Uh huh," DeAndre replied, distracted.

"You should have been there last night. It was quite a partay. Plenty of free booze. Dancing. Lanie was asking about you," Reg called from his room. DeAndre rifled through the kitchen drawers looking for paper that was big enough to fit his purpose.

"Is that right?" DeAndre couldn't care less about Lanie or any of the other girls he used to flirt around with. There had been a time when he never turned down an invite for a party—whether the invite came from the host or just from Reg looking for some gig to crash. He just wasn't interested anymore. While his best friend got wasted last night, he stayed up late sketching out plans for the mural on the side of Pa's shop. The others had approved it, and DeAndre wanted this tribute to his father to be perfect.

"She gave me her number. Told me to give it to you in case you lost it before."

"All right."

"What's with you today, D? You're sure not saying much."

"And you're sure saying a lot for a guy with a hangover." DeAndre found a large rectangular sticky note. It would do. He grabbed it, grabbed a sharpie, and headed for the door.

"Where you going now?" Reg was up now, standing in the doorway of his bedroom, his palm pressed to his forehead.

"Out. See you later."

Back in the abandoned ice cream shop, DeAndre debated what to write. He wasn't an eloquent man. He was a high school dropout. How could he communicate the depth of regret he felt? And on a sticky note. He pulled out his phone to check the time. He had to hurry.

I'm so sorry.

Looking at what he wrote, he scoffed. Lame. Stupid. Not enough.

But it was all he had. That and the bottle of wine he had bought. Checking and double-checking to make sure no one was watching, he climbed out of his hiding place and dashed across the street. He found the spot where he thought she had dropped her bottle of wine during the attack and placed his note there with his bottle sitting on top of it. He pulled the note out a little, making sure it was visible, hoping the green color would catch her eye. *Please don't miss the note.* Then he rushed back to the shop, climbed inside, and waited.

When church let out, DeAndre heard the trickling of voices down the street. The noise grew until it was a cascade of sound, each conversation indistinguishable from the distance. Natassa should be the only one walking in this direction. Everyone else either drove or lived in the apartment complex or duplexes on the other side.

His heart hammered as he waited, anticipating. His mouth felt dry, but he didn't have anything left to drink. The bottle of wine across the street glinted in the sunlight.

As he strained to hear the voices down the street, the wind blew an empty candy wrapper down the sidewalk, and he jumped at the sound. How embarrassing. He was glad Reg wasn't there to see that, thankful Reg knew nothing about this at all.

There. Voices coming closer. Footsteps on the street.

"Why'd you park so far away, sugar?"

"I don't know."

"Do you want me to walk you to your car?"

"That would be nice." A beat of silence. DeAndre leaned closer to the window. "Actually, no. I need to do this myself. Thanks anyway."

"You're sure you don't want to come over for lunch?"

"Not this time. Brandon wants me to come straight home. We haven't had much time to spend together as a family on Sundays lately."

"Well, that's understandable. Maybe next week."

"Maybe."

Then he heard it. *Smack. Smack. Smack.* Those flip-flops were coming closer. He leaned to his right, and he could see her. She wore a modest blue top and khakis, and she carried a beige purse that was much larger than the tiny little thing she'd carried that night. Her head was up, her phone was put away. She looked so different than she had that night.

She came closer to the wine bottle, and DeAndre leaned forward, rubbing his hands together. Then she was nearly upon it and hadn't even looked down. Would she trip over it? Pass it by? DeAndre held his breath.

And then she stopped. Looked down. Yelped. Stared at the bottle. Looked around wildly. DeAndre slipped back a notch just to be certain she wouldn't be able to see him. Then she bent down, grabbed the bottle and the note, and ran.

DeAndre stared at her retreating form as she dashed around the corner, feeling the disappointment pool inside of him like stagnant rainwater. What? That was it? *Well, of course. What did you expect? For her to shout, "You are forgiven," to the skies?* He stood up and kicked the beat-up chair over onto its side.

There was no forgiveness for him.

22

---

lank. Clank. Clank. She had stashed the wine bottle under the driver's seat before hastily driving away. Now every time she made a turn, the glass clanked against the bottom of her seat, grating on her nerves, driving her mad.

She trembled still. He had been watching her? Stalking her? She hadn't just been at the wrong place at the wrong time on her anniversary weekend. The rapist was not only a debased criminal; he was a psychopath. Where had he seen her? Where was he? What did he look like?

She checked the rearview mirror to make sure no one was following her. There were no cars directly behind her, and she didn't even know what she was looking for.

One thing was for sure: she was never setting foot on St. Anthony Street again. That thought brought Natassa to huge, sloppy tears. The lowlife not only violated her that night—now he'd stolen the one place she could find peace. St. Anthony's Baptist Church was abruptly snatched from her grasp. Would she ever see Bethany, her mama, again?

How could God let this happen to her? Mercy was supposed to be following her. Instead, a rapist was stalking her?

I'm so sorry.

Sorry? He was sorry? Yeah, well she was sorry too. Sorry she ever put on that stupid red dress. Sorry she ever bought it. Sorry she even thought about the wine and the strawberries. Sorry she desired another baby at all. Why hadn't she just been content with what she had? The what ifs tumbled through her mind. What if she had changed at the last minute? What if she'd just packed the dress instead of wearing it? What if she'd bought a bottle of wine from the shop up the street, in her own neighborhood? What if she hadn't been looking at her phone? If she had been paying attention, would the criminals have risked the crime? A dozen scenarios passed through her thoughts, each of them leading to a different outcome that night.

And then? She briefly touched her stomach. And then there would be no baby, at least not *this* baby. No baby and no Bethany. Who was she kidding? Even now, there would be no baby. Not for her to raise anyway. And now that she couldn't set foot in that neighborhood again, there would be no more conversations with Bethany either.

She had lost everything.

Clank. Clank. Clank.

Why did she grab the bottle? The note? She didn't know. Right now, she wanted to heave that blasted bottle out the window of her car, hear the glass shatter on the concrete since she couldn't bust the blasted thing over the psychopath's head.

Should she go to the police? She cringed, remembering the agony of filing a police report. She should tell Brandon, show him the note, the bottle. He would know what to do.

But then she would have to tell him where she found the bottle. And it was not at Breanna's church.

As she pulled off the highway onto the exit leading home,

she checked her rearview mirror once more. Nothing looked suspicious. It didn't seem like anyone had followed her. She wiped her wet cheeks with her trembling hands.

Clank. Clank. Clank.

Oh, God! What should I do?

* * *

Natassa did her best to pull herself together before heading inside. Sitting in her car in the garage, she fished tissues out of her purse. She dabbed them with water from a stray water bottle and attempted to rid her cheeks of smeared mascara. The rest of her eye makeup was still in place. She smiled at herself in the mirror, forcing a "How was church?" to see if it sounded convincing. It would do for the children, but Brandon would see right through it.

Knowing she could do no better, she took a couple of deep breaths and started for the house. She steered toward the side yard when she heard her children's voices around back. She found Brandon tackling David. Daniel piled on top of them both as Hope and Faith ran around the trio, giggling. Brandon tickled the boys, and the girls jumped in the fray. Natassa found a tumultuous smile. Wasn't everything she needed right in her own backyard?

Brandon saw her then and started to stand, only to get knocked down by the four of them ganging up on him. His laugh resounded, the air thick with it. Natassa closed her eyes and tried to keep herself from wishing there was space in that joy for the little one growing inside her. That was a futile train of thought.

"Okay, okay! Let me get up so I can say hi to Mommy!"

"Mommy!" The girls realized she was standing there and skipped over to her. "You're back! You're back!"

"I found a caterpillar and put it in a jar," Hope declared.

"Nuh uh. I found it." Faith crossed her arms and stuck out her lip.

"But you was scared to touch it!"

"Was not!"

"Well, I'd love to see it," Natassa interrupted.

"I'll go get it!" both girls said at once, and they were off.

"Hey, babe," Brandon said, coming alongside her. "How was your time with Breanna?"

Natassa remembered then how Brandon had asked her friend to ensure her compliance with the adoption plans. She shifted away from him slightly.

"Fine."

"What did you girls do?"

"Talked, mostly. I finally let her do my makeup." Natassa batted her eyes in Brandon's direction.

"Nice. What'd you talk about?"

Natassa was tired of the games. "Oh, come on Brandon. I think you know."

Brandon sighed and shifted his weight. "Breanna said you didn't want to talk about adoption agencies."

"Oh! Breanna said that, did she? You seem to talk to my best friend more than I do."

"I texted her to see how things were going. That's what she said back. It's not like we had some in-depth phone conversation. I'm not having an affair with her or anything if that's what you're thinking."

Natassa blinked. Stared. Then she blurted, "In order for me to be thinking something, it would have to have entered my mind, Brandon. Why would you even say something like that?"

He shrugged. "I thought that's what you were inferring."

"No!"

"Well, with what happened with your dad—"

The girls came running and collided into Natassa's legs.

"He's gone! Our caterpillar is gone! We looked everywhere!" Faith cried.

"Maybe he turned into a butterfly and flew away," Brandon said.

"No, Daddy! It doesn't happen that fast!"

Natassa stooped down and looked Faith in the eyes. "You're right, baby. That kind of change doesn't happen that fast. Let's see if I can help you find that caterpillar." Natassa let Faith and Hope lead her to where they had last seen their little friend, leaving Brandon in the distance.

* * *

Master took me to Lexington, but I never made it to the auction block. As soon as we entered town, Master ran into an old friend, and they went to the tavern, talking up a storm. He tied me up to the wagon and left me waiting outside while the sun beat down on me, making me feel like I's bread baking over the fire.

I don't know how long I was waiting out there, but they come out all loaded with spirits and slapping each other on the back. Then Master done untie the rope from his wagon and hand it to the other man while he handed over a fist full of bills.

"She's all yours."

"Thank you, William. It was great to see you! And great doing business with you."

"Indeed. I hope she works out well for you."

No one said a word to me, but all's the sudden I was on the back of a different wagon, not having a lick of an idea where I was going. I done cry my heart out then 'cause no one was paying any attention anyways.

We rode what seemed a good long ways until we pulled up to a house that was good and twice the size of the last Master's house, though still not as big as Old Master's plantation in South Carolina. This house made more sense to me straightaway, its red brick stretching tall as the sun, the steps large, the porch perched up high above the rest of the world. Them white columns felt like a familiar comfort, though they only be 'round the front porch and not hugging the whole house. The space around the front door be painted blue like the sky. I liked that. I could see a good size farm stretching in back, but there was still woods all around, like we was nestled in the wilderness.

The Master must have been following my gaze because he said, "We still have much land to clear."

I felt my eyes get all wide as I imagined myself trying to chop down a tree, and I said, "We?" then added "sir," like I's knew I was supposed to.

"Oh," he chuckled. "No, not you. That's not why I purchased you. My daughter, Mary, needs a companion. You will be her slave. She will be your Mistress."

"Yes, sir." I bowed my head, relieved to be able to remain a house servant. Then I done felt guilty for feeling like that, seeing as Mama was at that moment laboring in the field, hands calloused, back aching. Shouldn't I want to be in the fields? To be like Mama? To identify with her in that way? But no, I wanted the easy way out. While Mama ate her measly allotment of pork and beans, I would get to enjoy the leftovers from the Big House. While Mama visited the Big House when the Missus was away, I would get to live there, and without paying the price that Mama had to pay. I bit my lip to keep from sheddin' any more tears.

"Come on inside. I will introduce you to my wife and to Mary."

When we stepped inside, a tall woman, thin as a candlestick, met Master at the door and took his hat and his bag. My eyes searched for a big staircase, but I wouldn't be finding it. We was as high up as the house got. Instead, my gaze got caught up in the striped carpet and the fancy patterned wallpaper.

"Emma, would you please ask Miss Mary and Ms. Rachel to join us in the parlor?"

"Yes, Marster." As she walked down the hall, I noticed how she towered over everything in the house. She done be nearly as tall as Master, though with her being skinny she wasn't nearly as imposing. Still, I stood in awe of how a slave could fill up so much space. Seemed like she had busted out of her limits, which made something like hope sparkle inside me.

I followed Master into the parlor, my eyes working extra hard to take everything in. When I saw Missus Rachel walk into the room, my first thought was that this was what good and kind looked like. Her cheeks were rosy and not because she was riled up mad. It seemed like her heart done warmed them up. She looked at me, and though the first glance that passed over her eyes seemed all surprised-like, it took only a moment for her to smile.

"James, I thought you said there wasn't going to be another auction for a couple of weeks!"

"I didn't find her at an auction. I ran into William Marcus, who happened to be selling her."

"Selling her? Why?"

"Something about how they bought her for to nurse their baby through the night, but they no longer need her anymore as the baby has grown."

I guess they didn't want to say the real reason 'cause then maybe they wouldn't be able to get rid of me.

"Odd. Maybe they fell on hard times."

"Perhaps."

"Well, how old are you?" Missus Rachel asked me.

"I don't know, ma'am."

"Hmmm ... You look to be about eight or so. Does that sound right?"

"Maybe. I's not sure."

"Well, Mary is six. You will be her companion. You will do as she asks, but you will also help me when I ask you to." Miss Rachel looked behind her. "Mary? Where are you?"

A little girl with blonde ringlets peeked around the corner. She *had a twinkle of mischief in her eye, and I's trying to figure out if that was a good or bad thing.*

"Mary, come here."

The blonde girl came closer, and I tried to figure out if she be wearing a grin or a smirk.

Missus Rachel looked back at me. "What do they call you? What's your name?"

"Mercy, ma'am."

"Mercy? Oh, goodness. What a horrid name." She shook her head, and Mary scrunched up her nose. "We'll have to change that."

I think my mouth done slid open. A horrid name? That thought had never done crossed my mind. I loved my name, the name my mama gave me. The name my mama sang to me. Mama always said that everybody needed themselves some mercy. Did Missus Rachel think she didn't need no mercy in her house?

"What would you like to name your slave, Mary?"

"Emma!"

"No, honey, you already named a slave Emma. You have to choose a different name."

"Hmmm ..." Mary hopped from one foot to another like she was playing a game. "What about Anna? Annabelle!"

"Annabelle is a wonderful name, honey. Annabelle it is!" Missus Rachel clapped her hands together, grinning from ear to ear. Then she turned to me.

"Your name is now Annabelle, so that is what you will answer to."

I managed to say, "Yes, ma'am," but a couple tears snuck out of the corners of my eyes, mourning for the loss of my name and how it linked me to my mama. Hurting for how I's no more important than an animal and could be named by a stranger like a litter of kittens.

"What's the matter?" Missus Rachel asked.

I studied her face for a moment. I's not sure how to answer, if to answer. Here I thought she be kind and good, then she went and stole away my name first thing. Could I tell her how it bothered me so since she done asked me the question? Or would meanness leap out of her all unexpected-like? Figuring out who I's could trust ... I done never been sure of that one.

I bit my lip, crying harder.

"It's okay, Annabelle. You can tell me what's wrong."

"I's just miss my mama, that's all."

She nodded, a sad little smile on her face. "Where is your mama, Annabelle?"

"South Carolina."

"That's a long way away."

"Yes, ma'am."

"You've got to put the past behind you. There's nothing you can do about it. There's nothing any of us can do about the things that have happened in the past. We can only move forward. Your future is here, Annabelle."

"Yes, ma'am."

"Now, dry those tears. We won't have any of that around here. Emma will make you up a place to sleep at the foot of Mary's bed. It's too late for a tour tonight. But are you hungry?"

I nodded.

"I'll have Lucy prepare something for you. You can eat in the kitchen downstairs and then rest. You will start your duties tomorrow."

So, I ate and I slept on a soft mat, covered with a thick quilt. I woke up that morning as Mercy. I went to sleep as Annabelle. I felt like maybe Missus Rachel liked me and wouldn't whip me none, but that she didn't have no patience for hearing about my mama, so I best keep all that locked up inside my heart and not let it leak out.

* * *

The next morning when I came downstairs, Missus Rachel noticed something she ain't noticed the night before.

"Why, Annabelle. Where are your shoes?"

"I don't got none, ma'am."

"You don't have any, Annabelle. The proper way to say it would be, 'I don't have any shoes.' We prefer our house slaves to at least try to speak proper English."

I looked down at my bare feet. "I don't know how, ma'am."

"You'll catch on." It sounded as if maybe she was smiling, so I looked up and saw that she was indeed. "Now, about your shoes. You don't have any?"

"No, ma'am. I's don't have any," I said slowly and carefully. I looked up at Missus Rachel expectantly and was rewarded with the sound of a small giggle. "I's had some back when I was with my mama, but then they got all worned out when I's walked to Lexington, ma'am."

"What about at the last plantation you were at? Didn't they give you shoes?"

"No, ma'am."

"What did you do when you had to walk outside in the winter?"

"Cook found some rags to wrap around my feet. Then she didn't have to doctor them up so much."

"Oh, dear." Missus Rachel put her hand on her heart, as if I touched something in there. I didn't know a slave could get at a white person's heart none. Least not a Missus or a Master.

"Well," she said kind of breathless-like. "I'll have Eli make you a pair of shoes right away."

And she did too. They was the nicest things I had ever owned, and Mama didn't have to pay for them at all.

* * *

As I lay on my mat at the feet of Miss Mary's bed that night, I kept tossing that word around in my head. Proper. Missus Rachel said I needed to talk proper, but that wasn't the first time someone had said something like that to me. I reached into my sack and stroked the primer Mama gave me, picturing her face, and it all came back to me then.

I remembered how Mama wanted me to pay real close attention to how white folk talk and act, all proper-like. She said someday that might be my ticket to freedom—passing as white.

I's tried, but I reckon there's a piece of me that can't bear to let go of the slave in my tongue, seeing as it's my only link to Mama. It's a loyalty that would run against her wishes, and I know that in my head. But I also got a glint of rebellion in my eye passed from Pa. Even though we never did share the same blood, we's family just the same. When I look at the white folk I had known before coming to Missus Rachel, I don't want to be like them. I don't want to be a slave, but I don't want to be like those Masters either. Maybe I don't know what I want, the mixed blood in me mixing up my feelings and thoughts. I just want my mama to stroke my wild hair again and talk about how with all the pain in her life, I's her joy.

And freedom? Law, that was the furthest thing from my mind then. I didn't give it nary a thought. Not until the spark that burned in Emma done spread to me too.

23

———

Natassa wiped beads of sweat from the back of her neck. It was only the beginning of June, but summer had pounced with a vengeance. As she sat on her back porch watching the children play in the sprinkler, Breanna called.

"Come to the pool with us. It's a perfect day for it."

"I don't think so. Thanks anyway." Natassa shaded her eyes from the sun so she could see Faith better.

"Oh, come on. Please?"

"Not today."

"Why not?"

Natassa sighed. "Because if I wanted to go swimming, I'd have to put on a swimsuit."

"And?"

"And I just can't do that. Not yet. I don't know if I'll ever be able to wear something so revealing again." Natassa shuddered just thinking of being so exposed in front of all those people.

"Oh, Nat. Not even a modest one piece?"

"No, I don't think so."

A long pause. "Do you want us to take your kiddos? We'll take good care of them."

Natassa hesitated. "Hope can't swim yet."

"I'll keep her with me at all times. We'll hang out in the kiddie section."

"Promise?"

"I promise. You trust me, right?"

"Yes."

"Great. We'll pick them up in an hour. It'll give you and Brandon some time alone together."

She knew the thought should excite her, but it only served to make her nervous.

* * *

Natassa waved goodbye to the children, packed in the back of two separate cars since Breanna's car was too small to fit both sets of children. She closed the front door and locked it behind her. Now it was just her and Brandon.

Where *was* Brandon? She hadn't seen him for hours.

She began to quietly search the house, checking in each room. He wasn't in their bedroom, the living room, or the kitchen. She headed downstairs to the den.

She heard the shuffling of papers and the clink of glass before she saw him. Peeking around the corner, she found him hunched over the coffee table with papers strewn all around. His back was to her, but she could tell that his hair was sticking up on the sides. He took a swig of something from a small glass. Was that *alcohol*?

"Brandon, what are you doing?"

He jolted. "Natassa!"

"Brandon ..." she ventured.

"I've got to find him. I've got to." He slurred his words. As he shuffled papers around, a few fell to the floor. He banged his head on the coffee table as he bent down to pick them up. A string of curses filled the air.

"Who? You've got to find who, Brandon?" Her voice trembled. She was pretty sure she knew.

"He's a monster. A monster! He ruined everything. Me. You. Us." He waved his hands around emphatically. "This! Ruined. Everything."

Natassa took a step back. Brandon never drank, never more than a glass of wine at a time. He was drunk. She felt as if the floor was shifting beneath her. Her rock was crumbling before her eyes.

"Evidence. I need evidence. Brett and I both combed the neighborhood, but we have nothing to go on. Nothing. If anyone at Edison's saw anything, they're not talking. Without a description ..."

"I swear I never saw a thing."

"I believe you."

"What are those papers?"

"All the other cases of sexual assault in the city within the last few years. I'm looking for clues. Connections. Something."

"And?"

"I've got nothing. We need evidence."

Evidence.

Natassa thought about the bottle and the note, no doubt littered with the criminal's fingerprints. They would give Brandon and Brett something to go on. Her husband was unraveling in front of her, her world tilting off its axis.

"I'll be right back," Natassa said as she jogged out of the room, up the steps, and out the door to her car.

She flung open the driver's side door and felt under the seat for the bottle. Her hand grasped its smooth, thin neck, but as she pulled it out, the back of her hand brushed something else. What was under there?

Mercy's Journal. She pulled out the bottle and *Mercy's*

Journal, laying them next to each other on the driver's seat of the car. She looked between the two, feeling the pull of mercy and judgment.

I'm so sorry. He'd said.

The jogger at the park had cried out, "*Have mercy!*"

What if there was a double meaning behind it all?

She thought of the wine bottle shattering at the time of the attack, broken glass all over the sidewalk. Then she thought of the stained glass windows of the church, also made of broken glass, yet made whole and beautiful.

She thought of her husband, sitting on the sofa, drunk and tormented, desperate for evidence she could supply.

"Oh, God. What should I do?" Natassa whispered, hunched over the driver's seat.

The midday sun baked the garage, stifling Natassa with stuffy heat. She couldn't stand out here forever, waiting for a booming voice from on high.

She thrust the bottle and the journal back under the seat and went back inside empty-handed. Instead of going back to the den, she went to her bedroom, closed and locked the door, and cried herself to sleep.

* * *

I be used to bowing to every whim of a Master and Missus. What I ain't never had to do before then was bow to the whim of a girl younger than me who ain't had a lick of sense in her perty little head. Missus Rachel learned me how to braid Miss Mary's hair. She been soft and patient with me as I figured my way through that heap of blonde curls and kept telling Miss Mary to stop squirming around. She said I learned right quick and smiled at me all pleased, which made my insides feel warm and sweet. That was a good time, learning with Missus Rachel.

Soon, though, the learning was done, and I had to braid Miss

Mary's hair all by myself. She'd wiggle around like some worm in the garden, and I'd do my best to make that hair behave and do what I's want it to do, sticking in them fancy pins to make her look right pretty. When we's done, I'd be right proud of myself, and I'd think about how proud Missus Rachel would be of me and of her kind smile. Then I would make Miss Mary's bed or tidy her room and look back at her to find that her hair be loose round her shoulders, bouncing wild and free. She'd look at me with a gleam in her eyes and skip down the hall, and then I'd hear Missus Rachel calling, "Annabelle! You need to braid Mary's hair!"

And what could I say but "Yes, Missus Rachel"? Because Miss Mary could do no wrong in her mama's eyes, and if I pitted myself against that little girl, I thought I'd likely be finding myself a new place to live.

After a few days of being there, I ain't seen a lick of Master during daylight hours. I got curious as to his comings and goings, wondering what he did all day. I ain't never had a Master who didn't march around the house, letting everyone know he's the boss of everything under the sun. I figured Emma would know 'bout Master, seeing as how she was tall enough to see just 'bout everything that happened round there. She waited on the family at dinner and managed the affairs of the house. She got her nose in everyone's business. But I just couldn't gather courage up enough to talk to her just then. She fascinated me, but in an intimidating way. My eyes got all big when she'd walk into the room and my mouth got all shut up.

So, I asked Samantha instead. Samantha be Missus Rachel's lady's maid mostly, though she help Lucy in the kitchen sometimes too. Samantha was easier to talk to, seeing as how she work closely with Missus Rachel. Seems like some of Missus Rachel done rub off on her.

"Marster James? Why, child! He's in the field working."

"*Master? Working? What about the slaves? The field hands?*"

"*They working too, of course.*"

"*You mean he ain't got an overseer. He's driving them?*"

"*No, he's out there plowing right alongside of them. That's how they do it here in Kentucky. Most of 'em anyway.*"

I shook my head. Samantha had to be telling a tale. I never heard of such a thing. A Master working in the field right next to his slaves? I tried to picture Old Master in the rice paddies next to Mama and Pa. There wasn't no space in my head for such nonsense.

Yet, I paid attention that evening and came down the hall when I heard him come in the door. By the dirt on his trousers and smeared across his forehead, and the stench coming from him, I knew Samantha told the truth. He called to Missus Rachel to say he'd be cleaning up in the creek before dinner. She said something I couldn't hear, and they both laughed. I rushed back up the steps and hid myself in the corner for a minute.

Thoughts and feelings crashed around inside me again. I wanted to hate him. I had to hate him, didn't I? Didn't I need to find that ugly anger and grab hold of it? Remember the feeling of the lash, remember that it came forth from white hands, and loathe the whiteness around me? These people owned me. They saw nothing wrong with my bondage. I hated slavery, but I did not hate Missus Rachel. I hated slavery, but now it was hard to hate a Master who worked in the field with his slaves. I wanted my mama, but I didn't want to be sad all my life without her. I wanted my mama, but maybe I had a Master who was kind and good, like the old slave said. Maybe I could be happy here.

"*Annabelle! My braid fell out! Fix it for me!*" *Miss Mary stood a few feet away, a smirk on her face. I looked down to see mud on her shoes and muddy tracks all down the hallway.*

"*Yes, Miss Mary. But let me clean up the mud first.*"

"*No! I need my braid now!*"

"*Very well, Miss Mary.*"

And with that, Miss Mary ran into her room, leaving more mud tracks that I hoped I could clean up before Missus Rachel laid eyes on them.

* * *

I came downstairs to the kitchen one morning to see Lucy drinking something out of a mug.

"Is that coffee?" I asked, eagerness and yearning pulling on my insides.

"Sure is, child."

"They let you drink that?"

She nodded.

"Every day?"

She nodded.

"I want some!"

"Shoot, child. What you want with coffee?"

"Please! Please, Lucy!" I fell at her feet, grabbing at her apron and twisting it between my fingers as if I could wring mercy out of her that way.

"Goodness, Annabelle! What's gotten into you? I can give you a little coffee if you'll stop carrying on."

"Thank you! Thank you!"

She poured only enough to barely cover the bottom of the mug, but I didn't mind.

"Can I get cream? I need cream in my coffee!"

"Cream? Law, child. Now you done lost you mind for sure."

"Did you milk the cow yet this morning?"

"Sure did."

"Please let me have some cream."

She shook her head but said, "Just a little now. I need it for butter." She pointed to the milk churn.

I listened. Took only a slight amount of cream from the bucket and added it to my coffee. Then I stepped outside the back door so I could enjoy the moment of drinking my coffee alone. But not alone really, seeing as Mama was right near me. As near as she had been since I last saw her face.

* * *

Coffee was a special treat at Old Master's plantation in South Carolina. Betty handed out tin cups of it at Christmas and after a good harvest. Mama managed to get a cup of coffee a few more times a year as part of her negotiations. Slaves there looked forward to their coffee. They'd line up for it, holding out their hands like the beggars they were. Mama sat with me once outside our cabin, steaming cup in hand. She done looked in her cup. Then looked at her skin. Then looked in her cup and looked at my skin.

"It's so good. Coffee. It's dark like Pa's skin. Like most of the skin you see around here in the field."

"But not like my skin," I said.

"Do you feel different, Mercy?"

"Sometimes. But not when I'm with you. When I'm with you, I feel like I fit. Like I'm who I'm supposed to be. Where I'm supposed to be. When you're not next to me, it's like everything is mixed up."

"You're beautiful, Mercy. And you're exactly who you're supposed to be. I want you to remember that, even when I'm not right next to you. You've got everything you need inside you, baby girl."

Then she took me to the kitchen and dished out a bit of cream, pouring it in her coffee.

"There. That's better. You're the cream in my coffee, Mercy. You make everything richer."

Then she let me taste her coffee. And each time after, whenever she could get her hands on coffee, we sat together and took turns taking sips. I's the cream in her coffee. Not everyone had cream in their coffee, but she did. She had me. She always be happy to have me.

As I stood outside drinking that coffee that Lucy gave me, the tears started washing over my face. Was Mama drinking coffee anymore? Did she still put cream in hers? Was I still the cream in her coffee? Did she miss me as much as I missed her? I just wanted to tell her how much I missed her. How much I loved her still.

* * *

Miss Mary got her schooling by a tutor who came to the house every day. When the tutor came, I had to go to the kitchen to help Lucy out so I didn't pick up any learning. No one knew I could read already. I done listened to what Mama said. Mostly I just fetched water from the creek and wished I could be up in that room learning more. I had done read that little primer over and over again and wanted more than anything for something new to lay my eyes on. Miss Mary had some books, but I couldn't never get at them without her seeing me.

One afternoon, she was playing and she wanted to play school and be the teacher. She wanted me to be the student, so she done decided to teach me to write my initials A. W. for Annabelle Whittle. 'Course I already knowed how to do that, but I played along real good like I didn't know nothing of the sort. She got out her slate and showed me how to make an A. I acted like I's having a real hard time and doing it wrong. Then Missus Rachel walked in.

"What are you doing?"

"I'm playing teacher. I'm teaching Annabelle how to write her initials."

"Oh, honey, you can't do that!"

"Why not?"

"Well, it's not exactly against Kentucky law, but your Grandpa would not approve in the least. He cut off one of his slave's fingers for trying to write once. It's not the place of a slave to know how to read or write, dear. I don't want you to try to teach Annabelle again, do you understand?"

Miss Mary nodded, but I started shaking real bad. I looked down at my fingers and imagined them not being there. I thought about those slaves at the last place limping 'cause they had no toes. I felt like I might be sick right there in Miss Mary's room.

"Annabelle, are you okay?"

I tried to say, "Yes, ma'am," but I couldn't. My words wouldn't come out.

"Oh, dear. I didn't mean to scare you. I'm not going to cut off your fingers, Annabelle. My father is a strict man with certain ideas about how things should be. You don't have to worry. You're not one of the rebellious ones who is trying to usurp authority by learning how to read and write."

I managed to nod, but that shaking didn't stop on the inside of me.

* * *

When Old Master gave Mama that primer, I reckon he didn't think she could do a lick with it. She wouldn't have been able to neither if Winny hadn't stumbled upon her pouring over that lil book back in the weeds. Winny was learned real good, though I never figured out how. She lived on the Miller Plantation down the road, but she be married to Ben on our plantation. They wasn't even supposed to see each other 'cept on weekends when Ben got to visit overnight, but Winny was ever sneaking over to get a few moments with her husband. The Millers were more lax than Old Master, and truth be told, I think their Missus thought it romantic and such and chose to overlook such indiscretions. If it was Ben sneaking off, Old Master would have him tied to the whipping post.

At any rate, Winny saw Mama with her primer and offered to learn her some letters, so she wrote them out for her with a stick in the dirt. And that's how Mama done learned me too, with a stick in the dirt. Then we'd stomp away the evidence so no one would know what we'd been doing. But knowing how to stick them letters together into words, Mama had to do most of that figurin' out on her lonesome since Winny ain't even live with us. My mama had a brain on her that even slavery couldn't push down.

I don't understand how that can be a crime. How someone can cut off your fingers because your mind wants to sprout up and grow tall.

Late that night, I snuck out of the Big House and made my way to the creek. I had a candle in one hand and my primer in the other. Standing by the rushing waters, I let my tears loose as I kissed and stroked that book. My mama's very hands had touched that primer. Her very hands, soft and tender. I knew every word in that book by heart. I didn't need to read it no more, but I loved to feel the pages. I loved knowing how it connected me to Mama. It was the only thing I had of hers.

But if I's caught with that primer, I could lose my fingers.

I threw it in the creek and watched it dip away a little before the darkness ate it up. Sinking to my knees, I whispered what I done wanted to scream. "It ain't fair! It ain't fair! It ain't fair!"

24

Natassa sat at the table in the playroom, Faith on one side of her, Hope on the other. The girls rolled bright-green Play-Doh into flat sheets with rolling pins, pressing cookie cutters into the dough and holding them up for her inspection. Natassa kneaded a small lump of dough in front of her.

"Look, Mommy!" Hope exclaimed, holding up a figure of a girl with half of her leg hanging by a thread of stringy dough.

"Oh! A ballerina! She's beautiful!" Hope's smile widened at Natassa's praise, which caused Natassa's smile to broaden as well.

"Yeah, but ballerinas should be pink. Shouldn't they, Mom? Shouldn't ballerinas be pink?" Faith asked.

"I think all colors are beautiful," Natassa said with a catch in her voice. Would she be having this conversation with her children later, but in a different way? Talking to them about skin colors? Or ... not?

"Mommy? Why are you pushing your Play-Doh so hard? Are you making bread?" Faith asked.

"Oh. I guess I am." Natassa pushed a smile back to the surface.

"Mommy! Look what I made!" Hope held out a small green log shape.

Natassa mocked horror, pushing away from the table. "Oh no! A snake! Mommy wants to run away. I'm so scared of snakes."

"No, Mommy!" Faith said. "You're not supposed to run away from snakes. You're supposed to step on them."

"Step on them?"

"Yeah. Like Mrs. Walters said at church. 'You will trample upon lions and cobras; You will crush fierce lions and serpents under your feet!' Psalm 91:13. It was our memory verse. A cobra is a snake, and a serpent is a snake too. Mrs. Walters said so. And trample means to step on." Faith began stomping around the room.

"Wow. You did a great job memorizing the verse Faith Cakes. I'm proud of you." *Why can't I do that? Stomp on the snakes instead of running from them? Oh God, I don't want to be so afraid.*

Natassa snapped back to her present reality when she realized Hope was tugging on her sleeve.

"Yes, Honey Bunches?" Her daughter held the Play-Doh snake in her hand.

"It's not a snake! It's my caterpillar. Don't step on my very hungry caterpillar!"

"Oh! Look, Faith. It's the very hungry caterpillar. In that case, you girls had better get him some food because he's still hungry."

Faith came over for a closer look. "He's ugly," she said.

Natassa was about to scold Faith for her insensitive remark when Hope nodded her agreement.

"Most caterpillars aren't that pretty," Natassa admitted. "But then they change into a beautiful butterfly. So, we can look past a little ugly for now because we know great beauty is coming, right?"

"But when, Mommy? When do they turn beautiful?" Hope asked.

Natassa shrugged. "I don't know, Honey Bunches. It takes time. But it's worth it."

"We'd better go get him food!" And with Faith's declaration, the girls were off, racing to their play kitchen and grabbing armfuls of pretend food for the little Play-Doh caterpillar. Natassa watched them, her mind fumbling through the conversation she'd just had. When was beauty coming for her?

It takes time. But it's worth it.

* * *

It took me a good long while, half a season maybe, to get the courage to eek out a word to Emma. When I finally did, I wondered what took me so long, seeing as how it felt she be the big sister I never knew I had.

I's just standing in the parlor one day, gawking at her, wondering at how a slave could fill it so full like it was just as much hers as the Master's or Missus Rachel's.

"Whatcha looking at, child?" she asked me when she caught my eye.

"What's your ... your n—name?" I asked. I wanted to add "Your real name? The one your mama gave you before Miss Mary changed it to Emma," but I had enough trouble getting out the first part. My mouth remained awestruck.

She knew what I meant without me explaining none. Her hand stilled, her duster stopping in midair. Then she sunk down into Miss Rachel's black chair. The room seemed bigger somehow; she seemed smaller.

"Mary," she whispered.

"Mary? But ..."

"This house already had a Mary, and Law knows she takes up all the room there is. Just ain't room for two Marys now, is there? So, one of us had to go. Didn't matter none that I had my name for years before she been born. No one cared that I was on this here earth first. No. I been born a slave whether I wanted to or not, so I be the one giving up the name I gone by since I knew what be what. Queen Mary, I call her. She gets what she wants, don't she? Gets to give me a new name and gets to keep my old one."

"I's sorry. When it's just you and me together, I can call you Mary, and you can call me Mercy."

"You're sweet, child. But I been Emma for so long now, I nearly forgot. Someday you'll understand. Someone will call you Mercy, and you won't even turn your head, won't even know they be talking to you."

I shook my head. "Never."

She tossed me a sad smile. "Just wait and see."

* * *

Once my mouth got comfortable opening up around Emma, it's like nothing could stop me from blabbing on. I done asked her dozens of questions a day, and her answers fascinated me. Not in an intimidating way, like her very presence did at first, but in a way that opened up new possibilities with each word she spoke. She expanded my world.

Master and Missus Rachel came to Kentucky from Virginia. Missus Rachel's Ma and Pa owned a gigantic plantation there. Emma worked under Missus Rachel's Pa but was given to Missus Rachel as a wedding present. Master James had dreams of venturing west and whisked Missus Rachel away to the wild unknown of Kentucky. Emma said she be relieved to get as far away from Missus Rachel's Pa as she could, though she didn't give me no details. I remembered what Missus Rachel said, looked at my fingers, and swallowed my questions 'bout that man.

Emma worked as a field hand, first in Virginia and then in Kentucky. Somewhere between east and west, she fell in love with Richard, a fellow slave. They got married in the Big House in Kentucky and lived together in one of the cabins. Emma said reckoned they were as happy as a couple in slavery could be, but Richard didn't want to have no children born into slavery. He set his eyes on freedom and came up with a plan.

Richard ran away a year after they married. He promised he'd be back for Emma, but she never saw him again. Master and Missus Rachel brought her to the Big House to keep an eye on her. Never let her leave.

"Freedom's just on the other side of the Ohio River, and I's stuck here in this ole house," Emma said to me.

"This is the best house I've ever been in." I didn't like Emma talking 'bout freedom. What if she ran away too? I'd already done lost my mama. I didn't want to lose my Emma. Besides, there were much worse places to be. We had a good and kind Master. Couldn't she be content with that?

"Oh, you'se just a child. What do you know? There are worse Marsters and Missus for sure, but freedom, child! Freedom!"

I didn't know nothing about freedom one way or another. Didn't know what it looked like, what it tasted like. Didn't know enough to reach for it. But Emma got me thinking about the fact that, whatever this illusive freedom was, Mama wanted it for me. And if Mama wanted me to have it, then maybe it was something I should want too. But it took some time for roots to grow on that thought, and even more time for a bud to open up and taste fresh air and decide that, yes, maybe this is something worth striving for after all.

* * *

My first Christmas at Missus Rachel's house made me nearly forget I was a slave. Missus Rachel gave me a green calico dress. It came from the ragbag at church, a hand-me-down none of the white folk wanted, but it was the softest, finest clothing I'd ever owned. I kept twirlin' around, imagining I was royalty.

Master and Missus Rachel held a giant shindig for the holiday. Dozens of couples came, and there were oodles of children. I helped take their coats and bring them drinks, tasks normally reserved for Emma and Samantha. I felt all grown-up like and whisked into the magic of the season, admiring the guests in all their finery. We slaves ate good that night. We got all the leftovers, and Lucy outdid herself making quite a feast of pork ragout and braised lamb with all the fixin's and ten different pies for dessert. I stuffed my cheeks full as a chipmunk in the kitchen as the guests lingered over wine.

Then I was in for a surprise. Master called for Emma, and she came into the great room with a fiddle. She played song after song while the guests clapped and danced. I sat wide-eyed. Was there anything that woman couldn't do? She had a jar setting on the floor beside her, and guests would toss a few coins into it as she played.

As the evening wore on, the music got slower, and the children got cranky. Missus Rachel had me put Miss Mary to bed and grab blankets for some of the other children to lay on the couches. I was stiflin' yawns of my own by the time the guests were ready to leave. I gathered their coats and bid them goodbye. Although I felt 'bout ready to collapse onto my mat, Missus Rachel told Emma, Samantha, Lucy, and me to take all of the dishes to the kitchen and wash them. First Emma and me had to go down to the creek and fetch four buckets of water a piece to wash all them dishes in. After Master and Missus Rachel turned in, Lucy looked at my eyes half closed and sent me to bed.

"But Missus Rachel said—"

"I done know what she said, but you'se just a child. Go to bed. We'll finish up."

I didn't argue none. Just went up the stairs quietly humming Christmas carols to myself. Now I had a dream of my own. I wanted to play the fiddle.

* * *

As soon as I finished filling Miss Mary's water pitcher and emptying her washbasin and chamber pot the next day, I ran to ask Emma about it.

"I want to play the fiddle, too. Can you teach me to play the fiddle? What was that jar? Do you get to keep that money?"

Emma took me to her room off the back of the kitchen and showed me an even larger jar nearly chock-full of coins.

"This is my freedom jar. I'm saving up to buy my freedom. When I play here, I get to keep whatever coins people give me. When they hire me out, I get to keep half what they pay for me. When I get a thousand dollars, I can purchase my freedom. Then I can go find Richard, and we can start a family."

I held the jar in my hand and turned it around, admiring the way the sun glinted off the coins.

"This is all yours?"

"All mine! I gots something that's all mine."

"Teach me, Emma. Please, teach me how to play the fiddle."

"I would, child, but I only gots one fiddle, and I don't know how to get my hands on another one. Maybe if you ask the Missus, she can get you one. She's awfully fond of you."

My insides quivered at the thought of going to Missus Rachel and asking something so bold, but the wanting inside of me grew bigger than the fear.

When I asked Missus Rachel about the fiddle, I couldn't bring myself to look her in the eye. I practiced my plea time and time again, and then I delivered it while looking at her shoes. I tried to make it seem like I had her best interests at heart. Having two fiddlers would bring Missus Rachel more money than having only one. A second fiddler would certainly be useful. In reality, I wanted to be able to bring *some beauty to the world, and I didn't care a lick who benefited from it. I needed to contribute life and light and creativity, though I don't think I could express it as such at the time. It's one of the things slavery sucks out of the human soul, but here was an opportunity for a touch of restoration.*

Because I didn't look at her face, I couldn't rightly judge her response. She said, "Hmmm ... I'll see what I can do, Annabelle." Then she dismissed me to shine Miss Mary's shoes.

I didn't know what to make of that, but a few days later, she called me to the dining room as the family was finishing dinner.

"Annabelle, I have something for you." She presented me with a wooden case, smooth and smelling of spruce. "My mother gave me this violin, and she got it from her mother. It's Italian-made, a real work of craftsmanship."

"You're giving this to me?" I asked, hands shaking.

"Well, not giving it per se. Lending it for your use. You can learn to play it, and then you can play at parties with Emma. It is still mine, but you may use it. I trust that you will take good care of it." She arched her eyebrow, which did nothing to ease my nerves.

"I'm afraid to touch it, ma'am. It's too 'squisite for the likes of me."

"Exquisite? Indeed. But you have proven yourself to be trustworthy. I never did learn to play it, so it's never been put to use. I would much rather it make beautiful melodies than sit on a shelf."

"I ... I don't know what to say, ma'am."

"I believe 'Thank you' would be appropriate."

Missus Rachel smiled, and I bowed in appreciation. "Thank you! Thank you!"

"You are most welcome, Annabelle. I had it tuned just yesterday, so it should be ready. I trust Emma will be a patient tutor. It takes time to learn to play well, but I have no doubt that with persistence you can master the instrument."

"Yes, ma'am. I'll try real hard and keep at it." I kept on nodding and bowing, beside myself at receiving such a gift. Missus Rachel laughed and then got up and showed me where she kept it in the

parlor. She didn't want me keeping it in Miss Mary's room, lest Miss Mary get into it. I guess she did figure Miss Mary capable of doing some wrong after all.

"I'm so glad you are happy, Annabelle." Missus Rachel put her hands on my shoulders and looked at me with such delight jumping from her eyes. I nearly thought she was going to kiss me on my head, but of course she didn't. But I thought then that I was almost like her daughter. Almost, seeing as how she gave me a family heirloom. Lent it to me and wouldn't even let Miss Mary touch it.

That's how I started my own freedom jar. And that's how I got the means to betray the woman who treated me like family while I was her slave. Seems like you can't have loyalty and freedom. Not at the same time.

* * *

It took me years to learn to play that fiddle. Watching my dream grow wings was longer and harder than I ever thought possible. Emma worked with me most every night, just as patient as Missus Rachel said she'd be. My patience with myself stretched thin. I thought about Mama learnin' herself to read and wondered why I couldn't just pick up on the fiddle as easily as she picked up on her letters and words. I must have been eleven by the time things finally settled into place for me and I could pick up my bow and play something that resembled music. The beauty I wanted to make ended up to be something I had to go searching for.

And yet when I did it, when I learned to make my fiddle come to life, a whole new world opened up to me. Miss Mary might be as ornery as ever. My day might be filled to the brim with fetching, carrying, cleaning, and putting up with Miss Mary's whims. In every aspect of my life, I was still a slave. Yet, when I played that fiddle, I became the master of my own destiny for as long as the song lasted.

At first, I played mostly for the family after dinner. I didn't make a lick of a coin, but I got practiced real good. Missus Rachel seemed delighted with my progress, and that made all the long hours of rehearsing worth it to me.

My debut was a slave wedding, or rather the shindig held after the wedding. The wedding itself was held in the Big House, right in the parlor. Missus Rachel let the bride wear a makeshift veil she put together and an old white dress. Master lent the groom an old suit of his. Master did the ceremony, and a handful of slaves watched the couple jump the broom in the front room. Then all the slaves made their way to the barn for dancing. Emma and I provided the music.

I'd never been around the field hands before and never had I seen such a lively bunch. They danced the Double Shuffle, the Heel and Toe, the Buck and Wing, and the Patting Juba, patting their knees, clapping their hands, striking their shoulders while singing, and keeping time with their feet. Emma and I had to stop playing a time or two 'cause we be laughing too hard to keep time. Once, when I took a break for a drink of water, a boy took me by the hand and spun me around real good. I didn't know which way was what, but I didn't care. I ain't never had so much fun in my life. I'd never felt like I truly fit in a group of slaves, but I fit there in that barn. No one seemed to notice that my skin was lighter than most of theirs. They was all too busy enjoying themselves to care a lick about the differences between us.

I didn't make one coin from my first public fiddle playing, but to this day it be my favorite one. After that, Master and Missus Rachel started renting Emma and me out at parties. We got to keep half what we's made. My freedom jar started to fill up, and I began to learn about the world around me so much so I didn't question Emma wanting to cross the Ohio River anymore. Not every Master and Missus be like ours. Soon that reality would creep close to home, right into the Big House.

25

DeAndre wiped down the counter, only half listening to Rob and the others talking about their future dreams. He couldn't get Natassa Bloomington's face out of his mind, that horrified look she had when she saw the bottle and the note. Forgiveness withheld. Why did he even offer it?

Rob leaned over the counter, his elbows smudging the spot DeAndre just wiped down. "What are your plans, Dre?"

"Plans?"

"Yeah, plans. What do you want to do with your life?"

"Heck, I'm living my dream, right here."

They laughed. But he wasn't joking.

"Seriously, are you going to college?"

"College?" He chuckled. "No."

"Why not?"

Why not? Did they forget he wasn't like them?

"Boy, I didn't even finish high school."

"Oh." Rob was quiet for a moment. DeAndre went to the utility closet and grabbed the broom. He nearly ran into Rob on the way out.

"You could get your GED."

"There was a reason I dropped out. I wasn't a great student."

"We can help you." The others nodded their assent.

"For what?" He looked each of them in the eye for a moment, trying to convey with his gaze what a lifetime had taught him about the gap between them. "Why would I get a GED?"

"So you can go to college," Rob replied, undeterred.

DeAndre sighed. They didn't get it. "Can't afford college."

"But Java Joe's offers tuition reimbursement if you work full time. We'll talk to James, get him to up your hours. You can do it, Dre."

They looked so hopeful, so ... gullible. Like life had sung them a different song than the one DeAndre had been hearing since he was born. "Shoot, bro. You're wasting your time with me."

"No, man. I'm serious."

"Why do you care? Why would you go to all that trouble for me?"

Rob shrugged. "That's what friends do. They help each other out." He cornered DeAndre with his gaze. "So, what are you good at? What do you like to do?"

DeAndre refocused his attention to sweeping under tables. "Nothing. I'm good at showing up to work on time, and that's what I'm gonna do."

"There's got to be something you're passionate about."

DeAndre leaned on the pole of the dustpan, wondering how much to share.

"I paint."

"You paint? See! An artist! You could go to art school!"

DeAndre laughed. "You guys got your heads in the clouds."

Patrick came up to him, taking the broom and dustpan from him and asking, "So, what do you paint with? What medium? Oil paints? Canvases?"

"More like spray paint on buildings."

"Graffiti?" Patrick looked at Rob apprehensively.

"Yeah. Graffiti. You should check out the gang symbols I busted out on the walls of the bathroom." DeAndre grinned, but the nervous laughter that followed wasn't quite what he was after. He didn't know how to joke with these guys.

"You any good?" Rob asked after a beat.

"Why don't you come to my hood and see for yourself?"

"Really? You've got actual ... art on buildings down there?"

"Yeah, man."

"Couldn't you ... you know, get arrested for that?"

"What? You think I'm some gang tagger?"

They shook their heads no, but their nervous smiles betrayed them.

"Nah, it ain't like that. I got permission from the store-owners before doing any of my work. That way I never had to worry about the cops buffing it or busting me." Well, except for the St. Anthony's mural, but the cops stopped caring about that street a long time ago. His mural wasn't going anywhere.

"Well, let's go. Right now."

"You serious? I was just joshing around with you all."

"I'm serious! I want to see your art, Dre." The others nodded and chimed in their agreement.

"You expect me to drive you guys all the way down there, then drive back up here, then drive all the way back home? Just forget it. Some other time."

"You're working early shift tomorrow, right?"

"Yeah, I open."

"Then stay at our house tonight. It'll save you the trip."

DeAndre hesitated. He wasn't sure this was such a good idea.

"C'mon, man. We're your friends."

He looked at their eager expressions. For them, cruising

down to his hood was some big adventure. Those white boys were in for a culture shock.

"All right. Let's go."

With the last of the cleaning supplies stashed in the closet and the lights flipped off, the four of them piled into DeAndre's Corsica and headed south.

* * *

The boys were talkative for the majority of the ride but cooled their tongues the closer they got to DeAndre's hood. He planned to show them the eye first, then the bird, then the mural on St. Anthony Street. There were a dozen others throughout the city, but those three were the ones he was most proud of. After that, he would need to swing by his crib and grab his clothes for the next day before heading back to Crawford County.

He didn't know what to think, couldn't gauge why these white college boys from the coffee shop would take such an interest in him. What did they have to gain from befriending him? Why would they waste their time trying to help him study for a GED exam? What was in it for them? Was he just some token pity project to them?

But if they saw where he came from and didn't bolt, that was a good sign, wasn't it? And if they ran? At least he still had a job.

Art school. Yeah right. Sure, DeAndre could improve some boarded up buildings and bring a little color into a bland neighborhood, but be an artist? That sounded as high up as the moon to him. Maybe he could try and get his GED and then figure out what he might like to do at a trade school. There had to be something.

He slowed down and pulled over at the curb right next to

the eye looking up to heaven. Unlocking the door, he got out. "Exhibit one."

The boys didn't make a move. They exchanged glances, apprehension etched on their faces.

"You can get out. There hasn't been a drive-by shooting on this street in over a week." DeAndre's joke fell flat yet again. "Really, guys. It's safe to get out and look."

Slowly, the car doors opened, and his friends emerged.

"Whoa! You did that?" Rob asked.

"Yep."

"How did you learn to blend colors like that?"

DeAndre shrugged.

"That's amazing! I had no idea you had such talent. What are you doing pouring coffee?"

Were they serious? If they thought the eye was something special, they were gonna drop to the floor when they saw the mural on St. Anthony. Even the cardinal was more detailed than this. DeAndre didn't want to be cocky, but he felt a smile spreading across his face, and he couldn't rein it in. Might as well go with it.

After watching them admire his work for a few minutes, he walked back to the driver's side of the car and said, "You ain't seen nothing yet. Get in."

His prediction was spot on. The boys gushed over the cardinal, and they stood speechless at the St. Anthony Street mural, jaws hanging open. Much like Natassa Bloomington did that day, Rob raised his hand to touch it, then stopped himself.

"It's okay, bro. You can put your hand on it," DeAndre said.

"No, that's not right. You couldn't do that if it were in a museum."

"This ain't in a museum."

"It should be."

DeAndre waved his hand as if to blow off Rob's comment, but in truth, he let those words sink inside of him like a seed being planted. Was he really that good? Or were they just throwing out compliments to make him feel better? They seemed sincere, but he couldn't tell for sure.

After viewing the mural, they swung by his house so he could grab a change of clothes. Thankfully, Reg was gone, and he made it quick to avoid running into him. He wasn't sure what would happen if the two worlds he lived in collided.

Back in the car and headed toward Crawford County, conversation was stilted. DeAndre hadn't thought twice about bringing them by his crib, but now he wondered if seeing how he lived made them uncomfortable.

After a couple failed attempts at small talk, Rob ventured into conversation again. "So, is that where you grew up, Dre?"

"No. Reg and I moved there when I turned eighteen."

"So where were you raised then?"

DeAndre paused. His past attempts at humor had fallen flat, but this one might just work. He started belting out the lyrics to the theme song of *The Fresh Prince of Bel-Air*.

Sure enough, when he got to the chorus all the boys chimed in. Then Patrick threw some sweet beatboxing in the mix.

"Patrick! I had no clue you could do that!" DeAndre said when they finished the song.

"One of my hidden talents."

"Man! Reg would get a kick out of that."

Reg. Reg definitely would not approve of his new friends, even if Patrick could beatbox with the best of them. He meant to leave Reg a note saying he would be out tonight. He'd have to text him later.

"I'd like to meet your friend sometime," Rob said. "You two should come hang out at the house."

DeAndre smiled and said, "That'd be cool." But he doubted that would ever happen, with good reason.

* * *

DeAndre sat hunched over his kitchen table, a notebook directly in front of him and books sprawled across every inch of the table. Math was probably his weakest subject, so he wanted to tackle that first then move on to studying science. Now, solve for *n*.

Reg barged in the door, startling DeAndre so badly that his pencil flew from his hand onto the floor. "Where were you last night, D?"

Shoot. He had forgotten to text and had neglected to bring the charger for his phone. It died shortly after they'd rolled into Crawford County.

"Out with friends. Sorry, I meant to text you."

"Friends? What friends were you with? Your friends are my friends."

"Not these guys."

"Who are they?"

"Friends from work."

"White boys?"

"Yeah. So?"

"You were out with some white boys all night?"

"I crashed at their place last night. They rent a house near work, and I had to open this morning."

Reg stomped over to the table, his gaze drifting from one book to another. "What's all this crap?"

"Books."

"I can see that. You think I'm stupid? What are they for?"

"The boys from work are gonna help me get my GED. While I was at work this morning, my buddy Patrick went to the library and got these for me so I can study."

"You serious?"

"Yeah."

Reg cursed and slammed his hand on the table. "Why, D? Why would you go and get yourself some fancy GED?"

"So I can move up in the world," he said, exasperated.

"Up? You know what I think? You already too up for your own good. Rubbing elbows with some snobby rich white kids whose mamas still pick out their clothes for them. You got your head in a bunch of books now. What next? Never would have thought my best friend would go turn into an Oreo. Never would have thought. You're a traitor, that's what you are."

Reg swiped his hand across the table, knocking several books to the floor, and stormed out the front door.

26

———————

I walked into Emma's room one morning before the rooster even started crowing. I couldn't sleep, and when I went to the kitchen for a drink of water, I heard rustling and clinking coming from the room off the kitchen. Emma sat hunched over her freedom jar, coins in piles and stacks all across the floor.

"Whatcha doing?" I whispered.

"Law, child!" Emma gasped, holding her hand up to her chest. "You about done me in! What are you doing sneaking around?"

I shrugged, staring at the mess of coins laid up all around.

Emma sighed. "I ain't never gonna make it. Might as well face it. One hundred forty-three dollars and twenty-one cents. I done been fiddling for years, and a thousand dollars be as close as the moon to me."

I had almost six dollars by that time. One hundred and forty-three dollars seemed like enough to buy a Big House of her own.

"Keep going. You'll get there."

"Don't you see, child?" Emma looked at me like my head was 'bout to fall off my neck. "I've been working so I can earn my freedom and start a family with my husband, if I can even find the man. By the time I earn a thousand dollars, I'll be an old woman. Richard will *have moved on, found someone else. I'll never get to have a baby, raise a child. My life will be over before it even started."*

I knelt down next to her, running my fingers over a pile of coins, wishing with all I had in me I had some magic in my hands to make them sprout and grow. "I'm sorry, Emma."

"It ain't your problem, child. I'll just have to find another way is all."

"Can't you just run away? Cross the Ohio like your husband did?"

"It ain't that simple. They patrol nearly every inch of that river. If the paddy rollers get ya ... well, it be their job to make sure you never think of running again."

The situation seemed hopeless as I helped Emma stash her coins back into her freedom jar. I used to think the clinking sound of the coins was the sound of freedom, but there in Emma's room that morning I figured it was just another sound, like the crowing of the rooster or the lowing of the cow. Just another sound that meant life would continue as usual day in and day out with no hope of changing in the least.

I must have been nearly fourteen the day thoughts of freedom shifted from a smoldering flicker to a thirsty, desperate flame. Emma and I were fiddling at the Munsons' place for one of their spring parties in honor of some out-of-town guests. Neither of us was too keen on playing for the Munsons, seeing as how they treated their slaves the last time we fiddled for them. Law, did they prepare a feast for their guests! You could smell the roasting pheasants a mile down the road. And though they had leftovers to spare, they didn't give none of the slaves a lick of that good food. Their cook said the dogs got to eat the scraps, and the rest went to compost. The slaves ate cornbread mush and maybe a little beans if there were some to spare. That explained why all them slaves were as thin as Emma, though not nearly as tall.

I could see their bones jutting out under their thin, worn linsey-woolsey dresses. Them Munsons talked nicer to them dogs than they did to their slaves too. That be why Emma and I weren't so excited about playing there again. But we was hired out—not like we had a choice.

The alcohol flowed free as a river at this party, and the distinguished guests were acting less distinguished as the night went on. Sloppy drunk, Emma called them. They couldn't even talk proper like white folk were supposed to. I tried to pay them no mind. Just kept on fiddling, turning my attention to the songs and to the violin I had come to love.

Then one of the guests, so round in the middle his button wouldn't close, told Mrs. Munson he was retiring to his room. I breathed a sigh of relief, thankful that his brash commentary would be coming to an end. But then he made a request. Or rather, demand.

"I want a slave girl brought to my room." He stood up, stumbling into a side table.

"A slave girl?" Mrs. Munson asked, shifting in her seat, looking to her husband.

"Certainly, Grant," Mr. Munson said. "We will do whatever we can to ensure our guests are ... well taken care of. Which girl would please you?"

The horrid man scanned the room, and I watched every slave take a step back, slink behind a piece of furniture or another guest. Emma looked down, and I followed suit, continuing to play.

"That one!" I raised my eyes slightly to see who he chose. To my horror, his fat finger was pointed straight at me. I began to shake, my bow falling from my fiddle, the song unraveling.

"Certainly," I heard Mr. Munson say, as if from another room, another world. My mama's life flashed before me, and I wondered if I could kick and scratch. Could a beating possibly be worse than what he was suggesting?

Emma grabbed my hand. Squeezed so hard I couldn't feel nothing no more.

"Oh no!" Mrs. Munson said. "James and Rachel would never approve. I'm sorry, Grant. That's not our slave, or we would be happy to lend her services to you. She's a neighbor's slave."

"I'll compensate them, if that's what you're worried about."

"No, no. Her owners, they have different views. They wouldn't approve. Please, feel free to take any of our personal slave girls. I'm sure one of them will please you."

"What? They a bunch of nigger lovers?" The horrid man tottered toward me, spilling whiskey from his glass as he stumbled. He leaned close, grabbing my chin in his hand. "That's all you are. You know that, right? You're a pretty little filthy nigger. Just a slave. You're just a slave. Don't get all high and mighty because you had a white daddy." Then he pressed his portly lips on mine. I pulled back, but he pushed his mouth harder onto mine. Tears stung my eyes as I tried unsuccessfully to shake him off of me.

"Come on, Grant. Leave her alone. She's just a child," Mrs. Munson said.

He pulled back then, looked at me, and laughed. "A child? She's old enough to know the ways of the world."

"What about Sophia?" Mr. Munson asked, pulling a reluctant slave forward. She didn't look much older than me. Her head was bowed, but I could see her lip tremble.

"All right. She'll do." And he led poor Sophia back to his room. I thought about her the rest of the night, feeling sick to my stomach.

"Let's hear something more upbeat now, shall we?" Mrs. Munson requested. So, despite the fact that my insides were still all tied up, I played a reel so that the white folk could dance and clap. All while a young slave was being raped in the other room.

* * *

I don't reckon neither Emma nor I recovered from the incident by the time the Munsons' driver took us home, Emma shaking nearly as much as I was. "We gots to get out of here," she whispered.

I thought she meant away from the Munsons, and I nodded, thinking we couldn't roll away from their house fast enough.

"No, child. I mean it. We've got to run away. You and me. Soon."

"Run away?"

"Shhhh! Keep your voice down, child! You never know who's gonna turn you in for a price." She eyed the driver in front.

"Run away?" I whispered back.

"I'm gonna come up with a plan. We'll think of something. Something that doesn't take years of waiting and counting coins."

"What about the paddy rollers?" I asked, cringing.

"Shush, Annabelle! Let me think!"

That night started nearly a year of spinning a plan to escape. In the middle of the night, I'd sneak down to Emma's room using the narrow servants' steps, and we'd hash out possibilities. I didn't have much of anything to add, but I sure liked listening.

"What we need is a pass," Emma said one night.

"A pass?"

"Yeah. We gots to find someone who can write, who can write us a pass. Then they can sign Marster's name on it, and it'd be like we gots his permission to cross into Ohio."

I sat up straight. "I can—" Thankfully I caught myself before saying something I knew I couldn't be telling nobody. "I can find somebody who can write. I know someone."

"Who?"

"I can't tell. They don't want nobody to know."

"All right, child. This might work!"

But the next night, Emma sat all slumped in her bed. "It won't work. We'd have to get far enough away so that no one would know Marster James. Anyone who knows him knows he don't issue passes for his slaves. They'd catch us for sure. But if we could somehow get far enough away without anyone checking for our pass, well then they probably wouldn't let us cross anyway seeing as how they wouldn't know the Marster."

"Maybe they wouldn't ask questions if we gave them our money."

"Maybe." Emma shrugged. "Or maybe we'd end up in a slave pen. You just never can tell."

But her next idea seemed like the best one of all. I probably thought that because it reminded me of my mama's words. That's why I felt certain it would work and we'd be crossing into Ohio in a few short months. Emma would find her husband, and I'd be a part of their family. When they had a baby of their own, I'd be a big sister and love that baby just like I loved Baby Elizabeth. It wasn't the life I had with Mama, but it was a new life. A free life. And I'd be part of a family again.

* * *

I didn't mind missing out on sleep to hatch plans with Emma. Sleep didn't make itself friendly with me anyway. At night I'd see that man's plump face, see his fat finger pointing at me. He'd come after me to kiss me with his foul mouth while I struggled to get away. In vain. Always in vain. I'd hear him say, "You're a pretty little filthy nigger. You're just a slave. Just a slave." In my dream, I'd try to talk back to him, try to find the power I didn't have in real life. I'd try to tell him that's not all I was, that I meant something to somebody. I tried to say I was the cream in Mama's coffee. I wanted to say everybody needed a little bit of Mercy, 'cause that's what Mama always used to say, but in the dream, my words got all mixed up like I forgot who I was. I forgot my name. I forgot where I came from. So that man's words shouted louder than all the kind words my mama ever said to me, and I couldn't fight them. I'd wake up crying and try real hard to shush myself real quick before I woke Miss Mary up. Then I'd creep downstairs to Emma's room, where we'd whisper about running away from what I couldn't seem to face.

* * *

One night I sneaked into Emma's room to find the fire that I'd been afraid was about to get right snuffed out burning bright and hot again.

"Do you think you can braid your hair up? Like Miss Mary's?" Emma asked, stroking my wild hair as if she could tame it with her hand. "It's not like mine, or I could do it up for you."

"It's not like Miss Mary's neither." Seeing Emma's hopeful look turn downward into a scowl, I added. "But I'll try." I didn't know she meant for me to try right then and there, but she stared me down until I got her meaning.

Working on Miss Mary's hair was far less difficult now that she was older and less wiggly. Now she wasn't causing trouble for me in that way no more. Instead, she tossed her pretty little nose in the air and demanded that every inch of her hair be perfect. If it wasn't, she'd done tell me to do it again. Most days it took a handful of tries for me to get it to her liking, and then there was not a lick of thanks. Just "That will do, Annabelle." Sometimes I thought I wanted to cut her hair off while she slept. That wasn't a very nice thought for me to think, but I weren't Mercy no more, was I? But then I thought of Missus Rachel, and I was ashamed such a foul thing fluttered up out of my heart into my head. And I wondered, if I hadn't been born a slave, if I hadn't known cruelty at all, would only pure feelings take flight in me?

Anyway, Emma watched me as I struggled to tame my hair in a braid. Then she told me it wasn't good enough and demanded I try again. Over and over again, I worked my hair into submission until finally, Emma said, "That might work."

Only then did I ask, "What's this about?"

Emma dug under her quilt and produced a white bonnet with a lace fringe.

"Where—" I began, but she held up a finger. "No, child. Don't go asking questions. Just like you'se friend who knows how to write. It's best you not know where I got my hands on this beauty."

"It's lovely!" I said, tracing the handiwork with my fingers.

"Yes, it is. And it's yours."

"Mine?"

Emma put the bonnet on me and twirled me around. "There! Yes! We'll have to wait until fall. That way you can cover up well without anyone thinking a thing."

"Emma, what are you talking about?"

"It's my new plan. Our new plan, and I really think this one is going to work. Law, child! We's gonna be free!"

I grabbed her hands, holding tightly, and our eyes danced together in the candlelight, imagining the possibilities. "Tell me how."

"Covered up and with that bonnet, you'se look white, Annabelle. So we ain't gonna run at all. We gonna act like we got no reason to fear. You'se gonna be my Missus, and I gonna be you'se slave. We's gonna march right across free lines saying we visiting you'se family."

"I'm mighty young to be visiting family without my mama, ain't I?"

"Oh, Annabelle. You might feel like you'se just a child, but you'se nearly grown now. Besides, we'll think up a good story. No one will question you travelin' by yourself if there be an emergency."

"How are we gonna get away without Master and Missus Rachel posting a notice looking for us?"

"We wait until they go to town. They always take Samantha. Never you and never me. As soon as they leave, we head out. We'll be long gone before they get back."

I grinned up at her, craning my neck like I always had to do whenever I wanted our eyes to connect. "This might work!"

"It's got to, child! We just got to wait until harvest time."

27

Breanna showed up on Natassa's doorstep with Jesse on the last Monday of June.

"I invited myself over," she said, giving Natassa a quick hug before plopping her bag and purse on the floor by the front door.

"I see that. Come in. Jesse, the girls are in the playroom." That was all the direction he needed. He scampered off in the direction of the stairs. David and Daniel—along with Breanna's oldest son, Blake—were at sports summer camp.

Breanna headed straight for the kitchen, pouring herself a glass of water while talking over her shoulder. "Sorry for not calling first. I was just so excited I couldn't wait to talk to you, to tell you in person."

"What's up?" Natassa asked, cautiously curious.

Breanna rummaged through Natassa's pantry. "Got any chips? I'm starving."

"There are bite-size rice cakes to your left."

"Ugh. That'll have to do, I guess." Breanna tossed the bag on the island and straddled the barstool. She scrunched up her nose as she bit into a rice cake but didn't comment.

Breanna was eating her healthy food without complaint? Something was up.

"What's going on?"

"Oh! I'm just so excited. It's such a God thing. Don't you just love how He works all the details out so perfectly?"

"What details?" Natassa wasn't about to comment until she knew what details Breanna was referring to.

"I found them! They are perfect, so absolutely perfect. Marisa and Jason. They go to my church and run the marriage retreat weekend. Solid couple."

"Slow down, Breanna. Found who? Who did you find?"

"The couple to adopt your baby! They already adopted a little boy a few years ago—a little *black* boy, Natassa. Wouldn't that be perfect? Strong marriage, sibling of color, sweet family. They go to my church! You could still see her, have an open adoption—"

"Breanna, slow down! I told you I wasn't ready for this."

"Yeah, but that was a month ago, when you'd just found out. I thought you'd have time to warm up to the idea by now."

Natassa shook her head. "No."

"No? What do you mean no? Natassa, you're about to start your second trimester here. You've got to make some decisions. Are you listening to me? This is God-ordained! Marisa and Jason are a stellar couple—loving parents. I told them about your situation, and they don't mind that this is a child conceived by rape."

"You what?" The volume of Natassa's voice surprised her— and Breanna too, judging by Breanna's open-mouthed expression.

"We were talking, and they mentioned having just finished their home study and how they wanted to adopt again, and I told them about your situation."

"How could you? We haven't told anyone at church yet, hardly anyone at all. Only family."

"It's not like it's going to be a secret much longer! You're showing, Natassa! Those baggy clothes aren't going to hide it forever."

"It's not for you to tell! This isn't your life! You don't get to call the shots."

"Well, you're not doing anything! Sometimes you just need a little push in the right direction. I'm just trying to help."

"I don't want your help," Natassa said through clenched teeth.

An uncomfortable pause ensued, and Natassa kept herself from apologizing. She had to stand her ground. For once.

"Fine," Breanna finally said. "I don't want your disgusting rice cakes." Breanna rolled up the end of the bag, the crunching sound overly loud in the absence of conversation. She snapped the bag clip back in place and returned the snack to Natassa's pantry.

Natassa's face felt hot, and she stood and turned her back to Breanna, gathering courage for what she was about to say.

"You should go." There. She did it.

"Go?"

"Yes, go," Natassa said over her shoulder. "Jesse can stay and play since he just got here. I'll have Brandon take him home when he gets off work. That will give you and Brandon a great opportunity to talk about me behind my back and discuss how unreasonable I'm being."

"You're seriously kicking me out?"

Natassa bit her lip and nodded, not even sure if Breanna could see the gesture.

"Fine. You're infuriating. You know that, right? Here I am trying to be a good friend to you and help you through some hard decisions, and you kick me to the curb."

Natassa listened as Breanna said goodbye to Jesse and told him Brandon would bring him home later. She steeled herself to turn around, but she couldn't look Breanna in the eye.

"Have a great time at your mom's for the Fourth of July. I'm sure it'll be a blast," Breanna said before picking up her purse and bag, sliding out the door, and slamming it behind her.

* * *

Natassa fidgeted with her seat belt then pulled at the hem of her large blue-and-white striped top, shifting it lower over her growing belly.

"I'm dreading this." She kept her voice low, leaning over to Brandon in the driver's seat so that the children in back wouldn't hear their conversation. The boys were playing a game on one tablet, the girls watching a show on another, but she still wanted to be careful.

Brandon didn't say anything in return; he just gave her the sideways glance that he usually reserved for when she complained about her side of the family.

"I know. I know. You love my family. What you wouldn't give to be able to spend just one more holiday with your mother. But it's different for me, Brandon. I'm serious. You'll go watch the game with the guys and leave me to the wolves. They'll tear me apart." She put her head in her hands, fighting off a wave of nausea. "Oh, I feel sick. Can we turn around right now?"

"I won't leave you to the wolves."

"You will!"

"I won't. I promise."

He reached over and grabbed her hand, squeezing it tightly. She lifted her head and looked at him. His eyes were on the road so she couldn't search them, but she felt the resoluteness in his gaze. If he would stand with her, maybe she could make it out of there alive.

She needed him now more than ever. She hadn't counted the cost of kicking Breanna out last week, but she felt the emptiness in every crevice of her life. Her best friend had barged in and made herself at home in Natassa's house, planted herself firmly in Natassa's mess, and pledged that they would make it out together. How could there not be a gaping hole where Breanna used to be? She ached with loss and debated endlessly whether she had done the right thing.

But Breanna had betrayed her, shared confidential information with people who were complete strangers to Natassa, and she wouldn't stop shoving her agenda down Natassa's throat. Even if she claimed it was God's agenda, Natassa didn't believe it. Putting God's name on it didn't justify how Breanna was going about "helping."

If they couldn't see eye to eye, they had to part ways. At least for now.

But life was lonely without her.

No Breanna. No Bethany. She studied Brandon's profile. Her rock had crumbled in the den, but the steady set of his jaw assured her that the man beside her had pulled himself together, gathering strength that she hoped was enough for her to lean on. She had no one else left.

They pulled into Natassa's mother's driveway to find that Olivia and Maureen's families were already there. The house wasn't the best for hosting, but it was within viewing distance from the public fireworks display. Every year the sisters and their families gathered to watch fireworks on the Fourth of July from the comfort of the back porch. There were no trees in the backyard, and the view was unobstructed. They were close enough to still get the awe effect of the fireworks and far enough away that young children weren't bothered by the loud noises. This year Natassa didn't know which would be worse: battling crowds at the fairgrounds or facing her family inside.

True to his word, Brandon didn't join the other husbands in the family room. He stuck by Natassa's side and sat next to her as the women gathered around the kitchen table. Natassa angled herself so she could see the children playing in the backyard.

Natassa's mother slid everyone a glass of pink lemonade, complete with red, white, and blue umbrellas sticking out of them. She seemed overdressed in her navy pantsuit with a red handkerchief sticking out the front pocket of her white blouse. Then again, everything was rather formal at her mother's. While other families would be barbecuing hamburgers and hot dogs on this day, they would be dining on shrimp and artichoke hearts.

"Have you chosen the parents?" Leave it to her mother to abandon small talk and go right for the jugular.

"We haven't chosen the adoptive family yet. We're still narrowing it down," Brandon said.

"When do you expect to know?" her mother pressed.

"Soon." Natassa felt the weight of Brandon's reply. Soon. They needed to make some decisions soon. The children didn't even know about the pregnancy yet, but their time for secrecy was running out.

"It's a big decision. I guess not many people want a rape baby."

Natassa flinched, and her hand instinctively covered her expanding midsection. She wanted to guard her baby from such cruel words, wanted to tell her, *It's not true. I want you.*

"I'm sure we'll find someone." Brandon kept his voice light, but his body was rigid.

"Oh! Of course. Yes." Her mom smiled and nodded politely at all three girls.

Maureen leaned forward and entered the conversation. "So, what are you saying to people? Are you going to tell everyone what happened to you? About the ... the ..."

"The rape?" Natassa supplied.

"Yeah."

"We haven't decided what to tell people yet," Brandon said.

"Well, you'd better think quickly. You're starting to pooch out a bit, Natassa," her mother said, patting her hands on her own stomach for emphasis.

"I know! You could just act like it's a normal pregnancy and then say you lost the baby at birth." Maureen looked pleased with her plan.

"That could work," her mom said.

Olivia had been withdrawn since they'd arrived, but she interjected now. "Wouldn't you have to plan a funeral or something then? Or say you did? That's a pretty elaborate lie."

Natassa pleaded with Brandon with her eyes.

Her mother sighed dramatically. "Too bad you can't just go away somewhere until the baby is born like they used to do in the old days."

"Ladies," Brandon interjected, "I'm not sure how we're going to handle this, but we're going to get through it together, and honestly. Now, if you'll excuse us, we need to check on the girls."

He grabbed Natassa's hand and stood, guiding her out the sliding back door and to the porch overlooking the girls playing on the swing set and the boys throwing a football back and forth in the yard. She squeezed his hand and whispered her thanks.

"I told you I wouldn't feed you to the wolves."

"My protector."

"This time."

"I don't blame you for what happened. You know that, right?"

He kissed her forehead but didn't reply.

Natassa leaned into Brandon's strength for the rest of the day, fielding more intrusive questions from her family, and into the night when every boom from a firecracker made her feel as if she would jump out of her skin. She had not been prepared for the feelings of panic arising from the familiar noises of the holiday that should have been associated with freedom.

* * *

Emma done thought of everything. That's what I'd been thinking at the time. She thought up every feather we's be needing to make us wings to fly away. Her mind must have been working all the time, seeing every possible obstacle that could rise up to block our path. My own brain didn't have space for all's she came up with. She got me a little purse, as no white Master would be carrying about a jar of money with her. And she somehow exchanged out all those small coins for half dollars and bills. How she did these things, I never knew. My stomach clenched at the thought of asking. The more people who knew of our plans, the more who could turn us in. There weren't many who wouldn't flip their allegiance for the taste of favor.

"I think you should have your friend write me up a pass. Just in case we's get separated," Emma said to me one night, just before I sneaked back up to Miss Mary's room.

"Separated? What? Why would we get separated?" The quiver in my voice embarrassed me, as I's supposed to be playing the part of a white Missus in just a few short months. I had to be brave, but I didn't think I could be brave alone.

"Oh, don't worry none. I's just trying to think of everything there is to think 'bout, child. You without me, well you'se just a white woman traveling. Me without you? I'd get caught by the paddy rollers for sure."

I reached out to her and grabbed her hand. "But we's gonna stick together, me and you. You said. You said we's gonna be together the whole time."

"That's the plan, child. But sometimes things don't go by the plan. In case that happens, it would be good to have a pass. That's all I's saying." She squeezed my hand tight, and I let go for a minute to dry my tears then held fast again.

"But I don't know what a pass looks like," I said before I caught myself. I bit my lip then added, "How am I gonna tell her what to write?"

"You're sure she don't know?" There be only a flicker of light from the candle in the corner, but it seemed to me her brow bore suspicion.

"I don't think so."

"I know someone who has a pass. Let me see if I can get it to show you."

I nodded.

"Then you can tell her what to write," she added.

"Okay, Emma," I said before turning to creep upstairs. I was nestled under my quilt on my mat when understanding rose with the sun. If I were going to tell someone what to write on a pass, that meant I could read the pass. Emma knew. I'd given myself away and broken a promise I made to Mama.

I pictured Mama's face, growing blurrier in my memory with each year that went by, urging me to keep my knowing a secret. I squeezed my eyes shut tighter, pleading with my mind to draw the lines etching her cheeks, defining her forehead. Yearning to glimpse the small lines at the corners of her eyes. I had to apologize, and I needed to do it to her face, but the image wouldn't stick in my mind. It was like I kept trying to grab onto air, and in the end all I had was my own fingers.

"Annabelle, are you crying?" Miss Mary asked, her singsong tone a reminder that such tears weren't welcome in this home.

"No, ma'am," I said, drying my eyes with the edges of my quilt.

Mama used to tell me not to lie neither, but there wasn't no way I could get around that one no more.

* * *

I first knew something was wrong when Master and Missus Rachel be whispering in the dining room when it wasn't even meal time at all. I didn't hear a word of what was said, but Missus Rachel be *twisting her hands and looking all wide-eyed. Master's shoulders dropped low, and he kept rubbing his hat on his knee. My stomach got itself all tied up. Was it me? Did they know I could read? Were they's talking about how to best cut my fingers off? Or sell me to a slave trader? I tried to catch Emma's eye, but it was too high up.*

Three slaves died. Typhoid did them in. Lucy be the one to tell me why the house slaves be crying and why Master and Missus Rachel look sick with worry. For weeks we all walked around in a blur, speaking all hushed-like, as if not wanting to disrespect the departed. We was waiting, really. Waiting to see if all of us were going down to the grave with those field hands. Waiting to see if fate would grab hold of our ankles and pull us under even then.

After a few weeks, we started breathing a little easier. I snuck back into Emma's room, began to believe there was a future to plan for after all.

But then one morning Master James didn't come out of his room to go down to the field. It was as if the house itself held its breath and waited, all of us frozen in fear. The white doctor came and told Missus Rachel it was typhoid. When he said to her there was nothing to be done, she about melted on the floor. Samantha had to hold her up, speak strength to her. Told her of a medicine man, a slave on the neighboring farm. Missus Rachel cried out to send for him, and Samantha ran to go get him herself. Any one of us would have run however far we needed to for Master. Any one of us.

* * *

I had never seen a true African before, and from the time the African set foot in the Big House, my eyes stayed fixed on him. He bowed to us in greeting, and we bowed back, transfixed. Samantha led him into Master's room, and though I couldn't follow, my gaze remained on the closed door until he came out again.

From the time Samantha left until the time she returned with the medicine man, Emma and Lucy filled my head with stories of this

African miracle worker. "He doesn't speak much English," Lucy told me. "But he can blow out fire. It's secret magic." She meant that he could blow on a burn and make the heat and pain go right away. Emma said when white doctors gave people up for dead, the African brought them back to life.

He emerged from Master's room, and Samantha brought him down the narrow slave steps to the kitchen. Emma, Lucy, and I followed at his heels, crowding around, straining to see what magic he would pull out of the little sack he carried. He came to the table and emptied out his bag, laying bundles of herbs out across the surface. I squeezed in front of the others, right next to the medicine man, eager for a clear view of the action.

The candlelight illuminated his face, and I gasped. Three up-and-down cuts marked each cheek, making him look fierce. I put my own hand to my cheek without thinking. He glanced at me, and I quickly dropped my hand to my side, embarrassed.

"Yoruba," he said.

"What?"

"Yoruba. My tribe. Nigeria." He turned his attention back on his herbs then, mixing a few of them together and then mashing them up.

"Those are tribal markings, Annabelle," Samantha said. "Everyone in his tribe has similar markings. Different tribes have different markings. It's how they know who goes with what tribe."

But here he was, way out in Kentucky. Far away from his tribe. Far away from anyone else with up-and-down marks on their cheeks. My heart started aching as my eyes went over and over those cuts on his cheeks.

"What's your name?" I asked, surprised at the boldness of my voice.

"Ekundayo."

I tried to repeat it but fumbled. The corner of his mouth tipped in a smile.

"What does it mean?"

"Tears have become joy." He didn't look up, intent on his task as Lucy started boiling water for a tea. I bit my lip, shaking my head. One day this man was with his family, his tribe, in Nigeria. In Africa. Then someone snatched him up and brought him to America. Made him a slave. Tears becoming joy?

"Sounds backwards to me," I said.

He stilled. Closed his eyes. Nodded ever so slightly. Then he looked up at me, eyes clear. He reached his hand across the rugged table and grabbed my hand. His skin felt rough. Parched. Looking right at me, right into me, he said, "For now, child. For now." My breath caught. I didn't know what just happened, but I reckoned something did 'cause I felt a little jump inside of me.

He instructed Samantha to mix whiskey and butter together and give Master a few drops in his mouth. That didn't sound so magical to me, but he went on mixing and mashing herbs, so I held down my doubt.

"Name?" he asked, nodding at me.

"My name? Annabelle. Well, no. Not really. My name is Mercy."

"Mercy? Ah. My tribe, you Iyanuoluwa."

"Iyanu ... I can't say that."

"Iyanuoluwa. Mercy of God."

* * *

I don't know where the mercy of God went because Master James died a week later. I never saw Ekundayo again to ask him where his miracle powers ran off to or why his name seemed to be more backwards than ever. Missus Rachel had his funeral in the parlor. She done took the door off and laid him on it. Eli and some other field hands helped some. She laid out flowers all around him, whether because he deserved a bit of beauty or just to ward off the stench, I don't rightly know. Emma and me played the fiddle for his funeral, only it be some sorry playing with all the tears we be shedding. I tried to hold it together, as Master deserved some right pretty music *in his memory. All I could think about was that I had a good and kind Master, and he been taken away, likely 'cause he worked close to his slaves who'd been sick.*

From my time traveling 'round to different houses fiddling, I'd heard slaves talking about how you have to cry at your Master's funeral whether you like him or not. You've got to at least make it seem like you'se sorrowful or you could get in bad straights for sure. Some slaves wet the corners of their eyes with spittle to make it seem like they crying. But, you see, there ain't been no such nonsense at Master James's funeral. Every tear been true.

* * *

After the funeral, Missus Rachel called all the slaves up behind the Big House for a meeting. None of us had an inkling of what been decided. We all been too heavy with grief to lift our thoughts to the future.

Missus Rachel stood on the back porch, her mourning dress looking strange on her, like it be too heavy to fit her petite little frame. She'd cut some of Master's hair off and put it in her locket, and she wouldn't take her hand off that thing. Yet she tried to stand tall, tried to make her voice loud and strong as she spoke. Maybe only us in the house knew how small she really was when the rest of the slaves went back to the fields.

"As you know, my husband was the backbone of this farm, of this entire operation. I cannot run it without him. As such, my parents, Wilson and Veronica Merriweather, have volunteered to come from Virginia to Kentucky to aid me in running this farm. This is preferable to me selling the farm and moving myself. Several of you know Mr. and Mrs. Merriweather from your time with me in Virginia. I trust that you will be as loyal and hard-working for your new Master and Mistress as you were for my husband."

At that, there were much murmurings among the crowd. One of the field hands shouted, "You don't have to do this, Missus Rachel. We can run the farm for you'se. We mighty good at it."

"Thank you, Edward, but it is a big responsibility managing this large of a farm. My father has the experience necessary to prove successful." When more commotion broke out, Missus Rachel dismissed everyone back to work and slunk into the house, into her bedroom, where we could hear her weeping for the rest of the evening.

As for me, everything was unsettled within me. Missus Rachel's father was coming? The man who cut off his slave's fingers? I was more eager than ever to flee with Emma, across that river and away from that sorrow.

Emma came to me that night, all nervous-like. Skittish as a rabbit in the field.

"I think you need to get me that pass straightaway, Annabelle." Her eyes stayed up high, not bowing down to meet mine.

"I thought we wasn't leaving for another two months."

"I just want to have everything together. Just in case."

"In case what? Are we going to go earlier?"

"I don't know, child! Stop askin' so many questions. I know you can read and write. So write me up a pass right now. Tonight. Stop dawdling!"

"Okay, okay. You best not tell no one."

"I swear I won't. Just write me one up."

"You got something for me to look off of?"

Emma pulled a folded piece of paper from her pocket.

Please to let Helen Riley pass and repass to Ohio from the first until the fifth of September 1832 to Lexington, Kentucky.

"Okay, so I's just write this, but using your name?"

"And change the date. Today's June 20, 1840. And sign it with Missus Rachel's name."

So, I wrote the pass up for Emma.

The next day I wished to God I hadn't.

Because the next day Emma was gone.

28

———

Missus Rachel was all in a tizzy, pacing back and forth so that I thought she'd wear a hole clean through the dining room carpet. "Emma ran away! I can't believe it! I thought she was loyal, as loyal as they came. I trusted her! She'd been with me through ... well, through everything. Through my growing up, becoming a woman, getting married, moving out here to this godforsaken wilderness—" Missus Rachel burst into tears just then, sobbing into her skirt.

I'd been standing there, watching her, my head going back and forth as she paced, which matched up just fine with what was going on inside of me. I knew it wasn't my place to speak, but then again, Missus Rachel didn't seem to be following convention just then anyhow.

"She can't be gone, Missus Rachel. She can't! Not for good. She didn't take her freedom jar. She wouldn't leave without her freedom jar."

Missus Rachel patted her eyes and peered up at me. "Freedom jar?"

"Yes, ma'am. She been saving up all them coins from fiddling. Saving until she'd have the thousand dollars you done told her she *needed to buy her freedom. But if she was gonna run, surely she'd take that money with her. She wouldn't just leave it here. So, you see, she's probably just hiding out in the woods for a day or two like Eli did that one time. She'll come back."*

Missus Rachel let out a breath that had a trace of a humorless laugh on the end of it. "Freedom jar, huh? She thought to purchase her freedom?"

"Yes, ma'am. She done saved every coin she made, tucking them away."

"I might have mentioned something in passing," Missus Rachel said, waving her hand, "but I never could have given Emma manumission. She was far too valuable to me. No one could place a price on her in my eyes."

I squinted my eyes at the Missus, realization squeezing my insides tight, making it hard to breathe. "You mean you'se lied to her?"

"Oh, Annabelle. If she took something I said lightly in passing as gospel truth, whose fault is that? I put nothing in writing. No one is bound by contract if it's not in writing."

At that moment, my thinking got all switched around. Instead of pleading with God for Emma to come back, I prayed that she'd fly away swift and free.

I remember when I first saw that slave caravan when I's just a little girl and I thought that I's lucky to never have been shackled. What I didn't realize then was that slavery itself be a shackle on your very soul. I felt the weight of it then, even as I pictured Emma finally shaking free of it.

* * *

Missus Rachel's parents arrived about the same time as Emma and me had planned on running away. I could tell Missus Veronica was a lady of fine breeding even though she be covered by a thick layer of dust. She stood straight and stiff as if she be posing for a picture every moment. *Master Wilson marched in with gusto and snake eyes, peering at everything like he be trying to figure out who his enemy was. His footsteps sounded overly loud in the house and made the furniture shake a bit. Made me quiver inside too.*

"We're so sorry for not making the funeral, dear," Missus Rachel's mama told her.

"Oh, I understand, of course." Missus Rachel dabbed her eyes with a handkerchief while her mother patted her politely on the back. "It takes time to pack up a plantation and move across the country."

"Your father and I thought we could hold a memorial service to pay our respects to James. Does that sound favorable to you?"

"Oh, yes." Missus Rachel nodded, dabbing at her eyes faster now, her voice giving way. "That sounds lovely, Mother. Annabelle can play the violin, and we could all say a few words."

"Then it's settled. Tomorrow afternoon in the garden, we will honor James's memory and say our official goodbyes. Your father wanted to have some closure before taking over the farm and establishing his dominance. Can you have one of your slaves bring me some tea? I'm quite parched."

Missus Rachel called for me, and I served the new Master and Missus in the dining room, stepping into Emma's shoes as best I could. The teacups clinked as my hands shook, and Missus Rachel's father cast me a look of displeasure.

I done set up three chairs out back in the garden the next morning. All the slaves was invited to the service, an act of goodwill by the new Master and Missus. I been shaky all morning, thinking about playing for Master James again when the first time I didn't play so good at all. I hoped this time I'd do better, as I wanted to get on the new Master and Missus's good side.

When the time came, we slaves stood as Master Wilson presented Missus Rachel with a silver spoon, which he called a coffin spoon. He showed it off like it was something special. All's I could think was that Master James deserved a lot more than some silly spoon. What good was a spoon to him?

Missus Rachel nodded to me to play my mourning song, and I pulled out my fiddle. But as I struck my first note, I heard Master Wilson murmuring.

"Is that your violin, Rachel?"

"Yes."

"You're letting that dirty Negro touch your violin? The one your mother gave you?"

I pretended I didn't hear, but my playing told a different story.

"It was just sitting on the shelf, Father. I would much rather it be played. I'm only lending it to her to play. She knows it is not hers to own."

"I will not stand for this! That is a family heirloom! She needs to get her filthy hands off our family's property!"

I hit a wrong note, the squeaking echoing his offense to my ears.

"Father, can we talk about this later?"

"We most certainly cannot. She must find another instrument or cease altogether!"

Missus Veronica put a hand on Master's muscular arm as Missus Rachel rushed to my side. "Annabelle, did Emma leave her violin?"

"Yes, ma'am."

"Please go get it. Quickly. Play her violin instead."

I bit my lip and nodded, handing over the precious family heirloom and rushing to the house, tears streaming down my face. When Missus Rachel gave that to me, I'd nearly felt like a daughter. But I'd been a fool. A dirty Negro. I wasn't nothing but a dirty Negro who looked almost white. I didn't mean nothing to no one in this house. Didn't mean enough to Emma to take me with her. Didn't mean enough to Missus Rachel to stand up for me. My hands were filthy because they had Mama's blood in them? Fine. If that's what it meant to be black, I would much rather be filthy than be white like the new Master.

When I got back to the garden, Master Wilson was saying his words all calm and sweet like he was the best man in the world. I found out later no one else heard what had gone on. They's all assumed I got all choked up and had to leave for a bit before I could play again. I did play again, and I did a right good job putting the anger out of my mind and focusing on my missing Master James something fierce.

That evening, Master Wilson and the two Missus called Miss Mary and me to the parlor.

"We've come to a conclusion," Master Wilson said, his voice like a gavel. "Annabelle, you are not to touch the family violin again. Do you understand?"

"Yes, sir," I said, lowering my eyes and bowing my head.

"However, as it is a family heirloom, and as Rachel does want it played, we have decided that Mary will learn to play it. Annabelle, you will teach her how."

"But—" Mary started.

"Young lady," Master Wilson interrupted, "I don't know how you talked to your father, but under my rule, the only thing you are allowed to say when I give you an order is 'Yes, sir' or at the very least 'Yes, Grandfather.' Is that clear?"

"Yes, sir." Her teeth be all clenched, and I could tell she was gonna be saying a lot more in my ear later.

"Good. Then it's settled. Annabelle will start teaching lessons in the morning."

"Yes, sir," I said, curtsying. We both went down the hall to Miss Mary's room, Miss Mary stomping and me dragging my feet some, dreading trying to teach that dreadful girl anything.

Before I could even start fiddling lessons, Master Wilson called all the slaves to the back of the house for a meetin'.

"Your old Master was a good man, and I hear you served him well. He grew this farm to a decent size and ensured its success. However, he neglected to focus on the main cash crop for this climate: hemp. We are going to start growing hemp, and we are going to

expand this farm to ten times its size. This means you are going to work harder than you've ever worked in your life.

"I've been told you had half a day off on Saturdays. No more! You will work sunup to sundown on Saturdays, and if I feel you are not working hard enough throughout the week, you will put in a half day's work on Sundays as well. I've hired an overseer, and he will make sure there is no idleness among you. From here on out, things will be different. I expect full obedience and absolute diligence in all tasks. If you cooperate, you should not have a problem with me. If you do not—" Master Wilson struck a whip against the post of the house, and I shuddered. "Now, get to work!"

I scuttled inside and grabbed my fiddle from the parlor then rushed to Miss Mary's room and pleaded with her to grab her own. She did so but slouched in her chair.

"Miss Mary, you gotta sit up straight like this to make your violin sing." I tried to remember how Emma taught me, the words she used to inspire me.

"I don't want to learn this wretched instrument."

"Why not, Miss Mary? You can make beautiful music."

"I don't want to be like a slave. I don't want a slave to teach me anything."

My mind spun around, trying to think of something to get that girl to sit up in her seat and give it a try.

"Well, then," I finally said, "you'se just gonna have to get real good at it then. Real good, so you can prove that you'se better than me."

She sighed, rolled her eyes, and sat at the edge of her chair, listening as I told her how to hold her fiddle and what notes be what.

* * *

Mary's lessons would go good one day and downright awful the next. Maybe it had something to do with trying to teach a moody thirteen-year-old girl whose father had just passed. I tried to be sympathetic with her, seeing as she was going through so much change in her life, winds just swirling all about her and not caring a lick to ask her where she wanted to land. But, Law! She was making it right difficult to have tender feelings toward her.

After a few months, I knew she could play some notes right fine. She played them on her good days, yet when she was upset with the world, she'd screech mighty awful on her fiddle, making me want to cover my ears.

"Mary!" Master Wilson called one day. "Come here this instant!" Mary tossed her fiddle on her bed and dashed down the hall. I creeped after her, careful not to be seen.

"Why in God's name are you playing so awfully? That is dreadful to hear!" His face be all red, his hands in fists at his side.

"I'm just doing what Annabelle taught me to," Mary said, voice sweet as syrup.

"Annabelle!" he thundered.

I came into the parlor, trying to show Miss Mary my hurt through my eyes, but she wasn't looking at me. "When I told you to teach Mary the violin, I expected you to do your job with excellence. I know you are able to play decently. Therefore, you should be able to teach Mary to play decently. The only conclusion I can come up with is that you are being rebellious and insubordinate. That will not be tolerated in this house."

"Yes, sir."

"Come to my room so we can deal with this abominable behavior."

Trembling, I followed Master Wilson. I told myself I'd been whipped before and I'd done survived it. I'd make it through. But something in me knew this time would be different. All of me was shaking as he had me unbutton my dress and pull it down, exposing my bare back. I braced my hands against the wall, but nothing could have prepared me for the fury of that lash. With the first sting, I gasped and went down to my knees.

"Get up!" he commanded, and I did so, but my knees knocked together.

I didn't want to give him the satisfaction of hearing me cry out, but I couldn't hold it in as the lash stung my back again and again and again. I screamed and wailed and pleaded for mercy, but he kept whipping me until Missus Rachel knocked on the door.

"Father? What's going on?"

"Just disciplining a slave."

"Who is it? Father?"

Another lash, and I cried out, "Missus Rachel! Help me!"

"Annabelle?" Missus Rachel burst through the door and was at my side. "Father, my goodness! She's dripping blood all over the carpet!"

"I'm sorry. I should have taken her to the new whipping post outside."

"What did she do?" Missus Rachel looked from me to her father and back again, but neither of us answered.

"Here, Annabelle. Pull your dress up. Your punishment is quite through now. I will have Lucy dress your wounds."

"You're too soft, Rachel. Always have been," Master Wilson said before stomping out, shaking his head.

Missus Rachel let me go to bed early. I had to lay on my stomach 'cause there wasn't no way I could roll over on that back of mine. I was laying there on my mat, letting my tears flow when Miss Mary walked in. I turned my head the other way.

"Annabelle?" Mary knelt on the floor next to me. "Annabelle, I am so sorry. I didn't know he would do that to you, honest. I just wanted to get out of the lessons. I had no idea ..." She pulled down the upper corner of my dress to see just a small portion of my back. "Oh, my! Oh, Annabelle! I hate slavery. Do you know that? I hate it. I think it is evil."

I turned my head to face her then, surprised.

"In fact, I've decided. On my deathbed, I'm going to free all my slaves." She smiled, clearly pleased with herself. "Well? What do you have to say about that?"

I thought of myself, a couple years older than her. If I were still alive, how much use would freedom be to me then? But I knew what she wanted to hear. "That's mighty good of you, Miss Mary."

"Here. I brought you something." She placed a diary next to me, white and delicate with a fancy M on the front. "It was Daddy's. Well, not Daddy's. I mean, he gave it to me a few years ago. I'm not much for writing. You know that. I've had this thing for years and only wrote in two pages that whole time. I guess writing just feels like schoolwork to me. So, I tore out those first two pages, and I'm giving it to you. You know, so you can draw pictures in. It's an apology gift."

I got all choked up, thinking about how much I was going to love and use that diary all up and thinking of how that girl didn't have a lick of sense in her head to just give away something so easily that came from the hands of her father. But I'd take it. Law, I'd take it.

"Thank you, Miss Mary."

"And I won't cause you any more trouble with the lessons. I'll work hard and do well."

"That's good, Miss Mary."

"Okay, so, good night."

"Good night," I whispered, but I's far from sleep. I had so much thinking to do.

My back was puffy. I remembered seeing the puffy backs in the slave caravan. I tried so hard to be good, to find good. And here I thought I had done it, only to feel the heat of the lash lick my back. I couldn't win. I would never be enough—good enough, white enough, black enough, free enough. The lash would follow me all the days of my life. I pressed my fist into my mouth, softening the sound of the sob breaking up out of me.

Mama! Oh, how I wanted Mama right then. I couldn't even see her clearly in my mind, but the sense of her arms around me felt as fresh as ever. What would she say to me right now? What would she *say about all I'd been through since I left her side? I figured she'd say something she'd done said to me before, as Mama always been saying the same things over and over, so I tried to remember.*

And I did remember.

I remembered sitting in front of our cabin and drawing with my fingers in the dust. Mama came and sat down beside me.

"You know that's where we all came from, don't you, Mercy?"

"Where, Mama?"

"From dust. The preacher said God made the first man out of the dust of the earth. Every person here today done come from him, from Adam they's call him. The white man and the black man, all dust. Ain't not one of us made out of gold. We's all the same, really."

"Then what makes us special?"

"What makes you special, baby girl, is that God made you. He made you in His image. And you know, after He made that man out of dust, He breathed the breath of life into him. God's own breath made him come alive. So, you got the breath of God inside you too, baby girl. It's inside you. All you need, God has given you already. You just gotta learn to trust Him."

I blinked, the memory fading but the confidence remaining. Slowly sitting up on my bed, I realized something. Maybe everything I'd passed along the way been put there to push into me and pull out of me something I never even realized was there. Maybe I already did have everything I needed. Maybe freedom really was just on the other side of a river I was brave enough to cross.

29

"Natassa! It's good to see you. Where have you been?"

Natassa smiled politely and shook the older woman's hand, worrying that the baggy shirt she chose to wear coupled with the abdominal binder wouldn't be enough to hide her pregnant belly. "It's been a busy few months."

"We've missed you. I've seen Brandon and the children but haven't seen you for quite a while."

The four-minute meet and greet seemed to drag on for an eternity. *Hurry up and play the music, already!*

"I know. I know. How have you been?"

That at least got her talking about her husband's upcoming knee surgery and her grandson's high school graduation. Relieved to have the focus off of herself, Natassa asked follow-up questions until the band finally began to play the interlude. The hard part was over. Brandon promised they could leave as soon as the sermon was over, no small talk in the foyer. Under that condition—along with the condition that they take separate cars—Natassa agreed to go to church with the family for the first time since the attack. Though she promised to not jet out when uncomfortable, knowing that she had an escape in the form of her Audi made her feel a bit safer.

Still, everything felt strange, as if she were floating in a dream. The setting and routine were familiar, and yet they no longer felt akin to putting on a comfortable pair of yoga pants. She felt awkward and out of place, and God help her, all she could think about was hightailing it out of there to the old church building with stone steps, stained glass windows, and a resounding brass bell. She wanted to smell wood stain and old, musty hymnals. She wanted to hear organ music and dozens of voices rising higher than the stage, harmonizing boldly and with passion. She wanted to feel Bethany's arm linked securely in her own.

Brandon sat next to her, his Bible and bulletin on his lap, pen poised to take notes. He fit here, in this church, and she did not. Not anymore. She shifted in her cushioned chair, longing for the comfort of a wooden pew.

* * *

I done told Missus Rachel that Emma had left her freedom jar, but I ain't told her where I found it. When I woke up the morning we found out she'd left, I rolled over and bumped straight into it. I didn't know what it was straightaway 'cause something was wrapped up around it, but as I got to unwrapping it, I saw it was her jar with her money wrapped up in a map.

I thought for a good long while that she done left everything she had, but then I got around to counting it, and it turns out she left me forty dollars and twenty-nine cents. It might not have been everything, but it was quite a sacrifice. Now my brain been runnin' circles around this one, and I still can't figure out why she left that money and why she left me. If only Emma could write, I'd like to reckon she would have written me a note explaining her reasoning. But I's the only slave who can read and write around here, near as I can tell, so I guess I'll never know for sure. I do believe that she meant for me to use that money to break away from my cruel bondage. So that's just what I's planned to do.

Missus Rachel left Emma's room untouched, still holding out hope that Emma would walk back through those doors. She never did send the hounds after her, just vainly hoped in the goodwill between them to bind them together again. Since no one else set foot in Emma's room, it became a refuge of mine.

When I snuck in there at night for the first time, I found all of our things still hiding under her mat. The bonnet, the purse, the gloves— they be all accounted for. I gots a plan brewing. Now all I have to do is wait for the family to go to Lexington. I've done hid supplies in the woods while Miss Mary was doing her lessons. There's talk about Saturday being the day.

* * *

It's taken me months of writing to get all these thoughts on the paper of this journal. I've done snuck into Emma's room nearly every night, writing by candlelight, heart pounding at the thought of getting caught by Master Wilson and his whip. Yet it be his whip that fanned this spark of braveness in me, and every time I tiptoe down those stairs and into this room, it burns hotter. Brighter. Brighter than my fear. I done need to get these words out 'cause I can't afford to forget who I am.

All these words bring me to today. I hear it be Friday, and Missus Rachel says they planning to go into Lexington tomorrow. I'm planning on going to Louisville, 'cause that's where the Ohio River be. The river I'm now brave enough to cross.

* * *

Missus Rachel did go to Lexington today. Master Wilson went too, and Miss Mary. They took Samantha like they usually do. But Missus Veronica stayed behind to keep an eye on the slaves.

We ain't never had anyone stay to keep an eye on us before, not when the whole family went to town. Wasn't no need when we had a good Master. Missus Veronica kept her eyes on me like a hawk circling its prey. There wasn't no way I could fly away with Missus Veronica's eyes on me like that.

So, I'm still here in the Big House, dreaming the dream of freedom.

* * *

Ain't got nothing to write. I'm tired of writing. I wonder what Emma is doing right now. What does the air smell like in freedom territory?

* * *

I know I haven't written in here for a long time, but I'm writing today from the woods outside of Lexington! I did it! I escaped. I can't rightly see nary a thing I's writing, as it's dark as ink out here. I'm trustin' my fingers know well enough to write the story. I arrived in town yesterday with just enough time to apply for passage on tomorrow's stagecoach to Louisville. It will arrive at four o'clock this morning. I've not much time.

Missus Rachel and Miss Mary and Master Wilson was taking a trip to Cincinnati, and they was debating on taking me since it be free territory. Missus Rachel was saying it was fine and they should take me, as I would be of help to Miss Mary on the journey, but Master Wilson be dead set against it, saying I'd be looking to escape at the first opportunity. Miss Mary wanted me, so she be pouting and fussing, but then Master Wilson would give her a look that shut her up real good.

They's all this confusion as they went back and forth. Missus

Veronica would be staying back as usual, keeping an eye on the slaves back at the house, but she wasn't sure what was going on the same as the rest of them. So they's getting ready to leave and going out the door when they finally said I's staying at the Big House, but Missus Veronica didn't hear. So, I went out on the front porch and waved goodbye, then waited a few minutes and went back inside.

Missus Veronica be sipping tea in the dining room. I told her that Missus Rachel forgot her cloak and I needed to fetch it for her and run to catch up.

"They're bringing you then?" she asked.

"Oh, yes. Miss Mary insisted," I said. Then I grabbed Miss Rachel's cloak. Then, while Missus Veronica wasn't looking, I grabbed the family violin straight off the shelf in the parlor. I don't know why I did that. I just had the gumption, and I snatched it and dashed out the door. I ran off down the road for a minute just in case Missus Veronica be looking out the window then I dashed off to the woods, where I hid the canvas bag, purse, and food before.

The bag had a change of clothes Emma found for me. They look right fancy, like some rich white woman's clothes. With the bonnet, gloves, and boots, I will look right well off. The bread I hid in the bag is crusty and stale, but the jars of canned peaches and pears I snuck from the kitchen were fine for eating. I took several cans of beans as well and felt thankful for my foresight. However, lugging around all them jars and cans in that bag, plus a violin made my journey slow and tiresome.

I didn't change straightaway and stuck to the woods, sleeping during the day and traveling at night. I'd come out to the road just enough to make sure I was still going the right way. The dusty road to Lexington was well traveled, and they was signs as I got closer. When I started hearing more commotion, I knowed I be almost there. Then I cleaned up in a creek and changed into them fancy clothes. It took all my gumption to come out into the open and make my way in the world as a white woman, taking a stagecoach to Louisville. My stomach was tossing around, and my throat be squeezing so tight I *didn't know if I'd be able to squeak any words out of it at all. 'Cept I did. I made myself brave like Mama and marched into the general store to ask about the stagecoach. They directed me to the stage office, where I paid $3.50 for my fare. They told me to rightly expect an eleven-hour ride.*

I hear some commotion in the distance and had better get back into town so I don't miss my chance.

* * *

I'm on a steamer!

I cannot believe what bubbled up from the inside of me. I marched out of those woods, held my head high, and walked like I owned the right to be on the roads of Lexington without a pass. Who is this girl? Or is she a woman now? Nearly, at least. I'm only seventeen, but I feel like I've grown a decade in a day.

I paraded up to that stagecoach driver, looked him straight in the eye (Think of that!), and showed him my ticket to Louisville. The driver took my bag and the violin case, stowing them up top, and the next thing I knew I was riding in a stagecoach on my way to the Ohio River. The whole way, my heart be soaring, hope pulsing through my veins. I could taste freedom on the breeze. The only other person riding on the coach with me was an old man who slept the entire time. Relief settled over me to not have to make any sort of conversation. I'd been practicing talking proper but was still nervous about slipping up and the slave in me sneaking out. I'd never been to town, least not since I been a little girl, so I was right curious and wanted to look around while we'd be riding, but I pulled the shade down low just in case we ran across anyone who might recognize me from them parties I'd fiddled at.

When we got to Louisville, the swirl of sights and sounds done made me dizzy, and an overwhelmed feeling started to overtake me. Then my eyes beheld the Ohio River, and I 'bout landed flat on the ground. I ain't never imagined it could be so big! Might as well be an ocean for all's I could tell. How could any slave get across it? My bewilderment must have done showed in my face, because the stage-coach driver asked me where I was headed.

"I'm boarding a steamer," I said.

"By yourself? You're traveling alone?"

I had to come up with something real quick like, which ain't never been something I's good at, but I said, "I'm visiting a cousin who is deathly ill."

The worry in my face must have looked an awful lot like grief because his face melted in sympathy for me, and his shoulders drooped a bit. "I'm so sorry, Miss. Let me show you your steamer. I regret that you have to travel alone. Which one, Miss? Which steamer are you boarding?"

"Um ..."

"Don't you rightly know?" I's shook my head. "Where are you headed? East or West?"

I just stared at the man, mouth hanging open a bit 'cause I knew something was supposed to come out of it, but I hadn't a clue what to say. East or West? I just wanted to cross the river, didn't I? How did I do that?

"Northeast or Southwest?" he asked.

North or South? North or ... South? Mama? Mama.

"Southwest."

"Then you'll want the Blue Bell. She'll take you west. From there you can take another steamboat south on the Mississippi. You can go straight down to New Orleans on a Mississippi steamer!"

I hadn't a clue where New Orleans was, but I said, "Thank you kindly. That's perfect."

He hitched up his horses and walked me over to the Blue Bell. Excitement mixed with trepidation as I walked toward the magnificent boat. The blue deck and roof looked striking next to the bold red stripe painted across the boat at the waterline. The name "Blue Bell" was painted in an arc, bright-blue letters on gleaming white. The paddlewheel stood still, imposing. Impressive.

The stagecoach driver motioned for me to walk across the plank to the boat, following behind me. Once we crossed, he hailed for assistance, and the captain himself came to speak with me.

"You're just in time. We'll be setting off within the hour. Cabin or deck passage?" He looked me over and continued without giving me a chance to reply. "Why, you look like a lady of fine breeding. Cabin passage, I assume? That's for the best, I assure you. Last month another steamer boarded a deck passenger with cholera, and goodness if it didn't spread to half of those on deck. Goodness, me! And besides, up here you won't have to bother with the Irish and the Germans. Few immigrants can afford a stateroom. Now, where to, my lady?"

The stagecoach driver answered for me, for which I was mighty grateful, my tongue still not wishing to cooperate.

"To the Mississippi."

"Ah, yes. That will be twelve dollars, Miss."

I pulled the money from my purse and paid him without comment. I expected the fare to cost far more than twelve dollars, yet now I hadn't the least idea where exactly Mama was, much less how to get there and how much that trip would cost. My mind be jumbled up with wonderings even now.

"Wait here a moment, and the steward can show you to your stateroom," the captain said. I nodded and watched him disappear onto the boat before the stagecoach driver bid me farewell.

"Enjoy your trip west. Everyone's going west nowadays."

But not every slave was going south.

Natassa and Brandon sat in lawn chairs, watching David round third base and slide into home. Brandon cheered. Natassa whistled. Clapping resounded from the bleachers next to them, where Daniel sat with a couple of friends. Faith and Hope played with Barbie dolls in the grass nearby.

The sun glared menacingly. Natassa's thighs were sticking together, and she felt sweat building underneath her shirt where the abdominal binder was. Trying to be as discreet as possible, she undid the Velcro and pulled the binder toward her back until she was sitting on it. There. She could breathe again. But it was still so hot.

"You win," Brandon said.

Natassa pulled the ball cap down further over her forehead so she could see his face without the sun blinding her. "What are you talking about?"

"You wanted a fifth child. You win."

"Brandon, what do you mean?"

He took a long drink of his Mountain Dew and spit an ice cube back into the cup. He leaned toward her. "I know you don't want to give that baby up. But do it, Natassa. Pick a family. Make an adoption plan. Then I will give you that fifth baby you wanted. My baby. Our baby. When you're ready."

"You're serious?"

"Dead serious. It's called compromise, Natassa. It's what people do in marriage. You give a little, I give a little."

Natassa winced. "A lot."

He tilted his head to the side. "We both give a lot."

She sighed. "What do we tell people?"

"The truth, I guess. Or nothing at all. It's no one's business but ours."

"What do we tell the children?"

He looked to where the girls were playing, and she followed his gaze. They were so innocent. Were these among their last innocent moments?

"I don't know," he finally said. "We need to sit down and figure that out. Together."

David's team got their third out and took to the field. David stood at first base, the knees of his once white pants the color of russet potatoes. His red ball cap hung down low. He caught her eye and grinned. David. Her firstborn. Her little man. He was only nine years old. Far too young to know about something as awful as rape. And Daniel. She turned and watched him for a minute, joking around with his friends. He always threw his head back when he laughed. She wanted to bottle his childhood, not shatter it.

You win.

No.

Nobody won here.

She had to sit on her hands to keep herself from stroking her belly. Biting her lip, she told herself not to cry.

David got the runner out at first, and Brandon stood and cheered. Natassa clapped halfheartedly then wiped the sweat from her brow. The sun beat down upon them. She needed to reapply sunscreen on the girls.

Grabbing the tube from her bag, she called out to them. "Faith! Hope! Come here, please!" Hope was by her side in an instant, but Faith was not.

"Where's your sister?"

Hope shrugged.

Natassa surveyed the empty patch of grass the girls had been playing on just moments before. "You don't know where she is? Brandon, have you seen Faith?" Natassa asked, whipping around, scanning in all directions.

"She probably went to the playground."

Natassa jumped up, knocking her lawn chair over, and jogged toward the playground. "Faith? Faith!" She wove her way through a dozen children playing on swings and seesaws but didn't see her.

"Faith?" she heard Brandon call out behind her, concern lacing his voice.

She was out of breath and holding back tears. "Maybe I need to check the bathrooms?" Brandon nodded, but just then she looked up and saw her daughter at the top of the staircase in the castle tower at the entrance to the tallest slide.

"Mommy! Daddy! I'm a princess in the castle!"

Natassa covered her mouth and let out a cross between a sob and a laugh. Brandon wrapped his arms around her, breathing out slowly. He rubbed her arms then stepped back.

Just then, Jean walked toward them. Her son and David had been playing on the same team for two years and went to the same school. Jean's ponytail swung back and forth when she walked, and Natassa could hear her chomping on gum from yards away.

"Be friendly," Brandon whispered through his teeth.

"Hey, Natassa! Brandon! How are you?"

"We're good." Natassa pasted on a smile.

"I haven't seen you in a while, but I think I know why now! I didn't know you were expecting again! Congratulations!"

Natassa froze. She could feel the blood draining from her face. Brandon coughed.

"I didn't ... I didn't realize ... anybody could tell."

"Mom, you're pregnant?" Daniel asked. She hadn't seen him walk up and stand next to his father, but there he was—standing right next to his sisters.

"Mommy's going to have a baby?" Faith asked.

"A baby!" Hope jumped up and down, clapping.

"Oh, dear. I'm so sorry," Jean said. "I had no idea this was supposed to be a secret." She shifted her weight from one foot to another. "I'd better be going."

"It's true?" Daniel looked up at Brandon, and he nodded. Faith put her hand on Natassa's belly and squealed.

"I need to go," Natassa said, feeling pressure from all sides. She grabbed Brandon's hand and squeezed. "Hold onto Faith. Please! Watch her. Don't let her get out of your sight." Then she ran to her lawn chair, grabbed her bag, and rushed to her car.

30

————

y head pounds and my stomach twists within me. My cabin proves more than satisfactory, yet there is no true rest for those traveling on the river, even for us in first class. All night long, the engine puffs and roars. We stop frequently to take on cargo. Last night we took on some hogs, and their squealing kept me up half the night. Then there is the bell that clangs with each snag. After my ears cringe at the sound, I brace myself for the vessel's reeling, lurching sometimes only once, sometimes over and over again until I want to scream. Perhaps others more accustomed to such things can sleep through it. I cannot.

I cannot even enjoy the fine cuisine served in the dining room. I am out on deck right now, hoping the fresh air will calm my nerves and restore my appetite.

* * *

The last time I wrote, I had to be real careful as some lady seemed to be looking over my shoulder. Maybe I's just being suspicious of everyone around me, but she seemed to be standing awfully close, and she be the one asking me many questions at dinner. Not just asking questions, but talkin' 'bout anything and everything to anyone with ears on they's head. Miz Liza, they call her. She'd be just the kind to enjoy the story of a runaway slave on a steamboat. I gots to steer right clear of Miz Liza, indeed.

Remembering to use my white voice and act proper out in public is tuckering me out. Thinking about everything I say takes all the space in my mind. I think I's doing a right good job, though. I's trying not to talk too much, trying not to give myself away, so I mainly only come out of my room at mealtimes. While the other ladies talk by the fire of the ladies' cabin, I stay holed up. As much as I'd like to stretch my legs on land at wooding-up time, I dare not even line the railing to watch. The men have contests as to who can carry the largest pile of wood, and I hear everybody cheerin' for their favorites. I imagine it'd be fun to watch, but the less I'm seen, the safer I be.

I could ask to take my meals in my room, but I fear that'd make me more suspicious, so I figure it's best to dine with the other passengers. I don't come out until the meal bell, and whenever people press me, I say something about my cousin who's deathly ill and start dabbing my eyes. Then I excuse myself back to my stateroom. I ain't never have to worry 'bout not having tears at the right time. I just think of Mama and all the wanting inside of me for her and how I can't imagine how I will ever be able to find her in this big ole world.

I look at the map Emma gave me, and I's just lost in it. It helped me know how to get to Louisville is all. It had a big star right there, leading me to the river. But how to get to Mama? I ain't got a clue. I see South Carolina on that map, and I see the river I be traveling right now, and though I'm going a little South, I ain't getting much closer to her as near as I can see. Maybe I's even getting further. I got on that stagecoach feeling so big and grown up, and now I feel so small and alone.

* * *

I done had to come out of my stateroom onto the deck last night 'cause there been a lurch that knocked me clean out of bed. I heard screaming and feared we be sinking. I threw on Missus Rachel's cloak and rushed outside, thankful I'd slept in my braid.

Nearly everyone be out on deck, looking over the rail, asking what was going on. Turns out a log broke the spoke of the paddlewheel.

All at once, Miz Liza was right up next to me. I stepped back into the shadows, fearful as I didn't have my bonnet or gloves on.

"Don't you worry, Mary. It's just a log. They'll have the paddle-wheel fixed in no time. Now, at first, I thought all of the commotion was due to a boiler explosion, which is not uncommon on the river, you know. An explosion can kill hundreds of passengers. Hundreds, I daresay. So, suffice to say, I'm thankful it's only a log. My cousin's steamboat suffered an Indian attack, and I believe no less than fifteen deck passengers and two deckhands died in that attack. And of course, there's the prospect of sinking. Many a steamboat have hit a snag and sunk into the river. Now remind me again, Mary, have you traveled by steamboat before?"

Miz Liza took a step toward me again, even as I took another step back.

"Forgive me, Miz Liza, but it's quite late. Seeing as we are all safe, I'd like to try and get some sleep."

"Oh, of course dear. I'll see you at breakfast. You can tell me all about your traveling adventures then."

This morning, I done sat as far away from that dreadful lady as I could.

* * *

I overheard someone say we're nearly to the Tennessee River, and you'se can take that east. I reckon that's what I plan to do, stead of headin' down the Mississippi. That should get me closer to Mama if I'm looking at this map correctly. I don't rightly know when the next steamer takes off, but I will be happy to get my feet on solid ground, for however long that be.

When they's asked me what my name was, I told them Mary. I figured if I'm gonna play a part of a rich white young lady with her family's fiddle, I could just borrow Miss Mary's name for a bit. But now I be so mixed up in my head when someone calls out for me in the dining room. Mercy? Annabelle? Mary? Who am I? I just hope my grief is a good enough cover for me not always responding straightaway to a name I's not used to.

We's be sitting at dinner and some lady asked, "What are you having, Mary? The roast lamb? The boiled chicken?"

I didn't answer straightway, not recognizing she be talking to me. "Mary? Mary!"

"Oh! Oh, sorry. I think I'll have the roast turkey tonight." As the ladies round the table still eyed me like something be off, I added, "And the pound cake with figs and almonds for dessert. Don't you think that sounds delightful?"

At that, some nodded while others said the gooseberry pie was far better. At any rate, their attention be off me and onto the food, which be a right good thing.

* * *

Something just came to me in that strange place in between dreaming and waking, the sound of the bell and the lurching. Mama taking me down the river, me feeling a brew of fear and awe at its bubbling strength.

"This is the Pee Dee River, Mercy. It's what helps us to grow the rice. Beautiful, ain't it?"

"Yep. And big."

"It's good to depend on something bigger than yourself, baby girl."

"I hate it. The Pee Dee River."

"And why's that?"

"If there was no river, then there'd be no rice. Right, Mama? Then you and me would be no slaves."

"Ah, Mercy. If it wasn't rice, it'd be something else. Don't blame ole Pee Dee. She ain't done nothing to us. She's a beautiful river."

I sprang up in bed, the bell on the steamboat sounding like it be somewhere far off shore and not right above me. Georgetown. Old Master's plantation was in Georgetown. Off the Pee Dee River!

I snatched the map and scoured it, my eyes searching hungrily. There! The Pee Dee River! And there! Georgetown! And ... I looked at where the Tennessee River went to. Looked at where the Pee Dee River started. The two didn't touch each other. Not even close. And what was that bumpy thing in between them? Were those ... mountains?

How could I feel closer to finding Mama than ever before only to feel it would never happen at the same time? I'd get caught. Sent back. Or maybe I'd die alone in the mountains. And Mama? She would never know that I'd come for her.

I'd never had a pillow until coming to this cabin. My first pillow ever be soaked wet with tears.

I'm on the steamer The Sunrise *headed east on the Tennessee River now. I don't know what else to do. I know it won't get me where I need to go, but I don't know what will, and this will get me closer. It be costing me fourteen dollars for the 652 miles it takes to get to Knoxville, Tennessee, which be as far as this steamer can take me. The Sunrise be smaller than the Blue Bell. I don't rightly care either way as long as Miz Liza's not on it!*

At meals, all us cabin passengers sit 'round these big tables with them fancy tablecloths while the waiters serve us like we's kings and queens. Negro men and women in crisp white aprons. I can't rightly tell whether they be free or slave, and it bothers me something fierce that I can't make out the difference between the two. Seems like whether you get paid a measly amount or not at all, if you'se got dark in your skin or somewhere in your blood, your life's gonna be about serving the white men and ladies, bending to their every whim so they's can have calf's head soup and currant pie on fine china. I guess if you'se free, you end up with some money in you'se pocket and without a lash on you'se back, but it still seems short of what Mama wanted for me when she spoke of freedom.

Everyone makes small talk during meals and around the fire in the ladies' cabin. On the **Blue Bell**, *I's tried to talk as little as possible and tried to duck out as soon as I be done eating, lest I give myself away. Now, though, I be desperate for information. I need to find out how to get where I'm going, so as much as it makes my nerves jump to risk me talking, I's asking everyone where they're headed to. I try to sit with different people each meal to find out as many places as I can, hoping beyond hope someone will say they're going straight to Georgetown and I can figure out how they plan on getting over those mountains.*

I have no idea how long Missus Rachel and her father be gone to Cincinnati. She said maybe two weeks, maybe shorter, maybe longer, so there's no telling. Did they return? Do they know I'm gone? Are they looking for me? Did they put out notices? I wonder if they did, if the picture on them showed my hair wild and free and if anyone would recognize the girl who got on that stagecoach or the steamboat as one and the same. I try not to think about these things, but my mind keeps running back to them.

Lord, help me. I don't know what to do with myself. Sometimes I wish I'd never run off at all.

* * *

Tonight, I sat by a girl of sixteen named Susan. She be a talker, and we's came together like butter and bread, straightaway. Like we's always meant to be together. When she heard I had my own cabin all to myself, she about begged me to come over, tired to death of sharing a cabin with her Ma and Pa. So I invited her to my cabin to sit and talk after dinner, not thinking a lick about it since we's be so friendly together.

As soon as we's got to my cabin, she started prodding around, saying how's my cabin seemed bigger than hers, though I don't think that be true. I think it just seems that way since I be the only one in it. She saw my journal straightaway, as it sat on the desk and she picked it up, tracing her finger over the M on the front. My stomach dropped, and I about pounced on her to snatch it out of her hands.

"Oh, don't worry," she said. "I know better than to read someone's diary."

But I was worried, 'cause though I know better too, I can't be saying that if I came across one curiosity wouldn't get the best of me and prod me to open up a page and read a lick of what I know I best not be reading. And if she did so, would I be turned in? I guessed there wasn't a bond of friendship tight enough to endure such a betrayal.

Then she saw the jar of peaches I had packed. She picked it up and turned it in her hands, giggling. "Did you think they wouldn't feed us enough on this steamboat?"

"It's for my cousin. My mother's peaches, for my cousin."

"Oh, I see."

She eyed me and asked, "Don't you take off your gloves as soon as you get in your cabin? And do you always wear a bonnet? Are you always so proper?"

I just smiled back at her, as I didn't have no answer. She be walking around all restless like, and I could tell something be bothering her, all that bothering be coming out as questions and nonsense is all.

She finally sat on the wingback chair and I on my bed, and her heart just spilled out of her mouth. All her woes just tumbled on out. Her family had gone out west on the whim of her father and against the wishes of her mother. Her father wanted to build a life on the frontier, but it didn't turn out like he'd hoped, and the constant nagging of Susan's mother brought their spirits lower and lower until her father gave in and agreed to go back east. So they is headed back home, which pleases her ma to no end, but her pa is brooding, and Susan worries about their life east with him so displeased. She feels pulled between the two of them, stuck in the middle of the country somehow, one arm yanked west, the other yanked east, not knowing which she would choose, but not having a choice either way.

"And I'm sixteen! I should be getting married soon, but there's no beau in sight. We had no neighbors to speak of. We had to travel for miles and miles to see anyone at all, and the family nearest to us only had a toddler is all. Back home at least I'll have a fair chance at a match, if all the good ones aren't already taken. Oh, I fear they'll already be taken and I'll get stuck with some old widower of my father's choosing! What about you? Did you have a beau in Kentucky?"

I blinked, not prepared to answer such a question. I hadn't had a thought of starting a family of my own, only of getting back to the one I'd been torn from in the first place. But I recovered right quick and said, "No. I had the same problem as you, I'm afraid."

"Oh, I do hope we both make good matches back east. And soon! I don't want to be a spinster!"

She continued spilling out her woes, and I listened sympathetically, nodding and feeling my heart pull toward her until she said, "I think I have about the hardest life of anyone I've ever met." Something must have shown in my face, though I tried not to flinch.

"Oh, I'm sorry, Mary! How insensitive of me! I forgot. You said something about visiting a relative who is ill?"

I tried to recover my composure, remember who I was pretending to be. "Deathly ill."

"Oh dear."

I needed to change the subject before she started asking too many questions I wasn't ready to answer. "So where back east are you headed?"

"Hamburg, South Carolina."

"South Carolina?"

"Yes. Daddy's going to buy a new wagon and oxen when we dock in Chattanooga. We sold our old ones. Then we'll make our way back east, waving to every wagon we pass, wishing them the best of luck. It should take a week or two to make it back home, depending on how hard Daddy drives the oxen. Seeing as how he's not in much of a hurry to get back home ..." She trailed off as she looked around my cabin. Her eyes fell on my fiddle.

"Oh! A violin! Do you play?"

"Yes, I do."

"Can you play something? For me? Now?"

I was just about to tell her I would when I remembered that I best not take off my gloves in front of her, and I didn't reckon I could play with them on. "Maybe some other time."

"Daddy says it's not proper for a young lady to play the violin, but I don't see why not. You're from a proper family and you play. How did you learn?"

"A slave taught me."

"A slave? Oh my! Was that humiliating?"

I considered that for a moment. "She was a good slave. I liked her. I enjoyed learning from her."

"Was? Is she not your slave anymore?"

"She ... she ran away."

"Oh no! How awful! Oh, I hate stories like that, stories of slaves betraying their owners. I can't even imagine my slave Phebe doing such a thing to me. She's on deck, and she's as faithful as can be. I would be beside myself if she took off."

I reached inside me and grabbed the feelings that gripped me when I found out Emma left. "It was quite a loss."

Susan sighed and fanned herself with her fancy lace hand fan. "Oh, well. You'll be able to get another slave, won't you? I'm sure you will. Where are you headed?"

"Georgetown."

"So, you are going east when the whole world is going west as well. But alone? Why so far alone?"

I closed my eyes, searched for an answer. "My parents have passed as well. My cousin is all I have."

"You poor dear! How will you get there?"

Tears began to leak out the corners of my closed eyes. "Truth be told, I have no idea." The dam burst, and I began to weep.

Susan came and knelt in front of me, holding my gloved hand in hers. "I know. I know! You can come with us. There's a railroad now in Hamburg. My aunt wrote to us about it. It goes all the way to Charleston. From there you can catch a stagecoach to Georgetown. Oh, say you'll come with us!"

I nodded through my tears, daring to open my eyes. "Yes! Yes, I'll come with you. If your parents approve, of course."

"I know they will. Oh, this will be grand! It will be so great to have a friend along."

I squeezed her hand, managing to smile. Knowing I could only enjoy this friendship until Hamburg, but thankful for it just the same. And thankful for the hope beginning to take flight within me yet again—that I will see my mama again.

It's only right that I give Susan's pa some money for taking me along, but I don't know how much be proper, and I don't know how much I'm gonna need for the train and the stagecoach. I don't want to run out. So tonight, I did a right risky thing.

After Susan left, I waited to make sure she be gone for good. Then I took my braid out and mussed my hair. I took off my fancy clothes and put my slave clothes on, throwing Missus Rachel's cloak on over them and stuffing my wild hair under the bonnet. Fiddle in hand, I sneaked down to the deck, dragging my finger in soot on the way and rubbing it on my face. I found a discarded cup on the stairwell. When I was halfway down, I took off the cloak and bonnet and stuffed them in my fiddle case. And on the deck I played the fiddle for the spare change of some deck passengers.

Rowdy, they pushed into each other and occasionally into me as I played. The smell of liquor mixed with the stench of unwashed bodies and livestock, and I held my breath. Though room was scarce, some danced. Others tapped their feet. Some thanked me for drowning out the cries of the chillun. When my cup filled half up, I took it and slunk away, back up the steps, wiping my face with my hands and spittle as I went. When I got halfway up, I threw on the cloak and bonnet and braided my hair. I poured the coins into my fiddle case and threw the cup down the stairway.

I made it nearly to the boiler deck before the steward stopped me.

"Deck passengers are not allowed up here, Miss."

Heart hammering, I held my fiddle case behind my back and pulled out my stateroom key with the other hand, holding it out before him. "I apologize. I heard a dreadful noise and went to investigate. I'm returning to my room now."

"Oh. Very well," he said. And he walked away, allowing me to slip into my stateroom otherwise unnoticed.

See, Mama? My braveness hasn't gotten crushed completely. It just went into hiding for a bit.

* * *

I haven't had hardly a minute to myself—and no time to write— since Susan has hardly left my side. We got off the steamer in Chattanooga, Tennessee, and I'm traveling with her family and their two slaves on their wagon. We should arrive in Hamburg in two days.

As hard as it was to remember to be proper on the steamer, it be twice as hard here on the wagon, as Susan is with me every moment. My brain hadn't a minute to rest. I slipped up yesterday and feared I had given myself away, but as it turns out, I's already known.

Phebe and Olive, the slaves, been cooking the beans, and I went to scoop myself up some. They apologized for serving up beans again, and I said, "I ain't never tire of beans." I said that! Plum forgot to use my white voice. I felt my eyes getting wider, and I put my hand to my stomach to keep everything in from lurching out.

Phebe's mouth curved up on the side, all sly-like. "You ain't, huh?"

I tried to take it back, like that be possible. "I mean, I don't ..." but she just chuckled.

"We know what game you playing, Mary."

I looked between Phebe and Olive. Back and forth between them.

"That's a nice fiddle you have there. Real nice. Looks familiar. Looks like one some slave girl be playing on deck on the steamer."

"There are a lot of violins."

"Not like that there ain't!"

I ducked in close to them, trying to pull on their sympathies with my eyes. "Please! I'm just trying to find my mama. Please, don't tell!"

"Oh, shush. Why'd we go and be telling on one of our own? You sit down and enjoy them beans. We ain't whispering a thing to a soul."

I keep watching them, trying to trust they be telling the truth. I think they is. If they was going to tell, wouldn't they have done so by now?

Susan's sleeping now. Everyone be asleep but me. I tried to drift off, but my thoughts keep tumbling around in my head.

Susan asked me today what plantation I was headed to.

"Are you familiar with the plantations in Georgetown?" I asked her.

"No."

I pulled a name from the sky. "The Thymes Plantation."

"I shall visit you someday. We'll write back and forth. Promise me we'll remain great friends. Promise me."

It's a promise I made that slavery won't allow me to keep. When she goes writing to Mary at Thymes Plantation, she'll not find her. In another world, we could remain friends forever. In this world, the blackness in my blood, a color you can't even hardly see, will keep us apart forever.

* * *

We arrived in Hamburg as the first rays of the sun kissed the sky. I paid Susan's father five dollars. I wasn't sure if that be what's proper, but seeing as he nodded and thanked me warmly, it seems I wasn't too far off. The train left Hamburg at 6 a.m., so I had nary a bit of time to hug Susan goodbye, certainly not enough time to cherish that feeling as the last time I'd feel her friendship wrap around me, before I paid eight dollars for my train ticket and boarded the train for Charleston.

I turned around in my seat to watch Susan grow smaller and smaller behind me, reaching out my hand to wave, or maybe to try to grasp the wisp of a dream that be fading away. But soon she be gone, and I turned to face forward again to whatever my future might hold. And I was flying toward it at fifteen to twenty-five miles an hour, they said! Fast as the wind!

We stopped for breakfast at Aiken. I's kept to myself, not saying a word to anyone. Why should I risk being caught now? And for what? A glimpse of a friendship that would only last till Charleston? I was relieved to board the train again twenty minutes later and thankful when we arrived in Charleston shortly after two.

After arriving in Charleston, many of the passengers stopped to dine, but I counted my money and thought it best not to spend a lick of it on food until I knew what my plans were. When I got to the stage office, I been thankful for my foresight as passage to Georgetown done cost five dollars. And seeing as it left at five the next morning, I had to stay at an inn for the night. After I paid for the inn, I only had thirty-three cents left, so I figured I'd just have to be a bit hungry for a while. It's not like I'd never been hungry before. I just imagined I's still on that boat eating me some venison.

The stagecoach to Georgetown be crowded and bumpy. My knee kept knocking against the lady next to me, and I wondered if they's could hear my stomach complaining the whole way. I arrived in

Georgetown near dusk, weary from weeks of travel, still unsure of how to find Mama.

I asked someone in town the way to the Pee Dee River and then just began to walk, dragging the fiddle and my luggage with me. I prayed for God to guide me. I had to believe my heart remembered the way.

When I heard the sound of waters, I rested a bit on the bank. I found a spot in the woods to spend the night, eating the last jar of peaches, praying paddy rollers wouldn't find me. In the morning, I went back to the river, washed my face and my hands, and then found the road and started walking again. Pretty soon I saw a bend that looked familiar. I just felt like I needed to go right, so I did. After just a bit, I saw our field. When I walked up into it, after a bit, I saw our cabin. Mama's cabin. I went running, flinging the fiddle behind me, calling out "Mama!" the whole way.

I flung the cabin door open, my eyes searching around hungry for a glimpse of the woman I'd been missing for eleven years. It was empty. Bare. Barren. Mama was gone. I dropped to the dirt floor, too stunned to even cry. After all that way, she was gone. I just looked around the empty cabin, not even a clear thought in my head for a good long while.

Then I stood up, dusted myself off, walked out, and turned to face the Big House. It loomed just as large as I remembered, gleaming white in the sun. The porch wrapped all the way around with each pillar standing at attention, as if waiting to do Old Master's bidding. The steps to the right and to the left met at the center staircase to take you higher still into where the Master and Missus ruled over all. I trembled. Still, the answers were in there, so I needed to get in there as well.

I walked up to the Big House, heart beating its drum sound in my ears. But I held my shoulders square and knocked forcefully, my knuckles demanding answers.

An old slave I didn't recognize answered. He was hunched over, looking as though he needed a cane but having none, head cocked to the side. He didn't say nothing. Just looked up at me.

"I have business with Ms. Whitegrove. She's expecting me."

I released a long breath as he let me in and led me to the drawing room on the right without questioning me.

I set my luggage by the massive door and stood, hands clasped in front of me, waiting. The Missus came down the front steps and met me in the drawing room, looking like she'd gone through a war or two since I'd left.

"Who are you? I don't have an appointment with you. What do you want?" she asked, her voice coarse.

I forced myself to look her in the eye, playing the part of an equal. "I'm looking for a slave you once owned. Charity."

Her eyes squinted back at me, suspiciously. "I sold her," she said.

My stomach clenched, my mind scrambling over the miles I'd journeyed to find her, envisioning the miles I might have to travel still, searching. I had to find her. I couldn't come this far and not find her.

"Where is your husband?" I demanded.

"Husband?" She sneered. "Dead. Long dead. Why do you ask? Were you one of his many lovers? No. You're too young. Who are you?" She looked me up and down.

Who am I? Mary? Annabelle? I squared my shoulders, brought my eyes straight up to hers and said, "I'm Mercy."

"Mercy?" She cocked her head, as if searching through her memory.

"I came to find my mother."

Realization came over her. "And you ask about your father?" She done spit out the name "father" like it be a foul thing.

I softened my eyes, my stance. "Only if it might lead me to her. I have no affection for the man."

She paced slowly, and I felt the weight of my future in each step she took. Then she stopped and faced me. "I will tell you where she is

—if you show me your freedom papers. You did earn your freedom, didn't you? Or are you here as a fugitive?"

I looked around the Big House. I'd never set foot in it as a child, but now I admired everything the backs of slaves helped to build. It was larger than any other home I'd been in. The great big windows let in all the light from outside as them fancy drapes were pulled back. I looked out them windows into the garden, the garden slaves tended for the pleasure of the Missus. There on the mantle of the drawing room, right next to that porcelain doll, stood a picture of Old Master and Missus in their younger years. He'd been quite handsome with his moustache, and she looked at him with hopeful longing.

"It's hard loving somebody who doesn't love you back, isn't it? I mean, they do love you, in the way that they can right then with the part of their heart they're willing to share with you. But when it's not everything, it's not enough. Because love is supposed to be everything, you know?"

"Why have you come here? To torment me? I will call the authorities. I swear it." Her face be pinched and red, and I felt sorry for her, truly. Maybe she ain't never had no mama's words ringing in her ears when she needed them most.

"I didn't come to hurt you. If it weren't for you, I'd still be with my mama. Never would have had to leave. So, as far as I see it, I have every right to hate you. To hurt you. But my mama named me Mercy for a reason. Everybody needs a little Mercy. I know I do. And if I need Mercy, I need to be able to give it too."

She stopped pacing then and slumped onto the couch, all limp like a rag doll, like all the rigid fight got pulled out of her. I stared at her, the Missus that once loomed so large above me now sittin' like a wisp of a thing on that fancy green couch. I stood large over her now, yet with nary a couple words she could have me locked in a slave pen. I wasn't rightly sure who had the real power, but I felt like I had some anyhow.

I could hear my breathing and her breathing and my own heart beating as I waited.

When she spoke, she didn't look up at me none, and it came out as not much more than a whisper.

"Your mother is at the Miller Plantation down the road."

It be like the sun rose inside of me. I bowed at her feet and thanked her before taking off fast as I could. I wish I hadn't stolen the fiddle. I couldn't run so fast with it.

I ran through the field, searching among dozens and dozens of dark faces.

"Have you seen Charity?" I asked each of them. They only stared. One shook her head.

In the distance I saw her kerchief, blue with white little daisies.

"Mama! Mama!"

She turned toward me, awe written on a face that was etched with years of stories I knew nothing about.

"Mercy? Law, is that you, baby girl?"

"It's me! It's the cream in your coffee!"

"You came back to me!"

We fell into each other's arms, grabbing hold like we ain't never gonna let go again. She just kept saying, "Mercy, you followed me!" I don't know what she be talking 'bout since it seems more like I hunted her down across the whole country. But it don't rightly matter as long as we's together.

* * *

The Millers agreed to purchase me if Missus Rachel agrees. If they can come to an agreement, I will ask them to ship back the violin as well. I haven't decided whether to ship Missus Rachel's cloak back or keep it with me. It smells like her, which is right pleasant to me, and though I know it'd be wrong to hold onto what's not mine, I'd like to remember how a white woman almost loved me once. Nearly like a daughter.

* * *

Missus Rachel sold me to the Millers, and I can breathe easier now. Her father said it'd cost more to fetch me from South Carolina than I was worth, so he didn't put up a fight. Mama and I live in a cabin with Winny and Ben and their chillun. Winny has ten books, and she said I could read any of them anytime. We don't have to hide our learning, least not from the Master and Missus. They be good and kind and not the kind to snuff out the spark in us that wants to burn bright, long as we still work hard and do what we's told.

I keep thinking 'bout the miracle of finding my mama and all I went through for the two of us to be together. Mama keeps talking 'bout how the preacher says God split this big ole sea so Moses and His people could walk straight down through the middle of it to get free from this enemy army. Just split it right in two. I guess it seems crazy to some, but I believe it 'cause I done seen a sea split open for me so I could walk straight through to Mama. I reckon God did that one, too, and that He's just as good at doing miracles now as He was back then.

That's what I think about at night, lying next to Mama, my back aching from being in the rice paddies all day. I ain't never had to work so hard, yet I ain't never been so happy in my life.

31

DeAndre glanced out the window again, searching for the sight of Reg's car cruising into the driveway. He wasn't coming. Of course, he wasn't coming. Why had DeAndre gone and gotten his hopes up anyway? When Rob had asked him to invite Reg over to the house to watch movies and hang out Friday night, DeAndre initially shrugged it off as a stupid idea. There was no way he was going to get Reg to come waltzing into Crawford County.

But the more he thought about it, the more he figured Reg was just jealous of his new friends and afraid of being left out, left behind. If he could somehow bridge the gap between them, maybe Reg could see that the "white boys" weren't the enemy. Maybe DeAndre could get him to understand that there was space for both worlds in his life. He needed to do something to make things right between him and Reg. Maybe this was a way to make him understand.

"You want *me* to come hang with you and the white boys in their prep house in suburbia?" Reg asked when DeAndre brought it up.

"Yes. Please. Come meet them, Reg. I think you'll like them when you get to know them."

"And you think they'll like me?" His laugh was dry.

"Yeah, of course. How could they not like my best friend?"

"Give me the address and we'll see."

DeAndre kept checking out the window, but he didn't know why he bothered. Reg wouldn't show.

Patrick walked into the living room carrying three DVDs. "What do you want to watch first? I've got *Hitch*, *Hancock*, *Men in Black*."

"I'm sensing a theme here."

"I figured you liked Will Smith." He shrugged. "Hey, you started it." He broke into beatboxing a bit of the *Fresh Prince* theme song.

"It's all good." DeAndre had to give Patrick points for trying, even if he was trying a little too hard.

"*Hitch*," Rob called out from the kitchen. "It's hilarious."

"*Hitch* it is."

"Hey, Dre, do you want a Coke or Mr. Pibb?" Rob asked.

"A Pibb is fine." Not what he usually drank, but it would do.

They had settled on the couches, the movie just beginning, when there was a banging on the door.

Reg! DeAndre jumped up. "I'll get it!"

Reg stood on the doorstep, ball cap on backwards, jeans sitting low on his hips. "What's up, D? These your new digs?"

"Come in, Reg."

"Whoo-eee," Reg said, looking around. "You were right, D. These preppy snob boys got a sweet setup."

DeAndre looked nervously at his friends on the couch, who had paused the movie and were staring at them. "I never used those words. Reg, these are my friends—Rob, Patrick, and Eddie. And this is my buddy, Reg. We go way back."

Rob got up and awkwardly extended his hand to Reg. "Welcome."

Reg stared at his hand for a beat then briefly grasped it. He didn't smile.

"So," Rob said, "you're just in time. We were just getting ready to watch *Hitch*."

"Oh, watching a movie, huh? That's what you guys do for fun?"

"Yeah. Sometimes."

"D and I, we get our fun other ways. But I'll try a movie. Sounds quaint."

DeAndre coughed. Rob laughed nervously. "Would you like something to drink?" he asked.

"Drink! See? That's what I'm talking about!"

"We've got Coke and Mr. Pibb."

Reg busted out laughing. "Oh, that kind of drink? That ain't what we're used to, is it D? Mr. Pibb. You ain't got any beer? My man D and I live off beer. I've had to tell him to lay off it a time or two. You know how it is. And whiskey! That boy cannot hold his whiskey for nothing."

"That's enough, Reg."

"What? You gonna stand here and tell them it's not true? That you don't get drunk as a mug on your days off?"

"I haven't lately."

"Oh, yeah. You're Mr. High and Mighty now. I forgot. Over here drinking ... which one did you choose? A Coke or Mr. Pibb?"

"Just grab a drink and sit down and watch the movie," DeAndre said through clenched teeth.

"Chill. Chill. I was just joking with you. Go ahead and start the movie. I got to use it."

"The bathroom is down the hall to the left," Rob said.

When Reg was down the hall, DeAndre apologized. "I'm sorry, guys. I don't know what's gotten into him."

"No biggie," Rob said as he unpaused the movie.

Reg seemed to be taking forever. Then again, the room was more peaceful without him in it.

"Ummm hmmm," Reg said, sauntering into the room. "Now that's what I'm talking about." He pointed to the character Allegra on the screen. "That's one fine piece of meat right there. You might think that D and I only go for black women, but that ain't true. Red and yellow, black and white—they all precious in our sight. Right, bro? Wasn't the last girl you banged a white chick? In that sexy red dress?"

DeAndre felt like his ears were on fire. "Shut. Up."

"What, bro? It's not like I blame you. She was hot."

"I said shut up."

"I guess he doesn't want you guys to know how he is with the ladies. I guess he doesn't want you to know who he really is at all. Do you, D?"

DeAndre clenched his fist. "This was a bad idea. You need to leave."

"Leave? But your new buddy said I was welcome here."

DeAndre stood. "Not anymore. Get out, Reg."

"Fine. I'll go, but I think you should leave too. You don't belong here, D, and you know it." Reg stormed out, flinging the door open and neglecting to close it. DeAndre walked to the doorway and watched Reg's car peel out of the driveway and down the street. Closing the door, he leaned against it and sighed. So that's why Reg came. To ruin everything for him. To smear crap all over his new life and send him crawling back to his hood on his hands and knees.

He might as well hightail it out of there too. It wasn't like his new friends were going to want to hang with him now that they knew the truth. Because there was truth in everything Reg had said, even if he said it in all the wrong ways. Was he trying to be some chameleon? Blending into whatever surroundings he found himself in? Drinking a Pibb in one hood and whiskey in another, watching a movie here and committing a crime there. Reg was right. Those boys in there didn't know him at all.

DeAndre walked back in the living room, dragging his feet, shoulders slumped with the weight of what he was about to lose. But before he could open his mouth to say, "I should go," Rob interjected.

"So *that* is your best friend?"

"Yep." He hated that his admission sounded like an apology.

"Why? How? I don't mean to be rude, but you two are as different as night and day."

"We go way back."

"I get that. It's just ... he says we don't know you and, yeah, we don't know your past. But I think he's the one that doesn't really know you, Dre. Because all he knows *is* your past. I think—"

Rob was interrupted by a knock on the door. Reg? Did he realize what a royal jerk he had been? Had he come to apologize?

"I'll get it," DeAndre said, rushing toward the door.

A pizza delivery man stood on the front step. DeAndre sighed. "Pizza's here."

"Oh! The pizza. I completely forgot." He heard Patrick's voice behind him and stepped back to let him take over. "Wait, Rob, you're paying this time, right? It's $34.87 plus tip."

"Okay, hold on," Rob said as he headed back toward his room.

A couple minutes later, Rob called out, "Guys, have you seen my money? I had two twenties on my dresser." Patrick and Eddie both claimed not to have seen them.

"Dre? Can you come here?" Rob asked.

DeAndre went down the hallway to Rob's room, still distracted with replaying what had happened with Reg, wondering what he could have done differently to make peace between the two worlds.

"Dre? I had two twenty-dollar bills sitting on my dresser."

"I didn't touch them, man. I swear I didn't."

"No! No. I didn't think you did. But I think maybe it was Reg."

"Reg?"

"Well, yeah. He said he had to use the bathroom and then he was gone a long time. I'm telling you, I emptied my pockets when I got home and took the money out of my wallet, setting it aside for the pizza."

"Naw, man. Reg wouldn't do that."

"Really?"

"I mean, he's done some stupid stuff before, but he wouldn't do that to me. Not to my friends."

Rob didn't say anything, just raised his eyebrows so high DeAndre felt like a little boy again standing in front of his pa after doing something foolish. Would Reg throw him under the bus like that? Steal from his new friends? Make a fool of him in order to keep DeAndre all to himself?

Of course, he would.

DeAndre almost laughed at himself for not seeing it earlier. How could he have been so naïve? The streets of his hood weren't made of quicksand. His connections there were. And he was tired of sinking.

"Rob," Patrick called from down the hall, "the delivery man is waiting."

"Tell him to hold on a minute," Rob yelled back.

DeAndre felt pressure building inside of him. He needed to make a decision.

"I'll pay for the pizza." He dug out his wallet, grabbed a wad of bills from the paycheck he'd cashed the day before, and thrust them into Rob's hand.

"This is way more than forty bucks."

"It's also the deposit for my room. If you'll still have me." He didn't want to allow Reg to change his mind.

* * *

DeAndre couldn't believe he was doing this. Would it be the last time he drove this route from suburbia into the city, past Park Ave. into his hood? Wait. It wasn't *his* hood. Not anymore.

He wanted to spread his wings and fly, but how he wished Reg would soar with him. Why couldn't they do this thing together? Why did Reg insist on keeping those shackles on his feet?

Reg. When DeAndre sifted through his memories, everywhere he looked Reg stood with his cocky grin. Reg at nine, Reg at thirteen, Reg at twenty—he never changed much. The same spark of mischief glinted in his eyes, the same stubborn tilt of his chin told you not to mess with him. But his laugh—no one could bust a gut like Reg.

DeAndre sighed. God help him, he loved that boy, even if there were a million reasons why he shouldn't, or at least one good one. He couldn't help it. Their souls were tied together.

In the back of his mind, he saw ten-year-old Reg, his dirty overalls sporting a hole in the left knee the size of a tin can lid. Both of his big toes were poking out of his worn sneakers, but he didn't seem to notice. His 'fro made his head seem too small for his body, and the dirt on his chin and cheeks almost made it look like a five o'clock shadow crept up on his face. He and DeAndre sat in the alleyway next to DeAndre's apartment building, their backs against the brick wall.

"You know what we should do, D?"

"What's that?"

"We should become blood brothers for real." Reg pulled out his pocketknife and sliced his finger. "Now you do yours and we'll mix the blood together. A blood pact. Then we'll be best friends for life, always there for each other."

DeAndre took the knife and cut his index finger without hesitation, sucking in his breath at the sting of pain. It only hurt for a second. When the boys rubbed their fingers together then shook hands, the feeling of solidarity eased any discomfort.

And now what? DeAndre planned to march into the house the two of them shared for years and demand his blood back? Break the covenant he made?

He knew he had to do it, but his chest ached with the weight of it.

And he had some loose ends to tie up in that hood. He not only had to say goodbye to Reg, he had to say goodbye to Pa and one final goodbye to St. Anthony Street.

32

———

Natassa arrived out of breath and knocked on the door. Then as she remembered where she was and that she might be followed, she began to pound.

"Bethany! Bethany! It's me, Natassa! Let me in, please!"

She heard footsteps, then "Hold on, baby girl!" and the snap of the locks.

"Come in! Come in."

"I'm sorry for barging in like this," Natassa said, voice shaking. "I didn't know where else to go."

"Oh, don't you go apologizing none! I done said you was always welcome here." Bethany wrapped her in a bear hug, and Natassa leaned into her strength. "I've been missing you! Oh, how I've missed you! Now, you sit yourself down on the couch, and I'll make you some tea. You want some tea, sugar? Or lemonade?"

"Either is fine."

Bethany raised her eyebrows. "You don't have to do that with me. Just tell me what you want to drink."

"Water, actually. I normally just drink water."

"Well, that's a good thing 'cause I got plenty of that. That wasn't so hard, was it?"

"No." Natassa felt a little of the tension leave her shoulders, even as she still felt the world spinning out of control around her.

Bethany disappeared into the kitchen, giving Natassa a minute to get her bearings. She couldn't believe she'd actually come back here, driven through that neighborhood. Desperation pressed her forward, overriding reason. She didn't have anywhere else to go. Her heart and mind were tangled around the pain of what she felt she must do and the pull of her own desires. She needed wisdom, and she knew she could find it here.

Bethany came back a minute later, placing a glass of ice water into Natassa's hands and sitting down next to her. "Now tell your mama what's wrong."

"I can't hide this anymore," Natassa said, motioning to her stomach. "It's too big. Everyone wants me to give the baby up for adoption, which is better than having an abortion, so I should be thankful, right? I should be, but I'm not. I don't want to do it! And now Brandon says if I just give this baby up, he'll give me another one—his baby. Then I finished the journal, and I'm thinking that has to be it, right? I have to let her go. Maybe someday God will give her back to me, but oh, God, I don't know how I can bring myself to do this. It feels so wrong." Natassa buried her face in her hands.

"Oh, I see. You're looking for a formula. You read the journal and you done think you got the Good Lord figured out now. You found a box you can fit Him in." Bethany chuckled. "Well, sugar, let me tell you something. God's liable to bust out of any box you try to stuff Him into. He is not the God of formulas. He's the God of miracles."

"But I thought—"

"That's the problem right there. You've been doing too

much thinking and not enough listening. And probably not enough talking either. Did you ever sit down with that husband of yours and share your heart? Really share it without putting up defenses and expecting him to see into that pretty little head of yours?"

"I've tried! Kind of ... I mean ..."

"You pray to God, sugar. You ask Him to show you *your* path. Ask Him to give you the words to say. Then say them."

Natassa thought back to her conversations with Brandon, if she could even call them that. Very few words had even been said, very little of her heart had been shared, and not in truth. She had withheld information. She had devised plans. She assumed Brandon knew how she felt, but she had never told him how God's voice changed everything for her that day. He didn't know how she felt drawn to that church, that street. She had this whole other facet of her life he knew nothing about. How would she feel if he had done the same to her? A secret life? Could she open up to him?

"I'm afraid."

"Shoot! We's all afraid. You think Esther wasn't afraid when she went before the king to plead for her people? The only thing that separates warriors from cowards is their resolve to not let fear stop them. Do it afraid, baby girl."

Do it afraid. Was that her problem? That she didn't have confidence in herself, or rather in her God to come through? Was there a warrior in her, ferociously trusting that her God was bigger than her circumstances?

Bethany brushed the hair from Natassa's face. "Natassa, you got yourself an unusual name. God made you to stand out. Not blend in."

Natassa sat back and sipped her water, letting Bethany's comment seep into her soul. It was so ... so ... contrary to everything she had ever experienced.

The women sat in silence for quite some time, Natassa

praying about what to say to her husband. When she drained the last of her water, she stood. "I need to go. I have to go talk to Brandon."

"One more thing," Bethany said, standing as well. "Unforgiveness will chain you up. You know that, don't you, sugar?"

"Yes."

"Then do what you have to do to get free."

"Have mercy," Natassa whispered.

"What's that?" Bethany asked, cocking her head.

"Nothing. I understand."

"Do you need me to walk you down?"

"No. Not this time." Natassa put her hand on the door then turned back around. Can I borrow something to write with?"

* * *

It was a short drive, but Natassa didn't need time to contemplate what she was about to do. As she prayed in Bethany's apartment, she'd felt the Lord assure her that a psychopathic stalker had not left the bottle and note. No one was out to hunt her down; the man was hunting for mercy. From her.

Clink. Clink. Clink.

That bottle had grated on her ever since she stashed it under the driver's seat of her car. It was time to let it go.

She pulled her Audi directly up to the curb of St. Anthony Street, right where he'd left the bottle and note for her to find. She didn't know if he was watching, or if he would even find it. She hoped he would. She prayed he would.

She pulled the bottle and note out from under her seat and held the piece of paper in her hand. "Lord, You have given me mercy, even though I didn't deserve it. Right now, I choose to forgive this man. Let him find mercy in You."

Turning the note over, she took Bethany's marker and wrote *I forgive you.* She was about to get out of the car, when she added *God will forgive you too.* She opened her car door and, holding her head high, placed the note underneath the bottle.

"Let him see it, Lord."

Then she got back in her car and drove, relishing the silence. There was no more clinking. Only peace.

33

Reg's escort wasn't in the driveway when DeAndre pulled in. Just as well. DeAndre could pack in peace. He rammed the door open with his shoulder and looked around at what he'd be leaving. What a dump. Good riddance.

Well, he and Reg had enjoyed watching quite a few games on that cracked faux leather couch. And they had set off the fire alarm in that dingy kitchen more times than he could count while burning frozen pizza and popcorn. Memories of the two of them crowded around, vying for attention. This place wasn't so bad, was it?

He needed to pack.

It took him all of twenty minutes. Everything he owned fit inside three duffel bags. Now all he had to do was wait for Reg to come busting through the door.

* * *

DeAndre awoke to the first rays of dawn shining through the living room window. He sat up on the couch. Did he miss Reg coming home last night? He looked out the window. No escort. So, he never showed.

He had no idea where Reg was, but DeAndre had to get moving if he wanted to finish everything in one day. He picked up the duffel with his paint supplies in it and headed out.

The crispness of the early-morning air felt nearly fresh, as fresh as it got in the city anyway. DeAndre kicked stray cans as he walked. *One last time.* His throat was raw, and he cleared it, glad he didn't have to talk to anyone. When he'd brought up the idea of the mural for Pa's shop, he never thought it would be his way of saying goodbye. He thought he'd see his pa's face staring back at him as he walked by, drove by ... Pa's constant presence ever before him. But now ...

DeAndre's eyes started misting, and he blinked rapidly. This was ridiculous. He would paint a stunning tribute that would honor Pa's legacy and make him proud. No need for sentiment. He needed to man up.

When he got to Seventh and Elm, he checked to see if Reg was inside. All was quiet, so DeAndre went back around and started to paint. He began with his pa's face, the grin larger than life, a shallow dimple on the right side. DeAndre was painting from memory, and it had been so long since he'd seen his pa's face. He hoped the shape of the eyes was true to life. Were they really so large with animation, or was it only DeAndre's youth that made them seem so? At any rate, he wanted to paint the Pa his heart remembered.

After Pa's face, he worked on the lettering, the sharp lines speaking to him of Pa's integrity and uprightness. Finally, he painted a green Cadillac with its windows rolled down, music notes piling out of it. Onlookers could think what they wanted; DeAndre knew those were jazz notes filling the air.

Sweat poured down his face, neck, and back as the afternoon sun hammered down. Just a few final additions and he'd be done. He added definition in a few areas then stepped back.

And back some more. He crossed the street to have a better look.

Perfect. Just like he imagined.

He crossed back over and gathered his supplies, throwing them in the duffel bag. Standing in front of the painting of his pa's face, he took a deep breath.

"I love you, Pa. I always will." DeAndre held up his fist, gave one final gaze, and then turned and walked toward St. Anthony Street.

* * *

DeAndre still had paint cans in the abandoned ice cream shop that he wanted to take with him, but that wasn't his main motivation for walking to St. Anthony Street. What happened in that place still ate away at him. He didn't know how to move past it, but he knew he had to find a way.

He spent every Sunday here, listening to the church bell, finding himself unworthy to enter the building down the street, yet longing for redemption. He had tried to make things right, but his efforts exploded in his face. He still felt the shrapnel imbedded in his soul.

If only he could turn back time.

But since he couldn't, he needed closure. At least he could say goodbye and hope that with time he could move on.

He turned the corner, and the sun nearly blinded him, so bright. So hot. Relentless. He had already thrown four cans of spray paint into his bag when the glint of something across the street caught his eye.

What was ...?

He froze.

A bottle.

The duffel bag dropped onto the sidewalk with a thump, and he took off running. In the seconds it took for him to dash across the street, a dozen thoughts raced through his mind. The hopeful ones reached the finish line first. *Is there a note from her? Does she forgive me?*

Breath coming in hard puffs, he squatted down next to the bottle. There was a note! His hands shook as he picked it up and read it. Then DeAndre did something he hadn't done since he was a small boy: he began to sob.

DeAndre wiped his face with the palms of his hands and laughed. Laughed! The sun started its retreat, sneaking behind the steeple of the church. How long had he been sitting on the sidewalk bawling like a baby? He didn't know, but after holding it in for over ten years, he felt like he had lost pounds of weight. And after asking God to forgive him, he felt free. He left the bottle on the sidewalk and took the note, folding it and placing it in his wallet. He wanted to remember this moment forever.

"And God," he prayed before standing to his feet, "would You break whatever hold Reg seems to have over me? I don't want to be tied to him anymore."

DeAndre stood and looked across the street at the mural he'd painted. There he was, on his knees begging for mercy. And here he was on the other side having found it. Another laugh bubbled out of him, grateful to cross the threshold of his mouth. Freedom. He'd finally found it, and he didn't have to cross into another zip code to grab hold of it.

He crossed the street, grabbed the rest of his stuff, and walked back to the house he used to call home, his step much lighter than before. He felt like that red bird in his painting, about to take flight. As if nothing could bring him down.

Then he saw the house in the distance—and Reg's car in the driveway.

He slowed. This wasn't going to be easy.

"God, give me strength."

When he pushed the front door open, Reg leapt up from the couch. "There you are! The prodigal son returned."

Yes. He had.

"Did you come to your senses, D? Did you figure out where you belonged?"

"I sure did."

Reg nodded his approval. "Good. Welcome home."

"Hey, Reg, Rob had a couple of twenties sitting on his dresser that went missing. You wouldn't happen to know what happened to them, would you?"

"Shoot, D! Why would I know about some white boy's money?"

"So, you didn't, let's say, take a detour on your way to or from the bathroom and slip them in your pocket?"

Reg shrugged. "Why do you care anyway?"

"Because Rob is my friend."

"I thought I was your friend." When DeAndre didn't say anything, he continued. "That white boy didn't need that money anyway. Not like I do. Not like we do, D. He's probably always had everything spoon-fed to him, slept on silk sheets. Shoot, his daddy probably gave him a new caddy for his sixteenth birthday. It was only forty bucks. It's not like he's gonna miss it anyway."

"Stealing is wrong, Reg. You know that. You're trying to start something, and I see through you."

"Wrong is relative." Reg tilted his head up in a challenge, crossing his arms, squaring his stance. Daring DeAndre to come at him with some moral argument he thought he knew how to punch down. But DeAndre had a blow he knew Reg wouldn't see coming.

"I'm leaving."

"What you talkin' about, D? Where you going?" The glint in Reg's eye held strong, taunting him not to run from a fight.

"I'm moving out. Springing out of this hood once and for all."

"You're messing with me. What? All because I pocketed a couple bills? I'll give the money back, D. I was just playing around."

"No, not just because of the money. All this time I thought it was these streets bringing me down, but it was you, wasn't it? You're jaded and bitter, and it's a virus infecting everything around you, including me. Not anymore. I love you, Reg, but I gotta be free."

Reg's eyes widened in what looked like panic. "I thought we were brothers! Blood brothers. Loyal to the end?"

"Yeah, well ..." DeAndre vaguely remembered hearing in church about the power of the blood of Jesus. He couldn't articulate to Reg what he didn't completely understand himself. All he knew was that there was a blood pact that was stronger than the one he and Reg had made.

DeAndre grabbed his other two duffel bags from by the front door. "Goodbye, Reg."

As he walked down the driveway and threw his bags in the trunk of his car, Reg stood on the front porch yelling and cursing at him. "You're a traitor, you know that? No good lowlife. Your pa would be ashamed! An Oreo, that's what you are. Go ahead. Turn your back on me. All I ever did was look out for you your whole life."

DeAndre closed his car door on Reg's accusations and started the engine, drowning out his monologue. Their old neighbor Mr. Jamison stood on his top step, leaning on his cane, staring back and forth between the both of them. DeAndre smiled and waved as he backed out of the driveway.

He did it.

He did it.

He was free.

34

Natassa pulled into her driveway and shifted into park, not bothering to press the button and wait for the garage door to open. She needed to talk to Brandon. Now. Before she lost her nerve.

She'd spent the entire drive home praying about what to say then rehearsing how to say it, praying and rehearsing, praying and rehearsing until their house came into view. She could do this. She had to do this. She took a final deep breath as her keys fought with the lock on the door.

When she pushed open the door, silence greeted her, an eerie sense of calm. "Brandon?" Her flats echoed on the solid wood. "Girls?" The refrigerator hummed in the kitchen. "David? Daniel?" She strode to the back porch and surveyed the yard. No one.

Fishing through her purse, she found her phone, still on silent from the morning's church service. She must have turned the ringer off entirely because the vibrate feature was disabled. Twenty-two missed calls. Thirteen voicemails. Sixteen texts. All from Brandon. She didn't waste a minute sorting through them; she just dialed his number.

"Brandon, where are you?"

"Where am I? Where are you, Natassa? And don't give me any nonsense about being at your mom's house. I've called everyone I could think of, driven all across the county ... Where did you disappear to?"

"Brandon, calm down. I need to talk to you about that, and I will. When you come home. Just, come home. We need to talk."

"You're scaring me, Nat. You say you're in one place, but you're not. You don't answer your phone. You keep skipping church. What's wrong with you? If I didn't know you better, I'd think you were having an affair. You're ... you're not having an affair, are you?"

"What? No!" But she was in love. And she did have a secret life he knew nothing about. "Brandon, where are you?"

"I'm with Brett now. You're safe, right? You sound ... safe."

"Yes, I'm fine."

"Okay," Brandon let out a slow breath, relief trailing on the end of it. "In that case, I think I'm going to stay here awhile. Brett thinks he has a lead in your case. Maybe. It could be nothing, but someone from Edison's finally talked, mentioned something about a couple of guys who came in that night. Brett thought we could go down there and press them for more information, see if—"

"Brandon, no."

"No? What do you mean no?"

"You've got to let this go."

"Some creep attacked and violated my wife and is right at this moment free to roam the streets and you expect me to let it go? You really have lost your mind!"

Natassa sighed. "Can you please come home so we can talk about this? Wait, are the children with you at Brett's?"

"No, I dropped them off at Breanna's."

"Breanna and I aren't talking."

"How was I supposed to know that? You didn't say a word to me about it."

"I know." Glancing at her watch, she formulated a new plan. "On second thought, meet me at Bristol's in thirty minutes."

"What?"

"Bristol's. Thirty minutes."

Natassa hung up the phone then sent Breanna a quick text. THANK YOU FOR WATCHING THE CHILDREN. I AM OKAY. BRANDON AND I NEED TO TALK. OKAY IF WE PICK THEM UP L8R?

A minute later, her phone buzzed in her hand. SURE THING, CHICKA.

* * *

"Can I get the corner booth? That one. Right there." Natassa pointed to the small booth partially secluded by ferns. Bristol's would be crawling with people by seven o'clock, but it was only four thirty, and the waitress seated her right away at the table she requested. Now she just had to wait for Brandon to show. He would come, right?

She put her phone in front of her on the table. She hadn't heard from him since hanging up—she checked the time—thirty-two minutes earlier. *Please, God. Let him come.*

"Are you ready to order?" the waitress asked.

"No, I'm waiting for someone, and when he comes, we're going to need a few minutes, please."

At four forty she saw him walking toward her, caution in his eyes, his movements sharp and guarded. He sat down across from her, shoulders stiff, arms rigid.

"Hi, honey," she said, smiling in an attempt to ease the tension.

"What's this about?"

"There are just some things we need to talk about. That's all."

"Oh. That's all. That's all? Natassa, you're acting like a nutcase. You've seriously got me concerned you need some psychological help, like you've got multiple personalities or something. What is this 'Meet me at Bristol's in thirty minutes'? What's that?"

"Brandon, I'm fine. Look at me. I'm okay. I'm not having some breakdown. I've just realized some things, and I think we need to talk about them."

"Realized some things?"

"Yes. But now that you mention it, I do think it would be a good idea to go to counseling."

"Counseling? No. Why? There's no need to bring another person into our problems."

"Okay, but I was raped, Brandon. Blindsided, attacked, and raped. I know you want us to just move on like it never happened, but I think a little outside help is needed here. And it's not just that. Even before the ... disagreement about having another baby, fault lines were just under the surface of our marriage, waiting for a degree of friction to topple us. Honey, we have to learn how to communicate."

"I don't think I'm the one with that problem."

"Okay then. I'll put it this way. I am going to seek counseling. I would greatly appreciate it if you would support me by going with me."

"I'll think about it."

"Fair enough."

Brandon took a long drink of his water. Natassa watched his Adam's apple as he swallowed. "So, you want to start communicating with me?"

Natassa nodded.

"Where were you that day when you said you were at your mom's? When I called your mom today, looking for you, she said, 'Why would she come over here? Besides the Fourth of July, I haven't seen her since she and her sisters came over for lunch the day I talked to her about her options.' You lied to me, Natassa."

Natassa pictured Bethany's face and smiled. "I have another mom."

"What?" Brandon leaned forward. "You're adopted?"

"Yes." Natassa giggled, despite attempting to rein it in. "No. Not like that. It's not what you think."

Brandon stood up, hurling his napkin down on the table. "I see this is all some big joke to you." He strode toward the door, nearly ramming into a waitress on his way.

"Brandon!" Natassa yelled, sobering quickly and starting after him. "Don't walk away from me!"

"Why?" he asked, turning to face her, dozens of couples and families dining at their tables in between them. Forks stilled in midair as other conversations in the room stilted and eyes zeroed in on Brandon and Natassa. "You do it to me all the time. Every time the conversation gets even a little difficult, you bolt."

"I know. It's wrong of me. I want to change. I think I am ... changing."

"There's a little too much change going on for me right now." Brandon turned and barreled out the door.

Natassa followed. "Brandon! I'm not done with this conversation."

"I am."

He ran a hand through his hair and blew out a breath, staring into the distance. Then he walked over and sat on the bench in front of the restaurant, shoulders slumped. Approaching slowly, Natassa sat next to him.

They stared straight ahead as a couple walked toward the restaurant, hands gripped together and swinging between them. The man said something to the woman, and her laugh resounded through the parking lot.

A happy, carefree couple. At least it seems like it. I guess you never can tell. Natassa assumed acting was the largest unpaid profession in humanity.

She didn't want to be an actress anymore.

She took a deep breath and dove in. "I went down there. To the ... scene of the crime."

Brandon's head snapped around. "You what?"

"Well, first Breanna took me."

"You went looking for evidence without me?"

"No! No. Breanna got this idea in her head that if we drove down there, I could get over my fear, or at least make some progress in that regard. We just drove down the street, but when we did, we saw a church—a beautiful church, Brandon. It's historically old with these giant stone steps and iron railings. And the stained glass windows are breathtaking. It has this giant brass bell, and when it rings, it's like the sound is resounding inside of you, like it's calling you back to life."

Brandon was once again looking at her as if she had lost her mind. "And?"

"And I couldn't help but go back there. To the church. So I did on the day I went to my mom's for lunch."

"With Breanna?"

"No. By myself."

"You went into *that* neighborhood by yourself?"

She bit her lip and nodded.

"Natassa! You *are* crazy! Why? Why would you do that?"

"I told you. I had to see that church again."

"Had to?"

"It compelled me. I'd just found out that I was pregnant and ... okay, I know it doesn't make sense. I can't make it make sense. Bethany says that it doesn't have to."

"Bethany? Who the heck is Bethany?"

"Oh, I'm getting to that. When I went to that church, St. Anthony's Baptist Church, I met this older black lady named

Bethany. She calls me 'baby girl' and says that I'm family and that she's my mama. And she is! She's the only real spiritual mother I've ever had, Brandon, and I love her. She's the reason I went back."

"You went back? Again?"

"I went a few times. And to her apartment a couple times. That time I told you I was at my mom's. And today."

Brandon shook his head. "I can't believe this."

Natassa turned to him, her knee brushing against his, and took his hands in hers. "I am so sorry I kept this from you. And lied to you. I was so afraid that if I told you, you would take it all away from me, but it was wrong of me. Please forgive me."

Brandon's head was down, and Natassa couldn't see his face, but she saw his shoulders begin to tremble. Her stomach felt sour. *Is he crying? Did my sin break him?*

All of a sudden he threw his head back and laughed, startling Natassa into nervous laughter herself. "What?" she asked. "What is it?"

"So that's it? Here I was imagining all these worst-case scenarios, not the least of which was some seedy affair. Not that I thought you would actually do that to me, but I couldn't seem to come up with a logical explanation for your bizarre behavior. And all this time you were at church with some old black lady?" Brandon wiped the corner of his eyes with the back of his hand.

"You're not mad?"

"It seems wrong to be mad at you for going to church. I wish you would have just told me."

"Me too."

"But I understand why you didn't." He squeezed her hand. Though this seemed like a pleasant stopping point, she knew she had to continue.

"Brandon, there's more."

"Uh oh."

"The reason I am begging you to give up searching for evidence about the rapist is that I have forgiven him." She put her hand up to stop him from interrupting. "Now before you tell me that we have to catch the guy before he does this to someone else, I need to say that I really believe he is not going to. I believe he is truly sorry for what he did."

"How could you possibly know that?"

"Because he left me a note."

Natassa felt Brandon's nails digging into her hand as his muscles clenched. "Brandon, relax. Listen to me. When I walked down St. Anthony Street after church, I saw a wine bottle at the same spot where I dropped our bottle that night. Under the bottle was a note that said 'I'm so sorry.' It was from him, left for me. It had to be. Today I wrote him a note back that told him I forgive him and that God will too."

"A bottle. A note. Evidence, Natassa! Just what I was looking for! Why didn't you tell me?"

"Because he was sorry. Because he was looking for mercy."

"He. Doesn't. Deserve. It."

"I know."

"You know? You know. Then why did you let him off the hook?"

"What he did was deplorable. There's no excuse for it. I'm not defending his crime. I forgave him to let myself off the hook. I needed freedom."

"But there were two men, right? One who raped you and one who helped? What if the accomplice left the note? What if the rapist isn't sorry at all?"

"I never thought of that." Natassa could see the hard set of Brandon's jaw, feel the anger radiating from him. "Brandon, please. If there were a solid lead, if he were in custody, I guess I would testify against him. I don't know. But the fact is, we've got nothing to go on, and it's eating you alive. Let it go. God is our judge. God is his judge. He will take care of it. Please, please ... leave it in His hands."

Brandon stared at his hands for several minutes, and Natassa stared at him, watching his internal wrestling play out in the lines around his eyes and mouth, in the shifting of his jaw.

Finally, he spoke. "When Clarissa died—"

"Your sister?"

"Yes, my sister. Why do you say it like that?"

"Nothing. It's just ... you never talk about her. Never."

"It's not something you talk about."

Natassa put her hand on his shoulder.

"Brett and I were supposed to be looking after her. Did you know that?"

Natassa shook her head.

"'Take care of your sister.' The last words Mom said before we took off on our bikes, down to the gas station to get slushies. Brett and I, though, we started racing, egging each other on. We left Clarissa trailing behind. Didn't even look back until we heard the blare of the horn, the screech of the tires ... her scream ..."

"Oh, Brandon."

"It's no one's fault. That's what our parents told us over and over again as we wept in their arms at the hospital. They tried so hard to be strong for us. It was an accident. No one's fault. But Brett and I knew the truth. We knew it was our fault."

"Brandon, you were ten. David's age, honey. You were just a child."

"Old enough. Old enough to feel the weight of guilt."

Natassa grasped Brandon's hand again. "You've been carrying this around your whole life and you've never breathed a word of it to me?"

"You're not the only one who can keep secrets." He squeezed her hand tightly then brought it up to his mouth and kissed it. "I guess what happened to you brought it all up to the surface. I was supposed to watch out for Clarissa, and I failed her. I made a vow to protect you, and I failed you. I've been—I don't know—consumed, haunted, with finding who did this to you and putting him behind bars, thinking that maybe if I could do that, if I could come through this time, maybe I won't be such a complete failure."

"Brett too?"

"Yeah, I think Brett feels much the same way."

Natassa sighed. She wished she could leave the two of them a note under a bottle. There was mercy for them too. Mercy would follow them.

"Oh! The voice! I almost forgot about the voice!"

The corner of Brandon's mouth turned upward. "Oh great. You're hearing voices now?"

"Don't worry, only one." Natassa's stomach grumbled. "Sorry. Just hungry."

"Do you want to go back in and order?" Brandon asked.

Natassa looked back toward the restaurant, remembering the scene they made when they left. "Why don't we just pick up fast food and take it home?"

"Sure. We have separate cars. Do you want to pick the food up, or do you want me to?"

An idea began formulating in Natassa's mind. "You can pick it up. I'll meet you there." They started walking to their cars when she shouted, "Can you go to that little place on Maple Street and get me the club salad with ranch dressing, please?" Because that's what she wanted.

* * *

Natassa watched out Hope's window, eyes straining to see Brandon's gray car appear on their street. He should be home any minute. She pulled a small pink wooden chair up to the window and somehow managed to wedge her pregnant body into it by sitting forward, her knees jutting out by her chest. Good. She could still see the driveway. Hope's room afforded the best, and really only, vantage point of the driveway and at least half of the walkway to the front door.

There! Natassa felt her heart rate pick up as she watched Brandon's car approach the driveway. She leaned her elbows on Hope's windowsill, pressing her forehead against the glass. *Come on, Brandon. Pay attention. See it! Stop!* She knew she'd taken a risk by placing it there. If his mind was racing from their earlier conversation, distracting him so that he crashed into it, this whole thing would have the opposite effect. Possibly a catastrophic one.

She held her breath. *Stop, Brandon! Stop!*

He slammed on his brakes just inches away. Natassa released her breath and waited.

Brandon got out of his car and came around to the front of it, to where Natassa had placed Hope's bike. Natassa watched him squat down and pick up the note. He stayed there in a squatting position with his head down, and Natassa couldn't see his expression, could only guess what was going on in his mind as he processed the words on the note. *You are forgiven.* Then ... were his shoulders shaking? Was the note trembling in his hand, or was it only a breeze?

But then he looked up. Searching for her? She ducked back, wanting him to receive the note as if it were from God, not from her. The short glimpse she caught of him showed his wet face, unless her eyes were playing tricks on her.

She waited a minute and then tentatively peeked out the window again just in time to see him fold the note neatly into squares and tuck it into his billfold. Then he started walking toward the front door and stopped as he saw the first piece of bright-green construction paper taped to the concrete walkway in front of their home. MERCY. He walked a little farther and stopped at the next paper. WILL. He stepped over it and kept going until he came to the next paper a few feet farther down. FOLLOW. His gait was slightly slower as he came up to the last paper. YOU. He paused before stepping over it, then, as she hoped he would, he looked back toward the paper path. *Believe it, Brandon. Mercy will follow you. Believe it.*

Natassa rushed out of Hope's room and reached the bottom of the stairs just as Brandon swung the front door open. Their gazes connected. Her heart moved toward his.

"Natassa?" he asked, eyes misty, "What was that?"

"Sit." She motioned to the couch. "I'll explain."

"Wait. I left the food in the hot car."

"I'll grab it. You just sit. Rest."

Natassa dashed outside, grabbing the papers on the way, stashing the bike back in the garage, and grabbing their dinner from the car. Seeing Brandon got a salad too, she tossed both in the fridge when she came inside. Talk first. Eat later.

Brandon was on the couch, his head in his hands. She sat cross-legged beside him.

"When I took the pregnancy test and saw that it was positive, I was a blubbering mess, and despite what you might think I wasn't overjoyed. Terrified is more like it. But as I sat there worrying, God spoke to me. Just one simple sentence, Brandon, but it changed everything for me."

"What did He say?"

"Mercy will follow you."

Brandon let out something that resembled a mix of a cry and a groan, something that came from the deep and not the shallow. It sent a shiver down Natassa's spine.

"I saw a picture of this baby, Brandon. Well, not as a baby. As a little girl, holding my hand, trailing a couple steps behind me. Mercy, following me." She squeezed her eyes closed tight. "I want to keep this baby, Brandon. More than anything I've ever wanted in my entire life. I know there are a million reasons we shouldn't, and I understand why you don't. I do. But deep inside me, I feel like this is what God wants for us. I feel like this is His path for our lives."

She opened one eye to judge his reaction, her shoulders nearly up next to her ears with tension. She couldn't tell anything from his vacant expression. "Think of it as a way to protect the most vulnerable one of all."

She waited for his verdict.

"Did you tell him?" he finally said.

Natassa sat back, turning toward him. "Tell who? What?"

"Did you tell the rapist about the baby? In the note?"

"No. It seemed out of place in the moment. Do you think I should? I could go back. Put another note under the bottle."

"No." Brandon turned to face her and put both of his hands on her shoulders. "Natassa, you don't owe him anything. He was a ... an unsolicited sperm donor, not a father. You owe him nothing."

Natassa closed her eyes. Nodded. "You're right. You're right."

Brandon slid his hands from her shoulders down her arms until he held both of her hands in his. "But," Brandon kissed her hand, "this baby has a father. I am its father. Sorry, *her* father. Because I will be the one tucking her in at night and singing her songs and watching her twirl around in those little tutus you can't help but buy our girls. Please, Natassa. Please, Natassa. You asked me to let go of seeking the criminal for justice. Now I'm asking you to let go of seeking him for any further connection."

"Okay," Natassa said through tears. Sloppy, messy, beautiful tears.

* * *

Brandon and Natassa pulled into Breanna's driveway at quarter after ten. Both laughter and a few tears had interrupted their dinner when they finally got around to eating their mediocre salads with plastic forks. Natassa smiled, remembering how she'd wiped stray dressing off his chin with the flimsy napkin. They were going to make it.

As for her friendship with Breanna ...

Natassa and Brandon walked to the door together. He knocked. She waited. Jack answered the door. "Hey, guys, they're all on the couch. Your girls are zonked out."

"Thanks. I'll grab them," Brandon said, heading in that direction.

Jack gave Natassa a knowing half smile. "Breanna's in the kitchen."

Natassa nodded and went to find her.

Breanna sat at the kitchen table, a gallon of rocky road in front of her, spoon in hand. She said nothing—just held out another spoon to Natassa, who took it and sat down next to her. The carton was nearly empty, and Natassa scraped ice cream off the sides.

Breanna scrunched up her nose. "Sorry. I got a head start."

"Sorry we're so late. Thanks for watching the children."

"Give me the lowdown?"

"I forgave the rapist. Brandon is going to stop trying to hunt him down. I told him about the church. And we're keeping the baby."

"Wow. No wonder it took you so long."

"Breanna, I'm sorry I kicked you out. It's just ... I don't know how to stand up to you. You're so ... so strong, and I'm—"

Breanna reached over and squeezed Natassa's fingers. "Gaining strength every day."

Natassa knew it was true, but still she admitted, "I might need some time."

"It's okay, chicka. I'll be here when you need me."

35

———

"It looks ... Wow! Just wow! Amazing work, Dre!" Rob shook DeAndre's hand outside Java Joe's.

"Thanks, man. Just finished it last night."

The two men admired the mural on the wall outside of the coffee shop for a few minutes more before heading inside.

"Isn't it great?" James asked as the bell jingled over the door. "It's going to bring in more customers, just wait and see. Those colors are so eye-catching."

"It was my pleasure to do it, sir."

"I can't believe we're going to lose you so soon. My favorite employee," James said, slapping DeAndre lightly on the back.

"Hey!" Rob called out.

"It's only for a year," DeAndre said. When he'd received the acceptance letter to the Art Institute of Chicago, he felt like he could float with pride. Him. DeAndre Scott. Accepted. But he couldn't afford to go. He didn't know why he let Rob convince him to apply. Then James helped him fill out an application for a scholarship. When the letter arrived saying he'd received one full semester of a scholarship, well then floating turned to flying.

College lasted four years. His scholarship lasted for the spring semester. Somehow, he'd have to make up the difference, but he couldn't think about that today.

Today they were celebrating him passing his GED test and being accepted to the Art Institute. It was time to party in Crawford County before leaving "Whitey World" for another city—and a school that prided itself on diversity.

As they were passing out cake, James came up to DeAndre and handed him a card. "I almost forgot. This arrived here. Addressed to you."

Recognizing the handwriting, DeAndre ripped open the envelope. The outside of the typical greeting card said congratulations. DeAndre opened it to see Reg's sharp handwriting. "Congrats, D" with a rudimentary picture of a guy with a cloud around his head, a bird flying nearby. He couldn't help but smile.

* * *

Natassa's eyes kept drifting to the heavy doors of the fellowship hall, even as she attempted to steel herself against disappointment. *She's not coming. You know she's not. You haven't seen her in months. You've got to let her go.*

Yet Natassa longed for her best friend, even as the activity of the celebration swirled around her.

"Baby girl, why don't you stand there in the center and let us get a good look at that belly of yours." Natassa complied, smiling as the women around her studied her ballooning midsection and tore off sections of crepe paper for the guessing game. Whoever's crepe paper most closely fit over Natassa's belly would win a scented candle as a prize. She struck a pose, so thankful to be able to flaunt what she had been hiding for so long.

Her mother sat by herself at a table off to the side, nibbling on veggies with ranch dip. Natassa could guess what her thoughts were about the paper plates. The first thing she'd done upon entering the fellowship hall was remark on the blue decorations.

"Blue is a boy color, Natassa. You're having a girl. The decorations should be pink."

Natassa had shrugged and given her a peck on the cheek. "Hello to you too, Mom. I happen to like blue, and we thought the blue morning glories worked well as centerpieces."

"I still don't understand why you're having a baby shower for your fifth baby anyway."

"I know you don't. But thanks for coming anyway."

"Maureen can't make it. She had other obligations. She sent her gift with me."

Natassa had pressed her lips together and nodded. She'd expected as much, but it still stung. At least Olivia showed up. Not only that, but she dove into Natassa's other world, chatting with the other women and participating in the games. Her mother stood alone in her aloofness. Stubbornness? Pride? Or fear? Whatever it was, it kept her on the sidelines, no matter how many times Bethany tried to draw her in.

Natassa wanted to leave her there. She didn't deserve a place in her daughter's inner circle. And yet ...

"Hi, Mom," she said, walking over and sliding into the chair next to her mother. "You don't want to wager a guess on how big my belly is?"

"I don't play games, Natassa."

Actually, she did. Just not this kind.

"You don't seem to be enjoying yourself much."

"How did you meet this Britany lady again?"

"Bethany, Mom. Her name is Bethany, and I met her at this church, remember?"

"Oh, yes. Don't remind me! Well, she is very friendly, but

she doesn't know the first thing about throwing a baby shower. You remember the shower I threw you for David?"

"Of course, Mom. It was lovely. Absolutely perfect." She still remembered the delectable taste of the blackened shrimp avocado cucumber bites, one of the many appetizers her mother concocted for the occasion.

"If she's going to use paper napkins, the least she could do is purchase the thick kind that have the feel of real linen."

"Mom, today isn't about perfection. It's about celebration."

"If you expect me to be excited about this baby ..." her mouth twisted up as if she'd taken a bite of a lemon.

"I don't expect it. But I hope you'll come around."

Natassa stood, giving her mother a sad half smile before walking back toward the sea of chairs where the other women were gathered.

"Oh my gosh! You did it. You actually did it."

Natassa swung around at the sound of Breanna's voice. There her friend stood in the doorway of the fellowship hall, the sun behind her back casting an orange glow to the pink highlights in her hair.

It took Natassa a minute for understanding to dawn then she touched the ends of her own hair, cresting an inch above her shoulders. She'd had it cut over a month ago, and it hung a half an inch longer now than it did then.

"Do you like it?"

"Like it? I love it! It's ... it's ... you." Breanna threw a bag on the table and closed the distance between them, enveloping Natassa in a giant hug. "You look great! Like some glowing warrior princess."

Natassa held on tightly, laughing.

"Mazy, this is my best friend Breanna. Breanna, this is Mazy. She's the one who gave me this killer haircut."

"Hey, sugar! Can you come here a minute and let us measure your belly for real so we's can see who won the prize?"

"Sure thing, Bethany."

As Bethany measured Natassa's midsection, Natassa kept an eye on Breanna. A smile adorned her face as she continued to make conversation with Mazy, but Breanna kept shifting her weight from one foot to another. *She's definitely not comfortable.*

"Hey, sugar," Bethany whispered in her ear. "Looks like you and your friend could use a little time to catch up. Why don't you girls go dish up the ice cream in the kitchen?"

"Sounds like a great plan, Bethany. Thank you." Natassa started to go grab Breanna but then turned back and asked, "Who won the game?"

"Your sister. Looks like she knows you after all."

Natassa wondered at Bethany's strange comment but continued on to snatch Breanna. "Bre, you're needed in the kitchen. Ice cream is calling."

"Say no more." Breanna put a hand over her heart dramatically. "It was nice to meet you, Mazy," she added before following Natassa to the kitchen.

"All right, chicka. What are we doing? Putting rocky road into bowls?"

"Cookie dough."

"Say what? Cookie dough? That's sacrilegious."

Natassa shrugged. "People's tastes change sometimes, Bre. I really like cookie dough. Oh, and I've given up fancy coffee. Just so you know."

"You're killing me."

"Sorry. Any new food preferences on your end? Did you start eating rice cakes or carrots or something?"

Breanna just rolled her eyes. Natassa laughed, grabbing Styrofoam bowls and plastic spoons.

"Okay, seriously, you have to fill me in," Breanna said, sobering. "What did you and Brandon tell the children?"

"Brandon told them, 'A bad man put a baby in Mommy's tummy.'" Natassa cringed.

"What? Not what you wanted him to say?"

Natassa grabbed the ice cream from the freezer, and the two of them went to work dishing it into bowls. "It's not how I would have phrased it, no. I think God put the baby inside me. The man attacked me, hurt me, raped me, yes. But only God can author life. But," Natassa raised her shoulders in concession, "I wasn't about to contradict Brandon in front of the children. And I guess it's all in how you look at it. The important thing is that I jumped in and told them that God can take all the hard, bad things that happen in our lives and turn them into good, beautiful things and that this baby is God's way of doing that. I told them we are going to love this little girl with all our hearts."

"What did they say?"

"They had a lot of questions, like, 'So this is Mommy's baby but not Daddy's baby?'"

"Ouch."

"Brandon jumped in and said that he's adopting the baby as his own so she will be both Mommy and Daddy's baby."

"And what about when other people ask about her? Kids at school or people at church?"

"We told them that if it's someone we have a relationship with and they feel comfortable, they can just tell them the truth. If not, they can just say, 'She's my sister,' and leave it at that. I guess we'll have to work through the rest as we go."

"And you and Brandon? Are you working through things?"

"We're going to counseling together. It's a process."

She didn't feel like going into how much of a process it was, how they were on their third therapist, and how Brandon still would hardly say more than two sentences during the sessions. He said he didn't like opening up to strangers. If only she could get him to open up to her again.

"What about church?"

"We're going to St. Anthony's Church once a month for right now. I'm not sure where we'll land, but I'm thankful Brandon agreed to go." Natassa giggled, remembering how Bethany greeted him with a bear hug and a kiss on the cheek that left a fuchsia lipstick smear.

"I'm glad, Nat."

"Me too."

"Shall we go serve this scrumptious delicacy to your mother?" Breanna asked in a snobby accent, holding a tray of ice cream bowls.

Natassa laughed. "Hey, at least she came." Unlike Maureen. And Laura, Brett's wife. Her smile faded at the thought. But a few minutes later, as she was indulging in cake and ice cream surrounded by women who cared about her and the life growing within her, her spirit revived. She had so much to be thankful for.

"You want to say a few words, sugar?" Bethany asked.

"Oh! Okay. Well ... I just want to thank everyone for coming. It means a lot to me to have your love and support." Natassa sent a focused glance to her mother in an effort to gain the latter from her. "This past season has been the hardest time of my life. I never knew ... I didn't know I had it in me to make it through. But Bethany gave me this journal written by someone in her family named Mercy, and Bethany's Mercy said joy and pain aren't opposites. I think maybe that's true. I found strength from Mercy's story, especially in how it ended—"

"Shoot, sugar! You don't have a clue how it ended." Bethany's voice rang out, and all eyes turned to her.

"What do you mean? I told you I finished it." Natassa stared at her, brow knit in confusion.

"You think Mercy's story is done now? She's only a young woman where you left off. No, sugar. I done took a bunch of pages out of the back of that thing before I gave it to you."

"What? Why?"

"'Cause you weren't ready for all that yet, that's why."

"What do you mean? Can I have them now?"

"No, baby girl. You still ain't ready. But don't you worry none. I'll be giving them to you when you is ready for them."

The rest of the women looked back and forth between Natassa and Bethany as Natassa attempted to process feeling cheated out of the rest of *Mercy's Journal*. What did Bethany mean? She wasn't ready? Hadn't she come so far? Grown so much in the last few months?

Natassa didn't even realize Breanna had sneaked up beside her until she heard her friend whisper, "Stop moping. Don't be offended."

"I'm—"

"Don't even say you're not, chicka."

"Okay, fine. Give me another piece of cake."

Breanna came back a minute later and thrust a rice cake into Natassa's hand. Natassa burst out laughing. "Where did you—?"

"I found it in your purse," Breanna said.

Natassa's laughter rolled out of her, complete with tears streaming down her cheeks. Breanna followed suit. Natassa wrapped her friend in another hug.

"I've missed you."

"Right back at ya."

"Okay, ladies," Bethany's voice called out. "Before Natassa opens presents, we'd like to pray a blessing over her and this precious baby of hers. We believe all life is beautiful and every life deserves to be celebrated, which is why we are all here today. We're here to love on my baby girl. I done adopted Natassa. I fell in love with this girl the first time I met her. And now I gets to be a grandma again!" Soft chuckles reverberated throughout the fellowship hall.

"But I ain't Natassa's only mama, so can her other mama

please come up here with me and help me to pray a blessing over her and over this sweet baby girl that will be blessing this family?"

All eyes shifted to Natassa's mother, who stood stiffly and trudged to the front to stand next to Bethany. Her mouth was pressed tight in an awkward smile.

"All right, sugar. Can you have a seat right here in front of us, please?"

Natassa dried her still damp cheeks and sat in front of the two women who had formed and shaped her. Each woman laid a hand on her, and Bethany began to pray.

So quiet she would have missed it had she not been so close, Natassa heard her mother chime in with an "Amen." A grin spread wide across Natassa's face, but then she felt something else spreading.

Bethany continued reciting Psalm 23 while Natassa tried not to panic.

"Surely goodness and mercy shall follow me all the days of my life; And I will dwell in the house of the Lord forever."

"Mama?" Natassa eked out.

"Yes?" both women answered at once.

"My water broke."

ACKNOWLEDGMENTS

Writing a book has been compared to giving birth, and if that's the case, I owe immense gratitude to many "midwives" who helped me bring this new life to fruition, enabling it to gasp breath into the light of day.

To my dream team of readers – Melissa, Janell, Jill, Rene, Shannon, and Cassidy- thank you for sticking with me from those very first contractions. You spoke life over this thing and shaped it, gently but firmly. *Mercy Will Follow Me* would not be what it is without you and your input as well as your encouragement.

To my dear husband, Kevin, and our children, who have dealt with the ups and downs of living with the one carrying this story and have given me space to explore and create, thank you for loving me well.

And to the One who implants all good things in the hearts of His sons and daughters, thank You for entrusting me with these characters and stories, with this piece of Your heart.

ABOUT THE AUTHOR

S ARAH H ANKS HAS SPENT THE LAST EIGHT YEARS delightfully merging her two main passions—writing and equipping children—by writing a variety of Sunday school curricula for churches in her community. She wrote her first novel when she was seventeen and continued to write fiction "on the side" until recently deciding to pursue writing professionally.

She and her husband have eight children of their own, a couple of whom seem to have inherited their mother's love for playing with words and crafting stories.

Though Sarah dreams of a cabin by the beach, their family of ten lives together in beautiful chaos in St. Charles, Missouri. She buys ears plugs in bulk.

ALSO BY SARAH HANKS

Drifting In and Out of Sleep

Freshly Cut Grass

www.ingramcontent.com/pod-product-compliance
Lightning Source LLC
Chambersburg PA
CBHW031310210726
48287CB00005B/1490